THE MAP MAKER'S PROMISE

CATHERINE LAW

Boldwood

First published in Great Britain in 2024 by Boldwood Books Ltd.

Copyright © Catherine Law, 2024

Cover Design by Head Design Ltd

Cover Photography: Shutterstock, iStock, Alamy and Dreamstime

A CIP catalogue record for this book is available from the British Library.

Paperback ISBN 978-1-83751-572-1

Large Print ISBN 978-1-83751-571-4

Hardback ISBN 978-1-83751-570-7

Ebook ISBN 978-1-83751-574-5

Kindle ISBN 978-1-83751-573-8

Audio CD ISBN 978-1-83751-565-3

MP3 CD ISBN 978-1-83751-566-0

Digital audio download ISBN 978-1-83751-567-7

Boldwood Books Ltd
23 Bowerdean Street
London SW6 3TN
www.boldwoodbooks.com

PROLOGUE
MIRREN

The Highlands, Summer 1985

She did not remember her mother, but she remembered things *around* her mother. Objects and made-up scenes in her head. Sometimes the weather. In the way the light shone across the lochan close to the house where she'd been born. Growing up amid the unspoken absence, aware of the questions she could not ask, Mirren wondered if her mother had ever gazed out at the hills, the ever-changing watercolour and rippling water. Noticed the scent on an earthy autumn morning? Or had she ever been enchanted by such things or indeed with Mirren?

If Mirren thought about it, there weren't that many things connected with her mother that she could hold in her hand. She could count her aunt and uncle's wedding photograph, taken in 1930 and propped on the sideboard. The men in kilts and ruffled shirts, attracting attention no doubt outside the church in the quiet London suburb where Auntie Anne in bridal lace married Uncle Allistair. And the solitary bridesmaid, the bride's younger sister, Mirren's mother, a wee girl, her face a blur. She must have moved her head when the shutter closed. And all in black and white, like everything from those days, slipping away and fading.

And something else. The earrings – vintage, silver settings clasping curious gemstones of luminous white and green, as ethereal as a misty Highland morning and too precious, too conspicuous to wear. People would notice and ask the questions. And yet Mirren had been too young to remember her mother ever giving them to her. They lay in darkness in a purple, silk pouch in Auntie Anne's drawer, and it would be another fifteen years before Mirren even had her ears pierced.

The first time someone mentioned Mirren's mother, in a way that seemed normal and grown-up, it had not been Auntie Anne, or Uncle Allistair, but Cal McInnis, of all people, the man with white hair who ran the post office at Foyers.

He had picked up Mirren and his nephew, her pal Gregor, from school and driven them home along the top road between Inverness and Foyers. Mirren sat in the passenger seat and Gregor in the back, his thick, dark hair in need of a cut, but then that had often been the way. She could not recall why Cal McInnis had picked them up, for they usually caught the school bus. Something must have happened. The bus breaking down, or another long-forgotten disaster. To be polite, Mirren had asked him something about his post office at Foyers. And Cal McInnis said her mother's name.

Clare.

The word left a prickling over Mirren's scalp, an odd streaming in her limbs. She kept perfectly still, determined not to react, pretending not to notice what he'd said, or to have even heard, while small thumps of shock pounded, over and over.

'Coming all the way from London as she did, Clare was amazed that letters ever reached us out here,' Cal McInnis said. 'Your aunt and uncle have a proper address, I suppose, but no one seems to know it. The post still gets to you there, even when someone writes

The Frasers, Foyers, Inverness. I make sure of it. In any case, it's my job.' He glanced at her. 'It's a good way to remember, Mirren. Just tell them that, or *the last house on the lochan.* Should you ever get lost.'

The road ahead had continued to peel its way over the moorland, the patches of bog reflecting the sky, and the name *Clare* chimed between her ears. She watched the hills move close then far away, shadows in the distance, layers of grey, streaked with yellow gorse and deep wedges of forest. The great Loch Ness below; the enormous landscape that contained her world.

'Why should I ever get lost?'

Cal turned his head to look at her. He fell quiet for some moments as the car rumbled on. At last, he drew himself up straight, rearranged his hands on the steering wheel.

'If you're anything like your mother—'

A deer streamed through a dip beside the verge, stopping alert and frozen close to the edge. Cal slowed the car, pulled over, the indicator clacking although not another soul used the road.

'Do you no' want to have a look, hen? How about you, Gregor? C'mon away, lad, have a look.'

Mirren stared into wide, glossy animal eyes, as if she had snared the creature, caught it in her trap. Stretch out her hand and she'd feel the antlers, fierce and velvety. If she touched the deer, then she'd know the deer, and it might not forget her. She wound down the window but the sound of it startled the animal. It darted off, disappearing as if it had been an apparition, back into the bracken, as if it had never been.

* * *

Mirren, grown-up now, forty-something, her marriage in tatters, a daughter of her own, she often wondered why Cal McInnis, or anyone, would think she would be lost. Indeed, why she should ever leave, like her mother had done? Not with this place her home, the mist and the hills, and black, unfathomable Loch Ness lurking in the glen. This place, old and watchful.

For she, her mother Clare, and Auntie Anne were not from here, and yet the hills had adopted them, taken them in, one way or another. And over the years, from time to time, deer, caught fleetingly at the tail of Mirren's eye, reminded her of Clare. Or the memory of Clare, real or imagined, Mirren did not know.

PART I

1

CLARE

London, August 1940

It happened on one of those rare, still, summer evenings, with traffic noise muffled as if the city held its breath in admiration at the light lingering in the sky. The pearly-white façades along Regent Street had never looked so exquisite, the mansions of Fitzrovia elegant and resolute. And at the centre of it all, Broadcasting House, moored like an ocean liner on the curve of Portland Place, its great aerial on top sending messages of truth to the country, to the continent, to the world.

In the bowels of the building, the pips sounded on the hour as Clare hurried through the lobby. The shift change meant an energetic hubbub of BBC employees, dashing in, dashing out, and Clare felt buoyant as she mingled with them, her hat tilted just so, her heels clipping as she set off east along Riding House Street. She felt part of everything, that she belonged. Her new job set a bright path ahead of her. New people, new friends. Doing what she could, to the best of her ability, for the war effort.

'Let's have dinner,' Leo Bailey had said. A little place he knew on

Charlotte Street. He said he'd meet her there, had reserved his usual table. A treat, he said, a thank you for her sterling work.

Clare crossed the cobbles along the little enclave of eateries, pushed open the velvet-curtained door to the restaurant and stepped from sunlit late afternoon into a small, dim, and exclusive space, readied for the night, with the blackout down and candles lit. The quiet murmuring from patrons at the tables in the twilight sounded soporific, early-birds already into second courses, and halfway down bottles of wine.

Leo Bailey stood up and pulled out a chair for her before the waiter even stirred.

'Now then, Miss Clare Ashby. How are you?' His eyebrows raised in greeting, his smile wide, his high inflection on the 'you', as always, sounding like a promise.

'I am very well. Thank you. A lovely evening out there.' Clare felt conscious she might be babbling as the waiter fussed with her napkin, lay it over her lap – surprisingly good linen, heavy on her knees – and placed a small menu in her hand.

Leo's amused gaze seemed to be his way of agreeing with her.

'I thought about ordering the merlot,' he said, 'but then it depends on what you would like to eat.'

'The fish is good tonight,' said the waiter, hovering, and perhaps sensing Clare's hesitation before whirring off to another table.

She pretended to read the rest of the menu before saying perhaps she'd have it. Clare's mother always said that ladies should preferably have fish, not meat, and, on occasional family meals out (before the war of course) would order it for herself, Clare, and Clare's sister Anne, while their father usually had the beef.

'But then you can't have any merlot,' Leo said. 'Why don't you try the lamb cutlets? I am.'

'I will, then.' Clare set down the menu, relieved, her decision made and tension smoothing away. She felt expansive, her confidence rising, as if she had achieved something, had grown up a little.

Leo hailed the waiter back, ordered succinctly, leaned forward on the table, and presented Clare with another full, beaming smile.

'And so, Miss Ashby, how has your day been at the coalface of our glorious Empire Service?' he asked. The look he gave her felt rather different to the way he sought her attention in the office, as director of programmes, as her boss.

'Not too bad,' she said, relaxing and laughing at herself, at her run-of-the-mill, oh-so-British answer.

Leo's laugh blended with hers. 'Oh, come on, Clare, you can do better than that. What about that mountain of "scripts as broadcast" that landed on your desk at noon? I hope you have managed to plough through them all.'

'I certainly have,' she said, noting his relaxed use of her name. 'But all that typing, all that paperwork, and all that filing, that's just one part of it. As for the rest of it, well...'

Clare's secondment from Personnel to the radio service had dropped her that summer right into the middle of the war. News came through on ticker tape machines in the basement, the first-hand reports from RAF Fighter Command as airmen in Spitfires battled in the skies over southern England. Typing up, then hearing the bulletins, spoken with confident urgency, broadcasted to Europe and the world beyond, to people in troubled places where only voices can reach them, made Clare feel as if she was doing her bit, although on constant tenterhooks and in a thoroughly amateur way.

'Well... what rest of it?' Leo Bailey asked.

'It's hearing the announcer say, "London calling", and imagining listeners turning the dial, through the static, searching for his voice,' Clare said, with a sting of pride. 'That's what makes me want to turn up every day.'

He nodded in agreement, seemed to study her reaction. 'I am glad to hear it,' he said. 'More than glad. Ah, here is the wine.'

Clare watched him sit back while the waiter poured, trying to convince herself that she didn't find him attractive. He'd rolled his shirt sleeves up, a concession to the warm evening, and yet his tie, and his thick, brushed-back hair, remained immaculate. The clock on the wood-panelled wall stood at a quarter to six, and a faint shadow had appeared on his chin. His energy, his positivity, felt like a skin-deep coating, and Clare, settling into her seat as dinner proceeded, realised she had not sat like this before: so close to and directly in front of him. The workings of the office meant constant movement, and no time to notice the flecks of grey at his temples or the shape of his hands. She wondered precariously if, at nineteen and he in his early thirties, he found her young and foolish. But these days, she conceded, as the waiter impelled her to taste the wine, everyone was young, for the BBC had to fill its ranks somehow, recruiting sixteen-year-old school leavers who only had to pay tuppence for a cup of tea in the canteen.

The waiter left them, and Leo sipped, catching her eye and nodding with pleasure, leaving Clare unsure if he liked the taste of the wine, or the look of her more. Even so, she felt secretly pleased she had worn her new green dress.

'And Kay Pritchard is looking after you, I trust?' he said.

'Yes, she has rather taken me under her wing,' said Clare.

Kay Pritchard who, at twenty-five, a seasoned secretary and recently promoted to programme assistant, had admitted she felt positively ancient among the new-starter youth. She had given Clare a tour of the dusty archives of recorded discs, shown her the mixer and the fader, played her some sound effects, explained how she must respect the red On Air signal as if her life depended on it. Had shown her the ropes, in fact. And Clare suspected, probably felt a little sorry for her, wanting to peel her out of her shell.

But Clare admired Kay; liked the way she did her hair. She wondered if she noticed when Clare turned up with her own hair rolled over her temples, instead of the clip on one side holding the wayward section that never looked right.

'So, tell me,' Leo said, 'how do we compare to Personnel? I must say, I had a glowing report from Miss Stanford about you. Your efficiency. The swiftness and accuracy of your typing and shorthand. She did say she had rather shot herself in the foot for singing your praises. For that's when I decided to snap you up.'

But this hadn't been Clare's perception. Miss Stanford often gave her important projects to complete and had recommended her herself for the stint with the Empire Service.

He pressed on. 'So, I can't see you going back to Personnel, sticking it out there. Do you?'

'I'm not sure...' This suddenly sounded like an interview. And she didn't want to do Miss Stanford a disservice. 'It's another world entirely, up there on the fifth floor. Quiet, I'd say.'

'Dull?'

'More detached, perhaps. That sounds a little kinder.'

Leo Bailey looked amused. His eyes flickered as if seeing something else in her, reading her a little differently, satisfied with her answer. And Clare felt another layer of confidence settle over her.

The cutlets arrived, with boiled new potatoes and a sprig of parsley, the juices a little too pink for Clare's liking. Her mother would have sent them back. And yet, they tasted delicious.

'I haven't been out for a meal in such a long time,' she said, tucking in.

'What with the war and everything.'

'What with the war...' Clare laughed. 'So, thank you.'

'No, this is my thank you.' He topped up the wine. 'Come on, drink up. It has been a hell of a week, hasn't it?' he said, putting it mildly.

Clare nodded, sipping from her glass, her thoughts running ahead of her.

One of her tasks had been to transcribe an old speech of Churchill's, delivered when he became PM back in May. A copy for the archive. As she read the passages, and as she typed, his vocabulary sank deep, to somewhere necessary and instinctive, and her fingertips, usually flying around the keys, froze, seemed to forget what to do.

After the battle in France abates,
there will come the battle for our Island.

She made a mistake, typed 'r' instead of 'e'. Had to correct it. Thought she really should do better with such profundity. She found it hard to explain to herself how it made her feel, let alone anyone else. Frightened, yes, but part of a bigger picture. Hitler had said they'd capitulate by August, and yet here they were. But how could she, Little Miss Efficiency, admit her fear to Leo Bailey?

'A hell of a week, yes. We're all exhausted, aren't we, shut away in our offices,' she said, realising he was waiting for her to continue. 'But how on earth do the airmen and their crews feel, out there on the airfields, waiting for the bell to ring?'

'As the great man has said, it will be foolish to disguise the gravity of the hour.'

'And this is just it,' Clare said, warming up. 'This is what I have come to realise. I could feel useless to the cause, compared to what the RAF and the WRAF are doing. But my role with you is similar to my one with Miss Stanford.' She stopped to think, to try to explain. 'In Personnel, we recruit and look after the radio people, the sound men, the reporters, the announcers. We see to their day-to-day business. We make sure they get paid. We are the ones who leave them free to get on with their important job. And I realise that, as secretary in your department, I am doing much the same, on a different scale. Does that make any sense?'

'Yes, of course it does. You make perfect sense, Clare.'

The waiter cleared the plates and offered the choice of puddings. Leo raised his eyebrows at her in question, declined for them both, asked for two brandies.

Clare paused a beat before carrying on. 'I had heard Churchill's speech you asked me to type up on the wireless at home when it was first broadcast. My mother, listening with me, said, "But what are we going to do if the Germans get here?" And I was annoyed. I bristled, in fact. I said, "But Mum, we have to stop them getting here in the first place."'

'I like this... your nature. You are sensitive. But also, there, right there, I see your strength. You hide it well, however.' He paused, appraising her, seemed fascinated by her. 'Something tells me, Clare, that you are not an only child.' His voice lowered to a new level of intimacy, the sound of her name lingering. In the office, it was 'Miss Ashby'. She had no idea what to call him, here, across the dinner table.

'How can you tell?' She laughed, lightening up. 'But I might as well be. I am a bit of an afterthought, I suppose. Perhaps, as they say, a mistake.'

'Surely not.'

The thought of her parents having that afterthought made Clare squirm.

'My big sister Anne is ten years older than me.'

'That's a large gap.'

'And as Anne would say, she was an old, married woman while I was still a little girl, really. I was only ten when she married Allistair. And so, I often feel like I am. An only child. In some respects, often alone.'

Clare sat back in her chair, surprised. She'd never spoken about this before.

The brandy arrived and Leo pushed her glass across the linen towards her.

'You shouldn't have to be. Alone,' he said. 'If you think about it, it is what you think it is, don't you think?' He laughed, sitting back, mirroring her. 'That sounds a bit muddled, doesn't it? Needs a bit of editing.'

Clare felt a dragging sensation, which baffled her until it seemed to entwine itself with possibility and blossom into hope. She liked what he said to her; liked his consideration, and the focus of his gaze. All rather odd, a little mixed up. After all, he was her boss. She distracted herself with her brandy, was not going to admit it was the first time she'd ever had it. Rather enjoyed it, in fact.

As the spirit worked its magic, the restaurant chatter grew louder and formed a protective circle around them. At the centre of it, their own conversation grew quieter, meandered one moment, ricocheted the next, and Clare kept up with him, her poise shining when she talked about her job. She seemed to impress him, felt surprised when he laughed at a funny observation or two. She wondered if he'd give her a good report at the end of her stint. Expected he would.

Leo told her how he hadn't always been in radio. That he had trained as a draughtsman out of school but had become bored of drawing architect's plans in stuffy offices. When the corporation or, as it was then, the British Broadcasting Company launched, he applied for five different jobs, all of which he wasn't formally qualified for. 'But it all seemed so fresh and exciting; the engineering side of it, I suppose, drew me in. The start of the "brave new world". And I managed to charm the men in suits behind the desk. The dreaded appointments board. Got offered all five and made my choice. Trainee radio engineer, thank you very much.'

'And haven't looked back since,' Clare offered, matching his excited tone. His beaming expression seemed to be seeking her validation.

She glanced at her watch, felt disappointed, but decided she must go, for she'd told her mother she'd be home by eight.

'Thank you again, for dinner,' she said, her voice chipper, breaking the mood. 'And I really must—'

'Glad you have enjoyed it. And it has been my pleasure.' Leo spoke softly, hauling her back, his eyes firmly on her face. 'But do stop looking at your watch.'

His gaze seemed to stir her, make her wonder why he would have bothered taking her for a meal, why this whole thing had happened in the first place. She felt a burning on her cheeks, felt conscious that her mouth might be stained with red wine. When it came to her job, she felt fired up, but that conversation was over and, really, she ought to be going. She must get the Tube, and a bus at the other end, and a good night's sleep, to be ready to start again tomorrow morning in the world of radio broadcast for a country at war.

'Are you sure you have to go home now?' he asked. 'It will still be light as day out there.'

Clare supposed he meant there was more work to be done back at the office. She felt thirsty, and the brandy on top of the merlot had blunted her thoughts; she'd make typing mistakes, and that wouldn't look very good. She fiddled with her handbag, wondering if she ought to offer to pay the tip and what Kay Pritchard would do in such a situation.

'I'd really like a drink of water,' she said, looking around for the waiter.

'Let's not bother him with that.' He motioned for the bill. 'I have water, and a stash of some good coffee back at the office. But keep that under your hat, Miss Clare Ashby. Because it's not kosher.' He moved his hand, crossing the centre of the table. 'We can have coffee. And you can have your glass of water.'

Leo placed his palm over her forearm, quick and determined, as if this gesture made the decision, *was* the decision. It seemed preposterous to Clare, but maybe it was part of his management style. While he signed the bill and counted out some shillings for the tip, the pressure of his touch lingered and Clare felt a barrier crumbling, one that she had been struggling all evening to keep in place.

Leo stood up, put on his jacket, straightened his lapels and tipped his hat onto his head. He was his own man, taking his time, sure of himself. He went behind her chair, ready, as any gentleman might, to help her. Clare felt his hand press her arm, the palm curling around, a little flick of his fingertip. This touch spoke more words than he had all evening. She sat quite still, as if watching herself. She seemed to know what was going on, and yet it puzzled her, as the situation, indeed herself, and her whole life, changed into something else entirely.

2

CLARE

She told them she was going to bed, but halfway up the stairs, she sat down in the shadows, rested her head on her knees, and listened.

When Clare was younger, and her parents had gone out for the evening, to bridge, or drinks or some other suburban soirée, leaving Anne to babysit, she would not be able to sleep. She'd creep from her bed, sit here on the stairs, and wait for them to come home. Her toes chilled, the staircase a cold tunnel, funnelling draughts, the long evening hours ending with the sound of the key in the door and, spotting her, her parents' gasps of exasperation.

Clare shivered now, leaning her head against the banister, as night air seeped under the curtain drawn across the front door. Lamp light escaped around the half-open door of the sitting room below. She could hear them talking about her.

'She won't even say who the man is. So, no hope of any sort of settlement there,' her father grumbled. 'He might be a boy she knew from school, with nothing to his name anyway. Someone she has met at work. Do you know if she has a boyfriend, Anne?'

'I don't know, Dad, no,' said Clare's sister, sounding bruised and sad.

'You know what she's like. She never tells us anything.' This from her mother, a little muffled, as if smothered by a screwed-up handkerchief. 'There's nothing else for it. We'll have to find a private clinic, but what about the expense? Why is she putting us through this? What with everything else that's going on. My nerves are in tatters.'

'There are places where girls can go away and have babies, and it is all taken care of,' said Anne. Sensible Anne, here on her yearly visit from her home in Scotland. It had been touch and go, their parents speculating that it would be too troublesome and dangerous for their daughter to travel all the way from Inverness, what with the air raids and new rules about unnecessary travel. After all, what might the neighbours say? But Anne had insisted, in her usual no-nonsense way, and had booked the sleeper. Her voice, rounded with kindness, chimed from the sitting room. 'Perhaps we can think about that for Clare?'

'But that means there'll still be a baby. And then what? What will we tell people? Oh, the shame.' A hefty sigh from her mother. 'Soon enough, anyway, it will all become obvious. She won't be able to hide it like she's done so up to now. She'll have to leave her job. Heavens, what will everyone, the family, the street, think of us? What she's been up to?' In the darkness of the stairs, Clare could hear the shudder in her mother's voice. 'I wish this could all disappear.'

Clare dipped her head as if ducking from a blow.

Her mother sobbed audibly and her father, in the gentle way he reserved only for his wife, said, 'Now, now, Celia, don't distress yourself.'

'Oh, Michael...'

'Never mind the neighbours, and everyone,' her sister continued. 'We need to think of Clare. What is best for her?' Her voice was quiet, firm. And Clare, hearing her sister, felt a wrenching stir inside her chest.

'We *are* thinking of her. It's all I can do.' Her mother's voice peaked with indignation.

Anne cut in: 'Perhaps she wants the baby. Really wants it.'

But it seemed her mother didn't hear. 'Oh, heavens, Michael. What have we done to deserve this?'

Clare unpeeled herself from the stairs and made her way up, gripping the rail, her legs like liquid, her stomach flipping. In her box-room bedroom, she undressed in the dark, made more intense by the blackout, put on pyjamas, her hands shaking, and burrowed down between the sheets. The blankets felt stiff and heavy, offering little warmth. The air smelt of soot from the cold grate, and something else. She drew her hands to her face, and on her wrists, her perfume lingered.

She'd been wearing the perfume that evening at the restaurant, back in August. Anne had given it to her last Christmas. He had liked her perfume. He had told her she smelt young and delicious.

In the darkness of her bedroom, the fragrance changed into something cloying and thick. A trickle of nausea rose to her throat. The doctor had said that she would feel sick; it was one of the first signs.

Downstairs, the conversation faded, to be replaced by the sounds of cocoa being made in the kitchen, hot water bottles filled, a clattering of cups. Clare heard them coming up to bed; she knew each of their footsteps, the creak on the half landing. Low, conspiratorial voices. Her parents' bedroom door shut with a click and Clare sensed Anne pausing outside the box-room door, before going into the guest room, the front bedroom they used to share.

Clare curled up on her side, squeezed her eyes shut, longing for sleep, longing for their words to leave her head. She imagined the avenue outside her window, pitch-black, not a light showing. The semi-detached houses, the bay windows blank, an occasional car parked at the kerb. Back gardens turned over for vegetables and Anderson shelters. And above the chimney stacks, the vulnerable night sky. A sort of waiting feeling.

* * *

He'd asked her if she was all right, afterwards. And then had quickly hustled her through the late-summer dusk to Oxford Circus Underground, for it was late and she'd told her mother she'd be home much earlier. After all, they were only having dinner. The suburban sky had sunk into night by the time she let herself in the front door. Her parents were already in their dressing gowns, sitting either side of the hearth, her mother in curlers and hair net, the news bulletin on the radio.

'What time do you call this, Clare?' her father had said, flicking his newspaper down and peering at her over his spectacles, the cliché of his question seeming not to register with him. 'We thought you'd be home ages ago.'

'I had to stay behind. We had a lot on. More than I realised,' Clare replied, her voice over-bright as she stood in the sitting-room doorway. She hadn't mentioned that morning about having dinner with her boss, and couldn't bear to now. 'And then there was something wrong with the trains.'

'Miss Stanford works you hard, then,' said her mother, folding her knitting away.

'Mum, I'm not with Miss Stanford at the moment. I'm on secondment, to the Empire Service.' Clare had felt aghast that this had slipped her mother's mind. 'Remember.'

'Ah, yes, yes, of course. Well, I expect all this extra work is doing you and the country good. Anyway, there's a plate of dinner in the oven for you. If you don't want it now, it can keep for tomorrow.'

Lying now in the darkness of the box room, Clare felt as if pieces were flaking off her. Hot tears streaked from her eyes to soak her pillow as she longed to drift off. That summer, her parents had barely taken notice of her new role at work, had never asked how her days went. And, that evening when she came home late, hadn't spotted the bewildered look on her face, or the threads on the collar of her new green dress where the button had been.

* * *

The siren jerked her awake from scratchy, uneasy sleep, wailing from the school gate at the end of the avenue, its ominous drone finding its way into her bones. She pulled the blankets over her head, covering her ears, her insides shivering. She had felt like this, night after night, since early September, when the threat of air raids began, and she'd first realised something had changed in her body. Perhaps it would be better all round if she simply stayed here and, as her mother wished, disappeared.

Someone opened her door, and she felt a tap on her shoulder, insistent. Anne, always the one to break into her thoughts, hauled the covers back, the light from the hurricane lamp flashing on the ceiling.

'Clare, come on. Grab your eiderdown. Get some shoes on,' she urged. 'Bring the torch. Come downstairs with me.'

Clare wiped tears from her eyes with her pyjama sleeve and got out of bed to follow her sister. Anne's visit had made Clare's internal muddle intensify, and an unnecessary shyness folded over her. She hadn't seen Anne in a year, and had wondered if her sister would notice the oily soup inside her, the burden of her secret as soon as she arrived.

Her nausea returned, Clare took a deep breath as she went down the stairs, Anne's lamp lighting the way ahead. In the front dining room, her parents were setting up camp in the shelter built over the table, her mother complaining about her knees, and her father's face, lit by his torch, a ghostly lurid mask.

'There isn't room for all of us under here, I'm afraid,' he said. 'It'll be too much of a squeeze. And I don't think my lungs can take the damp of the Anderson. Not in this weather.'

'You could try the cupboard under the stairs, Anne,' piped up her mother from beneath the table. 'That's where the children next door go.'

'I don't think there'll be room for both of us,' said Anne. 'We'll go outside.'

'Make sure you keep the shelter door closed,' their father said. 'It's a little tricky.'

'Sorry, Anne,' said their mother, 'But it's not too bad out there. If you don't mind spiders. Surprising what you get used to. Although some things are beyond being tolerated.'

She glanced out from under the table at Clare, as if to check her whereabouts, her pinched face immobile in the gloom, her eyes two dark points. Clare, standing right beside Anne, believed herself to be invisible.

She was a diluted version of Anne, anyway: shorter, more slender, quiet, less robust. And yet they were unmistakably sisters, with the same smile and wavy hair, except Clare's was paler and not so much chestnut as dun-coloured. And it tended to frizz.

Outside, in the back garden, the siren warped the air. In the sky to the east, search lights needled the dark. Clare heard her neighbour the other side of the fence call out to someone inside his own house to remember the brandy. She hurried along the path with

Anne and ducked down the steps into the earthy hole covered with corrugated iron, built the year before by their father and the man next door. Clare thought it looked about the same size as a family plot in a graveyard.

They sat down opposite each other on two creaking camp beds and shut the door. Her father was right; the latch stuck a little. Clare fixed the thick blanket over the doorway. Anne set down a flask, two enamel cups, and a tin of biscuits. In the light of the lamp, Anne's face looked angular and pale against the waves of her hair.

'Allistair will be concerned,' she said, worry creeping around her eyes. 'He'll hear about this on the news. He'll feel helpless, and a bit cross, if you ask me. He didn't want me to come at all.'

'But I think we are safer out here,' Clare said, trying to sound chirpy, although her sister's fear unnerved her. She curled her legs up and pulled her eiderdown round. 'I never like taking my chances under the table. Because there's a whole house above to fall on top of me. And it does get awfully cramped in there with Mum and Dad.'

'It's just that I didn't get a chance to telephone Allistair this evening, like I usually do. What with everything else going on. The "family conference", as Mum called it.' Anne caught Clare's eye, held her stare for a moment. 'But I am glad that I'm here.'

'Really, Anne? You're glad?'

'I had no idea what I was walking into when I arrived. But someone needs to be thinking of you.' She glanced in the direction of the house. 'And they're not doing that.'

One morning, the week before, soon after Anne arrived, Anne had ambushed Clare as she came out of the lavatory where she'd been retching, trying to muffle involuntary crying. She'd pulled Clare into their old bedroom and whispered that she needed to go to the doctor, that she will make the appointment, that she will come with her.

'How do you know?' Clare had asked, aghast.

'You're my little sister.'

Huddled in the shelter, Clare heard something, looked upwards at reams of illuminated cobwebs strung from the corrugated ceiling. The drone of aircraft engines peeled across the edges of the sky, a whirring, metallic sound. A Luftwaffe squadron, creeping over the suburbs. And far off, a deep thudding; less a sound, more of a feeling, coming from inside the earth.

'Oh, dear God,' said Anne, putting her hands over her ears. 'What a coward I am. This is my first. It's been quiet for us up in the Highlands. It seems that the war is happening, elsewhere, to everyone else.' She whispered, as if lowering her voice might keep them safe. 'And now, I appear to be in the thick of it.'

'Not quite,' Clare said. 'This sounds like it is over in Wembley.'

Anne shuddered. 'Poor Wembley.'

'Perhaps we should have asked our neighbour if we could have some of his brandy.'

'We can do better than that,' said Anne, reaching for the flask, her hand shaking. 'We have Mum's cocoa.'

They laughed, despite everything. The emptiness between them, created by time and absence, began to fill, like water from a spring finding its way into a pool.

As Anne gamely poured the cocoa, her company felt brisk, solid, and comforting, as it had last week, when the doctor washed his hands and confirmed everything. Clare had heard Anne's intake of breath, and had experienced a brief cleansing flash of disbelief, a sort of hope he was wrong as he began to write on his notepad, followed by the plunging reality.

And, as bombs fell, two or three miles away, Clare wanted her sister to continue to talk in the way that she did, softly and urgently, for it seemed it would save them both from harm.

They cradled their mugs and sipped. Nibbled biscuits. The horror happening elsewhere and to other people.

'Clare,' Anne said, her eyes wide in the irregular light. 'Will you tell us, or at least me, who? Whose baby is it?'

Clare swallowed. The cocoa clogged her tongue, the milky sweetness sticky. Her sister's question – the thought of the answer and having to admit that truth – felt far worse, much more dangerous than the enemy bombers slicing up the sky.

'I'm so tired,' she uttered, wiping her sleeve over her face. 'Sorry, Anne. I can't. Not really. Not tonight.'

'Sleep then,' said Anne, and her voice cut through Clare with its kindness. 'I understand. We can both try, at least, to get some rest now.'

Anne switched off the lamp and Clare settled down on her camp bed, the darkness pressing into her eyes, blotting out almost everything, like a merciful release from her life. The siren had stopped, and the first wave of bombers had moved on, leaving an odd, dead stillness. Anne's bed creaked as she shuffled to find a comfortable spot and in the blackout, her voice sounding loud and disembodied.

'Where we are, Allistair and I, up near Foyers on the shore of the loch, it is wild and empty.' She sounded as if she were beginning a soothing bedtime story. 'It is safe. It is beautiful, Clare. I can't tell you how beautiful it is.'

'Do you miss it?' she asked, her voice low from under her covers. 'Do you wish you were there now?'

'Aye,' Anne said, and laughed. 'Listen to me! I've been in the Highlands too long!'

For seven years, Anne had lived above Loch Ness with her husband, Allistair. And how happy and how grown-up she was. Life in the Highlands had ruddied her face, given her strong calves, and honed her briskness. Clare had been bridesmaid, the little ten-year-old sister in pink, with the bride and groom outside the church in Harrow, and the Scottish men in kilted splendour. But when she gazed at the photograph on the bureau in the sitting room, she felt detached, a separate being to the child in the picture.

'Clare, will you come back with me? Come back to the Highlands?' Her voice was clear in the earthy darkness. 'You can have your baby there. If you want your baby. And Allistair and I, we will look after you. We will take care of you both.'

Clare couldn't answer, so she pretended to have fallen asleep.

'Clare?'

The horror gripped her again, a fizzing sense of dread, a deep coldness as the man they all wanted to know about crawled in beside her. The sense of care, of attention, transpiring into something opposite and unsavoury. And the reality of what had happened to her sat inside her like a brimming cup of poison.

Eventually, to the restful sound of Anne slumbering, Clare slept, her body giving in to itself, reminded in a deep part of her of the nights of her childhood when they shared the large bedroom, with Anne in the twin bed beside her. Clare stirred once, when the All Clear sounded in the early hours, and woke to the autumn dawn, chilled and aching.

As she lay there, staring at low, metal ceiling, Anne's questions returned, folding themselves around her mind: *Whose baby is it?*

And her answer, whispered to herself and as clear as the morning: *it's mine.*

3

Clare emerged from Oxford Circus Underground later than usual the following morning along with all the other hollow-eyed people, who perhaps felt lucky or intended to keep busy and simply get on with their day. Fine dust suspended thickly in the air, giving it a metallic tang. Nearby, bedraggled pigeons looked like they needed a good night's sleep, too.

As she hurried up Regent Street, towards Broadcasting House, bells on passing buses tinged and taxi horns honked like any other morning in the West End, endeavouring to make the day seem normal. Clare, propelled by this fantasy, showed her pass to the soldier sentry at the sandbagged entrance and again to the commissioner in the foyer, the solid grandness of the reception making her feel she'd arrived somewhere very important indeed. Head down, fearful of who she might bump into, she took the lift to the fifth floor, and the safety of her own department, where she'd been moved back to recently. She walked quickly along the linoleum corridor, passing a parade of varnished doors, returning tired 'good mornings' along the way, and opened the office door bearing the plaque:

Miss M. Stanford

'You're a sight for sore eyes,' Meryl Stanford said, rising from behind Clare's desk in the corner of the outer office. 'I have just taken a telephone message for you to deal with. It's here on the pad.'

'I'm sorry I'm late,' Clare said, hanging up her coat and hat on the stand hemmed in by green, metal filing cabinets. 'Was a little tricky this morning. The Metropolitan line has problems.'

'No apologies needed. What a night. I watched from my bedroom window for a bit until I was persuaded down into the shelter. Up at Hampstead, we have quite the view. Those poor devils in the East End got the worst of it.' Miss Stanford gave her a sharp look. 'Are you well?'

'All well, thank you.' Clare's lie sounded far too bright. 'I will put the kettle on.'

'That's the spirit,' Meryl said, pausing at the door to the inner office.

Clare found it hard to judge her boss's age: well into her thirties, she'd say, for her face gave her away, but with her tall, willowy figure, she could pass as a fashion model, walking as she did from the hips first.

'Mr Hedges is due here in about ten minutes for a meeting. Can you call his secretary on the phone to double check? You never know these days if people are going to turn up or not.'

Miss Stanford teased at the Liberty scarf around her throat, smoothed the lapel on her nipped-in jacket, and offered Clare a scrutinising look, followed by her immaculate smile, her signature red lipstick her battle dress. Meryl had done her time as a senior secretary in Personnel throughout the Thirties, she had confided, and, seeing as it was unheard of for a woman to progress like a man might, she thought she would never get anywhere. Until Britain declared war on Germany, and the men began to leave. Meryl Stanford filled a gap and proved herself to be more than worthy.

'You know, Clare,' she said. 'I'm relieved you're back from your blessed secondment with the Empire Service. The temp wasn't up to scratch, I'm afraid. You've already seen the misfiled carbon copies. I dare not imagine the state of some of those personal files. We'll be discovering mistakes for months.'

Clare smiled with mild satisfaction. She had been back with Miss Stanford for two weeks now, and it had taken her that long to straighten things out. But she felt glad of the extra work, for it filled her mind, albeit temporarily, with blissful, everyday humdrum.

'Oh, and there's a delivery for you, too. On your desk.' Meryl gathered up some files, went into her office and shut the door.

Clare quickly telephoned to check if Mr Hedges, head of personnel, was on his way. She took the kettle and went along the corridor, curving like that on a ship, to fill it at the sink in the pantry at the end, and put it on the little stove set up under the office window. The tape across the panes of glass, to stop them shattering when the bombs fell, obscured her view of Portland Place, and so, these days, the graceful Langham Hotel and the fine mansions along the street looked wonky and not quite right. She arranged cups and spooned tea, remembering that Roger Hedges liked sugar, which seemed extravagant during wartime. She knew what her parents would have to say about that. Out of habit, she sniffed the milk and recoiled. Her stomach fizzed with nausea, and she opened the window for a gulp of sooty air.

When Mr Hedges arrived, all brown-suited and silver-moustached, she followed him with the tea tray into Miss Stanford's office.

'Ah, welcome back, Miss Ashby. Enjoy yourself down in Empire Service?' he asked, settling into the chair in front of Meryl's desk, his false teeth clicking as he spoke. 'All those news bulletins, all the continuity. How was your time with Leo Bailey?'

The tray felt unexpectedly, incredibly heavy. Clare, fearful of it slipping from her hands, set it down on Meryl's desk with a crash.

'Thank you, Mr Hedges. It was interesting.' She hesitated, fixed her smile. The mention of his name, so casually, stupefied her. 'Broadcasting while Tube trains rumble underneath the studio floor – that was certainly a challenge.'

'An enjoyable one, nevertheless,' said Meryl.

Clare nodded, picturing the trains passing in tunnels beneath the building, remembering the gentle vibrations, thinking of the passengers below hanging onto straps, oblivious. She'd been fascinated by the transmission equipment, the microphones, the announcer in his booth, immaculate shirt and tie, the vocal exercises he performed before he spoke, his diction all impartiality and authority, his insistence on a fresh glass of water every half hour.

'You certainly get to know the Bakerloo line timetable, Mr Hedges,' Clare said.

'Good, good. Ha, well, they didn't really think that through, did they, when they built this place? As for Bailey. I like to sit back and watch his illustrious career unfold. He's come far and he'll go far. Started out as some sort of draughtsman. Now look at him. Seems to be good at everything he turns his hand to. He's quite the chap, isn't he?' He cut his laugh short as he waved Clare away and began to shuffle through the files on the desk. 'Now, Miss Stanford, let's press on with this.'

Clare left the office, closed the door behind her, and sat at her desk.

She glanced at the parcel, a small box neatly wrapped with brown paper and tied with string, then picked up the notepad to read the message that Meryl had written that morning. A routine call from a member of staff wanting a meeting to discuss their contract. She leafed through the diary, turning pages to find a suitable slot, and then lifted the receiver and dialled the extension number Meryl had written down. The telephone rang in the office at the other end, somewhere else in Broadcasting House, and while she waited for it to be answered, her eyes flicked back to her parcel. Her name and office number had been written in what looked like a woman's handwriting. It had been sent in the internal post. Clare wanted to throw it in the bin and to tear it open in equal measure, but she knew she ought to get on with her job.

In the receiver, someone said, 'Good morning' and she introduced herself, checked with whom she was speaking, and booked an appointment for them to see Miss Stanford next week.

Low voices came from the adjoining office. They would be a while, the meeting far from being wound up, for Mr Hedges usually began telling jokes with Meryl laughing politely when that was the case. Clare teased at the knotted string on the parcel, peeled the paper off, opened the box, and pulled out a bottle of Chanel No 5. It felt heavy, resting in her palm, radiating glamour and luxury. A note, attached to the neck, in his writing this time, not his secretary's, read:

For you, a suitably more grown-up perfume. Yours, LB

Clare opened her desk drawer, dropped the bottle, paper, string – the lot – in, and shut it.

* * *

While her own cup of tea grew cold, Clare sat staring at her in-tray, at the stack of letters and memorandums to type up, remembering the admiration in Mr Hedges' voice when he dropped Leo Bailey's name. How his words had curled with approval at the idea of Leo's achievements. It grated through Clare's mind. A former draughtsman? She'd learnt this much, but she knew so little of him, really. Except which wine he liked, how he took his coffee, and what it felt like to be sitting beside him on his sofa in the half-dark of his office on the third floor.

Clare shuddered and the bleakness inside her shifted and settled, a cold stone against her spine. She gazed, her eyes stinging with tears, at the dull-green filing cabinets ranged against the wall. All the personal files were locked away inside: the lower-grade staff in the two cabinets to the left, with directors and heads of departments in the one on the right. Clare had the keys to cabinet on the left, while Miss Stanford, as pertaining to her status, kept the keys for the managers' files inside the drawer in her office.

Except, that morning, Miss Stanford had left her keys on Clare's desk.

Clare glanced again at the closed door to the inner office. The meeting stretched on, and it may well be time for Clare to make them another pot of tea. But she sat still. She felt like weeping, but would not allow it. Creeping fury replaced despair, a simmering rage at his recklessness, his arrogance. For sending her a bottle of perfume in the internal post. For his presumptuous note. For the risk he took with her. And how he made her feel.

She picked up Meryl's keys and gingerly unlocked the cabinet on the right. The drawer labelled A to J made a metallic clanging as she pulled it open. She peeked on reflex at the closed office door behind her before fishing through bulging, buff files, the records of many an illustrious career. Holding her breath, she eased out Leo Bailey's folder.

As she took it over to her desk and opened the first page, her head filled with a peculiar rushing noise, like a hundred voices accusing her. This is where she would see the information of any member of staff; she would check it all before starting a letter or a report, the mundane and the everyday: someone's date of birth, their staff number, their next of kin. And yet the ordinary information listed here, written in over the years in different inks, and different hands, cut through her as little lightning shocks: his full name, Leonard Alexander Austen Bailey – sounding rather eminent – and his date of birth. He'd been born in 1908, the year her parents had married. And he lived in Marylebone. This much Clare knew, for it had come up in their conversation over the glasses of merlot, when he'd teased her for living out in the sticks in Harrow. He'd called her his suburban girl, and she'd countered that she quite liked the leafy avenues, but also loved coming into the city each working day.

'We need to get you a flat in London,' he'd said, carving into his lamb cutlets.

Her finger travelled down the first page of the file. His starting salary, back in 1928, at the birth of the BBC, made her pause with a tic of admiration. He'd come in at a respectable higher grade than most new starters. But as Mr Hedges had said, he was quite the chap.

Under next of kin, a name had been scored out: a man who shared his surname, so possibly his father, and most probably now deceased. Beside it, a new name written and dated 1930:

Mrs Jane Bailey

And in brackets, a predecessor in this office, from a time when Clare had still been at school, had written:

(wife).

Prickling cold crept up her throat. Her tongue stiffened, shock intensifying into a rush of dizziness. Clare shut the file, bundled it back into the cabinet, closed the door and locked it. Darts of anger turned inward. How could she not have guessed? Why had she been so stupid? What did he think he was doing? The terrible noise in her head deafened her and the poison began to boil over. The voices inside the inner office grew louder, Mr Hedges about to deliver a punchline. Her stomach turned itself inside out, nausea intense and urgent.

She left the office, hurried along the corridor to the ladies' and into the first cubicle just in time to be painfully, horribly sick.

As she pressed reams of scratchy, BBC-issue toilet paper over her face to suppress her tears and her gulping breaths, Clare's despair turned a full circle. And in her ears, ringing below the thunderous sound of the lavatory cistern, was the memory of Kay Pritchard's confiding voice over a cup of tea in the canteen on her first day at the Empire Service. Clare, nervous and in awe of everyone, had thought she was sharing an in-joke, hadn't thought any more of it.

'You've met Leo Bailey already, of course. He's a good boss. Quite a character,' she'd said, with a knowing twist of her lipsticked mouth, 'but whatever you do, if you ever go into his office, don't sit with him on his sofa.'

Clare went back along the corridor to her office as best she could on shaking legs, keeping her chin up, doing all she could to plaster on a brave, professional, secretary's face.

Mr Hedges had already left and Miss Stanford was in her room, on the telephone. Clare sat down at her desk, shattered, and yet felt a new, unexpected, driving sensation, as if being sick had rinsed something out of her.

She lifted the cover on her typewriter.

'I'm suitably grown-up now, am I?' she uttered under her breath in fury, arranging a sandwich of headed paper, carbon, and flimsy, and winding it into the machine.

Clare typed an immaculate letter of resignation, addressed to Miss Stanford, carbon-copied to Mr Hedges, and one for the file. The words were liberating, making her breathless. And yet, as she finished the envelope, sealed the letter inside, the simplicity of the task hit her, and her anger faded.

She listened to Meryl speaking on her telephone, holding her own with some director or other, the faint clatter of typewriters in other offices along the corridor: girls, just like her, getting on with their jobs. She'd joined the BBC two years before when the world had been hanging on to tentative peace. Working for this creaking, budget-strapped, eminent service felt like being part of a family, or stepping into a deep and comforting, although rather lukewarm, bath.

And Clare, dropping her letter into her boss's in-tray, felt like the fool Leo Bailey had made her: young and stupid, and about to step off a cliff.

4
_____

Saturday morning and the autumn sun shone like it ought to, piercing the mist with gold and cutting through the coal-smoke suburban air. Anne began to pack her suitcase, and after lunch, Clare's father took a bucket and the step ladder out into the back garden to inspect the two apple trees by the fence.

Clare put on her thick cardigan, wrapped a scarf around her neck, and went out the back door.

Her father glanced at her as she approached, skirting the air raid shelter, and then looked straight back at his task, not catching her eye.

As a child, she used to follow him around the garden, seeking out the flowers in the borders, pulling at weeds under his supervision. She'd help him harvest the apples, holding the bucket, counting the fruit. Some apples perfectly smooth and green, blushed with pink; some curious and misshapen, peppered with carbuncles. She could remember vividly the chill in her fingers as she sorted them, fascinated by how a perfect-looking fruit could surprise her with its bitterness as she bit into it. And she wondered which apple might be home to a worm, the peel sometimes not giving up its secret until her mother cut into it to make a pie. And as for the windfalls, puffing with brown decay on the soil under the tree, they were to be despised.

Clare stood by the step ladder as her father studiously ignored her. Her discomfort reminded her of something from the evening at the restaurant and Leo Bailey, saying that he wondered why she wasn't the apple of her parents' eyes. Surely, the favourite, the cherry on the top, the little one still at home?

And she'd said, 'It has never felt that way. As I said, an afterthought.'

Leo Bailey had looked aghast, couldn't believe her, had refilled her glass of wine. She'd thought this over-stepping, his breaking through, as empathy. But it had been pretence.

'You've made your decision then?' her father said, passing the bucket down to her.

She took it, surprised, feeling the vague conciliation in his gesture, and put the bucket straight onto the ground. It felt far too heavy to hold for long.

'I have, yes.'

'Pity you can't go with Anne today.' He came backwards down the steps, concentrating on dusting off his hands, before looking her full in the face. A slight breeze lifted his hair, rearranging the way he combed it, revealing his scalp.

'I offered to work longer than my week's notice,' Clare said, sensing her father's impatience to have her gone. 'They are very short-handed. And I owe it to Miss Stanford to stay on for as long as I can.'

'I take it you didn't give her the reason?'

'No, I did not.'

How could she admit to Meryl Stanford, to any of them, what had happened? What had *really* happened?

'She was very disappointed.'

'I expect she was,' he said, his tone edged in agreement.

Clare had told Meryl that she wanted to go and live with her sister in Scotland – for the duration – and Meryl, after expressing heartfelt understanding and regret, had asked for her forwarding address.

'I can't lie, Clare, this is a shame,' she'd said. 'You have so much potential here. Are you completely sure about this?'

And Clare had nodded, not able to offer any more. Leaving her job was the one thing she was sure about. She would have to, very soon, anyway.

In the back garden, they turned at a rapping sound – Clare's mother knocking on the back door window, waving at them to come in. She looked furious, although Clare knew she'd be simply fretting.

'Must be nearly time for Anne to be off,' her father said. He subtly rearranged his hair. 'Listen, Clare, we've decided, what with all of this...' He gestured towards her, although there was nothing to give her away, her stomach still as flat as a board. He failed to meet her eye. 'We are going to evacuate to Great-Aunt Emily's in Amersham. Your mother's nerves are shot to pieces here.'

'Really, Dad? Great-Aunt Emily?'

He glanced at her, momentarily amused at her observation, a look she'd once enjoyed, perhaps playing the fool for his attention. She knew he could only tolerate her mother's aunt.

'Needs must, I suppose.' He sighed, and his face tightened again. 'I shall only be there for weekends – I'll be here during the week for work.' He seemed to be mightily relieved at the prospect.

'It will be good for Mum to be out of London...' Clare said, prompting him, seeking reassurance, wanting him to say something more that might include her, while everything fell apart around her – her family, scattering; her home, emptying. They'd moved here, to this marvellous, new semi-detached on a leafy avenue in the

London suburbs, when she was about seven. And she could not remember living anywhere else.

'Listen, Dad, about what has happened, I truly can't bring myself to say that I—'

'Come on,' he said, busying himself by folding his step ladder. 'Mum will be worried about the taxi arriving and none of us being ready to say goodbye.'

Clare found Anne by the front door, checking through the small valise she would take into the sleeper compartment, finding space for the Thermos and sandwiches that her mother, bobbing fussily around, had pressed into her hands. Anne, in her thick coat, dressed already for the Highlands, her sturdy shoes, and a lick of lipstick, had full-bodied and steady appeal. And Clare knew her sister would never be harassed by travelling squaddies or sailors on leave. They wouldn't dare.

'I like the way you have rolled your hair these days, by the way,' Anne said. 'I don't think mine will go that way.'

'If you'd said, we could have tried. We don't have enough time now.'

'Plenty of time for that, later, up at Foyers,' Anne said, and gripped her hand. 'I will see you soon, Lumen.'

Clare beamed at her sister's pet-name for her; she hadn't used it in years. It had been borne from *Clare* meaning 'light', and Anne had loved doing Latin at school.

'Yes, well, indeed...' their mother muttered, seemingly embarrassed by her daughters' intimacy, and opening the front door unnecessarily. 'Now where is this blessed taxi?'

'Let's get this suitcase outside then,' Clare's father said, bustling through.

It all seemed to happen too quickly. The taxi pulled up and honked its horn. The boot was opened, and Anne's suitcase tipped inside it. Quick hugs all round, for no one in the Ashby family dared keep a taxi driver waiting. And they stood on the kerb waving to Anne peering out of the back window of the vehicle as it trundled off down the avenue, scattering fallen autumn leaves, slowed, turned right, and was gone.

Clare's father cleared his throat and seemed anxious to locate his handkerchief. Grabbing it, he turned it over in his hand, just in case, while her mother stared at the spot at the top of the road before shaking herself as if she had come to. Net curtains across the road moved a little, and the next-door neighbour stood at his bay window, peering out, possibly wondering at the swift arrival and departure of a car.

Clare heard her mother gasp and make a grab for her cardigan sleeve.

'Clare, come on, get back inside,' she said. 'Hurry up. People may see you getting upset.'

5

On the Monday, two weeks later, Meryl Stanford left for an early lunch at the Langham with Mr Hedges; it would be a long one, she told Clare, for they were discussing her replacement.

Clare contemplated the sandwich sitting on her desk and felt her nausea simmering again, like an annoying acquaintance who wouldn't take a hint. She sucked a mint instead, sifted through the buff files in her in-tray, tucked a couple under her arm and left the office.

She took the stairs down to the third floor, where wood panelling declared the directors' importance and a carpet deadened the footfalls of the staff serving them. One or two people glanced her way, not recognising her, but Clare gave them a confident smile, her fingertips leaving damp prints on the cardboard files clutched in her hands. She'd brought them as a diversion to any queries as to why she was making her way along the hallowed halls to Leo Bailey's office.

The desk belonging to his secretary, Miss Halliwell, a renowned dragon, was empty. Moving easily past this first hurdle made Clare shudder with relief. She had not considered how she might have begun to explain herself to the formidable woman who guarded her boss with fervour bordering on obsession. Had Miss Halliwell questioned having to package up a bottle of Chanel No 5 the other week and addressing it to a young secretary in Personnel? Or had she, like everyone else, indulged her boss, turned a blind eye to his bemusing whims?

The door to Leo's own office stood open.

Clare paused on the threshold for a moment, watching him working at his desk, cutting his pen over a typewritten report, sifting pages, his head nodding over his choice of words and amendments. It felt curiously powerful to observe him without him realising, even for those brief seconds. He ran a brisk hand through the hair over his temple. His attractiveness, like an energy fuelling him, persisted, and she felt herself quake at the memory of knowing him in the way that she did. Remembering the way his skin smelled. How it felt to be held by him. That strange knowing sensation of something, however brief, shared between them. She clutched the files to her chest, words escaping her, hoping anger would be her armour.

At the corner of her eye sat the sofa, cushions plumped, the coffee table in front of it tidy, clear of cups, periodicals stacked neatly. She dared herself to look at the floor beneath it, wondering if the cleaners had thought for a second who the lost button had belonged to.

Leo must have sensed her, or noticed the imperceptible change in the light, her shadow perhaps on the wall, for he stopped, his pen poised and in danger of dropping a blot of ink, spoiling the report on his desk. He looked up with a brief snap of annoyance at being disturbed.

'Clare,' he said, his voice light and professional. 'Goodness, you made me jump.' He screwed the lid back on his pen, put it down, and gave her a flat, wary look. 'What brings you here?'

What indeed? Clare wanted to see him; she wanted to speak to him, have some sort of discourse that might shed light on what had become of her. A need for clarity had driven her here to his office. Her wanting to make something so utterly awful feel normal: something she could cope with. And live with. But, it seemed, he had no idea.

His eyes brightened. 'Are those files for me?'

Clare gestured with them, glad that they formed a barrier. Since she'd left his department, she had managed to avoid him. And, she assumed that because she had not acknowledged the perfume, he had been avoiding her. Once or twice, she'd caught a glimpse of him hurrying into a lift, or into an office, and she'd cringed, checked herself and turned on her heel, exhaling anger. But now, here alone with him, pent-up rage melted into confusion, and a shivering trace of fear.

She swallowed. 'No, Leo, they're not.'

He frowned, looked annoyed.

'Then what can I do for you?' he asked, clipped and business-like.

'Sorry, I can see you're busy,' she said, meeting his detached tone, managing to sound contained despite turmoil humming in her head. 'But I wanted to know, to ask. You see, I need to know...' She took a breath to steady herself, not quite believing what she was about to say. 'Would you like us to have dinner again?'

'What?' His face broadened in surprise, his good looks returning with his smile. 'Oh, well, I can't see why not.' He seemed to warm up. 'Lunch might be better, though. I'll have a word with Miss Halliwell, check my diary.' He sat back in his chair, as if to get a better view of her, remembering something. 'Ah, and of course, you are leaving us. I saw it in the Personnel Memo the other week. So, yes, we can have a jolly lunch if you like? You'll have to tell me about your new job. I'm sure you'll be excellent. I take it you have a new job, is that right?'

'A jolly lunch?' she repeated, aghast.

He hadn't sounded at all surprised that she was leaving. He hadn't asked why.

The reason sat on the top of her tongue but she couldn't bring herself to come out with it. His veneer, how he presented himself, his lack of sentiment and care, worked to negate and diminish her. Speaking the truth of the situation he had brought on her would only make things worse. She couldn't put herself through any more of it.

'Ah, Clare, you look all hurt,' Leo said, moving out from behind his desk to lean casually against it. He set his gaze on her, his eyes deepening in colour and his composure tugged at her, made her anger surge again. An unwanted blush bloomed up her throat. 'From the look on your face, perhaps lunch and most definitely dinner would not be appropriate. Perhaps we have misunderstood each other from the start.'

Something brightened inside her, a sort of relief at his half-hearted acknowledgement. But, straight away, she realised he had no idea what he had done, how he had seduced her, tricked her, used her, and pretended. Or if did have an idea, he did not care. She could not bear to look at the sofa. Had it been a normal event for him? Had it been something he went about as a matter of course? Her fingertips felt clammy, the files in her hands in danger of slipping from her grasp.

'Perhaps,' he said, lowering his voice, glancing at the open office door, his tone dismissive, 'this hasn't been what either of us thought it was.'

Leo walked over as if to close the door.

'There's no need to close the door, Leo. Miss Halliwell isn't out there to overhear.'

Clare thought about what Kay Pritchard had said about resisting sitting on the sofa with him. Poor Kay Pritchard. And yet the light in that girl's eyes had still looked like hero-worship.

Clare buckled down, finding strength.

'I'm going now, and I'm glad I'm leaving,' she said, her words hard against her teeth. 'Forget about it. Lunch, dinner, whatever. Forget it.'

Leo paused, standing close to her. She heard him breathing, could see the fine weave of his suit, the freshness of his shirt.

'You got my parcel, Clare? The perfume? You're not wearing it.'

Clare wanted to laugh. She almost admired him, his nerve. How he rode along on his talent, his cocky reputation, so admired by the likes of Roger Hedges and even Meryl Stanford.

'No, I thought I'd save it for a special occasion,' she said, hearing her own fickleness, hating herself for going along with his charade, when on the tip of her tongue hung the questions: *And what about your wife? What about Jane Bailey? Does she wear Chanel No 5?*

'I hope you find that special occasion, Clare.'

He looked sorry for her, almost wistful. He lifted a hand as if to touch her shoulder.

She stepped back and his hand fell short.

'As I said, I'm going.'

'We better say goodbye then.'

'Don't bother.' Clare turned and walked out of his office.

'Well— good luck!' he called, as if to cover himself and for a second, sounding full of doubt.

She did not answer. She did not look back.

That Friday, on her last day, a medley of colleagues crammed into Miss Stanford's office for cheese straws, baked by somebody's mother – Clare forgot who – and tots of sherry and a little pop of champagne procured by Mr Hedges from the director's dining room. Meryl Stanford gave the speech. Anyone else doing it would have made Clare's toes curl, but Miss Stanford was genuinely saddened, and Clare knew this because her boss would not look at her.

'What a loss it is to our department,' Meryl said, with poised, slender elegance, her teary eyes fixed on the other faces, 'to the Corporation. To us all.'

'And yet,' said Mr Hedges, with a strange movement in his moustache, 'it is most certainly Scotland's gain.'

People raised their glasses towards Clare and gave a little cheer. The girls from Programmes gathered round her, asking, but where was she going to live? Was she going into the forces? And wasn't there an airfield at Inverness? Do we have a BBC office in the Highlands? They'd take her on, surely. Earnest secretaries from Personnel uttered that they weren't surprised she was leaving if she had a chance to get out of London. The post room boy wondered why there wasn't any cake.

Clare explained again, tiring of her own voice, that her parents had decided to evacuate, and, really, things at home had changed an awful lot. She painted the unflattering picture of Great-Aunt Emily to sympathetic nods and grimaces of understanding. And there was no room for Clare at her cottage in Amersham, sadly. It made sense to go and stay with Anne. Yes, she was close to her sister, even though there was ten years between them. There would be much to do up there in the Highlands. She would try to get a job in local defences, or something, to do some good. She embroidered her story, hoping it didn't sound too detailed, or too extreme. But then, what was too extreme in times of war? And all the while, she kept her eye on the door, praying Leo Bailey did not decide to make an appearance.

As the gathering wound down, Clare lost track of the time. It was hard to tell what time it was once the blackout went up, and in the middle of October, this would be done by the brown-coated orderlies at sixteen hundred hours on the dot. People scattered, said their farewells and keep-in-touches. Miss Stanford had to dash off for dinner, regrettably, or she would have taken Clare for a drink at the Langham.

'This is my address,' she said in the deserted office, handing Clare a slip on which she'd written in her copperplate hand. 'I have your sister's and now you have mine. Belts and braces, with the postal service these days, is the best way to go.'

Miss Stanford hugged Clare, long and firm, the brooch on her scented, Jaegar wool coat digging into Clare's shoulder, the fur collar tickling Clare's nose.

A trill of her kid-gloved hand and off she went.

Clare had promised Miss Stanford she'd finish typing up a report on staff shortages and overtime budgets, to be sent over to Mr Hedges for first thing Monday morning, so she got straight on to it. Afterwards, she tidied her desk, wrote notes for the incoming temp, and opened the bottom drawer for a final time. The perfume bottle teased and trivialised her. She couldn't leave that for someone else to find. She stuffed it in her handbag, snapping it shut.

As she buttoned her coat, the alarm went for the second time in ten minutes, decreeing that all staff had to proceed, quickest route possible but without using the lifts, into the basement. She put on her hat, fired by her instinct to flee, to not get caught up with everyone and go to the exit instead. She'd make it to the Underground, and find solace in strangers, and not people who would feel they had to make conversation.

The fifth-floor corridor held a strange, deserted hush, for most of Personnel had left at their usual contracted hour, but, in the stairwell, she slotted herself into the weary trail of people winding their way down, voices lowered in respect to the lurking danger.

The building shuddered, as if it had shivered in fright, the lights flickered, and someone said, 'Here we go again.'

'There's been reports of parachute bombs,' said another. 'They come down in silence, settle, wait to explode, sometimes hours later.'

'Then, is this to be battle instructions?'

'Only if there are stormtroopers attached to the parachutes.'

'Never mind finest hour, sounds like final hour.'

Clare shut the conversations out, wanting to batten down and leave all this behind.

Her stomach flipped. Leo Bailey had emerged with Kay Pritchard from the door to a floor below her, his arm resting lightly on Kay's back, guiding her. Clare stopped for the briefest beat on the stair, but a tap from someone behind nudged her on. She wondered at the power, the fury in her stare, as for no reason, Leo glanced back up the stairs, his eyes locking on hers. He raised his eyebrows in an enquiring way, how he would do when he wanted to start a conversation. Lines of exhaustion scored his face. He looked somehow smaller, older, and fearful, and so fitted in perfectly with the rest of them as he turned, continuing on his way.

Something fierce cut through Clare and she fought it, couldn't express it, for who knew what might happen in front of all these people? And still, she plodded on down the stairs, her anguish ticking at the back of her throat.

At the doorway to Reception, she slipped through, hearing him calling, 'Clare, Miss Ashby, wait. Are you not going to the basement? Clare?' An echo up the stairwell.

Outside, in the blackout, buildings looked blank and muted in the backdrop of arcing white flares and pinkish smoke somewhere towards Piccadilly billowing against the night. The pale stone of

The Langham gleamed like a beacon. The guns up at Regent's Park blasted, and searchlights scraped the sky. And above it all, and beneath Clare's skin, the gnawing sound of the bombers.

She could see the faint, yellow glow from the entrance to Oxford Circus Underground, but bombs had begun to fall, and the ground thumped like something monstrous and heavy-footed approaching. The thought of being below, beneath its force, grinded her stomach.

She turned and scooted left down a pitch-black side street, the white-washed lines along the kerbs guiding her. In Cavendish Square, the sky widened, lighter than the ground and the full fury of the raid opened above her. The dreadful, menacing whistling. Explosions ripping the air. She stopped, couldn't help herself, and watched, pulled in by the show. The grand mansions loomed black against black, and above her, a whole new universe of falling, bursting stars split the sky.

Clare shook herself, fixed her mind on Baker Street Station and on the notion that she could get a train back to Harrow, somehow. She continued to pound along the empty street, wondered how soon she'd be spotted by an ARP and ordered to take shelter, and how they all kept going in this nightmare, back at the BBC, the ticker tape spilling out its information, transmitters swapped one to another so the voices will not go off the air. The stalwarts at their posts or waiting it out in the basement.

The look in Leo's eyes came back to her, that glance up the stairwell. A suggestion of care. And three months earlier, on that evening in his office, she had seen that look, and it had drawn her in, and assured her. His conversation lively and sparking. Her presence there a duty. Something she ought to be doing, sitting on her boss's sofa with a nightcap coffee. Something grown-up and expected of her, in this thrilling, new, broadcasting world.

'*Whatever you do...*' Kay Pritchard had said.

It had been far from care.

* * *

The smell of cordite, here on the street, stung her nostrils like smelling salts. And on she hurried, crossing Marylebone High Street. Leo's home address flickered behind her eyes, like a script she was typing, and she realised where she was going. They had laughed, that evening, over the fact he could walk to work in ten minutes, perfect for early-morning starts and late-night radio emergencies. But he'd not told her his address; she'd memorised it from her single simple glance at his file. And one thing Miss Stanford admired her for, had indeed hired her for, was her memory.

'I'd describe it as photographic,' Meryl had said.

Clare pushed open the main door to the mansion block, mindful of not allowing the mustard-coloured light in the foyer to escape. The cage-lift door stood open, but she took the stairs, her handbag containing the perfume bottle feeling heavy and bulky as she ascended. Fury returned and she welcomed it, like a quenching breath of fresh air. She had let it go, momentarily, by putting herself into danger, subjecting herself to the raid, the fire in the sky.

She paused on a landing, her hand pressed to her chest, feeding off the renewed rage inside her.

That hot, August evening with Leo, she had felt as if, in her mind, she had been moving swiftly along a passageway, with just one door at the end. It had felt good to be walking beside him back to Broadcasting House. He had made her feel solid, no longer invisible. She didn't need to play up to get his attention. All she had to be, it seemed, was herself.

The third floor at Broadcasting House had been quiet, the staff busy in the basement studios. His office, panelled with smooth wood, appeared haven-like in the glow of the forty-watt-bulb lamp on the desk. Leo had indicated the sofa, had sat at its opposite end facing her, his arm relaxed along the back. His coffee had tasted exceptionally good, and his conversation, encompassing art and music, had circled around her, enlightened her. Relaxed her. She'd seemed to charm him. He asked all the right questions. He'd even fetched a glass of water.

But the air had shifted once more, the atmosphere changed, like it had in the restaurant. He had taken the coffee cup from her hand, even though she had not finished, and set it down on the table.

Remembering, Clare caught her breath.

She had become weightless, watching herself from above as he reached towards her, his hand around the back of her neck, heavy there. His body like a wall, bigger than her, closing in. The buttons across the shoulder of her dress, fiddly and difficult.

'I like your perfume,' he'd uttered close to her ear. 'You smell young and delicious.'

She had liked him, had thought he admired her. She thought he cared. And dinner, wine, and coffee, surely, had merely been his way of showing it. Of thanking her. After all, she was a fine and efficient secretary. She'd heard the ping of the button as it hit the parquet. His mouth closed over hers, kissing deeply. She'd pulled away; she uttered as best she could that she didn't want him to do that. She'd tried to peel herself back and away from him. She didn't like him; she didn't know him at all.

At Leo Bailey's mansion block, the front doors along the passageway were painted regulation brown, and outside his flat, a console with a vase of rust-coloured chrysanthemums and a stand containing a man's black umbrella propped cosily against a woman's in navy blue. Such everyday, commonplace things, their significance flashing through Clare's temples. His wife. Had Jane Bailey any idea who she'd married?

Clare opened her handbag and rummaged inside it, her scalp

tightening with fear that the front door might be flung open at any moment. But surely no fool, not even Jane Bailey, would be home, with the air raid booming outside. Even so, on their return, if the flats survived, someone would find it, either Leo or Jane, wonder at it, or better still, know its meaning.

The doormat declared:

Welcome

Sucking in her breath with a buoyant flash of excitement, Clare set down the bottle of Chanel No 5 and made her escape, her steps ringing on the tiled stairs.

Outside, the street felt quiet and strange, a static tension in the air, the raid at a low ebb. She felt giddy, disorientated. She shivered with cold, wanted, more than anything, to be at home, wanted to get herself, and the little life inside her, to the safety of the bay-windowed semi on the leafy avenue. But trailing her way up to Baker Street, she remembered her parents were that evening packing for Great-Aunt Emily's, and her childhood home as she knew it would soon disappear. The night shimmered around her, an untold hell. Clare and her baby, alone.

6

CLARE

The Highlands, October 1940

A bank of cloud moved across the sky over the Royal Highland Hotel next to the station, splitting the sky in half and threatening to shut out the pale sun. Clare, waiting for Anne and hollowed out from lack of sleep, fancied the clouds looked like a great closing eyelid.

She felt crushingly tired, but at least now her feet rested on solid ground. She'd been juddering along in the train for the last twelve hours trying to sleep in her cramped couchette with the soupy-yellow lamp while the wheels rumbled beneath her spine. The pitch-black night outside, if she'd dared to lift the blind a chink, hemmed her in like suffocating velvet.

When the train had halted in sidings in the early morning, she'd seen cranes on the skyline and a roofscape with a mass of chimneys, and assumed she'd arrived in Glasgow, although to confuse any parachuting enemy, all station signs had been removed. She'd fallen into a sleep brimming with tetchy dreaming, before waking two hours later to a wild landscape of green glens, tumbling rivers, and wide, glimmering lochs. And she'd found herself relaxing into her smile, mesmerised by the purple and grey hills rolling to the horizon, tantalising her with promises of freedom.

A rusty, old van rumbled in over the cobbles of the station forecourt, with Anne at the wheel, tooting the horn, shaking Clare from her daydream.

'You made it, you made it,' Anne cried, cranking the handbrake and leaping out in her smart, fitted tweeds, in conflict with the state of the mud-splattered vehicle.

'I did, I did,' Clare said, allowing Anne to pull her into a tight embrace, then take charge of her suitcase and settle her in the passenger seat.

'God, you look done in, Lumen. Let's get you home. And before you ask, Allistair has our car for work; this is our neighbour's van – Allistair's cousin's husband's – and the gear stick is like stirring porridge.'

Anne drove proficiently, revving between the gear changes, manoeuvring the tall stick. She turned corners through streets of grey stone and alongside a river spanned by bridges, the sky pierced with dark steeples, until Inverness faded, and the view began to widen again. Clare caught a glimpse of Loch Ness, enormous, black, motionless, cut in by cliffs and stony foreshores but soon enough, towering pinewoods swallowed the road.

'We're at the head of the Great Glen, here at Inverness: the fault that slices through Scotland,' Anne said. 'It teases you, doesn't it?'

'What teases you?' Clare asked sleepily.

'The loch, Lumen. But it's there right enough, filling the depths. It shows itself, then disappears, as we drive our way along. It never fails to surprise me, even after all these years. The vastness of it. You never quite fathom it, really, however hard you look.'

Clare peered around Anne, through the driver's window, and said, 'Gone again.'

They started to ascend and soon the woods lay below them, and below that, somewhere, the loch. The road curved and peeled its way over moorland elevated above the huge glen. A small loch – Loch Mhor, Anne told her, pronouncing it perfectly – and other bodies of water, little lochans, reflected the sky in undulating heathland of gorse and bracken. And on the horizon were deep wedges of forest and the constant, distant hills, painted in layers of green and grey, shadows against the pewter sky.

'We're a good twenty miles from Inverness, but I'm glad we can get you home and settled before dark,' said Anne, glancing up at the cloud which now sealed the sky and skimmed the hills. 'Evening up here in the northlands draws in long before teatime in autumn.'

Eventually, Clare spotted the road sign for Foyers to the right, but Anne turned left and followed a narrow road, ribbon-like over the rough heath.

Noticing Clare's confusion, Anne said, 'Foyers proper is down near the shore of the loch. And we're up here, the last house on the lochan.'

Stone fences either side grew tighter as the road shadowed the shore of a miniature loch. Passing a scattering of houses, Anne slowed down onto a track sheltered by a line of dripping aspens and stopped in front of a solid, grey manse with tufts of errant grass on its roof and a stand of pines creaking behind it. The dusk had caught up with them, glittering raindrops splattered the windscreen and Clare had the glorious feeling that she had arrived somewhere settled and very old.

'Out you hop. I'll get your suitcase, and will take the van back to Isla's,' said Anne. 'Won't be long. Allistair is not home yet. The kitchen will be warm. The blackout's down; I left a lamp burning. On you go.'

'But I don't have a key, Anne,' Clare said, getting out.

'Ah, it's never locked.'

Clare stood for a moment in the deepening twilight as the engine faded off back down the track. The air smelt pure, with a tang of leaf mould and spruce, with an earthy chill at the back of it. Clare breathed in and breathed out fully for the first time in months.

She opened the front door and found her way across the wide, rather baronial hallway and through to the kitchen at the back, where the grate in the range glowed red, and an old-fashioned oil lamp burnt steadily in the corner. A tabby cat stirred in a chair by the hearth, stretching out his paws and uttering a drowsy greeting. Clare peeled off her coat, stripped her gloves, and walked to the window.

Peering around the blackout, she could make out the darkening garden, with terraces of granite cushioned by heather, and rainy mist pinning the evening sky to the tops of the distant hills. She wondered who might have seen the pinprick of light she'd risked showing across the immense landscape. Her new home, and she couldn't be anywhere safer or anywhere more removed from her younger life.

* * *

Anne bustled in, lit more lamps, and set to work on a good, strong cup of tea.

'You must be scunnered, as Allistair would say. You'll be wanting soup, no doubt,' she said. 'And I have some fresh bread and butter. We need to get the colour back into your cheeks, Lumen. Now you're here, it shouldn't take long.'

Clare sat at the table and watched her sister busy herself, while the tabby plonked down onto the floor and curled himself around her calves. Their conversation skirted the reason she was here, sticking with her journey, their parents, how readily they, or rather their mother, had settled at Great-Aunt Emily's at Amersham. For their father, they concluded, it would be a different matter. The superficial practicalities suited Clare. She felt too weary, too yes, *scunnered*, to consider her reality: being here in Scotland with her sister, the prospect of the baby.

Anne set a mug of brown tea and a bowl of soup before her, and cut her a hunk of bread.

'Eat up, and then I will take you upstairs and show you your bedroom. When Allistair gets home, we can all sit in the parlour together while he has his supper. We like the wireless in the evenings.'

As Clare spooned her soup, she asked Anne if Allistair still worked at the same school in Inverness.

'Yes, the boys' grammar. Head of English now. He'll complain and tell you he doesn't enjoy it, but I know he does really.'

'How do you know?'

'He wouldn't do it if he didn't.'

Anne's smile creased her face, radiating confidence. Of course, Anne knew what Allistair would or wouldn't do. She had been married to him for ten years, had known him even longer. Understanding another person, so richly and intimately and happily, seemed to Clare something other people did, something she had no hope of achieving. After all, the only part of the man linked with her, for life, that she understood, or that he had decided to show her, proved to be the worst, most appalling part of himself.

Despair returned, like a shadow catching up with her, and on reflex, she let her hand rest on her slightly swelling stomach as if to comfort the child that must bear this legacy.

'And you're still tutoring?' Clare asked, rallying a little.

'I am indeed,' said Anne, fixing her eyes on Clare's face, determined – she decided – not to look where her hand had been. 'Two or three students a week. They sit around this kitchen table, drinking tea, eating my biscuits, and I get them to analyse *Far From the Madding Crowd.*'

Clare found herself smiling. 'I like the sound of that.'

'It's cosy, and they're good company,' Anne said. 'It keeps me out of mischief, Allistair says.'

'Don't you miss teaching in a school?'

'Of course, I do. But I had to give up once I married. That's the rules, or rather the way of the world. But we had thought, of course, that there'd be other things to occupy me.' Anne's eyes brightened with moisture. 'Ten years and no baby.' She sighed, failed to continue with her train of thought. 'But, *wheesht*, enough of that, Mrs Anne Fraser.'

Anne cleared the plates and led the way up the robust, oaken staircase, around the half landing and on up into the shadows of a passageway.

'You're just in here,' she said, opening a door into a pleasant bedroom smelling of polish and lavender. A small hearth held a scoop of glowing coals behind a fireguard. 'Ah good, Isla has lit the fire for you. I wondered if she'd remember.'

A queen-sized bed with a cushiony eiderdown sat in a gleaming expanse of lino, with rag rugs scattered like stepping-stones.

'The cousin whose husband owns the van?' asked Clare, tiredness returning.

Anne hoisted her suitcase onto a chest of drawers under the window. 'Isla, yes, Allistair's cousin. It's her van. Or rather, Isla's husband's van. She lives down the road. We passed her place earlier, Lochan Cottage. Now settle in, no need to hurry.' For the first time, Anne glanced towards Clare's tummy and went to say something, but decided against it. 'Your bathroom is just next door.'

Clare eyed her suitcase, contemplated unpacking. She'd brought her warmest clothes for the winter, leaving her new, ruined, green dress behind. She never wanted to wear it again.

She had hoped tea and soup would have perked her up, but exhaustion seemed to pucker like waves over her body. She sat on the bed for some moments, wondering if that would do her some good. The curtains were closed, but Clare could hear the wind in the branches of the pines outside, a plaintive, continuous soughing. Beyond, nightfall had an echoing presence of its own.

She changed into her pyjamas and dressing gown, socks, and slippers, combed out her hair and decided a wash might work a miracle. After rummaging in her case for her sponge bag, she left the room, and opened the next door along the landing. Flicking the light switch, she walked in, stopped, and took a step back. She'd clearly gone into the wrong room, and on reflex, began to close the door, but hesitated, her hand resting on the handle. She poked her head back around and stared. She saw a cot in the corner, a nursing chair beside it. A stack of knitted blankets in sugary shades sat at the foot of the cot, a lacy shawl folded over the arm of the chair. On the walls, papered with a pattern of naïve flowers, framed prints of Rupert the Bear had been hung rather too high for a child to appreciate. But then again, Allistair, bless him, stood over six foot tall.

Clare backed out, snapped the light off, and found the bathroom, locked the door. Sitting on the edge of the bath, she fixated on the slender, black and white tiles set in a line around the walls, listened to the drip of the cold tap, could smell the moist, floral scent of the bar of soap on the basin, and began to shiver. Her thoughts crunched together in her head, confusion and alarm at the nursery's established feel chattering for attention, her heartbeat tripping and stuttering.

She heard the front door open below and Allistair's voice along the hallway calling his, 'Hello, hen,' to Anne. They'd only had about three weeks since Anne returned from Harrow to get to work decorating. How could anyone secure the baby's equipment so quickly these days, especially here in the wilds of Scotland?

Clare found her flannel, ran it under the cold tap and pressed it to her face. As she took ragged breaths through the cloth, her shock sank into odd numb realisation as her sister's words returned to her: *ten years and no baby*.

She looked around the bathroom in a daze, seeing the future that she had found herself in for the first time.

She brushed her hair again, wanting to seem normal and presentable, and made her way downstairs, following their voices and the path of lamp light from the parlour.

'Ah here she is, little Lumen,' said Allistair, leaping to his feet from his fireside chair, his height generous and impressive as he bestowed on Clare his sturdy embrace. 'How long has it been? Look at you. My God, you are all grown-up now. But surely, I must have seen you some time in the last ten years? Since our wedding?' He glanced at Anne.

'You did. It was father's fortieth birthday back home, in Harrow. In '33, I think,' said Anne, 'so Clare would have been about twelve.'

'I remember,' said Clare, although not admitting to being unable to place the occasion. But she recalled her brother-in-law's energy, her sisterly admiration for him. His large, kindly presence at the house, his laugh loud, his accent singsong and precise, an unfamiliar sound in the London borough of Harrow. 'I apologise for being in my dressing gown, Allistair, but I'm just about ready for bed.'

'Och, I don't blame you. And we don't stand on ceremony here,' said Allistair. 'You've had a fair old journey. But this is your home now; sit yourself down, that's it.'

'Relax by the fire, Clare; here, take my chair,' said Anne. 'We can have cocoa and listen to the news.'

Anne went off to busy herself in the kitchen, Allistair tuned in the wireless and Clare sat in an armchair opposite as a scattering of broadcasted words found its way through the static. Anne's chair felt supremely comfortable, the parlour rich with texture, with a tartan rug covering the footstool and the panelling glowing in the lamplight. The tabby had stalked in and found a warm spot by the fire, its presence peaceful. By the door stood an old screen to guard against draughts, its decorated surface depicting a menagerie of wild animals. Clare spotted red squirrels, a fox, badgers, and a deer emerging from a dark, oil-painted pine forest. She smiled, knew it warranted closer inspection, but felt pleasantly too tired to do so. She felt herself expand into the room's four corners, warmed at last. Small flames licking around the hearth gave off a bewitching, earthy aroma. She breathed in greedily and sensed a yearning, a sort of homesickness, but knew it couldn't be the case because their own fire in the sitting room in Harrow had never smelt like that.

'What are you burning there in the grate, Allistair?'

'Peat, Clare,' he said. 'They cut it just down the road. We get quite a good price for it, of course. We have a sprinkling of neighbours here. And you'll meet Cousin Isla soon, no doubt. You'll meet everyone, such as we are, all in good time.'

'Ah yes, Isla. I've already had the pleasure of the van,' Clare said, and felt her voice break at the prospect of community, of compassion. 'You and Anne. You've both been so very kind to me. I don't know how I...'

Allistair looked at her. 'Anne is mighty glad you're here.' He spoke softly. 'We both are. We think it will do us all the world of good, all round, to have you to stay. Ah, here we are!' Allistair's eyes brightened, widening adoringly as Anne came back in. 'Here you are, hen, in time for the news.'

Anne set down the tray and handed round the cocoa – 'better than Mum's?' Anne asked Clare with a glint in her eye – and they sipped and listened to the bulletin. Clare felt drowsy, in a cherished, cradled way, enjoying the crackle of the burning peat and its scent that seemed to come from a fabled, ancient place, or at least made her feel she'd arrived where she had always longed to be. Perhaps, here then, she thought, stealing a glance at her companions' faces, perhaps here in the last house on the lochan, beyond Foyers, above the loch, on the edge of the Great Glen, she had found it.

The cat noticed her, leaped up onto her lap and settled there. Tears wetted Clare's eyes, surprising her. She didn't feel entirely sure where they had come from. She dabbed quickly with her handkerchief.

'Clare, I'm sorry, are you all right? Is Hamish bothering you?' asked Anne. 'You must be so very tired and overcome. It has been quite a time for you.'

Clare nodded, then shook her head, dabbed some more.

'No, Hamish is fine. He's lovely.'

'Maybe hearing this bulletin from the BBC is making you homesick,' said Allistair, kindly. 'Leaving your job and everything. It must have been very exciting for you, working in radio, down in the Smoke, despite of all the danger. Perhaps you wish you were back there?'

'That's certainly not it.' Clare gave a sleepy half smile.

She wouldn't be anywhere else.

7

MIRREN

The Highlands, Summer 1985

Standing at the window, in the bedroom that until last month had been *their* bedroom, Mirren watched a pleasure boat chugging up the loch, diminishing into the vastness on its way to show holiday-makers the ruin of Castle Urquhart. Their own stone house, with its treasured views across the dark water, sat elevated on the road out of Inverness, here at the head of the Great Glen. It stood, Victorian, solid, and intact, at least for now, because Gregor hadn't started the formalities of the separation. He had, simply, decided to leave Mirren and their daughter Kirstine and the home they'd shared for years, packed a suitcase and gone. But not that thoroughly, Mirren noted as she opened the wardrobe door. He'd left behind his dress shirt and the kilt that had been his father's and worn on special occasions. And a belt coiled in the dust at the bottom of the wardrobe.

Despite a few empty drawers and hangers, Gregor remained. Conversations lingered, so many messy and unarticulated feelings lying around, as if dropped carelessly, like an odd sock on the way to the laundry. All, Mirren assumed, to be picked up, tidied away, and dealt with another day.

She shut the wardrobe and waited for the boat, carrying its cargo of tourists, bent on glimpsing the monster or at least having their imaginations teased and ignited, to disappear, before beginning her chores. She wiped over the mirror, rearranging dust, and half-heartedly moved things on the dressing table to polish around them. The little porcelain dish, given to her by Anne one Christmas, tinkled with a hoard of earrings, including her precious green gemstone ones and an old necklace and, it seemed, her pair of nail scissors. She'd wondered where they'd got to. She picked them up, puzzled, spotted beard hairs clinging to the blades. Oh, she wished he wouldn't do that: use her scissors, not clean them, and put them back in the wrong place. She turned to the bedroom door, ready to yell down the stairs to him that she really wished he *wouldn't*.

Mirren stopped herself in time, catching a glimpse of her enraged face in the mirror, her head of curls that she hadn't bothered with that morning, frizzing away. She knew exactly who she'd got unruly hair from, for she remembered that much about her mother, or perhaps it had been from a photograph, or something someone had told her once. As for her eyes, that fierce, wide-set gaze of hers, no one would ever dare place it.

She marched into the bathroom, dipped her fingertips in the tub of her 'goop', as Kirstine called it, and tackled her hair, masking its springiness, its fuzziness, changing its nature. Maybe that had been the problem, the reason why Gregor had packed up and left her: the bickering, the anger, *and* the constant disguise.

Mirren heard footsteps on the path, a key in the door – Kirstine back already. And she'd hardly started on the bedroom, hadn't even got the hoover out.

'Mum, I couldn't get the bread you wanted, so we'll have to

make do with Hovis,' Kirstine called on her way along the hall. 'I know it's not your favourite. But I got that shortbread you like.'

Her daughter's enthusiasm for her favourite biscuits sparked a warm, wet buzzing behind her eyes. She braced herself, checked the tears, smoothed her hair as best she could, placed a smile and went downstairs.

'There you are,' said Kirstine, in pedal pushers and with shirt sleeves rolled up, thick, straight hair – inherited from Gregor – in a high ponytail, embracing a little rockabilly chic in the middle of the Eighties.

'Here I am.' Oddly, vacantly, Mirren didn't feel entirely sure where she was.

'I'll deal with the shopping, but you can put the kettle on if you like.'

Mirren lifted the kettle to check how much water it contained, flicked the switch, and leaned against the kitchen table to watch her daughter load packages into the fridge.

'How was the bus?' she asked.

'Smelly,' Kirstine said. 'Curiously, always the same smell.'

'Sorry you had to get the bus. It's just that it's Dad's turn to have the car this weekend. I had told him that we needed it, as we hadn't managed to do the big shop during the week, but—'

Kirstine knocked a cupboard door shut with her hip and peered at Mirren. 'It's okay. I can catch a bus with the best of them.'

'But you had all that shopping.'

'I managed, Mum. I'm a big girl now.'

Kirstine threw a courageous, twisted smile at her, and Mirren felt such an onslaught of attachment and yearning that she didn't know what to do with herself. She pretended to check inside a cupboard, hiding her face, her grief melting and funnelling down into a real, physical sensation of Gregor's absence. Damn and blast that man, she thought. He has broken our family.

'You okay, Mum?'

'No.' Even so, Mirren turned and smiled.

'Silly question. I shouldn't ask. But, you see, I must.' Kirstine's direct glance seemed to be seeking clues. 'Sit down; I'll do this. Or at least fetch the cups for me.'

But Mirren stood, transfixed with admiration for her daughter. Kirstine was a McInnis, right enough, with her rounded cheeks, clear gaze, and that glorious skin with its extra layer of creaminess beneath the surface. And, even though Kirstine tanned easily, as did her father, who these days might be described as being on his way to sun-kissed silver fox, she preferred not to, her complexion remaining translucent and pale.

Mirren not being quite so keen on her daughter's black eye liner and spiky lashes proved the least of her worries this last week or so. Although she quite liked the blue mascara she'd had been wearing yesterday – 'It's post-punk, Mum' – the chirpiness in Kirstine's manner, even the bounce in her step, seemed astonishing. The eyeliner was probably a phase, and, Mirren deduced, possibly a show of courage. She had applied far too much for today's trip to the supermarket in Inverness.

Mirren stirred herself, fetched two cups from the mug tree and opened the packet of shortbread, peeling the wrapping decorated with obligatory red tartan and a black Scottie dog.

'Auntie Anne phoned just after you popped out,' said Mirren, before taking a sugary bite, relishing the comfort as sweetness dissolved on her tongue. 'Aunt Isla's not doing so well.'

Kirstine sighed, nodded, a vertical line pleating her young forehead. She sat down, poured the tea.

'Poor old soul. She must be ninety.'

'Eighty-nine,' said Mirren.

'Are they moving her to that place in Fort Augustus?'

'I didn't ask. Anne may have told me. I couldn't take it all in really. On the telephone, it's worse. These days. My mind just wanders...'

'Not surprised. Is...' Kirstine took a sip, thinking. 'Has Dad been in touch today?'

'No, not... no, I would tell you if he had, Kirstine.'

Tears glittered in Kirstine's eyes.

'It's just every time the phone rings, I think it may be him. Asking to come back.'

Mirren stared at her daughter. Two months shy of eighteen, one moment Kirstine acted as parent, scrutinising Mirren when she thought she didn't notice for signs of distress or tears; the next, the little girl again. She had come in the other day from walking around the garden, and Mirren knew she'd been out there singing to herself and smelling the flowers. The flowers Gregor had planned, planted, tended. Kirstine had often done this as a child and would come in with tell-tale pollen on her nose, hauling up a memory for Mirren, something delightful and playful, but now gone.

'Only he knows why he'd rather live in a garret flat at the wrong end of Inverness than here with us,' Mirren uttered, trying to hide her bitterness, and having no other answer to Kirstine's confession about the ringing telephone. Although, Mirren knew that she herself had something to do with Gregor's departure.

'Perhaps we can give him the space that he needs,' Mirren hated herself for spooling out hackneyed catchphrases but carried on regardless, 'if time alone is what he wants...'

Anne had said, give Gregor his due; at least he waited until their daughter was old enough before launching his early-onset mid-life crisis bolt from the blue. But Mirren felt a daughter is never old enough for this. And she wished she, herself, could take on the burden, wished her limbs didn't feel so weakened by it, her head so heavy on her shoulders, and constantly aching. But she had failed, because she could tell, watching Kirstine sip gingerly at her tea and wince back tears, that for her daughter, the only world she had ever known had slipped away. And how desperately she tried to hide it.

* * *

No one had seemed at all surprised when Gregor McInnis had started courting Mirren. It had been the summer of 1957, when Mirren had turned sixteen and she, too, sported a high, although ragged and curly, ponytail. And Gregor, two years older, seemingly adored her. After all, he had been on her compass since before she'd started school. Auntie Anne and Uncle Allistair had always known his Uncle Cal – everyone around Foyers knew Cal McInnis from the post office – since time immemorial.

All through school, Gregor would save a seat for Mirren beside him on the bus as it travelled half the length of Loch Ness from Foyers to Inverness and back again. He'd walk her safely, albeit silently, to and from the gates. Not many words exchanged, but he said, later, much later, that they didn't really need to say much, did they?

Mirren often wondered, through the years they spent together, whether Anne had taken him aside one day when she started school and asked him to keep an eye on her. Had his own mother pressed him to look out for wee Mirren from the last house on the lochan. After all, children can be so cruel.

It started with whispers in the lower-school playground, behind hands, and with eyes locking onto their target. Even girls she thought her friends. And it built momentum, compounded into kids telling her, chanting at her: *your parents are not your real parents*. But Mirren already knew and tried to explain. Yes, Anne and Allistair were her aunt and uncle. Her mother was away – no, not lost, and not dead; it was because of the war – and would someday come back for her. But they didn't listen, instead making crowing sounds, ploughing on out of earshot of the teachers or dinner ladies, taunting, repeating her name: *Mirren Ashby, Mirren Ashby, your parents' name is Fraser*. Telling her she was *illegal*.

But then Gregor came all the way over from the other side of the playground, taller than most and with all that handsome, dark hair, and the bullies peeled away. Even wearing spectacles made Gregor appear more confident. He carried the look so well. And the bullies didn't dare. Even so, some nights, wee Mirren Ashby, in the darkness of her bedroom at the last house on the lochan, thought the police might pound on the door and come for her. Because she wasn't meant to be here.

Gregor had been sitting on the back seat of Cal McInnis's car when his uncle had driven her home from school that strange, unsettling day. Quiet and watching, Gregor had sat behind her, contained in his own world, and yet including her in it. She wanted to ask Gregor, but never had: did he, too, remember seeing the deer by the side of the road?

'Mum...?' Kirstine's voice cut through Mirren's spiralling thoughts. She looked up from her empty teacup. 'Did you no' hear me? I said, do you want me to hoover?'

'No, no, I need to get busy.' Mirren roused herself. 'The day is half done already. Haven't you college work to do? Yes, you have, Kirstine Anne McInnis. I can tell by that look on your face. Let's both get on with it, shall we?'

She left her daughter spreading out her textbooks on the kitchen table and trying to find a suitable biro. Upstairs, she let the roar of the vacuum cleaner's motor drown out the world, moving from room to room, wishing each one didn't greet her with memories, happy or sad.

When Gregor asked Mirren to marry him in the summer of 1961, she was, by then, officially Mirren Fraser, adopted by Anne and Allistair, and twenty years old, training to be a librarian, and he a grown-up twenty-two. And everyone, from Anne and Allistair to Cal McInnis, Gregor's mother, and good old Auntie Isla, rubbed their hands with glee and started planning. Mirren relived the strange, cold, crushing feeling. She was to be the bride and at the centre of everyone's judging gaze.

In those days, *all* the young women had glorious, straight hair set in bouffants or cropped and urchin-like. Mirren had browsed the Mary Quant fashion spread in the Sunday newspaper feeling an odd mix of envy and inadequacy. Mirren and her frizzy hair simply did not fit. She tried her best, shortened her skirts, but constant trips to the hairdressers were out of the question. Anne suggested she could iron her hair. She'd read something about it in the *Women's Weekly*.

'*I-ron* her hair!' Allistair had laughed heartily. 'You'll blow the fuses!'

Gregor had assured Mirren she'd look bonnie whatever she did or wore. Yet, still, she tried everything she could with her hair, to change it and alter herself. And Gregor persisted. His care wrapped layers of goodness around her, his solid tenderness like a salve over her trembling inadequacies through twenty-four years of marriage. From their horrid little flat in the city centre, to the two-up, two-down in a nicer part of town. For their daughter's birth, or at least, outside pacing the hospital corridor or smoking in the father's room. And finally, their move to the potentially beautiful, Victorian, detached, 'doer-upper' house with views of Loch Ness. Gregor remained by her side, a steadiness through all the mundane ups and downs. Until he decided he no longer wanted to be.

The hoover was giving off that funky smell because the bag needed changing. But that was Gregor's job. Would have to be dealt with another day. Despite what he'd said when they were younger, Mirren thought as she worked the cleaner with pent-up fury, perhaps they should have talked more. But now, she could not think of a thing to say to him.

Mirren finished her chores in *their* bedroom, skirting the bed, using the attachment in the tight spaces around the dressing table, her technique vigorous and clumsy, anger rising as she knocked against the wooden legs. The machine was old, hard to manoeuvre, its engine high-pitched and whining, the hose a life of its own. As she bent to check for dust along the skirting, the attachment rammed into the dressing table and her dish of jewellery flew, scattering its contents. She didn't press the off button fast enough and heard the tell-tale rattle of whatever had landed on the carpet being sucked into oblivion.

Mirren switched off and in the sudden, cleansing quiet, knelt on the carpet, running her hands over the pile. She still wore her wedding ring; she hadn't been churlish enough yet to leave it in the dish and it remained safely on her finger. But, she realised, as she raked over what pieces had escaped the suction, one of her mother's gemstone earrings had gone.

Usually, they lay secure in their old, purple, silk pouch, tucked away in a drawer. How negligent she had become. How utterly careless. Mirren exhaled a whine of pain and frustration and yanked the plug out of the wall. She couldn't have one without the other.

Sitting on the bed, she dropped her face into her hands, refusing to cry, to give in. For a long while, she'd been too frightened to wear the earrings in case she lost them. But this last year or so, wanting to enjoy them, she'd released them from their pouch. The silver surround knotted in a Celtic pattern clasped ovals of semi-precious stone, the pale-green gem with serpentine patterns, quarried from the Isles and the Highlands. Scottish marble, Isla had informed her years ago, protected the wearer against misfortune. Mirren wanted to laugh. Her mother had, apparently, given them to her when Mirren was a bairn. She'd come all the way from London to the Highlands to collect her and take her home. But had decided to, inexplicably, cruelly, leave without her.

Mirren needed air. She opened the window, glanced down, and jolted. The familiar figure, with greying hair and wide shoulders, and his annoying, casual walk, made his way beneath the bay to the corner of the house, heading for the back of the house.

'What on earth...?' Mirren exhaled. 'What's he doing? He should have let me know...'

She clattered down the stairs, along the hall and into the kitchen in time to see Kirstine slipping out the back door and into the garden.

'Dad?' Kirstine called, her high, excited voice trailing after her.

But Gregor evidently did not hear his daughter, continuing his beeline for the shed. Mirren followed, the back door banging open at her push.

'Dad!' Kirstine called again, halfway across the lawn, and he stopped and turned in surprise.

'Hello, hen. I rang the bell,' he uttered, gesturing lamely, his eyes wide and nonplussed behind his spectacles.

'Mum was hoovering. I didn't hear.'

Mirren caught up with Kirstine, out of breath, her heart racing. She placed a hand on her daughter's arm, making her jump. Gregor had been to the barber. His eyebrows looked trim, his close beard neatly shaped. He had some sort of new polo shirt on. In yellow. And, Mirren wondered, had he whitened his *teeth*?

Kirstine, also breathless and a flash of joy brightening her face, burst out, 'Have you come back, Dad?'

'Och no, hen.' He shrugged. 'I just came to fetch some things from the shed. I'm putting some shelves up. The landlord allows it, apparently.'

'But I thought— you see, I— never mind.' Kirstine gasped, stricken, and turned sharply back into the house.

Mirren flashed Gregor a fierce look, anger blooming like a rash over her body.

'What is it you think you are doing?' she asked evenly.

They stood on the grass paces apart like people engaged in a duel.

'I did ring the bell. You didn't hear. I thought you wouldn't mind. You see, I need my spirit level and a couple of screwdrivers—'

'Not that, although I *do* mind. You should have called first,' Mirren cut in, feeling her eyes wetted with anger. 'You should have rung the bell for longer. You should have hammered. No, what I mean is *this*, all of this. What are you *doing*, Gregor?'

He looked down, away, interested suddenly in the garden borders ripe with summer flowers, his eyes travelling slowly, regretfully around his former domain. When he faced her again, he looked saddened and quite small.

'I don't know, Mirren,' he said. 'I don't know. That's why I went. Because I simply don't know any more. You and I— You see, I need some time...'

'Have all the time you want,' Mirren said. 'Take your time, clear the shed for all I care. Just make sure you lock up again and shut the gate on your way out.'

* * *

Later that evening, Mirren and Kirstine sat side by side on the sofa in the front room, curtains half drawn against the pearly-light midsummer sky because a double bill of *Tales of the Unexpected* was due to start on the television and they wanted the mood to be of the night.

Each had a tall, ice-cold Cinzano and lemonade on a woven coaster and a bowl of crisps to go with it. Through the large, bay window, pin-prick lights from a boat retreating over the loch appeared to sit on their own shimmering layer against the dusk. The hills beyond and the pale horizon gleamed like a painting.

Evenings like this made Mirren think of the old screen in Anne and Allistair's parlour. She'd dreamt once, as a little girl, that she'd crawled right into it and sat with the animals, the otters and foxes and rabbits in their wild, twilight realms. She had sought, particularly, the company of the deer, but she proved too flighty, too scared of Mirren to stay for long.

They had the sound down, waiting for the *Nine O'Clock News* to end, and Mirren tried to guess what the newscaster might be saying about Ronald Reagan, trying to push Gregor and his stupid visit from her mind. But how could she, when the trace of him, the feelings she'd always had for him, still lingered with her, along with his golf trophies in the glass cabinet and his *Guinness Book of Records* on the coffee table?

'Mum, come on, you look miles away. It's about to start.' Kirstine got up to turn the knob on the television set. Sitting back down, waving her fingers as if conducting the theme tune, she picked up her drink and gestured to Mirren.

They chinked their glasses and took a good, long sip in unison.

'I wonder if it's a repeat,' said Mirren.

'No, we haven't seen it.'

Mirren felt her daughter's strong gaze against the side of her cheek but dared not look at her. After all, Roald Dahl sat in his huge chair to begin his story.

'It's all right, Mum,' Kirstine said, her voice rich with maturity. 'You're not to worry. I won't be leaving you.'

8

CLARE

The Highlands, November 1940

Clare woke on her first morning at the last house on the lochan to a rain-washed sky and a fresh, clear sunrise skimming the tops of the hills. She opened her window a chink and let in the peaty, chill air. The sound of a hidden burn, surging somewhere beyond the garden wall, loosened the silence, and the tall pines along the boundary creaked, their dark shapes feathering the pale sky. A sensation of solitude, the sense of space outside her bedroom window, felt enormous and pleasingly secure. It made her feel looked after, as Anne had promised, and Clare wanted to embrace the new sensation.

After breakfast at the kitchen table and a good, strong cup of tea, and after Allistair had left for the school in Inverness for the day, Anne suggested they take a walk around the lochan.

'Then you can get to know the place, find your own way around. There are some beautiful places to go for a walk and that's without even visiting the Falls of Foyers,' she said. 'But that's for another day.' She indicated Clare's shoes. 'They won't do. I have some good boots I can lend you. And you may as well keep them. And don't forget your hat, scarf, and gloves. It's not as warm as it looks out there.'

Easing Anne's boots on, with two extra pairs of socks as they were two sizes too big, Clare said, 'The Falls sound lovely. Something to look forward to.'

'All in good time,' said Anne.

Buttoned up and snug in her coat, wearing one of Anne's warm, Scottish bonnets, Clare walked along beside her sister, squinting in the low light. She put her hand up to shield her eyes.

'Make the most of it,' said Anne. 'In a month's time, the solstice sun barely shows itself above the horizon. We should bask in it while we can.'

They crossed the lane and Anne forged ahead along a path skirting the water, her long strides picking up speed, the breeze teasing her hair from beneath her knitted hat, clearly in her element. The wintry sunlight shimmered across the surface of the lochan, which resembled a small lake, teased by the constant breeze. Brown, broken reeds softened the banks, punctuated by huddles of naked trees holding violet shadows between their trunks. Anne and Clare's feet crunched on fallen leaves that littered the ground. Close to the edge, where it lapped the scree, the water looked earthy and clean, and icy cold.

Clare matched her sister's pace, surprised that she could keep up with her. She liked the little loch; felt she could easily walk around it. It looked swimmable from one side to the other, the right size for her, and entirely manageable, compared to colossal Loch Ness lurking down in the Great Glen. She gave a happy, satisfied sigh.

Anne looked around. 'How are you feeling?'

'Oh, I'm fine to carry on. I know I'm panting a bit, but I need the exercise. It's so good to be stretching my legs, out in all this fresh air.

I feel I can really breathe up here, compared to London. London was...' She hesitated at the flash of unsavoury memory, her words failing her. She rushed on, 'And the views, Anne, this place. This is simply beautiful. The space, and the peace. Everything new. I can't explain...'

Clare usually saw magic in everything. The rain on the Tube train window, the crocuses in spring in the lawn at home, the crust on her mother's pie – nothing ever seemed to bore her. Her fascination and her attention to detail – her teachers, and indeed Miss Stanford, had often said – was remarkable. But, gazing around at the far-reaching landscape, she realised she hadn't felt this way in a long while. And could imagine that here, even in bad weather, there would still be magnificence.

'I didn't mean that, exactly, Lumen,' said Anne, 'although it is wonderful to hear you are feeling well. I felt worried last night; you looked so utterly done in.'

'Well, there must be something in the water, for it is doing me good already. And I slept like a log.'

'Let's sit here for a wee while, though, I don't want you over-doing it,' Anne said, leading Clare to a fallen tree in the shelter of a lone spruce. She patted the seat. 'This is Allistair's and my favourite spot. Well, one of them anyway. He'll take us to the Falls. He knows the best, safest path as it's a steep climb beside the waterfall, all the way down to the shore of Loch Ness, and even worse on the way back up. Punishing, in fact. We can save that for much later on...' Anne stole a glance at her, 'after the baby is here.'

The word prickled the air and Clare found that for a moment, she had forgotten. Walking and breathing in pure, Highland air had sent her morning sickness packing. She waited, gazed out across the lochan, and let the truth of her situation sink back into her, the baby sleeping inside her.

'Back home, it was all so tense and rushed with Mum and Dad

around,' Anne ploughed on. 'We didn't really get to talk, did we, Clare? You and me. Not properly.'

'And *they* clearly didn't want to talk about it,' said Clare, hearing her own bitterness, that little shake of fear. 'Not in any way that might be of any help to me.'

Anne sighed. 'I've come to learn there's a lot of things that are not up for discussion, according to our parents. Only the practicalities, it seems. And what it means to them.'

'Yes,' said Clare. 'I sat on the stairs that evening. During the *family conference*. I heard.'

'You did?' Anne's eyes filled with tears. 'I didn't realise you'd overheard. That must have been awful.' She wavered. 'They won't even talk to *me*.'

Something in the way her sister spoke jolted Clare. 'About what, Anne?'

'Listen to me, a fine one to talk,' she said, shaking her head, giving a little laugh. 'Because... you, I have never told you this. Somehow, I thought you might know, or guess, as you got older. But that was unfair of me. For why would you? *They* would never say anything, I knew that. And some things need to be addressed and faced. Some things need to be in the open, or it sends us all mad.'

'Anne,' Clare said, puzzled, 'is this about the nursery?'

Her sister dipped her head, as if caught out. 'Ah, you saw it? We were going to come to that.'

'I did. By mistake. I got a bit lost on the landing last night. I'm sorry. But it can't be, can it? You didn't do that for me, did you?'

Anne shuddered, seeming to sink inside herself. 'No. No, we didn't. But it is for you and the new baby now.'

Clare waited, beginning to understand. She let the moment drift, gazed across the lochan to the sheltering hills. The breeze had stilled, and the silence felt immense. A bird called, with a hard, raucous voice somewhere from the top of the pine.

Anne took a breath. 'Not long after we married, I fell pregnant.' She spoke as if she was speaking to a much younger person: a child, in fact. She settled back in her seat, her face brightened, remembering. 'And it was of course, wonderful, the natural way of the world. How things are meant to be. Newlywed, newly pregnant. Allistair was cock-a-hoop. Couldn't wait to tell everybody. And I was blooming. But six months in, I had this feeling. I knew something was wrong.' Anne's eyes latched onto Clare's. The two women shared their mother's colouring, pupils a clear, almost ethereal blue. Anne's pupils deepened in colour, shimmered with tears. 'The doctor told me. He told me... and Allistair had just finished decorating the nursery.'

'I had no idea,' Clare uttered, her words inadequate, failing to match the enormity of what her sister had said. 'Oh, Anne.'

She tried to remember, forcing her mind back to the year after Anne's wedding. She alone at home with her parents, her big sister hundreds of miles away, grown-up and gone. Clare had been shifted into the box room and the bedroom with the bay window that she and Anne had once shared was to be decorated, reserved for guests. And yet the only person who ever visited, apart from Anne once or twice a year, was Great-Aunt Emily.

Clare's small world had circled from school at the end of the road to homework at the dining-room table, reading on her bed under the box-room window on a Saturday morning, errands to the parade of shops, oblivious. She didn't know anything about her sister's pain; she couldn't have helped her. Had never been equipped to.

'Anne...' She sighed again, embarrassed that she couldn't muster anything else to say.

'You were young. How could I tell you? It would have been unfair to burden you. And I can see why Mum and Dad wouldn't have brought it up. But then again, they have never mentioned it to me since. Not properly. Not in a way that might help me. Even when we had the conversation that you overheard from the stairs, the significance did not strike them.'

'Significance?'

'When they suggested that you get rid of the baby. Be done with it. They were ignorant to how that might make you, or me, feel.'

Clare thought of herself, shivering in the dark on the stairs, hearing them talk about her. Her parents' outrage, and the sadness in Anne's voice as she sought to protect Clare, safeguard her little sister.

And now, Anne said, 'I'm not going to ask. You can tell me what happened, tell me about the baby's father, only when you are ready to.'

Her sister's kindness, bound by sadness, confused Clare. She wanted to shake the muddle out of her head. And be honest with her: tell her exactly what happened. But that evening in London remained as a dark mirror that she did not want to look into, for she would not like what she saw in the reflection.

Anne patted Clare on the knee, breaking into her thoughts. 'Come on, Lumen, let's walk. There's more to life than sitting and moping. We'll make it around the lochan in no time and go back for a nice cup of tea. And Isla said she'll pop round with a cake.'

Clare gulped in the crisp air, feeling relieved to be walking again, as if the motion was taking her further away from the past, and the tense heat of August in the city, and all that followed. She felt grateful that Anne sensed not to press her. In time, Clare reminded herself. She would tell her in time.

'Now see that little group of pines over there,' said Anne. 'That's where we've spotted red squirrels...'

Clare turned her head to look but saw a plane, suddenly, a flash of metal against the northern sky. The memory of the air raid, that last night in London, flared in her mind. Her throat closed tight. She gripped her sister's coat sleeve, fighting fear.

'Oh God, Anne, we need to take cover. We need to run.'

'Ho, my running days are over, and you are in no fit state to—' She followed Clare's stare, shielded her eyes to peer at the horizon, and laughed. 'It's one of ours, Lumen. A flight out of RAF Longman, the other side of Inverness. They take off this way when the wind is in a certain direction. Look, it's banking around. It'll be up over the Moray Firth in no time. Off to the Orkneys with supplies, food, and such, for the islanders. Oh goodness, that's really shaken you, hasn't it? You're trembling.'

Anne gently turned Clare by her shoulders, set her back the way they had come.

'Let's go straight back. Hot cup of tea. You can have my sugar ration. You look like you've seen a ghost.'

Clare rallied, trying to match her sister's lighter mood. 'It's just a shock. I didn't expect. London was awful. I was caught in a terrible raid, and... I thought I'd got away from it all here. And yet...'

'And yet, it is still with you, isn't it?'

Anne left her statement to settle in the air. She linked Clare's arm, leading the way back.

Clare glanced over her shoulder. The plane had gone, the skies wide and empty as before. The hills as brooding and as reassuring as ever. They reached the lane again, crossed over, and the manse waited for them, solid and comforting, a haven for her in all her chaos. She had escaped the Blitz and the bombing, the worst of the war, and yet, like everything else, part of it had followed her here.

As they walked up the path, two squat Highland terriers emerged from the rockery near the front door, tufted bellies close to the ground and their long, whiskery snouts rooting through leaf litter.

'Isla's here,' said Anne. 'Along with Jock and Jess, I see.'

One of the dogs pressed its wet nose to Clare's knee, jet-black eyes appraising her. The other scuffed around her shoes, sniffing. She tentatively encouraged the dog – Jess or Jock, she couldn't say – to move away and followed Anne into the house, hearing the kettle singing as they walked across the hall, the clattering of doggy claws behind them.

A woman with silvery streaked hair woven into a thick plait that lay over her shoulder rose from the hearth-side chair.

'As promised, I brought cake,' she said. 'And this must be the sister. All the way from the Smoke down across the border. I see what you mean, Annie; ah yes, I can see...' Her gaze dropped to Clare's gently swelling stomach, unobtrusive within the folds of her coat. 'I can see the likeness between you two. I'm Isla MacKenzie. The cousin.' She offered a small hand to Clare, clear-green eyes peering at her from a delicately lined face. 'Och, you're taller than I expected. But most people are taller than me, ha! How are you, dear?' Her voice, as soft and warm as her hand, seemed to rustle from her throat.

'I'm well, thank you. I'm Clare,' she said, thinking that she barely showed, especially to a stranger, so Anne must have filled Isla in.

'Aye, I have heard so much about you. Over the years. And Annie is right. You are so alike and yet so different.' Isla's whole face seemed to rise with her smile, her eyes like sparkling buttons. 'The wee girl back home in England-shire. And at last, you've come to see us. You've come for peace and quiet?'

'She has,' said Anne, stripping her gloves and holding her hands to the range.

'Then you're very welcome, my dear,' said Isla. 'You'll certainly find peace and quiet here.'

'I hope I do,' said Clare.

Isla MacKenzie seemed entirely at home. Her squat frame, wide bottom clad in plaid trousers, moved with ease around Anne's kitchen, stepping around the pattering dogs, spooning tea into Anne's large, brown teapot, steeping it in steaming water from the kettle.

'Dundee cake?' Anne said, sitting at the table, hauling out a chair beside her for Clare. 'Isla is spoiling us, Clare. It's her specialty.'

'I thought I would for our visitor,' said Isla. 'I've used the last of my dried fruit. Hoping Cal McInnis will have some in again soon. Before Christmas, let's hope.'

At Isla's silent command, a precise movement of her hand, the two terriers settled down below the chair where Hamish the cat lay, stripy limbs and tail coiled in sleep. Sensing them, he lifted his head and blinked in outrage.

'Not so much a visitor,' Clare ventured, feeling at ease enough to start cutting into the cake. She lay slices on plates and pushed one sideways to her sister, catching her eye. 'I will probably be here for a good while yet.'

Anne nodded. 'We both, Allistair and I, hope you will.'

'Adopted by the mountains.' Isla sighed with pleasure as she poured tea. 'Aye, that's what happened to Annie all those years ago. She came with Allistair, set one foot here in the Highlands, and she cannot prise herself away. They call you home, don't they, Annie? The hills. They call you home. Now dogs, stay down, and don't harangue Hamish.'

As Clare sipped at her tea, she sensed her sister keeping watch, searching her face for lingering signs of distress. But Clare hid her pain, tucked it away, to assay in her own time.

'Now, Clare,' said Isla, scratching the black head of one of the dogs who'd decided to sit at her knee and look hopeful. 'What brings you here to us? Apart from the obvious.'

Clare gave another unwitting glance to Anne, wondering how much to say. 'Our parents, they wanted to evacuate to our mother's aunt, and I recently got caught in a raid in London, and as you can imagine, I wanted to leave. I had to leave.'

'I heard all about your job at the BBC,' Isla said, her eyes wide, clearly impressed.

'Yes, it was—' Clare stuttered over her surprise. She had no idea that Anne would have spoken to Isla so much about her. 'But I thought I'd leave it to more capable people. Perhaps I can do some war work up here.'

'Och yes. Maybe. Perhaps. In time.' Isla pressed her hand to the teapot's side, checking its temperature, and gave Clare her firm consideration. 'But first, you must take care of yourself. And the wee one you have inside you. And second, more tea.'

9

CLARE

The Highlands, December 1940

Winter settled in, hard and cold, and daylight hours felt like precious gifts.

That Saturday, now that school had broken up for the Christmas holidays, Allistair said he'd drive them over to the Falls so Clare could get her bearings, stretch her legs.

'Now he's at a loose end and no bairns to supervise,' said Anne, 'he'll want to organise us lasses.'

'Loose end?' Allistair laughed. 'Have you seen the piles of marking I've to do? Anyway, Clare, you can take in some *cauld* air, clear the cobwebs. You'll find it'll do the world of good. Be just what you need.'

They drove across the heathland, up to the main road, and crossed over to a lane snaking down through pines and browning fern. And, even though Clare felt they descended a good many feet in the car, when they reached the hamlet of Foyers, with its one shop-cum-post office and a handful of houses hidden among trees, they remained elevated, the forested, craggy sides of the great loch below them still.

'I'll just pop into Cal McInnis's a mo, see if there is any post,' said Anne. 'You two go on.'

Clare heard the bell on the village shop door ping, followed by a hearty greeting for her sister, and beneath her, as she walked beside Allistair into the woods, a surging rolling of water inside the stillness of the trees.

They meandered down wooded pathways, the ground a soft bed of needles, their way marked by stones and boulders and all around them, close-set, towering pines. The sound of the Falls grew louder, then deadened, then heightened, as they switched back along the contours of the steep loch side, the air fresh with a moist, peaty aroma in the cold shade.

Allistair led the way, checking over his shoulder every half minute for her. 'Look out for squirrels,' he said in a whisper in case they heard him.

Clare wanted to tell him she felt fine and not to worry so, but let him enjoy his big-brotherly concern. She looked this way and that, at the tops of trees silhouetted against fragments of sky way above her head, to the crooks of branches nearby, searching. But she didn't know where to focus, for the enormity of the place, its serenity, and its patience distracted her, stirring her into appreciating its age-old, unchanging peace.

And around the next corner, she experienced the thrill and fullness of the Falls. Wet stone, dripping fern, mossy boulders and water crashing over, falling thick and dark, roaring down to the depths of the gorge, to a cauldron of white. It sent up mists of spray, like breath on a freezing morning. Clare's face felt tingling and damp, clean air in her nose, her skin refreshed within seconds.

'Here they are, *Eas na Smuide*,' said Allistair as they stood on the lookout. 'The Smoking Falls.'

'The mist, yes, like smoke,' she said, grasping the wet bars of the iron railings, which stood between her and the terrific force of nature. She leaned a little, wanting to track the water's path down, to see where it emptied itself, eventually, peacefully, into the great loch beyond. But she could see no further than the rocks and the deep, black pool.

She felt Allistair's brief touch on her sleeve, as if he wanted to steady her. 'I think this will be as far as we'll go, Clare. Any further down and we'll have to come all the way back up again. And with you in your condition...'

Clare blushed, though agreeing with him, she fixed her gaze on the crashing water. She felt glad, and relieved, that he had mentioned her *condition*. At last, the reality: the need to speak about it. And, sometime in the summer or beyond, Clare decided, she'd be able to walk all the way down to the bottom of the Falls on her own, and all the way up again. She would be free.

They made their slow way back out of the gorge and met Anne as she came out of the shop with a basket of groceries and a newspaper. A man with a shock of silver-white hair held the door for her, laughing cheerily.

'Who's that,' Clare asked, lowering her voice, '*old man*?'

'*Wheesht*, Clare, that's Cal McInnis. He's only thirty. The same age as Anne.' Allistair laughed. 'Don't let her hear you say that! Cal's shopkeeper, postmaster, keeps an eye on the rations. Keeps us in check. Hello, pal,' Allistair called. 'How are you?'

'So, this is Clare.' Cal strode over, a lightness in his step, his cheeks ballooning with his smile, his hand reaching ahead of him, ready to shake hers. 'I've heard so much about you. Hope you've settled in all right. Did you enjoy your walk? The Falls are bonnie, aren't they?'

'They are. But what a steep climb! I'm in need of a cup of tea and sit down,' she said, trying not to gaze too hard at his striking hair, unexpectedly attracted by its luminosity.

'Aye, always helps.' Cal's dark-brown eyes glittered as he looked at her and his smile curled the corners of his mouth. 'I can certainly put the kettle on again. Anne? Allistair?'

'We'd better get back,' Anne said. 'But thank you, Cal.'

'Another time then.' Cal glanced at Clare's stomach, and nodded, as if confirming for himself. Most people did this and looked away in pity. But he smiled warmly at her, unflinching, as if he saw past it in that one, bright moment, and saw her, the real Clare. 'You take care of yourself, hen.'

As she walked back to the car, Cal's words lingered, and the honesty of his compassion stayed with her, like a glistening wash over her skin. She stole a glance over her shoulder. He had busily set to changing the newspaper billboard outside his shop, adjusting its position with a deftness and pride. She had a dozen questions to ask Anne and Allistair about him. But reminded herself that she'd felt fascination, had been pulled in like this before.

In the car, Anne said, 'We've been drinking tea and discussing the news, Cal and I. It never gets any better.' She turned around in the passenger seat to look at Clare. 'You looked quite taken with his hair, Lumen. It's been like that since he was at school. He was your year, wasn't he, Allistair? At the grammar?'

'The year below, Anne. Aye. His hair turned white, it seemed at the time, overnight.' Allistair drove them back up the lane away from Foyers. 'Happened when he found out his father had died with the Highlanders on the Somme. He was only six years old. Poor lad. Extraordinary such a thing can happen. And it always made him stick out. Carries it well, though. Hasn't he got a good head of it? Lucky fellow.'

Clare contemplated what had happened to Cal McInnis as a boy, and her own troubles diminished in comparison. How insular she'd become, she thought. And it bothered her that someone else's grief may ease her own. In the least, she decided, it put hers in perspective.

She asked Anne what she meant about the latest news.

'Well, it says here, that after what happened to Coventry and Southampton, those massive air raids, we've sent the RAF to bomb our first German city.' Anne glanced at a headline. 'Mannheim.'

Clare had never heard of the place. She felt uncomfortable. An unknown city, an unknown enemy.

'Reprisal,' uttered Allistair. 'Tit for tat. The question is, when will it end? We could go on like this forever.'

'Not forever, Allistair, surely.'

They were silent, until Allistair turned onto the top road.

'And, Clare, I thought you might want to know,' Anne went on. 'There's a report here about Broadcasting House being damaged again the other day. No fatalities this time, but it mentions the air raid that happened back in the middle of October. Wasn't that in your last week there?'

'It was,' said Clare, fixing her eyes on the horizon, loath to think any more about it. 'It was the evening I left. Hold on, did you say, no fatalities *this time*?'

Anne swivelled in the passenger seat to look at her. 'Oh God, Lumen, I am so glad you are here. Hearing things like this must really bring it home. I realise now how bad it must have been. You poor thing.'

'Let me see,' said Clare, holding her hand out for the newspaper.

'I thought reading in the car gave you a headache,' her sister said, passing it anyway.

Clare found the story and quickly scanned it. The report said that because of this latest incident, a second direct hit on Broadcasting House, the BBC was moving some departments to different premises. The printed type set it out plain as fact: during October's air raid, the Corporation suffered seven fatalities. But no names had been listed, or any other details, really, of that night. It seemed to be done with, in a few sentences.

'I didn't realise that staff had been killed in October,' Clare uttered. 'It... it doesn't say who.'

'Ach no, they won't give names in the newspaper,' said Anne.

As they neared the manse, the sky began to darken, a brisk breeze from the north bowing the aspens and sweeping away the scant daylight hours. Clare hoped that Miss Stanford had found shelter that October night, wherever she had gone for dinner; she imagined that Roger Hedges had no doubt already been on his way home. The post boy? He surely would not have taken any chances. As for Kay Pritchard? She had been going down to the basement, with... Clare swallowed, her thoughts teetering towards something bleak. Kay had been making her escape along with Leo Bailey, and all the others on that terrible evening. And Clare had fled the scene, had stumbled on through darkened streets. With fire and fury exploding over her head, she'd found herself at his mansion flat. She'd sought futile and – thinking about it – childish revenge. She felt ashamed.

'You're right, Anne. I better stop reading.' She folded the newspaper. 'It has given me a headache.'

'I'll wait until we get home to give you Mother's letter, then,' Anne said with a half laugh to brighten the mood. 'Our post came in with the delivery at Cal McInnis's just this morning.'

* * *

They sat in the kitchen, blackout down, lamps on, finishing the last of Isla's Dundee cake, eking it out as, according to Cal McInnis, there wasn't any dried fruit to be had for miles. Soft swing music from the wireless filled the dark corners and Allistair sat at the table, surrounded by his stacks of exercise books.

Anne's letter from their mother had been addressed to:

Mrs Allistair Fraser

and Clare, glancing at the envelope, pondered on how a woman must lose her identity when she married: how much of her was erased. She no longer had her own surname, let alone her first name on correspondence. But, listening as her sister read out some choice anecdotes that her mother had written from Great-Aunt Emily's, Clare decided that Anne, these last few weeks, had emerged for her as a vibrant, stronger entity. Not a person who appeared a mere once a year in her life. Clare had found her sister again.

In Clare's own short, terse letter, addressed to:

Miss C Ashby, c/o Mrs Allistair Fraser,

her mother suggested she read Anne's letter to get the news on life in Amersham,

away from the bombs.

She didn't ask Clare how she might be. Simply asked:

what are you telling people up there?

'Have a look at this,' Clare said, showing Anne, trying to smile about it, but feeling the familiar heavy sense of loss, of disappointment, creep up on her again.

'Ha, she has a way, doesn't she, our mother? Asked the same thing of me.' Anne gestured with her own letter.

Allistair looked up. 'What you tell "people" is up to you, Clare.'

He waited, expecting Clare to respond, and she felt keenly that she still had not yet told Anne or Allistair the truth. How could she? She could barely face it herself.

'There's not that many people around, anyway, as you see,' Allistair went on, kindly. 'But we are welcoming folk, not quick to judge. We accept that we all have our own stories, especially these days. You may be a widowed war bride for all they know. But you approach it however you wish. We are here to support you. Through it all.'

'It's none of their business anyway,' Anne said. 'But people are nice. You'll see.'

* * *

The day before Christmas Eve, Anne was expecting two students from Foyers for a kitchen-table tutorial, so Clare strolled down to Isla's for the morning. Snow had fallen heavily through the night, and lay in powdery, crystalline drifts, silvern in the weakened solstice sun that grazed the horizon. Cloaked in white, the landscape appeared new and mercurial; the contours shifted, the map transformed.

Clare sucked in the chilled, metallic-smelling air, her ears echoing with profound silence, the only sound a brave robin giving it his all and the tender crunching of her boots on snow. The thick, stone walls of Lochan Cottage were painted white and, today, seamless with the terrain.

As Clare walked up the path, which Isla must have scraped clear already, Isla opened the door and Jock and Jess bounded out to greet her, black fur against the white, snuffing her ankles and raking her knees with their paws.

'Are they bothering you? I'll shut them out if you like,' said Isla, dressed in woollen trousers with a huge man's jumper on, a thick belt around her middle. Her long plait this morning was coiled on top of her head.

'Oh no, please don't. It's too cold for that,' Clare said.

'They're sturdy, wee beasties,' she said, 'but we'll take pity on them. Come through and sit in the parlour. I'll make tea, unless...' Isla glanced at her. 'You'd like a wee *swally*?'

'A what?'

'A tipple. A dram. Seeing as it's almost Christmas.'

'Isla!' laughed Clare. 'It's ten thirty in the morning!'

'Aye, right enough.' Isla chuckled. 'But you won't mind if I have one. I cleared the path and need something warm inside me.'

She showed Clare through to the pale-grey room at the front which offered a new perspective of the snowscape. The space was simple and frugal, patched but comfortable, with the fire in the hearth giving off the same peaty warmth as at the manse. Along the stone fireplace, cuttings of spruce and fir gave off their scent and Christmas cards had been planted among the fronds. The dogs settled down over Clare's feet, adding another layer of warmth, and Isla brought in the tray from the kitchen.

'Och, what would Annie say, me offering you a whisky? Is it not frowned upon these days, for expectant mothers to drink? With my four girls, I'm surprised they didn't come out mildly pickled.'

Clare gave a gasp and Isla winked at her.

'I'm joking.'

She poured herself a small tot from a near-empty bottle, holding it until the last drop eased itself out.

'Ah, there we go, all done. Apart from the angel's share,' she said, fixing the cork back in and setting the bottle on the hearth stone.

'What's that, Isla?'

'Whatever's left in the bottle, or the barrel, when you think you've emptied it out. The whisky vapours. That's the angel's share. Something ephemeral, intangible, not for us mortals.'

'I like that,' Clare said.

'Something we can't quite grab hold of. But we know to sample it would be sublime.'

They sat for a moment, Isla sipping demurely at her morning tipple, Clare watching the flames bubble in the modest hearth, hearing the hollow tick of the clock. She realised that in the six weeks that she had been here, she had yet to meet the owner of the van that had brought her over from Inverness.

'So, is your husband at home?' she asked, glancing through the doorway to the tiny hall.

'Och no, he left me three years ago.' Isla smiled at Clare's horrified reaction. 'Ah, don't you worry, hen,' she said. 'I'm free and well rid. It took a while, mind, my God it did. He just came in one day, said he'd met some woman, and was moving to Spey Bridge to be with her. The last of our children had just left home to get married. *Bastard.* At least he left behind his ropey old van. And a handy jumper or two.' She plucked at her shoulder. 'And I kept my dignity. I'm still married to him. I won't give him that. He can't have his freedom. I am still Mrs MacKenzie. That should annoy *her* no end.'

'My goodness, Isla. I am so sorry.'

'Don't be sorry. It seems that, in the end, Mr MacKenzie wasn't one of us.'

Clare, wondering how a family of six could have lived in this little house anyway, said, 'And you have four girls? All grown-up, then?'

'Aye, all scattered and married. I am a grannie thrice over already.' Isla rested her compassionate gaze on Clare. 'And I see, my dear, you are beginning to show.' She set her empty tumbler down. 'I have some things for you. Let me fetch them.'

She came back downstairs with a bundle of clothes.

'Maternity dresses,' she said, tipping them onto Clare's lap. 'A wee bit old-fashioned, but you can alter them if you like. Annie's a whizz on her sewing machine. And there's all sorts in there. I was expecting throughout the year: spring, winter, summer. Always seemed to be in the family way.'

'Really?'

'He was at me all the time.'

'Oh.'

Clare could feel Leo's hands on her shoulders, hear the soft rip of the stitches, the tiny ping of the button. Her insides turned cold, remembering the fear and how she tried to make it all seem normal. The dogs shifted their weight on her feet, as if detecting her distress. One raised his head to check on her, and settled back with a comforting groan.

Clare touched the dresses on her lap, feeling the good, woven wool, tears prickling her eyes, sensing utter kindness and acceptance. Here, safe and among friends. She knew she could confide in Isla.

'Anne showed me the nursery,' she said. 'Or rather, I stumbled into it, the day I arrived. She'd kept it, she told me, from when she was first married. It is so sad. I really had no idea. I was too young, you see.'

'Aye, that was just the first.'

'What?'

'Oh, she didn't tell you? Poor Annie had more pregnancies over the years. They never came to fruition. Never got anywhere near as far as that first one. And thank God for that, I suppose. But each time, I prayed. She kept the nursery. And I kept those maternity dresses for her.' Isla sighed. 'Annie would often hug me, said she hoped my luck, my ease of falling, would rub off on her.'

'There is still time for Anne, isn't there?'

'Och no. The doctor said. No more. For her own sake.'

Clare flinched, remembering her parents discussing so casually in the sitting room at home the whereabouts of private clinics, to 'get rid' and make it all go away. She thought of the alternative – the young girls who were sent to homes where they had their babies and then had to give them up, or rather, they were taken from them at a few weeks old.

'You've been a real friend to my sister, Isla, thank you. She said that when she came here with Allistair, she felt welcomed and settled, and I can see what she meant,' said Clare, relishing the gentle intimacy of Isla's hospitality. 'She was accepted by you, by you all.'

'Aye, *she* is one of us.'

And then maybe, Clare thought, as she began to sort the dresses, holding them up and laying them over the arm of the chair while Isla went to put the kettle back on the range, she and her own baby would be welcomed into the fold, too.

10

MARCH 1941

Spring came late to the Highlands, but when it arrived, it painted, within days it seemed, the heath in new shades of green, and dappled the aspens with fluttering leaves. Snow melted from the lower land but remained on the highest hills, a keepsake to the cold and dark. With each passing day, Clare felt her body swell and change, the baby pulsing and kicking, frightening her. She caught herself looking down at her stomach as if it did not belong to her. She felt out of her depth and, frankly, bizarre.

Since the beginning of March, she had been watching a pair of jackdaws from her bedroom window landing in the pine trees at the back of the house, a tuft of bracken or a clutch of twigs in their beaks. She watched the birds converse and collaborate, building their nest bit by bit in a nook in the branches. As the sky grew lighter and the days longer, they settled, quiet some moments, raucous and throaty the next. And, like her, waiting.

She stood there now, when Anne tapped on the door and came into her bedroom, Hamish sneaking in behind her to find his usual spot, the somewhat grubby dip on Clare's eiderdown.

'There you are,' Anne said. 'A letter's arrived for you.'

She handed it to Clare, giving her a pointed look.

'I'm not expecting anything,' Clare said, noticing the hand-writing and the London postmark. 'Ah, my old boss. Miss Stanford.'

'Well, that's nice,' said Anne, sounding disappointed.

Meryl had sent a card at Christmas, with a brief message and no particular news, which had meant, Clare decided, that all was as well as could be expected at the BBC, with the people there she had known.

Clare toyed with her old boss's letter, turning it over in her hands. She wanted to know how Meryl was, of course; she wanted to hear about life among her posh neighbours up in Hampstead, whether she'd been swimming yet this year in the Pond. But she knew that there may be snippets of things that she did not want to know.

'I'll read it later,' said Clare, putting the envelope away. 'In the meantime, let me pin your hair for you, Anne. There's not a lot else I can do around the house these days.'

Anne sat at the dressing table and Clare stood behind her, brushing her hair, sensing her sister's frustration. She wondered if Anne had expected someone else to write to her: the elusive lad from school, perhaps, the mysterious boyfriend. But there had been no boyfriend for Clare. No one had ever touched her; not until she went into Leo Bailey's office on that August evening. The eternal question of who the baby's father might be, Clare imagined, simmered on the tip of her sister's tongue. But she felt unable to talk about it, the admission like something caught at the back of her throat.

'There must be some useful work for me, in Inverness, at the WI, or somewhere. Isn't Isla a member?' Clare asked brightly, as she reached for a hairgrip. 'Once... once all this is over.'

'Over?' Anne said, puzzled.

'You know, once the baby is here. Something to do. To help with the war effort.' She wanted to fill her mind with something else; she wanted to fight back.

'Oh, Lumen,' Anne laughed. 'When the baby is here, *that* will be what you do.' She caught Clare's eye in the mirror, her face gleaming with hopeful pleasure. 'Although you know that Allistair and I will take care of the baby as little or as much as you want us to.'

Clare glanced away, uncomfortable at her sister's intensity, the rawness of her hope. She spotted a bird, or at least a flutter of black wings in the pines. She wondered if the jackdaws felt the same way. Had they done this before, nesting and brooding; were they well practised? Or was it, for them, simply nature taking over? Didn't Allistair say that jackdaws made their choice, mated for life? And yet here she was, floundering through her own mistakes, hoping her instinct would pull her through.

Her thoughts spoke to the baby, that weight clinging inside her: *I will try to love you. I will do my best.*

'Of course, you must. You and Allistair, help me take care of the baby. Anne... it will be wonderful,' Clare said, not convinced, her vision hazy with tears as she dressed her sister's hair.

Clare insisted on going into Fort Augustus on her own. Anne had arranged the appointment with the doctor and made noises about accompanying her, but Clare put her foot down, as much as she could with her older sister.

'Come on, Anne, let Clare be a grown-up,' Allistair had said that morning before heading off to work. 'She's not ten years old any more.'

Even so, Anne walked with her up to the bus stop on the top

road, giving her an old envelope on the back of which she had written the timetable.

'Two buses a day?' Clare said, as she watched in hope for a vehicle to appear in the distance, trundling along from Inverness. 'I might do better thumbing a lift.'

'Two there, two back. Gives you time to have tea in the wee café by the canal. You can't miss Doctor McLeod's house. It's the big one. Now, will you be warm enough in just that mac because you can't really do the buttons up, can you? You've got your purse and plenty of change.' Anne burst into laughter. 'Yes, all right, all right, stop it, Anne, I hear you say!'

Clare found a seat near the front of the bus and, relieved to sit down, waved animatedly to her sister through the window. The walk up to the top road had got more difficult in the last week or so. The baby wore her out. Now, as the bus bumped along, the child seemed to wake and began to kick, letting its presence be known, in case Clare had in some way forgotten. She tried to relish the moments she had to herself. Anne and Allistair meant well, did everything for her, sometimes too much. But even now, Clare thought, as the bus took her along the Great Glen and down into the village of Fort Augustus straddling the canal at the head of Loch Ness, she could never go far, never be truly alone. Not with Leo's child growing inside her.

* * *

Calling her 'Mrs Ashby', the doctor's receptionist looked her up and down and told her she appeared to be exceedingly early for her appointment, and that Doctor McLeod was running late, that she had better take a seat. She gave her a clipboard with forms to fill in.

'May I borrow a pen?' Clare asked.

The receptionist sighed and rummaged in a drawer. Passing it over, she pointedly looked at Clare's ring finger and succeeded in not catching her eye. Clare wondered if she shouldn't borrow Anne's wedding ring when she went out, to spare her the uncomfortable and judging glances.

The doctor had a more considered and patient air, asking her to sit, releasing the forms from the clipboard, and peering at her through his specs with a benevolent, professional expression.

'You evacuated to us from London, Mrs, Miss, er, Clare,' he said as he shuffled through the forms. 'I'll call you Clare; is that all right with you?'

'Yes, of course. I'd rather— you see—'

'And you're with your sister and brother-in-law, that's right? Ah yes, Mr and Mrs Fraser up there, in the last house on the lochan. Very good. They'll look after you, right enough. As I will too.'

'Thank you.' Clare could only manage a whisper. Her eyes stung at his kindness. Warm tears spilled out, began to wet her face. She wondered if he'd notice.

'Now, from the look of you, I think we can expect confinement in around six to eight weeks. If you hop on the couch, Clare, I will gently feel your tummy and be able to let you know that everything is fine and well with the babby. There's no need, ah yes, I see...'

Doctor McLeod waited while Clare found her handkerchief and pressed it over her face, hiding from him. He wrote his notes in her file, in his practised way, until she finished quietly crying, mopped her face, and tried to smile.

'All ready?' he said.

'No, I'm not,' she uttered, attempting humour. 'But yes, I will certainly try to be.'

* * *

Afterwards, Clare found the café that Anne had mentioned, and taking a table in the window, ordered tea. Allistair had said she might have time to walk alongside the canal, the waterway of the Great Glen, see the five locks that rose through the village, but the baby tended to dictate what she did these days, and she decided she'd rather rest.

Ordering her second pot, Clare caught sight of a familiar figure crossing the road. Cal McInnis, his pale hair a beacon in the overcast – and as Allistair would say, verging on *dreich* – day. The Foyers shopkeeper, evidently on an afternoon off, walked with a woman guiding a pushchair, and they paused by the café window, chatting, while the small boy twisted in his seat to reach a chubby hand up to his mother. They seemed to be saying familial goodbyes. Cal pecked the woman on the cheek and ruffled the lad's hair.

As he turned to go, he caught sight of Clare through the window, his eyes widening in pleasant surprise. He lifted his hand in salute to her, gave her a broad smile, and went on his way.

She still had half an hour until the bus was due, so paid her bill and strolled along the street, across the bridge over the canal, and lingered outside the window of the little gift shop. Trinkets and postcards created a rather frugal display, a handful of teacups inscribed with *Loch Ness*: slim pickings in time of war. But the cushion pinned with half a dozen earrings, with a label underneath stating:

Sterling Silver and Scottish Marble

caught her eye. Clare counted the notes in her purse and went into the shop, a desire to own an object, however small, lovely and pretty, and just for her.

The shopkeeper slotted them into a purple, silk pouch, wished her a good afternoon, and Clare walked down to the bus shelter.

The fresh, spring day, which had started like it might have promise, had not improved, and low, grey cloud clung to the top of the hills, sinking into rain. A driver passing in his car, tyres hissing over the wet road, slowed and stopped, tooting the horn. She wondered who he wanted, as rain continued to drum on the shelter roof. The horn sounded again, the window wound down and someone called her name.

'I wouldn't have left you sitting there, rain or shine,' Cal McInnis said, as she settled into the passenger seat. 'You looked troubled, as if you'd lost something. But the bus would have been along just now, right enough. They try their best to keep to their schedule.' He gave her another honest, direct look. 'Are you all right?'

'Yes, yes,' she uttered weakly, not believing it herself.

In the close confines of Cal McInnis's car, and out of the rain, Clare sensed the intensity of how not all right she felt. It started at the surgery, with the doctor reminding her of her sister and brother-in-law's nurturing of her and then the doctor himself demonstrating his own patience. And yet kindness made her feel worse, almost bereft. Tears prickled her eyes again and she turned her face to the window.

'Sorry, my coat is making your car wet,' she said, lightly.

'Aye, it is, but no bother.'

Cal left her to her thoughts, driving out of Fort Augustus, the windscreen wipers creaking, passing the gates of the rambling, old monastery in its park, with glimpses of the deep water beyond. The road began its ascent up to the higher heathlands.

'I expect you're glad to be here, away from London and the bombing,' he said, relaxing into conversation. 'I see they're still getting it. And now Glasgow, too. My younger brother left last week with the Highlanders for North Africa. I've just been to see my sister-in-law and their urchin, that's wee Gregor; check she is doing all right. Oh yes, you must have seen them.'

'I did.'

Clare felt stunted, and shy of him. Not sure how to proceed. She knew she ought to ask more about his brother, and how he felt about him leaving, but that seemed a banal question, and she did not know him well enough. And it must feel raw for him, for all of his family, after losing his father in the last war. Allistair had mentioned that, as a postmaster, Cal was exempt and Anne had added, 'And probably too old anyway.'

Allistair had almost spat out his tea. 'He's younger than me, as well you know!'

Clare could not place Cal. A neighbour, yes, and someone who knew Anne and Allistair like he must know everyone around here, who happened to be giving her a lift home. Certainly not a friend, and yet, he seemed to be an entirely relaxed and a gracious feature in this world that she felt herself being accepted in.

They drove on for some moments, before – as if he'd read her thoughts – he tried again.

'I hope you've settled in all right?'

She peeked at him. His face looked open and placid, his silver-white hair really quite remarkable. Clare felt herself begin to admire him, his attentiveness, and his untroubled air. And yet she had the sudden realisation that he was only a handful of years younger than Leo Bailey. She shuddered at the unwitting association.

'Cold?' Cal asked. 'Sorry, the heater is broken.'

'It's fine,' she said, 'It really is.'

Clare watched the raindrops streaming down the car windows, the road ahead a wet blur. She thought of the distance between here and her old life, except she felt she had not made the crossing yet, had not arrived completely. She had been scared of stepping in. But gazing at the horizon, at the mighty, ageless hills, and sitting beside Cal McInnis in the car, being taken back to her new home, she sensed familiarity.

She sighed, letting go.

'When I first came here, that long, long train journey through the night...' she said, as if starting a story. 'And, then as Anne drove me along from Inverness, in Isla's funny old van, I felt as if I was going further and further, deeper into a strange place, deeper into the middle of nowhere. But that's unfair to say, because this is *somewhere*. And it is beautiful.'

Cal chuckled. 'Despite the rain, I know.'

'It is *remote*, I should say. It is different, and I needed difference.' Clare hesitated and her mouth seemed be moving on its own. 'Here, I am removed from my life in London, and my... troubles. But they are still with me.'

'They are, of course, Clare. But you are in safe hands here.'

Cal's tone encouraged her, and, with his own kind reticence, he seemed to be saying so much more. But Clare's mind circled back on itself.

'You said, before that I looked like I'd lost something.'

'Och, it was an attempt at humour,' he said.

'But you were right. I have done. Somewhere along the line, but I don't know when it happened.' Clare stopped. She knew she'd have to dig out courage to continue. 'Anyway, it has led me to this.' She looked down at her swollen stomach protruding through her unbuttoned mac. 'I didn't want to be in this situation, Cal.'

He looked at her, for as long as was safe while driving the top road. 'I can see that.'

'I'm an unmarried mother-to-be. And I didn't consent to it.'

The car slowed as it crested a rise, as if losing power.

'You didn't...?' he said and uttered something inaudible through his teeth.

He caught her eye, and the colour of his irises confused her.

She'd thought them deep-brown, but they were flecked with a curious gold.

'But people, some people,' she said, thinking about the doctor's receptionist, about her own mother, her father, 'seem to be acting like it is my fault. And I have to pretend. And it's exhausting.'

Clare felt the vehicle coming to a halt, pulling into the side of the road.

'Please don't stop the car, please,' she cried. 'Keep going.'

'I thought you might want to...'

'No, I cannot talk about it,' she snapped. 'I simply can't.'

They drove on in silence. Clare hadn't wanted to speak sharply, but she could not help it, not in that moment, even in the face of his gentle concern.

Outside the last house on the lochan, Clare thanked Cal McInnis, wished him a pleasant evening and got out the car as quickly as she could, but felt it polite to at least wait for him to turn the car around and head off back down the lane before walking up to the manse. Hamish the cat, prowling along the hedgerow for voles, chirruped a hello and wound himself around her ankles.

Cal paused the car and raised a hand in farewell. But through the windscreen, she could not read his expression, and felt perhaps it best left that way.

11

MAY 1941

Clare listened hard to what Doctor McLeod was saying, trying to follow his instruction. It seemed utterly complicated, and yet also the most natural of matters, if only she would concentrate.

Isla leaned over her, her soft hands smoothing her hair, as she encouraged her, comforted her. Clare tried to not cry out, but Isla told her that she could, that she ought to. That she must.

'I've done this four times, my dear, and look, I'm all right. Despite the mid-morning *swallies*.'

Clare wanted to laugh, to please Isla. She wondered how she would bear the pain if it went on for much longer.

'Isla, the air raid in London. I got through it, you know?' She tried to smile up at her, but her teeth felt fixed in a grimace. 'I survived it. I escaped.'

'You did, you did, hen. And you will this. Now breathe. That's my lassie.'

'Where's Anne?'

'Waiting outside. Do you want her?'

Clare nodded, her mouth compressed with a pent-up scream as

a convulsion of pain rode around her body. The grinding agony seemed to punish her, to scoop out her insides. She gripped Isla's hand, and everything became a blur and a sudden and awful rush. The doctor bent to his work and Anne slipped in to sit in the chair in the corner, putting on a brave face, smiling through her worry, trying not to get in anyone's way.

There came a soft, mewing cry from somewhere near Clare.

'Is she all right?' Anne asked, and Doctor McLeod said, 'Yes, Mrs Fraser, they are both all right.'

Clare sank back into her pillow, hearing the faint crying growing louder and determined as the doctor busied himself.

Her exhaustion seemed bent on drowning her, sitting on top of her like an almighty weight. Isla wiped her face with a cool flannel and helped her sit up, while Anne perched on the side of the bed and placed the bundle, cleaned and wrapped in the shawl fetched from the nursery, in her arms. Clare remained silent, feeling the tucked-up warmth and weight of the child, a curious potency, in her hands. Anne carefully moved the shawl away from the baby's face and Isla and Anne watched her as she contemplated her child.

'A little girl,' Isla whispered. 'Poor, exhausted, wee thing. Both of you.'

'Look what you've done, Lumen. You are wonderful.' Anne gave her a look of awe, of admiration: a look that said that Clare had been somewhere that Anne could never go.

Once Doctor McLeod seemed satisfied that mother and baby were doing well, he packed his bag.

'Sleep when the baby sleeps, Clare,' he said, patting her hand, 'is the best advice I can give you. And now I will take my leave. Back tomorrow to check up on you. You are in capable hands, I see.'

Anne thanked him, for Clare had no energy to speak, wanting desperately to go to sleep, fighting exhaustion with all her might.

Looking down at her daughter's moments-old features, her closed, wide-set eyes, the arch of her eyebrow, the shape of her tiny chin, she realised that she had, evidently, not survived after all. The past pummelled inside her head, switching her thoughts to somewhere she did not want to be.

Without a word, she passed the baby back to her sister, who also looked into the child's face, seeking something, before tenderly, reluctantly, lowering her into the cot by the bed.

'I expect you'd like to freshen up,' said Isla, bringing a bowl of water and a towel, and helping Clare wash her face, spray on a little cologne.

Clare caught sight of her reflection in the mirror on the dressing table and barely recognised herself. Her face a stricken, pale mask. Eyes unfocused with fatigue. She felt like someone else.

Anne perched on the side of the bed and smoothed a stray curl of hair behind Clare's ear.

'Allistair is wondering if he can come in, by the way. He wants to see for himself how you both are. He has made a pot of tea.'

Clare, too weary to speak, nodded, and Anne bustled off to fetch him.

Isla, watching Clare rest her head back and close her eyes, said, 'Now, my dear, try not to drift off. You'll need to feed her soon.'

Clare felt sick with weakness, but did her best to concentrate.

'Isla,' she said, her voice croaking. 'What is your middle name?'

'Mirren, dear.'

'That... that is unusual. I've never heard it before.'

'It means *beloved*. And I have been, in my day.'

'Can I steal it from you?'

'It will be an honour, hen,' said Isla, her face beaming. 'It runs in our family. Now, would you like another cuddle with beloved little Mirren?'

Before Clare could answer, Isla settled the baby back onto her lap.

'I know what you all want to ask me,' Clare said, gingerly finding the baby's hands, cradling them in her fingers, getting used to her, the person she created. 'But her surname is Ashby.'

'Only tell us when you want to,' Isla said. 'I won't press you. And I am sure your sister won't. But then there is the question of the birth certificate.'

Anne opened the door and Allistair bumped in with the tray of tea. 'My, my, Clare, can it be possible that you look both tired and radiant at the same time? And I mean, hearty congratulations. You clever lass. I think this will perk you up.'

'Thank you, Allistair.' Clare smiled faintly. 'You always make a good cup of tea.'

'Here, let me...' Anne eased the baby out of her arms, and Allistair handed her a cup and saucer.

Anne held the bundle high on her chest as Clare sipped, her face inches from the baby's, her smile joyous, as if it would hurt her to look away.

'Ah, Lumen, you are getting your colour back. As for this little one.' She carefully passed the baby to her husband.

'Allistair and Anne,' Clare said, 'meet your niece, Mirren Anne Ashby.'

The couple both sighed and laughed with delight at the same time and Allistair, wide-eyed and speechless, scrutinised the baby, a mere scrap in his large, gangly arms.

Clare shut her eyes, trying to conjure the emotion she'd experienced while sheltering with Anne in the Anderson in the back garden in Harrow. Anne, then, had dared ask her whose baby she was carrying, and Clare had answered, silently and to herself: *the baby is mine.*

But now, exhausted to the point of her body crumbling, about to disappear, Clare did not feel so fiercely resolute as she had then, and worried she never would again.

Terrified, she set her cup down, the saucer rattling, and closed her eyes again. She let the joyful, excited chattering of her family drift around her as she fell into a mercifully dreamless sleep.

12

JUNE 1941

A few weeks later, Clare sat in the parlour with Mirren snuffling in her arms, suckling prettily, the clock inching its way to pale midnight. She hadn't bothered with the blackout, for she didn't need to switch on the lamp. Midsummer in the northlands at first seemed enchanting, a welcome contrast to the dark winter, but day rolled into day, and Clare longed for the balance to be reset, for the extremes to level out.

Mirren was a good, placid baby. And beautiful. Everyone said so: the scattered neighbours, at least those few people living nearby who came to visit. They didn't ask too many questions. They all loved Mirren, but they weren't here, Clare thought, gazing at her daughter's face, pearly in the twilight, through the long hours of day and night.

'Sleep when she sleeps,' the doctor had said. But how could she do the impossible when the sky didn't darken? The day seemed never to be done, but simply paused in an eerie, grainy dusk before lightening again.

That morning, having stolen a handful of hours' sleep, Clare felt the same as she had done the day before, and the day before that: tired and on tenterhooks, her grumbling unease, a constant in the background like a chorus of conflicting voices telling her she wasn't doing it right. And her hunger for rest never seemed satisfied.

Anne had left her breakfast on the kitchen table before she went out, but Clare's stomach churned at the thought of food. She ate what she could, and put Mirren down in her crib in the parlour and, miracle, after a few snuffly moments, she fell asleep.

Heading across to the sofa, with the idea that she'd close her eyes for a few moments, Clare spotted Cal McInnis through the window, heading towards the house. Anyone else, and she might have been dismayed. But his appearance felt like a cloud evaporating. She waved at him to come in.

He opened the front door carefully, mindful of making any undue noise, and poked his head into the parlour.

'Good morning, Clare. I won't stay. I've just dropped by with the post,' he whispered. 'And to see how you are.' He dipped his head to look at her, cautiously, as if checking on something for himself.

She hadn't seen him since three months before, when he'd dropped her off at the manse and she'd spoken sharply to him. But his uncomplicated expression told her that no longer mattered.

'Come in, come in,' she mouthed, playfully resting her finger over her lips, and pointed at the crib. Mirren had awoken at the sound of their voices but lay happily gazing at the lace canopy.

'What a bonnie wee bairn she is,' Cal said, peering in. 'Would you look at those eyes. They'll break some hearts later.'

'Thank you for coming by, Cal,' she said, immediately conscious of her sleep-deprived face and unwashed hair. 'It is very kind.'

'Ach, think nothing of it. And how are you?'

'Fair to middling,' she said. 'That's the best I can give you.'

They both laughed softly. Mirren chirruped from the crib.

'It's normal,' he said, 'or so I have been told.'

'I don't feel anything is normal at the moment. Sorry, Cal, you have caught me at a bad moment.' Self-consciously, she ran a hand through her hair. 'I feel like I'm letting the side down. Allistair's at the school. Anne had to go out, and I haven't had a chance to get washed and dressed. Mirren doesn't like to be alone, you see. It's as if she knows when I leave the room, even creeping on tip-toes. This sixth sense of hers also happens when she is fast asleep. She wakes, and she cries. And I have to come back for her. I can't leave her wailing. It does bad things to me.'

'So, you sit here with her, not daring to move?'

'Just about.'

'Bad things?' he asked.

Clare stiffened, realising how that sounded. 'Oh, I mean, it makes me feel odd. And so very tired.' She wanted to add, *and not the person I thought I was.*

'Again, as I am sure Isla would tell you, all normal.' Cal smiled. 'On you go, upstairs, have a bath. I will sit here with her.'

Clare looked at him, amazed. 'Are you sure? Aren't you busy?'

'Nothing that cannot wait. And remember I have a nephew, wee Gregor, so I am used to babies.' He pulled a comic face. 'To a certain extent, mind.'

As they shared gentle laughter, Clare's exhaustion gave way to contentment, and she felt a rush of freedom and something extraordinary that she had never had before: utter trust.

'I won't be long,' she said, and suddenly, it felt so easy.

'It's fine, Clare, take your time.'

* * *

Upstairs, she ran the taps, mindful of the line Allistair had painted inside the tub to show the level of the water allowed for baths – according to the government information leaflet – and scattered

Anne's scented salts. Since the baby, her skin seemed to have shrunk around her body, irritating her. But as she sank into the warm bathwater, knowing Cal sat downstairs with Mirren, her tired limbs relaxed and the ripples in her mind smoothed out.

But within moments, her thoughts switched again and Clare worried it would prove too relaxing, that she'd drift off to sleep. The window stood open, and she breathed in the tender air coming straight from the hills. As the roar of the tank refilling itself abated, the piping of the birds outside drifted through. And she heard Cal downstairs singing to Mirren, low and happily – an old folksong or lullaby, Clare could not say. She nodded and smiled to herself, sensing completeness, a belonging.

And yet it felt unfamiliar, and too difficult to bear.

She washed quickly, got out of the bath, and grabbed a towel. Mirren below began to cry, and in a surge of anger, Clare struggled back into her clothes, her damp skin not helping matters. The front door creaked; Anne had come home, and Clare heard her cheerful greeting to Cal, a questioning, and a gentle chiding. Clare guessed that Anne had taken Mirren in her arms for the crying softened and fell into contented gurgles.

Clare hurried back into her bedroom and ran her brush through her hair, wanting to present a vision of poised and perfect motherhood. She picked up the silk pouch and tipped the contents out into her palm, toying with the idea of putting the earrings on. But the watery-green gems seemed far too precious, and inappropriate for her to wear. The prickly, restless feeling returned, pinning itself into her skin and, feeling unworthy of their beauty, she put the earrings way.

As Clare went down the stairs, she heard Cal's voice drifting from the kitchen.

'Aye, she's having a bath. I was the babysitter... Och no, I said, it's no bother.'

'She struggles—' from Anne. 'I was worried to leave her for long, to be honest. Ah, I think she's—'

They both stopped talking, looked around as Clare entered the room. She dissolved their discomfort with a forced, cheery: 'Hello.'

'That's better,' Clare said. 'Thank you so much, Cal. Now how is the little one?'

Clare scooped Mirren from Anne and immediately, the baby braced, beginning to wail.

'I'll fetch her dummy,' said Anne, going out of the room to find it.

'Oh, I can't get this right,' Clare uttered, fighting despair, knowing she could not, should not, show it. Not in front of Cal – or anyone.

'You are doing fine, Clare,' he said. She glanced at him, as if captured by him, his belief in her, his ordinary, comforting words ringing with truth. 'And I better leave you all in peace, be on my way.'

But he waited for Anne to return with the dummy first, and stood for a moment in the kitchen doorway, looking back as if to check, to make sure. Satisfied that Clare seemed to be in some way fine, he said his goodbye.

Later that evening, Clare persuaded Anne to go to bed and leave her to it for, she felt, she must try harder. Mirren had been fractious but seemed to settle. She finished her feed and, now while Clare sat in the parlour armchair, the baby dozed in her arms. Clare knew she should follow doctor's orders and try to get some rest. She knew she should take Mirren upstairs and settle her in her cot. After all, Cal had said she was doing fine.

But instead, she gazed at the screen near the door, at the wild animals lurking, moving within their own painted shadows. They would have done it right, she decided. The fox and the deer, the rabbit; their instincts were true, their behaviour natural, whether adjusting to summer light and winter darkness or nurturing their young. As for the real-life jackdaws in the pines beyond the garden wall, they had done their job – for last time she looked, the nest seemed empty.

She glanced at Meryl's latest letter lying on the low table – brought earlier by Cal – realising that she was looking everywhere but at her baby. Bonnie, yes, Cal had said. But for Clare, baffling. The sensation of Mirren in her arms, that precious, disruptive little bundle, the sweet scent of her and her tender, folding limbs, created a strange unease, a sort of splitting inside her. She knew that love, fierce, involuntary love, lay somewhere. It had to, for she was not only a mother, but simply human. But, rising above it all, like a recurring dream, came the memory of the evening in London. And she could not look the memory, or her baby, in the eye.

Careful not to disturb Mirren in her arms, and yet longing for a distraction, Clare reached for Meryl's letter. She'd skimmed over it earlier, hadn't taken it in. Now, she made herself concentrate, think about life beyond the feeding, winding, the cradling, and the tears.

Breezily, Meryl enquired how Clare was faring. Was she busy, enjoying life in the Highlands? What sort of work was she doing? Clare could hear her old boss's upbeat voice, firing positive little darts around her. And Meryl herself had some news. She'd left the BBC.

Clare sat up straight, squinting at the letter in the evening twilight, the clock on the mantel delicately chiming. Mirren let out a stifled, milk-dream mew as Clare rearranged her embrace. Clare read how Meryl now worked for the Air Ministry, her skills in Personnel being put to good use recruiting for a special project, to be set up at a secret location somewhere in the south of England.

No more information, of course, could be divulged. She wondered if Clare might be interested in an administrative job. Her skills would most certainly be useful. She would, of course, have to resign the Official Secrets Act.

Meryl signed off:

Write soon and let me know if you are interested. I very much think you will be.

Clare folded the letter away, rested her head back against the chair and closed her eyes. Mirren was sleeping and Clare knew she should too, but her thoughts simply wouldn't let her, and the light in the sky exasperated her. The idea felt preposterous. She couldn't take a job like that. She had a child. And she couldn't go to *somewhere in England,* she couldn't leave Mirren behind. Because one day, surely, she will be doing fine. And, what would everyone think?

* * *

Summer unfurled, the hills turning purple with blooming heather; some days sunny, some *dreich*, and some simply nondescript. Mirren seemed to grow a little overnight, a tad heavier every morning, and Allistair announced that he would make a sling for Clare, a sort of papoose, so that she could easily take Mirren with her wherever she went. The good-as-new pram that had been stowed in the cupboard under the stairs for goodness-knows how long had been deemed inappropriate for the stony pathways. And Clare had no excuse now to leave Mirren behind when she went for a walk.

So, with Anne occupied with her tutoring, and Allistair busy in the garden or preparing lessons for the new school year, Clare would hitch Mirren into the sling fashioned from good, strong canvas and walk around the lochan with her strapped to her chest.

More often than not, Anne would call out, 'You'll not go far, will you...' with Clare's breezy response: 'I promise.'

Other days, if Clare heard that Isla planned to drive her van on an errand to Inverness, or perhaps to Fort Augustus to visit one of her daughters, she'd catch a lift with her to the main top road. She'd wave Isla off and then walk the half hour or so back along the lane, watching little birds rise and drop into the heath over the top of her daughter's downy head.

But even though she breathed soft, Highland air, and drowned in the sublime, shimmering landscape, Clare's detachment, the splitting inside her, drove deeper. And how she fought it. She whispered near Mirren's ear, filling her evolving mind with the hope that she herself did not feel. She spoke to her about the hills and the heather, and the birds she could see – the pipits, the stonechats and the skylark. She told Mirren about the monster dwelling in the black water in the Great Glen, she told her about her auntie and uncle, and how they took care of her, of them both.

'Your name means *beloved*, Mirren,' Clare whispered. 'And so you must be.'

And by the time Clare reached the last house on the lochan, Mirren was sleeping sweetly, her cheeks full and rosy, her hair ruffled by gentle breezes, and Anne looked overjoyed to see them.

'Ah, you're home.' She sighed, throwing open the front door, as if expecting the worst.

Yet Clare simply felt relieved that Anne would unwrap the baby and bustle off with her; glad that another day was almost done. And hoping that perhaps, tonight, she would feel better. Perhaps tonight, she would sleep.

13

Early in August, the air base organised a dance at Inverness town hall to raise funds, with a swing band, a raffle, and a Lindy Hop competition. WRAFs and airmen were being bussed in from Longman, and some of Allistair's teacher friends were going, plus a handful of folk from Foyers. Anne had written it on the calendar weeks before.

'Will you be all right on your own?' she asked, tidying schoolbooks from the kitchen table.

'It's just one evening,' Clare said with uncertainty. She'd just got in from a walk. She gingerly unwrapped drowsy Mirren from the sling and set her in her cradle on the armchair by the kitchen range.

'But we thought we'd stay the night with Allistair's friends, as it will be late, and a long drive home,' Anne pondered. 'Perhaps we shouldn't go.'

'Och, Anne, you're looking forward to it,' Allistair said, coming in from the garden and washing his hands at the sink. 'And it has to happen at some point. Us being away for a night. And Anne, it is just one night. Let Clare get on with it. She'll be fine.'

Mirren started to grizzle. Allistair brisky dried his hands, scooped her up and within moments, the baby moulded herself into his huge arms, placid and content.

'I will be fine,' Clare echoed her brother-in-law, wondering why she did not have his gift with her own daughter. 'We will be fine.'

Anne gave her a sharp look, not quite registering the tone of her voice.

'Now, come on, Anne,' Clare said breezily, 'it's half-past four and you ought to be getting ready. Let me do your hair. And I'm quite good with lipstick these days.'

Anne acquiesced. 'All right, all right...' She laughed.

'Something tells me it's you who doesn't really want to go because you'll be parted from Mirren,' Allistair said, laughing.

'Aye, he speaks the truth,' Anne uttered, pausing by the cradle to check her little niece, running a fingertip over her chubby hand.

Upstairs, sitting at Clare's dressing table, Anne said, 'I haven't been dancing in years. I think I may have forgotten how. I can't help thinking you should go in my place. I mean, there I am, an old, married woman, and you still so young. Officers from Longfield will be there. You might meet a nice one.'

Anne caught her eye in the mirror, wanting perhaps for her question to lead on to some sort of outburst from Clare, a confession. She waited, but Clare vigorously brushed her sister's hair and offered a put-on laugh. The idea of another man close to her, and touching her, giving her any sort of attention, made her sweat.

'I think I'm better off here for now,' she said, her fingers expertly dealing with Anne's unruly hair. 'Here with Mirren.'

Anne gave a satisfied sigh and a wistful smile.

'As long as you are all right...'

'Come on, Anne,' Allistair called up the stairs. 'By the time we get there, they will be playing the National Anthem.'

'Five minutes, Allistair,' Anne called. She put her hand on Clare's arm. 'You will be fine?'

'I'll pop down to Isla's if I feel lonely.'

'Ach no, she is spending the evening at her daughter's at Fort Augustus; did she not tell you? That's why I am twitchy.'

'Anne, please. Go and enjoy yourself. I will see you tomorrow.'

Clare stood at the door to say goodbye, holding Mirren and lifting her little arm to wave it. Her sister seemed almost unrecognisable in her best dress and a little too much lipstick, her eyes wide with urgent apprehension and Allistair splendid in his best shirt, waistcoat, and kilt. She waited for the car engine to fade and for the birdsong to fill the sky again, before turning back inside.

Up in the nursery, Clare settled Mirren down in the cot. It had been moved back in here from her bedroom soon after the birth; Anne had said it was good to set the rules for the baby early on, to get a routine in place. Clare checked the blackout. As well as blocking the light from any watching enemy, it ensured the nursery remained dim and restful for Mirren. She drew the curtains, admiring Anne's handiwork, the fine hand-stitching, the fabric that she would have driven to Inverness for one day, perhaps a decade ago, chosen, measured, cut, before she set to work.

'Auntie Anne made these curtains for you, Mirren,' Clare said. 'They had been expecting you, or a little soul like you, for years. They loved you, it seems, before they knew you. You see? *Beloved.*'

She shut the nursery door and stood on the landing, listening. Mirren burbled for a moment, seemed to drift to sleep, releasing her. Clare went downstairs and out into the garden, relishing a snippet of freedom. The granite terraces bloomed with lavender. Bees congregated, surely exhausted, Clare decided, by the length of their working day. Beyond the pines, the hillside expanded, sloping away and up, shimmering where it met the pale sky. And way over, in the next glen, a glimpse of purple heather.

Clare saw movement: a group of deer traversing the rise, blending with, and ruling their domain. And Mirren began to cry, softly at first, but the pitch rose, finding its way out of her nursery, out of the house and into Clare's head.

She went in, up the stairs and into the darkened room. Even in the twilight, she could see Mirren's pale, outraged face, her eyes open and fearful. Such a beautiful child, but she had nothing of the Ashby in her that Clare could see, as if she didn't belong with them.

She lifted her out and rocked her like she'd seen Anne and Allistair do, for they both seemed very good at it. Mirren continued to wail and Clare remembered Anne's question, 'Whose baby is it?' in the air raid shelter and her answer, whispered to herself hours later: 'It's mine.'

What a fraudulent thing to say, even to herself. It must have been a fantasy, a reflex, perhaps, that happens to newly pregnant mothers, to make sure that they want and will care for the baby growing inside them. But the doctors didn't talk about that. In fact, they didn't tell her anything, really, about feelings, and the bond that, as Mirren grew more fractious, a squirming nuisance, simply did not exist.

Clare tried to remember all the things Anne had told her she must do. The baby should be dry, clean, and fed, and then she would sleep. If only it could be that simple. Clare laid Mirren down on the table in the corner to change her nappy, although she barely knew how. Anne always took over: Mirren's layette clean and pristine, new socks and vests and booties every day, the washing line pretty with them in the sunshine.

The baby did not stop crying, her little fists pummelling at the air, her mouth a gummy chasm. And tears, real tears, of someone in pain.

The truth cracked open in front of Clare. She was a terrible mother. She didn't deserve to be one.

Clare dressed Mirren, inexpertly, took her downstairs and bundled her up into the sling. She strapped her to her chest, and still she howled. Clare hurried out of the house and down the road, a trembling fear to do harm pursuing her. She caught Isla just in time as she pulled out onto the lane in her van.

'She won't settle,' Clare said, panting, as Isla wound down her window. 'I know you're on your way to Fort Augustus. Would you mind dropping me at the top road?'

'Aye, it's a fine evening, and the walk back should do it. Hop in,' Isla said. 'Jock, Jess, behave. We have company.'

Clare sat on the wide front seat, with the Scotties between her and Isla, the dogs watching attentively through the windscreen their progress along the lane.

'Aye, she's a madam,' said Isla, manoeuvring the huge gear stick, as Mirren caught her breath mid cry, and let out a series of tentative grizzles. 'You wait, Clare, this is nothing. She will be sitting up soon, and crawling. Toddling around. You won't keep up with her, my dear. You'll be fare running after her.' Isla chuckled. 'Be happy and content with how she is now, when a simple walk will send her to sleep.'

Clare glanced down at her daughter as her crying took another turn, her brick-red cheek squashed against her sling, hot little tears squeezing from her eyes. Clare wanted her to shush, for the crying felt like a scolding, a reminder of her humiliation, her downfall, and how tongues may wag. As they jiggled along in the van, Clare thought about her mother's only concern. What would the neighbours say? Even though people here in the Highlands smiled and wished her well, what were they thinking?

'Anne and Allistair get off all right?' Isla asked as she pulled up at the junction.

'Yes,' Clare said, her bright smile a lie. 'Anne looked very glamorous.'

'Ah, that sister of yours. She is besotted with the babby. But it'll do good for them to have a break, I expect, even for one night.'

'Yes. I mean, I have barely changed a nappy in weeks. I'd almost forgotten how.'

Clare laughed with Isla, covering the feeling that she might be drowning in it, not coping, even though she ought to be with all that help. For isn't that what real mothers did?

'On you go,' Isla said. 'You get that wee bairn home and we will see you both soon.'

Clare got out of the van. Isla revved the engine and turned left, in the direction of Fort Augustus. The dogs pressed their noses to the window, their stumpy tails lashing. Clare waited on the roadside, waving as they disappeared along the road, sure that Isla would be watching in her rear-view mirror for as long as she could.

She sensed Mirren relax, comforted, perhaps by the sudden quiet. But her own body grew tense, rigid, overwhelmed by the feeling of being small and alone in this remote wilderness, responsible for an even smaller creature. The empty landscape opened around her, and there seemed to be too much light, too much beauty. And yet, the glorious evening felt as bleak as the future that spooled ahead of her. In that future, she would have to explain Mirren to people, constantly, and she felt utterly tired at the prospect of it.

And how could she tell her daughter, when she inevitably asked, the grown-up girl in the unspeakable years that lay ahead, that her birth certificate said *father unknown*? It was the truth. Clare did not know him. Mirren, however, resembled him in so many ways.

* * *

Isla's van had been swallowed by the hills, the lane leading back across the heath to the last house on the lochan waiting for her. But Clare turned, crossed the top road, and headed down towards Foyers.

'We haven't seen Loch Ness yet, Mirren,' she said. 'Remember, I told you about the monster? Ten months here, and I've never even stood on its shore.'

The narrow road to Foyers, sheltered by woodland, wound its way through banks of fern glowing green among the pines. An orchestra of vespers' birdsong peeled and whistled, and Clare felt protected here. The air smelt clean and earthy. And no one knew where she was, or where she was heading, and she'd never felt so reassuringly anonymous.

The tiny hamlet looked as deserted as always. Outside the McInnis shop-cum-post office, the newspaper billboard stated that the Germans had made inroads into Russia.

Cal came out, locked the door, and glanced in surprise at Clare, standing stock-still. She hadn't seen him in a few weeks, not since he'd popped in with the letter from Meryl.

He gave her a wave, a hearty, 'Good evening,' trying to hide the puzzled look on his face. His, 'How ye doin'?' seemed like he wanted to ask her something else.

She said nothing, waved back, and carried on walking. She turned onto the woodland track that led to the Falls and followed the way Allistair had taken her, all those months ago. The headline on the billboard set her to wondering what horrors would be coming through on the ticker tape in the basement of Broadcasting House. What things the newscasters, and the newspapers, stacked in Cal's shop, could not possibly report. She wrapped her arms protectively around the papoose and thought briefly of Meryl's letter. What secret operation 'somewhere in England' would want Clare's help?

Mirren had quietened, seemingly mesmerised by the light scattering through the canopy above them.

'Look out for squirrels,' Clare whispered to Mirren.

When she reached the viewpoint, she stood by the railings and eagerly inhaled. Inky shadows filled the spaces between pine and fern. The waterfall did not feel as loud or as ferocious as it had last autumn; Allistair said only the other day that summer had been dry so far. Even so, the peaty, moist air thrilled her.

'I want to go further,' Clare said aloud. 'We're going all the way down to the great loch, Mirren. But, I must remember, we do have to come all the way back up again.'

She set off along the steep path down the ravine, with its large, flat boulders for a staircase, and the floor a soft fragrant carpet of fir needles and fallen cones. Mirren, her head snug beneath Clare's chin, seemed alert and listening as the sound of the Falls receded and emerged, her eyes wide, her tears dried.

'Don't worry, we'll make it back up,' Clare said, remembering Mirren's birth and how she had got through it. And how she had survived other things. Other matters that she could not bear to turn her mind to.

The path began to level out and Clare left the sanctuary of the trees and the ravine, walking beside the shallow, widening river tumbling over rocks and pebbles on its way to the loch. The peace here seemed like an offering, reminding her: she and her baby were completely alone.

And there, before her – fabled Loch Ness. At least, one segment of it. Clare walked over the beach towards its shore, her shoes crunching on scree. The water looked immense, heavy, silky, and black, glowing under the light of the early-evening sky. She knew that wherever she stood, at whatever point along its vast, far-reaching banks, she could never take in its fullness, would never see it in its entirety. Something in the silver light of dusk spoke to a memory: that same summer evening in an entirely different place. The office in the city, and what he'd said to her, how he'd drawn her in.

'What a fool I am,' Clare whispered to Mirren, gazing across the water to the dark banks on the other side. 'What a fool for believing.'

She should have been insulted by his charm and seen through it. Seen the person that he wasn't. But he'd told her she smelt wonderful, delicious, whatever it had been. She should have paused, given it some thought. Not let flattery run away with her. She should have known. For a moment, she had felt desire. But immediately realised it to be something else in disguise, and not what she'd wanted, not in this way.

'I pulled away, Mirren. I pulled away,' she said, near his child's ear.

And yet he continued anyway, breaking the trust of a young and foolish girl. Hustling her to the Tube station afterwards, the extent of his concern.

Clare squatted by the shore, trying to find a new perspective. Little waves idled over the scree. She wondered what mystery lay beneath that ancient body of water. She could see why people revered it, and believed in the monster.

She reached to dip her hand in and trailed her fingers. The cold surprised her. She stared, transfixed by the living glow coming from the water. And its harsh, enormous beauty forced tears from her eyes. How small she felt. How insignificant. There seemed no point and no meaning to this exquisite world, to any of it. What was the reason for this majesty when there were people in the world like that? Like Leo Bailey, forever connected to her.

The weight of Mirren strapped to her made Clare wobble a little as she crouched by the water's edge. She held tighter to her daughter, trying to hold onto her pristine little body, but only felt distance between them, a terrifying detachment. She undid the binds of the sling, loosening the papoose, tears running unchecked, scorching her face. The white summer night revealed far too much. The light showed Clare what she had become. And the shame of it. At least in the blackout, the utter darkness, she could hide.

A chasm, as deep and as black as the loch, cracked open inside her, with Clare, the essence of herself, left as a tiny speck of panic. How could she carry on like this, with such harrowing *absence*?

She shifted onto her knees, the stones digging into her bones, her arms aching with her burden. What happened to her had been her fault and she cradled her own punishment in her arms. The water seemed the answer. The only way to quench despair. Clare watched waves surge and retreat beneath Mirren as she held her over the loch. She would fall too, into the depths, a reverse christening, an offering, giving them both up to the monster.

'It's like Isla said about the angel's share,' she whispered. Her clothing from her knees down was soaked, and heavy. Tugging at her. 'And I've had the angel's share of you, Mirren. That's all I'm to be allowed.'

Mirren, eyes shut and an almost-smile on her pert lips, seemed untroubled, tranquilised by the presence of the water below her.

'And you are my beloved...' Clare uttered. Blinded by weeping, she hesitated, gulping panicked breaths.

Mirren, drowsy and relaxed, began to tip from her arms.

A crunching sound behind her.

Footsteps approached quickly over the pebbly shore. Clare twitched her head. Heard her name. A hard shout. Felt a hand heavy on her shoulder and a voice near her ear. Cal McInnis saying something she could not understand.

She froze, felt herself being lifted like a parcel, Clare and Mirren as one, away from the water's edge, Cal talking to her constantly, gently, and she could not fathom the words. They sounded instinctive and reassuring, something to be cherished.

She gave in, let him guide her away from the loch. He made her sit on a boulder under the pines along the shore and he carefully eased Mirren from her arms. Released suddenly, her duty done, Clare bent double on the hard, solid rock, bewildered and ashamed, her palms over her temples, sobs racking her body, tearing at her throat.

Cal worked out how to strap the baby onto himself, all the while standing over Clare as if to block her from seeing the great, looming loch, keeping his eyes on her. Like some sort of miracle, Mirren fell immediately and contentedly asleep against his chest.

He gazed down at Clare in the deepening twilight, a whole storybook of questions playing out over his face. But he didn't ask them. Clare gazed up at him, stupefied, but she knew that if she focused on the flecks in his eyes, that somehow, maybe one day, everything could be all right.

Cal jerked his head in silent question, and Clare nodded. She walked with him, slowly, tentatively, back across the scree, and up the ravine. He never asked her why. He simply strode ahead with Mirren, and sometimes stopped to wait for her, turning to check that she was following. Clare held the hand that he extended to her as he helped her step up the stone stairway and negotiate sharp slopes. She watched him carry and care for her baby and her tears dried onto her face. She felt transformed, as if she no longer carried her burden. And below, by the dark loch, the waves continued to break onto the shore, as if nothing at all had happened.

They reached the top, leaving the pinewoods whispering behind them.

'Come away to the house, Clare,' Cal said, his voice clear in the near-darkness. 'I will telephone Anne.'

'They're not in,' she uttered, catching her breath, her legs as weak as straw and in danger of buckling.

'Och, the dance. I remember. Isla?'

'At her daughter's.'

'Here, you take her.' He gestured with his Mirren-bundle.

Clare stepped back, raised her hands, shivering. 'No, no, I can't.'

Cal flashed a look at her, sharp with concern.

'You're in shock. Come away. You need to rest.'

He walked across the deserted road to his cottage attached to the post office, its white walls glowing in the dusk, and she followed unquestioningly, her mind a dazed fog.

Cal sat her down in his snug parlour, lit the lamp, and without asking, set Mirren on her lap. She tentatively cradled her baby, knowing why he had done so, yet still worried about harming her by simply touching. And yet Mirren trusted her, snuffling in a half-dream. Clare gazed at her daughter's face with a sudden, strange lightness, a reacquaintance. She listened to Cal fixing her a hot toddy and toasting bread in the kitchen out the back. As she sipped and nibbled, she felt her strength seeping back.

Cal emptied a drawer from his bureau and created a nest for Mirren, folding a blanket and placing it inside. He set it on the floor by the armchair, eased the baby from her arms and settled her down. Clare watched him, in a trance of admiration.

'When you've finished your supper, you go to my bed,' he said. 'I will sit here all night and watch over her so that you can sleep. And in the morning, I trust, I hope, you will feel better.'

Clare felt no reason to question him and took herself off up the narrow, wooden staircase. Once again, as he'd done at the last house on the lochan, Cal had taken on Mirren's care, and in doing so, Clare's care too.

The simple, immaculate bachelor's room contained only the necessary pieces of furniture. Old-fashioned and rudimentary, but comforting, the room seemed like a retreat from the world. As Clare sat on the bed and slipped off her shoes, she felt reminded of being looked after, reminded of hope.

Curling up under the lambswool blanket, so supple it fitted around her body as if it was part of her, she thought of Cal sitting downstairs, watching over Mirren. And realised that she had never asked what had made him follow her, down through the pines, down to the water's edge.

But she would. She would in the morning.

Mirren lay safely now, downstairs with Cal, and the bed, sublimely comfortable, cradled Clare towards sleep. She closed her eyes on the blinding horror of the day. Her breathing and her heartbeat matched the bedside clock's slow ticking and she slept.

'All quiet,' Cal said, as he drove along the avenue of aspens, rich with fluttering summer green. He parked on the gravel, cranked the handbrake. 'We made it. It's still nice and early. Car's not here. No one is home.'

Holding Mirren on her lap, Clare glanced at him. He seemed relieved that Anne and Allistair would not be there to press questions, to wonder and worry; that Isla's cottage along the lane also stood empty. He looked happy to have his duty towards Clare and Mirren over with.

'Thank you, Cal,' she said. 'For everything.'

'Ach, think nothing of it.'

'But it... it wasn't *nothing*,' she uttered. Something terrible had happened to her, and Cal had noticed.

'Come on, you need to rest.' He got out of the car and came

around to open the passenger door for her, taking Mirren from her to make it easier.

'Will you not come in for a cup of tea?'

'No, no.' As Cal passed Mirren back, his hands brushed Clare's. He apologised. 'Need to get on.'

He turned his head, his attention caught by a raptor circling the heathland, and the thought of asking him why he'd followed her now felt wrong. All the questions Clare had pondered on over the last few months, about him, about his life, over that cup of tea, faded. Perhaps she should not impinge on Cal's privacy. For, in the light of day, it felt like prying. And, anyway, he wouldn't want to talk; he'd been up all night watching over Mirren.

The baby chirruped pleasantly as Clare hitched her higher in her arms.

'Best get the wee one indoors. She must be *scunnered*,' Cal said. 'As must you be.'

His dark, golden-flecked eyes sought hers for one small moment, before looking away. And, as he got back into his car, he became the aloof man again, the family friend leading his quiet life, performing his service for the folks of Foyers. Yet he had appeared in her life, and crossed her path at the right and critical time. And she did not want him to go.

'Yes, the wee one certainly needs a bath,' Clare said with false cheer.

'Take care,' he said through the open car window, and it sounded like an ending.

'Thank you, Cal,' she uttered.

He nodded, once and formally – a recognition – and Clare watched his car head back down the drive, eventually becoming swallowed by the aspens and the great, purple landscape beyond, until she could no longer see or hear it. She stood rooted to the spot, sensing the passing of present into past, while the heath birds continued to pipe and the bird of prey hovered, its wings flicking.

Mirren snuffled against her neck, and she planted a kiss on her soft little head, breathing in her baby scent.

'That man took care of us,' Clare whispered, and a rush of warm, guiltless joy overwhelmed her, coming from a place she'd never noticed before. She sensed a cherishing that would always be there, giving her the strength to say to her baby, 'And I vow, little one, to take care of you.'

But there seemed to be only one way she could do this.

Clare let herself into the quiet house and carried Mirren upstairs to her cot, her steps light, and the spaces inside her no longer empty but glowing, as if somehow, she could see the way ahead. That by simply knowing Cal McInnis, she better knew herself. She had arrived home, both she and Mirren safe. And no one need ever know what had happened.

She left her daughter in her cot to chortle happily to herself and went into her bedroom. Not twelve hours before, these rooms had been filled with danger and madness. Now, this morning, they appeared pleasingly ordinary and, she admitted, rather dull. Clare looked from the window at the stand of pines, the rich green concealing the jackdaws' nest. By now, the chicks would be fledged, and on their way into their own life.

Her pile of correspondence sat neatly on her dressing table. Clare sifted through it, discarding her mother's pithy missives, and found Meryl Stanford's letter. She felt as if a storm had broken a long, hot, stifling spell of weather.

14

MIRREN

The Highlands, Summer 1985

With the library closed on Wednesdays, Mirren had the day to herself. It made up for Saturdays, their busiest day, although going to work in that hallowed, silent, organised space had always been her solace. The cataloguing, the rustle of pages, the gentle stamping of books. The quiet voices, the occasional *shush*. Working her way around the shelves with her trolley, A to Z and sometimes, for a change Z to A, Mirren held on to the sensible matters in her mind: finding Daphne du Maurier next to D. H. Lawrence and putting her in the right place; locating the Ladybird book on the night sky for the wee girl doing a project.

The comforting routine of her working day stopped her mind brimming with questions she could not answer. And also, she decided, neither could Gregor. But being alone at home with the day stretching ahead had become a different matter. Standing at her bedroom window to assess what the weather promised, she forced herself to read the sky, check the clouds in the west, to focus on the time she had for herself. Overcast, she noted, with a sort of cool, nondescript blankness; the nature of the Scottish weather, so that when the sun found its way through, and cloud shadows moved over the hills, everything seemed agreeable again, even if it was only for a moment.

In any case, Mirren thought, she had better take a mac.

She allowed herself a smile. Although her voice sounded soft, and her vowels long, rolling her Rs occasionally, she wasn't entirely Scottish. Granted, she had been born not five miles from here, in the last house on the lochan, but the land was not in her blood. And yet she felt at home. Gregor once said that she'd been adopted by the hills. She loved that expression, but he wouldn't claim it; said it was something people round here said.

As Mirren secured her hair back from her forehead with a band, she caught sight of her wedding ring on her finger. What had made her fall in love with Gregor? His humility, his honesty? Or had it been that he simply had always been around and she did not wish to look any further? She didn't like the idea of that.

'I suppose it's staying on for now, Gregor.'

With flask and sandwiches packed up and walking boots on, she decided to see how far she got. Catch the bus to Foyers, and walking up to Loch Mhor with its little kirk high on the heathland could be possible, if the rain held off. She got as far as the bottom of the front path when Cal McInnis pulled up in his car.

Out he hopped in smart trews and shirt, always appearing good for his age. Mirren greeted him warmly, realising she knew exactly how Gregor will look when he reaches his mid-seventies.

'Off on a walk, I see,' Cal said.

'Yes, but it can wait,' she replied. 'Did Gregor send you?'

'No, no, not at all. I've come to see how you are for myself. I don't need him to tell me to do the right thing.'

'I'm sorry,' she said, hating the disappointment that Gregor hadn't asked his uncle to check how she was. 'We had harsh words, or rather, I had harsh words with him last time he was here. But he'd only come for some tools,' she added lamely, thinking she needed to explain. 'I just thought maybe...'

Cal nodded at her backpack. 'I can go with you, for a wee while if you like... if you want company. Or to talk. Harsh words or not.'

'Okay.' Mirren set aside the idea of catching the bus. 'Let's go for a walk up the hill for a while.'

Cal agreed, grabbing a jumper from his car before they took the track that wound its way up through the woods behind Mirren's house.

* * *

The steep path inevitably stifled conversation and they walked for some time in silence, boots crunching over pine needles, disturbing the smell of spruce. There felt no need to talk anyway; Cal's level-headed and peaceful presence seemed appropriate for Mirren's mood. Jackdaws called, their jarring shrieks echoing through the trees, and Mirren and Cal eventually emerged from the tranquil shade, blinking in a burst of unexpected sunshine. They found a comfortable-looking log to rest on.

'There's tea enough for two,' Mirren said, unscrewing her flask. 'If you don't mind sharing the cup.'

'That's smashing,' he said, always easy in her company.

They sipped and passed the cup, with Cal patiently contemplating the view.

'You wanted to find out how I am?' Mirren said, eventually.

'Aye. That nephew of mine...' Cal uttered, stirring himself. 'I don't get it.'

Mirren sighed. The cheese sandwiches she'd made an hour or so before had sweated in their foil wrapper and did not look so appealing now.

'Neither do I, Cal, neither do I,' she said. 'This whole thing. It has been appalling. Disturbing. For Kirstine too, remember.'

'I've not forgotten Kirstine,' he said. 'But how are you doing?'

Mirren swallowed some tea, hating the plasticky taste from the flask, feeling as if the pain of Gregor leaving lay poised and waiting for her, behind a door. Would telling his uncle this be a welcome release, or in some way disloyal?

'I don't think that I have felt it yet, properly. The impact of him leaving,' she said, easing herself into her confession. 'But it all feels so inexplicable. His reasons seem so lightweight and hackneyed. I feel he is hiding something.'

'An affair?' Cal asked, turning to her in astonishment.

'No, no. Oh, I don't know. But he does seem to be sprucing himself up these days.' Mirren heard the bitter twang in her voice. 'But that aside...' She glanced at Cal. 'So many other things seemed to be coming up, parading themselves in front of me. Unrelated stuff. As if my mind has decided to show me the worst parts of my life, like a badly edited cine film flickering on the wall.' Realising how intimate her admission sounded, Mirren let out a deflecting laugh. 'Remember when Allistair used to give us a cine show on a Saturday evening?'

'Aye, I remember.' Cal chuckled, relieved, Mirren thought, at the change of subject. 'The Highland Games at Braemar, except everything in the distance. The caber looking like a matchstick. And you and Gregor, two bairns in a paddling pool somewhere. That time Allistair tried to film the Falls of Foyers and nearly dropped the damn camera in. Aye, I remember. But I know what you mean...' he said, lowering his voice in his slow, thoughtful way, 'trauma like this... what Gregor has done has sparked deeper memories. You are, Mirren, being reminded of something.'

Mirren tried a bite of sandwich, but it clagged her mouth.

'I may have to feed the jackdaws with this,' she said.

Again, Cal waited. These days, his shoulders looked a bit more rounded, his arms less robust, his belly a little pronounced. But his face still had a freshness, his eyes that golden sparkle, and his hair – as white for as long as Mirren could remember and of which he seemed justifiably proud – swept-back thickly over his head.

'I do remember something, Cal,' she said, treading carefully. 'This came back to me the recently. You giving me and Gregor a lift home from school. And this wasn't normal because we usually got the bus. It seems so clear in my mind, it all playing out, but I have no idea why it happened. And why it should come back to me now. I assume the bus broke down or something.'

'No, lass, it wasn't anything to do with the bus.'

Cal fell back into typical McInnis silence. But the tone of his voice sent a cold quaking through Mirren's limbs. A sort of unsettling, acutely physical.

'It wasn't?' she prompted, her mouth dry.

'Nay, lass.' Cal looked at her, to assess if she seemed ready for him to continue. 'You were in the lower school; Gregor the year or so above you. The school had telephoned Anne to say it would be best if someone came to pick you up,' he said. 'Allistair, of course, was over at the boys' grammar and couldn't leave. Isla probably in Fort Augustus or somewhere. So Anne called me. I shut the shop, put up a sign, *back in two hours*.'

'Oh, Cal.'

'There was no question.'

'But why did they call?' Mirren asked, answers and reasons streaming through her mind.

'The bullies had got the better of you, the wee bastards. The teacher found you in the lower-school toilets, crouched in the corner. You would not speak,' he said, 'seemed unable to cry.'

Mirren nodded, remembering the rest before Cal could finish. She could feel the cold pipes against her back, the lagging crusted and hairy. She could smell the dirt and dampness under the cleaner's sink, the stale whiff of the old, grey mop. Could hear the thunder of chains being pulled, the earthy stench of the lavatories. That it felt better, safer, to be huddled in that corner, than out in the corridor, or in the playground, or anywhere else for that matter where there were other children. And she had wet herself. The warmness, brief and flooding, quickly turning sour and cold.

'It must have been the name-calling,' she said. 'My different surname then, you see. Ashby, not Fraser. I remember one boy snarling at me. Taunting me. Christ, they were awful.'

Cal turned to look at her, and she saw his understanding of her pain flickering in his eyes.

'But you would not go anywhere without Gregor,' Cal continued, comforting her. 'And so Gregor was fetched from his class and allowed to come home too. I bet he loved that.'

'That's when we saw the deer,' Mirren said, brightening at the memory. 'The deer, beside the road.'

'Ach, I don't remember.'

'But how old was I, Cal?'

'It was around forty-eight, I'd say. So...'

'So, about seven or eight.'

'After that, Anne and Allistair decided they should apply to adopt you, make it official. Change your surname to Fraser, hoping you could feel more settled and happy. Once and for all. Things had reached a bit of a head...' He breathed a relieved sigh, as if a burden of knowledge had lifted from him.

'I remember some of it, sort of around that time. But I never knew how it all came together. That it happened like that. Thing is, I didn't know I was unhappy. I just felt strange.'

Now, sitting here next to Cal nearly forty years later, the same aching detachment, the not-belonging, approached with stealth and threatened to upend her, again.

'They wanted you to call them Mum and Dad.' Cal looked at her. 'But you never really did, did you?'

'I did when I mentioned them to other people. I used to say it quickly, as if it would be less of a lie. Because I always knew Anne wasn't my mother.' Mirren shut her eyes, as if this would stay the memory. 'They had been clear about that from ever since I could remember. But they never talked about her. My mother. It's almost as if I didn't know her name. Until you said it, Cal.' She looked at him. 'You said her name. That time. In the car.'

He did not respond, and the jackdaws in the woods began to shriek again.

Mirren picked up a fresh pine cone from the ground, its covering tight and perfectly formed. She shook it, heard the rattling seeds.

'Don't tell me you don't remember,' she said, his silence this time unbearable.

'I do remember.'

'You said something odd. About my mother getting lost, or going missing, or something.' Mirren's mind's eye filled with the deer poised by the side of the road, its eyes glossy and fixed for those mesmerising moments. Her connection with a wild creature, brief, wonderous, privileged. 'You said her name. And no one else ever used it.'

Cal made a noise in his throat, a sort of groan, which he tried to disguise by coughing.

'I missed her. There, I said it.' He looked like he was in pain, trying to ease it by speaking. 'And so, it was the same for me. No one would talk about her, I suspect, in case it upset you.'

'Why did she go, Cal? Why did she leave me?'

'Ach, Mirren...'

'She came back for me, didn't she? But then left without me.'

'You remember that? My God. It wasn't much before the bullying. And if that was in the autumn term, she must have come back sometime that summer.'

'Why didn't she take me with her?' Mirren cried out, bewildered, like a child.

The memories had been separate all this time, burning different holes into her mind. The bullying and the taunting, and seeing the deer. And then, watching her mother leave without her. But now they fused into one hot, appalling mess at the base of her skull, a weight pressing down, ready to floor her.

'Ach, I can't answer you, hen. Only she knows. It's not that...' Cal caught her eye and his expression looked fierce with pain. 'It's not that she didn't love you, Mirren.'

Mirren fought tears, shook her head, moved her shoulders, and raised her hand to bat the memories, the very idea of them, away.

'No, no, I can't...'

Mirren squeezed her eyes shut and saw her mother standing below in the rain in front of the last house on the lochan. Seven-or-eight-year-old Mirren, watching through her bedroom window. Not understanding. The adults milling about – Anne, Allistair, and another man – a sense of confusion, of something wrong, their attention on her mother. Behind them, the aspens along the drive shimmered wet with the gentle rain that obscured the hills with white vapour.

Her mother's eyes had been pinned wide, her body rigid as if spiked with shock, only her head moved with minute, juddering shakes. The stranger stood beside her and seemed to be trying to say goodbye to Anne and Allistair for her because she could not do so for weeping. Anne, also crying, glanced up at Mirren's bedroom window while Allistair looked like he was bearing up and being strong.

Something had caught her mother's eye. She followed Anne's gaze and saw Mirren at the window. Her mouth gaped, as if in a silent scream. And Mirren crept so close to the rain-splattered windowpane that her breath misted the glass. Anne moved towards her mother as if to block her view, put her arms out to her, but she tore herself from her grip. She shook herself free and climbed into the back of Allistair's car, slamming the door.

Mirren could feel Cal's hand rest gently on her shoulder as if he were trying to contain her, stop her shaking.

'None of us thought you remembered that time – when Clare came back but left without you.'

'But the thing is, Cal. I do. I do now.' Mirren's voice trailed into a sob.

Cal sighed hard, regret spooling in his words. 'You see, I wasn't family. Not then. It perhaps was none of my business. What could I say? Perhaps Anne and Allistair thought, hoped, that you were too young, and would forget. No one spoke about it.'

'And they still won't,' Mirren uttered. 'And I can't stop remembering. I can't stop wondering.'

PART II

15

CLARE

London and The Chilterns, October 1941

It was a dark early morning and Clare got off the sleeper to King's Cross echoing with clanging and shunting, milk churns being offloaded, porters ferrying luggage and the first commuters in suits and hats heading into town. She took the Northern Line and emerged at Hampstead, high above the city to air touched with an autumnal chill.

Gnarled trees scattered leaves over cobbles as she made her way along streets of grand villas and town houses, their iron railings still intact and not ripped out to make Spitfires. Residents in this rarefied place, Clare decided, evidently had clout. After all, old money spoke volumes.

A woman passed her, pushing a pram, and Clare glanced at her beleaguered face, feeling sadness, tinged with wrenching guilt. She quickened her pace before she could catch a glimpse of the baby, pondering why people, tired of living in the countryside as evacuees, returned to London with their children when they could have perhaps, left them behind. She hurried on, telling herself Mirren was safe with Anne and Allistair, far safer, and better off without her. Her sister had agreed, all too readily, that Clare should take the job, move away, and leave her daughter with her. And the idea of Clare coming back to visit regularly had been raised and gently dismissed. After all, travelling in wartime proved to be so infernally difficult.

Miss Stanford's flat was the top floor of a house, and Clare was to cut through a steep, narrow alleyway and cross a cobbled lane to reach it. Meryl hadn't mentioned she lived in a graceful, Georgian villa with a tall, iron gate, a gravel path across a pristine lawn and an unduly wide front door, next to which you must pull a handle to ring the bell.

'Goodness, it is marvellous to see you,' Meryl cried, all immaculate and slender as she heaved open the door. 'Come on in. My God, you look good. All that Highland air, Clare, you have a colour in your cheeks I've not seen before. And they must be feeding you well up there.'

'This place is beautiful,' said Clare, stepping into the cool, black-and-white tiled hall.

'And you are of course wondering how an ex-BBC employee could afford to live in such a house?' Meryl laughed as she led the way up the exquisitely curved staircase. A series of graceful windows on each half landing threw sunlight in over the pale walls. 'But this is my godmother Betty's house; she has the first two floors, I the top. She's a funny old thing. Very old-fashioned. And rather deaf, too,' she added, seeing Clare's concerned expression. 'These windows, for example, as lovely as they are, need to be covered each evening with the blackout. And I've said, many a time, let's just leave the screens up, but every morning, she wants the house *dressed*, as she says, for the day. And back to how it was before all this inconvenience.'

Clare laughed softly as they turned onto the next flight. 'To describe the war as inconvenient is rather an understatement, Miss Stanford. Does she,' she joked, 'have a butler?'

'Used to. Until he left her for the King's Royal Rifle Corps. I'll give you an example of the deafness. When the raids were at their worst, I had to go and shake her awake. She barely heard the sirens. Now, this is me.'

Meryl showed Clare along the top landing and through the door of an apartment. She gestured for her to walk along a short corridor into a sitting room. It had a tighter and more snug feel than the expansive stairwell, with lower ceilings, but windows that looked out over Hampstead Heath and the London skyline beyond. Coal smoke hung over the irregular landscape of rooftops, chimney pots and the pale dome of St Paul's, with the mighty cranes of the East End docks silhouetted on the horizon.

'This was originally the nursery and servants' rooms,' Meryl said. 'They certainly had the best views in the house. Now, would you like some breakfast, Clare, before we get down to formalities? You must be famished. Please, take a seat.'

Clare, realising how hungry she felt, said she could manage something. The meagre breakfast offered on the train at six that morning had not made a difference. She perched on the sofa and gazed around the room, keeping her scrutiny swift and polite. A collection of framed art graced the wallpaper, ceramic figures of birds lining the mantel, while a small coal fire glimmered in the hearth below. How odd it felt to be here in her old boss's home, seeing her ornaments and discovering her taste in paintings.

'First things first,' Meryl called from the adjoining kitchenette where she clattered plates and cutlery. 'You must stop with the *Miss Stanford*. My name is Meryl, Clare, as well you know.'

'Why yes, of course,' Clare said, leaning forward to call back.

Meryl set a tray down on the coffee table for her, handed her a plate and poured tea.

'We're the other way round here, aren't we?' Meryl laughed, offering her the toast rack. 'You used to do the tea-making. I expect you don't miss that part of your job.'

'I can't say I do.'

Meryl sat down opposite and stared openly at her in a sort of wonder, smiling broadly, a glint in her eye.

'My, a lot of water has passed under the bridge since we last saw each other. I am glad you are here, still intact.'

'I am but...' Clare hesitated, thinking about the nature of the water that had passed under so many crumbling bridges. She scraped a dab of butter over a piece of toast. 'I was shocked to hear about the fatalities at Broadcasting House – a year ago nearly, isn't it? The night I left. That awful air raid. I only realised the extent of it later when I was settled in Scotland. I hope... I hope that we didn't lose anyone close?'

'A terrible, terrible night, but no. Our department remained unscathed. But I had to deal with the aftermath. The families of the staff members we lost. Possibly the worst few months of my career. I have a few more grey hairs, I can tell you.' Meryl grimaced and indicated her face. 'And these aren't laughter lines, Clare.'

Clare sipped the good, strong tea, cleared her throat. 'I did hear some departments have been moved out?'

'They did, down to the Strand. It was a difficult and disruptive time, and still is for everyone, everywhere. You can probably tell that all of this was the impetus for me to leave and join the Air Ministry. I wanted to do something different, something positive. Not that what the good old Beeb does isn't. And I haven't regretted it. It has been wholly interesting so far.'

Clare sat up, alert with anticipation. 'I feel the same, Meryl. I realise I have been rather...' She paused. 'How can I put this... isolated up there with my sister. And a little... redundant. As lovely and as welcoming as she has been.'

Shame held her tongue. This had been the moment to tell Meryl about Mirren, but she let it slip past, as if her daughter did not exist. Had no significance. For having Mirren might make her boss think differently about her, see her in a different light. Decide she would not risk employing such a flighty person, someone who would leave a child behind, who got themselves into difficulty in the first place. And who could be wrenched back home at any moment.

'I dare say,' said Meryl, reaching for a buff file on the table. 'I am heartily glad that you agreed to meet with me.' She waited, her eyes flicking to the windows, and her fine-boned face rumpled with anxiety. 'Actually, there was an incident the evening you left, the night of the raid—' she began, but shook herself out of her thoughts. 'But heavens, I'm forgetting myself. Best to keep mum. In Personnel, war or no war, we both know discretion is the rule.'

'Absolutely.'

'Which is why I know I can trust you with this job with the Air Ministry.'

Clare set her cup down, used the napkin and folded her hands on her lap, ready to listen.

'I must warn you and reiterate in the strongest terms, that everything we say here in this room is top secret,' Meryl went on. 'You will first sign the Official Secrets Act.' She handed Clare a document, her tone now clipped and efficient, the Miss Stanford of old. 'Having my home as my office these days is perfect for meetings like this. Especially as dear Betty downstairs will not hear a word we say.'

She waited while Clare read and signed the paperwork, familiar with its wording from her days at Broadcasting House.

'Now, if you are happy for me to proceed,' said Meryl, taking the papers back and shoving them into the file, 'you must be dying for me to explain?'

* * *

Clare caught the train from Marylebone Station to Buckinghamshire and High Wycombe, the place 'somewhere in the south of England' that Meryl had spoken about. The taxi – which Meryl had insisted hailing down and paying for in Hampstead – had taken Clare down past Regent's Park and along the Euston Road, above the series of streets and short cuts she'd stumbled along the evening of the raid. She spotted, in brief glimpses, bombsites, shattered buildings and homes destroyed, but many, she noted, were miraculously intact, not a hair out of place.

On the train, she turned her mind from that night, for it proved too horrendous and exhausting to give it her time, and she tried to concentrate on everything Meryl had told her. Which, in all honesty, had not been much.

'It's map making, for the RAF,' she'd said. 'You will support the cartographers, and artists. An administrative role, but vital, Clare. It is one of the plans, as is all of our work, to help shorten the war. They are target maps for Bomber Command. I'm sure you will guess why we are producing them. And, you'll be living in a pretty spot, tucked into the Chiltern Hills. That is all I will tell you for now. At High Wycombe, you will report to the police station. And you will be shown to your billet. Oh, and Clare,' Meryl said, as she helped her into the taxi with her suitcase, 'it helps if you can ride a bicycle.'

As the train trundled alongside the Tube tracks out through the suburbs of Kilburn and Wembley, with the white towers of the stadium in the distance, Clare found herself reliving part of her old journey home from work. It seemed a lifetime ago.

The train halted at Harrow, and she gazed up at the hill topped by its trees and its church, and the suburban avenues of her childhood spreading beyond before the engine built up steam again and chugged on into Buckinghamshire.

A while later, the train stopped, and she recognised Amersham Station. Clare pulled the window down to peer out along the platform, wondering. Her parents lived here now with Great-Aunt Emily in the village at the bottom of the hill, and may well be catching a train somewhere, or strolling around, going about their business with no idea that she was passing through. Her mother's infrequent letters had dwindled, and there had never been any suggestion of a visit to see Mirren. But this detachment, enforced by wartime, suited Clare. And she couldn't tell her parents about her new job anyway if they ever appeared interested enough to ask.

The sergeant behind the desk at the police station in High Wycombe indicated that she should take a seat and made a telephone call, speaking with terse precision to the person on the other end of the line.

'You will be collected shortly, Miss Ashby,' he said after replacing the receiver.

She waited, wondering how long his interpretation of 'shortly' would be. Local folk came and went to report such events as boys being spotted scrumping apples and a car being parked for over a week too near the crossroads, until an airman in RAF blue strolled in and saluted the sergeant in a mildly bored manner. At the policeman's gesture, he turned to Clare and his expression altered, his fresh features rearranging themselves in an effort not to smile too broadly, his eyes brightening beneath the peak of his cap. He seemed far too young to be in uniform.

'Miss Ashby, I'm flying officer Havill,' he said, picking up her suitcase. 'Please, come with me.'

Clare followed him out to the staff car and went to the passenger door.

'Right you are, Miss Ashby,' he said, having opened the rear door for her. 'The back suspension on this one is questionable. You will be more comfortable at the front. And I won't feel so much like a chauffeur.'

He shoved her suitcase into the back and leant over quickly to hold the car door for her, waiting for her to settle before shutting it.

'Have you travelled far today?' he asked as he drove them out of the town, onto a road that cut through the bottom of a valley with beechwoods clothing the steep hillsides in varying shades of gold. The sky had begun to dim over the Chilterns with the early-autumn twilight.

'I'm not sure I am allowed to tell you,' she said. 'You might be testing me.'

'That's the right answer,' he laughed. 'We have to be so careful, don't we? But once you have been debriefed by Mr Dawson – he's ex-army and in charge of the civilians on site – you will get more of a lie of the land in how everyone fits together, what we can talk about, and what we can't. You'll relax into it. It is tough and demanding, Miss Ashby; you will have to keep your wits about you, which I see won't be a problem. You'll find yourself working all hours, but we do have a lark too. I'm Bertie, by the way. We may as well get formalities over and done with.'

'Hello, Bertie.'

Clare gave a small, tucked-in smile. She felt surprisingly serene, rising above her goading guilt at leaving her old life behind like forgotten luggage.

With every mile Bertie drove her down the country road, her new life unfolded before her. Miss Stanford's trust in her, the belief in her that no one else had ever shown her, bolstered Clare enough, despite her simmering nerves, for her to enjoy the drive and Bertie

Havill's unexpectedly convivial company. The opportunity felt like a gift.

They drove along a smaller lane for at least a mile beside an old, metal fence which marked the boundary of a country estate. Beyond it rolled parkland punctuated by lone oaks and stands of beeches, and speckled with grazing sheep.

'I feel like I should ask you how long you have been in the RAF, to make conversation, but again such a question might be off limits,' said Clare, 'so I will content myself with saying that it is certainly beautiful around here.'

'That it is. Have you ever been in Buckinghamshire before, Miss Ashby?'

'Now, now,' she said, 'I am not answering any more of your questions.'

Bertie paused for a beat and they both laughed together.

Ahead, Clare noticed the road rising on a sharp incline.

'The person who recruited me said I would need a bicycle to get around, but I don't fancy that hill much.'

'It depends where you are billeted, I suppose,' he said. 'Look at it this way: if you lived in the village up there, Cryers Hill, coming to work will be a breeze. But going home again – my God!'

'Sounds like it should be called Crying Hill,' said Clare.

Laughing, the airman slowed the car and stopped at gates where a sentry checked Clare's paperwork and saluted them through. The track lead over undulating grounds, past a little church, stables, and estate buildings. Bertie pulled the car up behind a towering yew hedge, next to a shed for a motley selection of bicycles.

'Welcome to Hillside.'

'So, the elusive destination...'

'Leave your suitcase for now, Miss Ashby, because I will be taking you to your billet later.' He checked some paperwork. 'Ah, it's bad news, I'm afraid. You are to stay with Mrs Bell up at Cryers Hill.'

'I take it that the punishingly steep hill is the bad news,' said Clare. 'And not my landlady.'

'Not for me to say,' Bertie laughed. 'But, anyway, here we are. Jolly old Hillside.'

* * *

Bertie, tall and smart in RAF blue, walked with her over the gravel. They went through an opening in the hedge and onto a path sweeping around a circular lawn planted with elderly trees. Clare caught glimpses of the russet-brick Victorian manor house, its tall windows catching the last of the evening light, and its surprisingly modest but welcoming arched porchway.

'This was once Benjamin Disraeli's home,' said Bertie. 'I wonder what he would have made of us rabble invading his salons and parlours.'

'He was Jewish, wasn't he?' Clare said. 'I am sure he would have approved.'

They went through the porch which Clare imagined at Christmas time, long ago, would have been gleaming with decorated fir trees. At the door, an Air Ministry constable confirmed who Clare said she was, and she went with Bertie across an elegantly dusky and, again, quite modest, entrance hall with fireplace, parquet floor and deep-red walls.

Gothic arches framed a series of doorways, where, from rooms leading off an inner hallway, Clare heard voices, a typewriter clacking, the general murmur of a busy office day. A man with rolled-up documents under his arm strode past, and a woman, trundling along with a tea trolley, offered Clare a smile.

Bertie tapped on a door, waited for the command, opened it, saluted briskly, and retreated.

Mr Dawson, a short and robust man with surprising energy, regulation army moustache and round glasses, came from behind his desk to shake Clare's hand.

'Now, now, Miss Ashby, I hear you have travelled far today, but we will furnish you with tea and sandwiches while I brief you. There is a great deal to take in, and I can't, I am afraid,' he gave her a wry smile, 'keep it brief. Mrs Askell will be along shortly with some refreshment.'

Clare sat down, straight-backed, and folded her hands on her lap, feeling suddenly and immensely tired. The day had sunk into evening, disorientating her, and with the blackout down and lamps on, she felt as if she had entered yet another wakeful twenty-four hours. But she must concentrate, and take it all in. This, now, being here at last at Hillside and listening to Mr Dawson, the reason she had left the Highlands: this, now, was why she had deserted her daughter.

Mr Dawson sat behind his desk and handed her a sheet of paper with details of her billet – the working hours, that lunch will cost one shilling and six pence, and tea one pence a cup, from her civilian wage of four pounds a fortnight. The lady with the trolley wheeled it in, handed Clare a plate of sandwiches and Clare began to rummage in her handbag for her purse.

'No, lovey, it's your first day; these are on us,' Mrs Askell said, setting down a large mug of tea and bustling out again.

'Now down to business, Miss Ashby,' said Mr Dawson.

He clasped his hands and rested them on his blotter, lifting them and placing them to punctuate and accentuate all that he had to impart. The war, he told her, had been going on for two years, as well they knew, and it was, frankly, not going favourably. Britain stood alone with her Commonwealth allies. The enemy was on the doorstep.

'The Blitz, Miss Ashby, appears to have abated, as Hitler has turned his attention to Russia. And Bomber Command are raiding Germany and its occupied territories almost every night. And yet, many of those munitions are wasted. Fall short of their targets. Miss them altogether. And we are losing our crews, I would say, Miss Ashby, at an appalling rate, and for no good reason.'

Clare wondered whether the reason bombs falling onto schools, hospitals, houses, onto a person running down the London side streets desperate to find her way home, could ever be considered good.

'And so, this is where Hillside comes in,' said Mr Dawson.

He explained how, in fine weather, reconnaissance planes flew regularly over Germany to take aerial photographs, which the RAF spent a great deal of time examining to identify potential targets.

'Factories, docks, railways, and certain cities selected for...' Mr Dawson cleared his throat, 'strategic reasons. The photographs come here to Hillside where the maps for our bombing crews are produced. Your job, Miss Ashby, is to work alongside the Intelligence Section—'

Clare, surprised by the gravity of the department name, uttered, 'Oh!'

Mr Dawson paused and pointed to the wall. 'They're just next door in Disraeli's Library and in the Garden Hall, across the corridor. You will compare the new photographs against the existing maps we have of the areas, some of which go back to the Twenties, and indicate where they need updating. And they will be passed onto the Drawing Offices. Such is the accuracy needed; it is time-consuming, as you can well imagine. Our cartographers can only produce about two maps a week. They are then printed in our print shop here at Hillside, thousands of copies, and distributed to airfields all around the country. And the aircrews study them, take them on board... But, Miss Ashby, we will leave the rest of it for another day.'

'Thank you, Mr Dawson,' Clare said, her eyes flickering with tiredness, her head so full to the brim with information, she worried it would overflow and she would not be able to remember a single thing he'd said.

She took a breath, tried to remember the reasons why she decided to take the job, how she could in some way help the war effort, do some good, and try to become a more worthwhile person. And maybe, one day, a better mother. One day, tell Mirren all about it.

'Away to your billet, Miss Ashby,' said Mr Dawson. 'You look done in. Havill will drive you. He should be hanging around out there. See you tomorrow, bright and early. Eight forty-five sharp.'

Bertie dropped Clare off at a brick-and-flint cottage in the village of Cryers Hill, the sort of dwelling she'd imagine with roses around its door in summer and, in winter, a roaring fire in the inglenook. She got out of the car, thanking Bertie.

After he set her suitcase on the doorstep and said cheerio, Clare felt mildly bereft, for the day had felt like it would never end, and Bertie had helped smooth things over. But she put it down to exhaustion.

As the sound of his car drifted off into the night and she lifted the brass knocker, she knew she'd well and truly arrived at the start of her new life.

A woman opened the door and gestured for Clare to hurry.

'Come in quickly, or the ARP will have a go.'

'Pleased to meet you, Mrs Bell? I'm Clare Ashby.'

The woman turned from hauling her blackout curtain back across the door. 'Well, you don't sound Scottish.'

'That's because I'm not.'

'I heard you were,' she harrumphed. 'I suppose it is all some sort of cover story. They don't trust any of us really. We provide an excellent service for all you people coming here, and they keep us royally in the dark for our pains. Hang your coat and hat on that hook on the left. Your bedroom's upstairs, first on the right. Lavatory is out back. It's way past teatime but I could heat you up some soup.'

'I have been living in Scotland, arrived this morning,' Clare said, feeling the need to explain, to appease her. Her suitcase felt incredibly heavy. She set it down. 'And thank you, Mrs Bell, soup would be lovely.'

'Oh.' The woman's face fell with disappointment, clearly expecting Clare to decline. She folded her arms over her flowery tabard, her eyes glaring through spectacles. 'And you can't leave that there.'

'Upstairs on the right, you say?' Clare said as brightly as she could, determined to counter the rudeness. She picked up her suitcase and went to climb the narrow staircase.

'Shoes off!' Mrs Bell said. 'As you can see, this is a very old house and we have bare floorboards, and they make an awful racket.'

Clare sat on the bottom stair and eased off her shoes, which she then placed under the spot where she'd hung her coat. She longed for her bed, any bed, where she could lay down and be finished with the day.

'I think I'll go straight up, Mrs Bell. But thank you for the offer of soup.'

The woman didn't bother to hide her relief.

'Breakfast is in the dining room at seven. Good night.'

Not waiting for Clare's response, Mrs Bell walked through a door along the hallway, where a radio was playing, and shut it.

Clare's bedroom had a single bed, with chamber pot underneath, wardrobe and washstand. It was frugal but spotless, the result of Mrs Bell's no-shoe policy, no doubt, the bed made up with tight, pristine sheets. The cottage was certainly old, with trusses in the walls sinking into plaster in a pleasing framework, and the ceiling heavily beamed. Clare lit the lamp, resolving to start afresh with Mrs Bell tomorrow, and drew essentials out of her suitcase. She hung up a blouse, and found her book, knowing that reading a few paragraphs would be sure to send her to sleep.

Snug in her nightie, with the book on her lap, her head propped by pillows, she turned to her bookmark. Something fell from under the flyleaf onto the eiderdown.

Clare picked it up. Inhaled sharply.

A photograph. Mirren dressed in the bonnet knitted by Isla, and the smock made by Anne years before for her own longed-for child, lying on a sheepskin rug in a photographer's studio. The reason why Anne and Isla took Mirren off on a trip to Inverness the other week, and why Anne had asked her what book she was going to pack.

Clare's eyes screwed up with pain, her body pierced by a shuddering of longing.

The photographer had captured Mirren's curious glance at his camera. Clare imagined Anne and Isla cooing and waving at her from behind his elbow, her wide eyes gleaming in black-and-white joy, her gummy smile radiating, one hand reaching chubbily for the lens. Someone had carefully brushed her dusting of fine hair.

Clare propped the print on her bedside table and suddenly, the initial shock, the scratching of guilt, melted into something else richer and more tender. As she switched off the lamp, lay down and turned over for sleep, ready to face her new life, she believed it to be how a mother might feel. She believed it to be love.

16

For a place as hush-hush and top secret as Hillside, it felt alive with activity, Clare thought as she finished her checks with the cheery constable on the gates and walked up through the grounds. People on bicycles wheeled by along the path on their way to work to the sound of good naturedly tinging bells and a van rumbled off from a Nissen hut, its driver raising his hand as he passed.

She reported to Mr Dawson, as requested, and he took her through into the library and showed her the desk where she'd be working. She had never stood in such a richly decorated room before. Dark-wood cabinets rose from parquet floor to elaborate-plastered ceiling, shelves packed with Disraeli's precious and age-old books. The grand, marble fireplace was scrolled and decorated, and around the place, rather incongruously, stood filing cabinets and huge, Air Ministry plan chests containing, she guessed, maps of Germany and its occupied territories.

'Good morning, Mr Dawson. Miss Ashby?'

Clare turned to see a brisk, tall, angular man with an exceedingly sharp haircut and wearing a smart, brown suit come through the archway that led from an adjoining salon.

'Lieutenant Richard Fariner, intelligence section,' he said, with a distinct patrician clip in his voice. 'Please take a seat.'

'Miss Ashby is one of Miss Stanford's protégées,' said Mr Dawson. 'Comes highly recommended.'

And with that, he left, and Clare's confidence, which should have been boosted by his comment, began to swerve and plunge. But she took a deep breath, paid attention to the lieutenant, and focused on the reasons she had come to Hillside in the first place.

'Now then,' said Fariner. 'Let's get on, shall we? Lots to do.' He opened one of the plan chests, shuffled out a large photograph, and placed it before her on the desk. He sniffed loudly. 'Before we begin, Miss Ashby, cups of tea are always placed on the side table over there. There's a high risk of china coming into contact with elbows, you see, and spillages, ruining precious information.'

'Understood, lieutenant.'

He sniffed again and she wondered why his fine upbringing had not taught him to refrain. However, she appreciated his straightforwardness and her spirits lifted. She settled behind her desk, frowning in concentration as she listened hard to the logical and meaningful details he conveyed with nasal punctuation. She realised, within moments, that Fariner was only ever going to give her the necessary information about her small part in the whole enormous chain of events. And this suited her perfectly.

'Let's start with this one, shall we?' he said, presenting her with a recent aerial photograph of Hamburg. 'So, Miss Ashby, the fellows over at RAF Medmenham, the interpreters, have identified the potential targets on the photograph. See here.' Fariner tapped it with his finger. 'And this,' he extracted another, much larger, document, 'is our most recent map of the same area, drawn in 1935. I need you to study the aerial photograph and compare it against the existing map. There are other maps of Hamburg here to assist you. I need you to be able to tell me of any differences. New landmarks, buildings, road structures, railways. And you mark them up on this overlay that we place over the map, here.' He pulled out a transparent sheet. 'So our cartographers can produce the target maps for the bombing crews. And, hey presto.'

Clare looked up at him, expecting him to continue with that train of thought.

Instead, he said, 'I will give you an hour to do as much as you can on this one. Let's see how well you do.'

'Is this a test then, lieutenant?' Clare said, picking up a pencil from the pot on the desk.

'Yes, Miss Ashby. But forget the pencil. I want it done thoroughly and accurately, first time, in red ink.'

'A test indeed, thank you, lieutenant.'

Clare set to work, using the photograph's bird's-eye view of the city with the mighty River Elba snaking through, rolling to the North Sea. Comparing the map to the photograph, she noted the canals and the parkland, the churches, and the schools. A large lake sat at the centre of the city, and she imagined it surrounded by shady trees and pathways, the water iced over in winter and blooming with children playing in the summer.

She froze, her nib poised and in danger of dripping ink as she pictured the ordinary people, the children, who had no choice. A sickening feeling dragged through her, a terrible sense of power and shame. She placed the pen back in its stand, took a shuddering breath, and waited.

Outside Disraeli's library windows, the autumn day resumed. A robin sang, and beyond the terrace, the lawn lay in the October sunshine, the grass scattered with the first fallen leaves and edged with clipped, cushiony evergreens. Clare saw movement, a burst of energy within a flower bed and a small, black Scottie dog sprang out, snuffling its way along the path, and a woman dressed in headscarf and mac came into view hurrying after him, the lead swinging in her hand – an unexpected and ordinary little vignette taking place behind where Lieutenant Fariner sat beavering away at his own desk.

Clare focused on the view until her mind settled, her troubled imaginings, the pressing concerns of war, shifted to one side. But never, she knew, to be forgotten. Instead, she thought of Isla and her own Scotties, and of Mirren. Her instinct urged her to reach for her handbag and pull out the photograph that Anne had hidden. But Clare crushed the feeling. She reminded herself of the job in hand.

Leafing through the stack of maps that Fariner had left with her, she set back to her task, carefully outlining on the overlying sheet, the docks, and the factories and the railway lines. The possible targets for Bomber Command.

Someone knocked on the door and Bertie Havill, smart in his uniform, came in with a stack of paperwork.

'Morning, Miss Ashby,' he said, all formality. 'Lieutenant, I have the maps of the Rhine here, sent in from the Geological Society.'

'Very good. Put them on the cabinet,' said Fariner. 'Miss Ashby, you can file them later. And, when you have finished what you are doing now, perhaps Havill can take you on a tour of the house. Get your bearings, meet the other bods in the other departments.'

'Certainly, sir,' Bertie said, and Clare caught the sudden delight in his voice.

Without his forage cap this morning, she could see more of his face, his cropped-short, sandy-blond hair, and his clear, pale-grey eyes. She mirrored his smile.

'I have finished this, sir,' she said.

'Quick work, Miss Ashby. Put it in my in-tray,' Fariner said, and gave them both a quizzical, amused look. 'Off you go.'

Feeling as if she were handing in homework, Clare did as he asked and followed Bertie out of the room.

'Who does the Scottie dog in the garden belong to?' she asked, as they walked into the hallway.

'Sergeant Hadfield and his wife,' Bertie replied. 'He's in charge of the constables and the security of the place. You'll meet him anon, I expect. They live in an apartment upstairs somewhere. Mrs Hadfield cooks our lunches. Here, let me show you where the most important part of Hillside is first: the mess room and canteen.'

They walked across the entrance hall and Clare paused to admire it. Yesterday, tiredness had prevented her noticing the white plasterwork of the ceiling curving down to meet the gothic archways, giving the space a cloistered air. Doorways lead into rooms, from which emanated a hushed and studious air.

'Through there are some of the drawing offices. They can wait,' said Bertie, leading the way along a smaller back corridor.

He pointed out the photographic library, the camera room, and bromide room. A vague clattering of utensils, the murmuring of voices, and the smell of lunch being prepared drifted along. A WAAF girl with blonde hair and neat, blue uniform bumped out of the room with a tray of cups.

'Ah, here's Julia,' said Bertie.

'Goodness me, Bertie Havill, got time on your hands, have you, to be getting in our way?' she said sharply, although her eyes sparkled.

'Carrying out my duties, Julia, that's all. This is Miss Ashby, working for Fariner, and this is her first day.'

'I'd shake your hand, dear, but as you can see...' She lifted the tray a tad higher. 'I won't say welcome to the madhouse, as you won't believe me. It all looks so sedate and serious but underneath it all...' She laughed. 'All I can say is, give the Ice House Boys a wide birth. They are pranksters extraordinaire. Don't ever agree to pose for a photograph for them.'

'Goodness, why on earth should I?'

'They only ever have done that to us fellows,' said Bertie. He threw a look at Clare. 'I'll explain later. But put it this way: they know not to mess with the girls. Especially you, Julia.'

'I will make a note not to.' Clare laughed. 'Whoever are they? These Ice House Boys?'

'All in good time, Miss Ashby. All in good time. Julia, do you still have your bicycle?'

'Yes, it's the rusty old green one in the corner of the shed.'

'And you don't need it?'

'No, thank goodness. I'm billeted down the road at Downley now. I can walk it in fifteen minutes.'

'Can Clare have it?'

'Of course, she can. Be my guest.' Julia smiled at Clare. 'Tyres need pumping. But then, Bertie, I am sure you have a pump somewhere around. Or at least...' She lowered her voice for Clare. 'He will always know where to procure one. Now if you're both done with me, this tray weighs a ton.'

Julia said cheerio, adding that Mrs Hadfield was up to her eyes in the canteen, so best not to bother her.

They poked their heads in for Clare to have a quick look and then went back to the main hall, where the occasional bod crossed in a calm, confident fashion and disappeared through a doorway. Away from her desk and the reason for making the maps, Clare could feel the buoyancy and the chumminess of the place. If the staff did not relish that feeling, she realised, they would go mad with misery.

'There's a really pleasant busy-ness to this place; reminds me of the BBC,' she said. 'I like it.'

Bertie winked. 'You mean the broken biscuit company?' He put his fingers on his lips. 'Now, through here are the hallowed drawing offices,' he half whispered. 'And there are also a couple upstairs.

Have a quick look. But is best not to raise voices. Remember that when you are going to and fro.'

Clare followed Bertie into what could have been one of Disraeli's salons, but cleared of fine furniture and curtains. The staff, four or five men and two women, were perched on high stools at neat rows of tables, intent on their work at their drawing boards under Anglepoise lamps. Clare sensed the concentrated hush, heard the scratching of pens, a faint clatter of their instruments as they drew the target maps. The shutters stood wide open, letting in as much daylight as possible, and the ceiling was strung with lights.

Seeing Clare glance up, Bertie said quietly, 'All the ceilings have been painted white to keep it as bright as possible.'

At the sound of his voice, one or two raised their heads and threw Clare a curious but friendly smile. Bertie gestured that they should leave them to it.

In the hallway, he said, 'Best you get back to Fariner. I am due to go and collect another new recruit from the police station this afternoon. See you later.'

By the time she returned, Lieutenant Fariner had her next task ready for her on her desk.

'Now that I know that you can do the job quickly and competently, Miss Ashby, I want you to do your work from now on slowly and methodically, drafting first in pencil. This way, I know I will get even better results.'

Clare, after hearing his round-about compliment, sharpened her pencil and settled into the work, her knowledge of the cities and towns of Bavaria, Hanover and the Rhine expanding as the afternoon ticked on.

* * *

Later, at five forty-five knock-off, she met Julia out by the bicycle shed.

'Gosh, it is in a bit of a state,' Julia said as she wheeled out the bike, 'but I see Bertie has dealt with the tyres. And, thank goodness, he's fixed the lamp. And yes, it still complies with blackout rules.' She pulled out a handkerchief and dusted off cobwebs. 'It is a bone shaker, but it should see you right.'

Clare wondered if now might not be a good time to confess she had barely ridden a bike before. Her parents had never allowed her to have one but, as a child, she had occasionally ridden on her friend's three-wheeler up and down the avenue.

'It's been a while, so there might be some wobbles,' said Clare, as she perched gingerly on the wooden seat and tested the brake. 'But thank you, Julia.'

'Don't mention it. Any problems with it, see Bertie. He knows all about fixing stuff. He is good like that.' Julia gave her an amused smile with a twinkle in her eyes. 'Listen, we're meeting at the Woodsman's Arms in Downley on Friday evening. The village behind the estate,' she added. 'A few of us are billeted there. Come and meet everyone, away from this place.'

Clare thanked Julia and set off tentatively through the deepening dusk along the roadway out of the estate, certain that she'd have to push the bicycle up to Cryers Hill, but already looking forward to her journey down again tomorrow morning. Although, she reminded herself with a wry smile, there was an evening with the delightful Mrs Bell to get through first.

As she pedalled along in the cooling twilight, her confidence simmered. She passed staff making their way on foot, their torches held downwards, offering cheery farewells as she passed by. Around her, the Chiltern hills formed a bulky darkness against the evening sky, and for a moment, she thought of the Highlands, the wide heathland, the last house on the lochan and Cal. She imagined him closing up his shop at Foyers for the day and heading next door to his home. She remembered the first time she'd seen him, greeting her there from the doorway, his quick walk over to her, and the acceptance in his smile, his unconditional kindness. And what he did for her, down on the shore of Loch Ness.

A vehicle approached along the estate road, bumping over the uneven surface, and Clare recognised Bertie's staff car. She began to wave, tinging her bell for good measure.

Bertie slowed down as he drove past, his face beaming at her through the windscreen, and gave her a comical thumbs-up. His passenger in the back seat looked her way, and Clare's smile stuttered. The shape of the person's head, the way he held himself, a stillness in his arrogance forced a dreadful nausea to rise inside her, an indistinct panic, a feeling that would only be stopped, she thought, if she burst into tears. But she would not give him that part of herself, would not let it show. She would not break down, even though staring at her in astonishment from the car as she wobbled by sat Leo Bailey.

17

The mess room at lunchtime the next day brimmed with chatter and laughter. Clare sat with Bertie and two other RAF lads, Frank and Jim, who Bertie introduced as the Ice House Boys. Hot meals served by Mrs Hadfield and the WAAF girls, Julia and Susanna were devoured and huge cups of tea sipped and replenished. The place was full and lively. Everyone seemed to know everyone. Except, at the end of a long table in the corner, Leo Bailey sat silently and alone, eating his lunch.

'Ah, at last,' Clare said, and coughed in the cigarette smoke drifting around the tables. 'The infamous Ice House Boys.'

She shifted awkwardly in her seat, so all Leo would see of her was her back, the side of her face at most, and she focused her attention on her companions.

'And I still don't know why you're called the Ice House Boys,' she said, the skin on the back of her neck prickling as she fixed on a bright smile for the lads. 'Would you care to enlighten me?'

Her cheery conversation did nothing to stay the shock of seeing Leo. First, yesterday in Bertie's car. And now here in the mess room. The distress and the disbelief continued in snaking waves through her body, like the shivering of a fever, and she wondered how on earth she could maintain her composure if this would forever be life at Hillside. The effort to speak normally, and convivially, made her weak.

'It's after the small building in the grounds where we work. Our studio. We photograph and enlarge the target maps,' said Frank, who looked like he might have only just started shaving. 'There's about eight of us. Breathing in all the chemicals makes it twice the fun. It's a bit of a squeeze down there, I tell you.'

'Down there? So, what is this place?' Clare asked. 'I am intrigued.'

Even though she'd guessed already, she focused on Jim with all her might while he explained, willing him to keep the conversation going.

'In Victorian times, at grand houses like these, they had ice houses to store, you've guessed it, ice,' said Jim, seemingly the younger of the two boys but by the way he tapped out his cigarette and flicked his lighter, he was trying his hardest to appear older. 'Apparently, Disraeli shipped his over from Norway. Kept it there to plonk in his whiskey.'

'How the other half live...' Clare said.

At the tail of her eye, she saw Leo Bailey look her way again. He sat there eating and sipping like someone wanting attention but not willing to do anything about it. In that moment, her shock, and her fear of him, sunk into bitter hatred. She kept her gaze fully on Jim as if her life depended on it.

'The good thing is,' Jim said, 'we're off the Sergeant's radar most of the time. We have some larks, I can tell you. Play some pranks.'

'I can well imagine,' said Clare.

Jim nudged his friend. 'Tell her, Bertie.'

'Yeah, they got me...' Bertie pulled a straight face, even though he seemed to be bursting. 'My first day, I was sent on an errand there to collect something or other. So, it's this odd little dome-shaped building, half underground, tucked away, a chilly cellar if you will.'

'Perfect for storing ice, then?' Clare asked, determined to give Bertie her full attention, to avoid the chance, or the error, of catching Leo's eye.

'So down the steps I went,' said Bertie. 'Frank, here, the delightful Frank, said he wanted to take my photograph, told me to smile for the camera. Asked me to stand in a particular spot. And Jim...'

Jim, sitting opposite Clare, was compressed by laughter. 'You didn't look up, Bertie,' he said. 'You should have looked up.'

'Jim tipped a whole bucket of water down the ice chute onto my head, just as Frank clicked the shutter.'

The others fell about, relishing the story for the umpteenth time. And Clare tried to laugh the hardest.

Bertie composed himself enough to put his hand on Clare's arm.

'They wouldn't do it to the girls.'

'Yes,' Clare said. 'As Julia mentioned, they wouldn't dare.'

'Did I just hear my name?' Julia sat down at the table, wiping her hands on a tea towel. 'My shift's over. There better be some tea left in that pot, Frank.'

Frank pushed the teapot along the table and, without asking, fished out a cigarette for her.

Clare poured Julia's tea. 'They were just filling me in on Ice House tomfoolery.'

Julia rolled her eyes and lit her cigarette. 'Yes, they get the visitors and new recruits every time,' she said. 'Although, I don't think you should attempt it with that new draftsman sitting over there.' She twitched her head in Leo's direction. 'He looks like a VIP.'

Clare dared to look. He wore civilian shirt and tie, his hair peppered more intensely with grey. In the hard light of the mess room, the lines in his face seemed deeper, carved with more ferocity than before. And yet, as he noticed Julia looking over at him, gaining the attention he'd been seeking, he remained handsome, distinguished, and bright eyed.

Julia stood up. 'I'll fetch him over. He can have his pudding with us.'

Clare's insides stiffened, her stomach flipping. The world she had run away from, the events that had snared her, returned full circle to torment her. She felt cowed and confused as fate converged over her head.

Leo's face lit up as Julia approached. He engaged with her, nodding away, as if butter wouldn't melt. His gaze flicked passed Julia to Clare with an odd, strangled look of hope and admiration. He had no idea that a young baby with the same eyes, the same smile as his, lay gurgling in her cot some 500 miles away.

A rush of despair made Clare light-headed, and yet she wanted to laugh at the farce playing out before her.

'I have to go,' she said, standing, her chair scraping loudly.

'See you later,' Bertie said.

'Can I have your pudding then?' Jim asked.

She did not have the strength nor the will to answer either of them, so she turned and walked quickly out of the door.

That evening, Clare wrote to Anne to thank her for the photograph of Mirren, but was unable to tell her own news. She could not say where she was, or what work she was doing. As far as Anne and Allistair were concerned, she was back with Miss Stanford, somewhere in the south of England – her correspondence arriving via a War Office post box number.

As she posted her letter the next morning, loneliness shivered through her. She could no longer share her life with the people who cared about her.

Clare kept her head down, tucked away behind her desk, hoping there would be no good reason for Leo Bailey to come into the library where she worked. And, as she ferried folders containing the photographs that she'd checked, and that Lieutenant Fariner had signed off, across to the Garden Hall for the intelligence staff, she became adept at glancing neither right nor left, nor engaging with anyone. And once the folders were taken off her hands and the jobs allocated to the drawing offices, Clare did not have to venture any further.

Avoiding the mess room, she ate her sandwiches in the garden, finding quiet corners and evergreen nooks from where she could watch Mrs Hadfield walk her Scottie dog, wondering if her new friends might see her as stand-offish, perhaps a little snobby. In any case, she hoped her colleagues found her efficient and professional, while every day she battled with Leo's presence, and the churning inside her.

Anne's reply to her letter, a week or so later, described Mirren as thriving, blooming, and growing a little more each day, her little character forming and evolving, her laughter as bright as sunshine. How they took her for walks around the lochan, and down to Isla's. How the nurse at the doctor's in Fort Augustus delighted in her when she went for her six-month check-up. And how people stopped Anne in the street to lean over the pram – a Silver Cross, no less – bought brand-new, a gift from Cal McInnis.

He didn't realise we had our own one, stored under the stairs, but what a kind gesture.

Holding the letter, perched on the end of her bed in Mrs Bell's smallest bedroom, Clare wondered if the strangers assumed Mirren belonged to Anne. And, if so, did Anne correct them? She inhaled, closed her eyes, imagining the creamy scent of Mirren's skin, her little limbs full and ripe, fighting the twist of jealousy.

In other news, our parents are going off to the West Country soon for a few weeks. Perhaps you'd like to pay Great-Aunt Emily a visit?

Clare chuckled, dismissing the very idea. What would Great-Aunt Emily want with a visit from her? Surely, she would barely remember her.

Isla and the dogs send their love, as does Allistair. And Cal has dropped around a few times, asking after you.

Anne continued, never being able to finish a letter:

P.S. You could write to Cal yourself? Thank him for the pram?

Little did Anne know how much Clare had to thank him for. But she did as her sister asked. She fished out her writing pad and wrote a brief, formal note to Cal. She told him how grateful she was for the pram, adding what a generous and kind gift it had been and that she felt sure that Mirren would enjoy being wheeled around in it.

She signed off and sealed the envelope, wishing she'd been able to acknowledge his care, to thank him for following her down to the loch that evening. For noticing. For saving Mirren's life. Indeed, her own. But speaking or writing about such solemn feelings threatened to trivialise them and make them lose their meaning. And so, the words escaped her.

18

Sunday morning, the middle of November, and Clare cycled down Cryers Hill into the valley where the last traces of mist drifted, her tyres hissing over wet leaves, her nose chilled and red. Mrs Bell had been as cold and silent as ever while serving breakfast, leaving her feeling unsettled. Tiredness dragged through her limbs. She hadn't slept well. Last night had been clear, a high, black sky and a rich moon, and she'd heard the bombers, she guessed from an air base in the Midlands; from the throbbing vibration as they passed over, they sounded like they'd gained height already. She imagined the planes arranging into formation, the navigators setting co-ordinates, and she lay in bed, half-congratulating herself that she could identify them from the noise they made: the putt-putt of the Spitfire's engine, and, now, the thick drone of the Wellington.

The wind had changed direction in the early hours, the dew settled, the mist rose over the valley beds, and the planes had limped home, empty of their load, a straggling and depleted squadron. And Clare, as if it was any ordinary Sunday, rose early and set off on her bicycle down the hill into the town, where she left it at the station and caught a train to Amersham.

The people in the carriage all endeavoured to read their news-papers, pass the time of day or carry on as normal, as if there was no war, while Clare sat among them, deeply aware of her own contribution to last night's raids on Germany. None of her fellow passengers gave her more than a passing glance, and yet the maps she helped produce had been up there with the navigators and the bomb aimers.

Bertie had shown her a finished batch from the print room, ready to be dispatched to Bomber Command. The maps' simplicity, the restriction of colour, made them easy on the eye for Clare, and vital for the navigator and the bomb aimer to make out in the orange glow of the cockpit lamp. The target sat in the centre, painted magenta, with concentric circles radiating out at one-mile intervals to focus the bomber's sights. Roads were shown in black, water in white, and woodland in grey. All other things on the earth eradicated.

She glanced at the headline on the man's newspaper opposite. More reports of the Desert Rats fighting Rommel in North Africa, and Russia defending their capital from German advances. But through the dirty train window, the skies of Buckinghamshire looked empty and ordinary.

When the train stopped at Amersham, she got off and walked down a long hill, passing new bungalows and houses not more than a decade old. The place had boomed when the Metropolitan line had been extended out here for city workers and their families to live. A Metro-Land idyll indeed. At the bottom of the valley in the Old Town, the high street, lined with a medley of brick and flint cottages and Georgian façades, appeared wide enough for carriages in days gone by to pass each other with ease on their way to the marketplace. She saw past the taped windows and white lines painted along the kerb, and imagined the road strewn with straw and piles of horse dung, and ladies in bonnets chatting here and there with red-coated soldiers.

Now that she'd arrived, her trepidation seemed to shadow her along the pavement. Clare wasn't one for simply turning up at someone's house, let alone someone she had not seen in years. Who she could barely remember. And she never would have considered it if Anne hadn't suggested it in her letter, and even then had laughed at the very idea. But a long Sunday alone at Mrs Bell's had felt far too awful to bear. In the face of everything else unfolding in her life and playing out around her in a world she could not control, this seemed like a good way to spend her day off. She realised that she needed family connection, however distant, however removed.

All manner of mismatched properties lined the street. Cottages built in red brick criss-crossed by wooden struts sat cheek-by-jowl with white-stucco houses with pleasing symmetry, window boxes and fanlights over the doors.

Clare checked the address she'd written down. Town Cottage was the latter, double-fronted no less, and squeezed up next to a narrow, cobbled alley. She paused for a moment, remembering her father speaking in his disparaging, mocking manner about her mother's supposedly prickly aunt, and hoped he'd been exaggerating. She hoped that Emily wouldn't mind her calling on her. She wondered, indeed, if she was even in.

Clare pulled the miniature chain on the little, metal doorbell. It tinkled prettily, and the door opened almost immediately, as if Great-Aunt Emily had been waiting by her window on the lookout.

'Hello, dear.' The woman in neat cashmere and woollen skirt, gestured her in, bangles chiming over slender wrists.

'Aunt Emily, I'm Clare,' she said, poised on the doorstep. 'You remember me?'

'Of course I remember you. Come in. We have the place to ourselves.' She fluttered her hand in the air to a chorus of jingling, and her delicate, rose perfume scented the air. 'But I suspect that's why you came. Please, go through.'

Clare's great-aunt stood back to let her pass along the snug, stone-flagged hallway and into the front parlour where, indeed, a plump window seat had been built under the sash window and the warm scent of beeswax emanated from the fine furniture. Standing on her Turkish rug, Emily appeared more aged and slight, and narrower than Clare recalled. Above quintessential pearls, the skin around her neckline looked soft and crimped, but her cheeks were smooth and powdered, and her eyes the same lucid blue as Clare's mother's, although they had less of a scorching searchlight within them. Emily smiled, pressed Clare's hand warmly with her own, and motioned for her to take a seat on one of the tightly unholstered armchairs.

'Now, Anne mentioned in her last letter that she'd suggested you visit.' Emily sat down opposite. 'And I guessed it would be a Sunday, as I thought that might be your day off. And possibly, that you'd come while your parents are away.'

Clare glanced at the older woman to check she'd heard her correctly.

'It is a shame to have missed them,' Clare began, but stopped when saw Emily's amused, questioning look, the tilt of her head. 'Well, I haven't seen them in a long while, not since—' She halted, unsure as how to continue. 'Not since a year ago, when I moved up to be with Anne.'

'All the better for us. I can give you my undivided attention. It was never like that when I visited the house in Harrow, you know. You were a lot younger of course, and never took any notice me. You were often playing in the garden or upstairs, your nose in a book. Or off at the park with your friends. And your mother and Anne rather did take up a lot of my energy. But now, we can talk undisturbed. I can get to know you properly. You always were my favourite, Clare.' She reached and patted her knee briskly, as if to punctuate her sentiments. 'Tea?'

Emily went to leave the room but paused by the doorway to appraise Clare.

'My goodness,' she said, half to herself, 'haven't you grown up beautifully?' and disappeared off into the kitchen, all vigorous and refined, leaving her scent behind.

Clare took a moment to glance around the room. A small dining table stood near French windows looking out to a courtyard garden at the back. The little hearth was stacked with coal ready to light later on, the latest *Radio Times* issue waiting on the arm of the chair. Bookshelves in alcoves either side of the hearth were stuffed with Austen, Brontë and Agatha Christie.

'And I must apologise,' Emily said, as she came back in with a tray set with china, slices of lemon and a teapot secure under a knitted cosy.

'For what, Aunt Emily?'

'For showing my age, just then, saying *haven't you grown up*. What must you think of me? A silly old woman, I should imagine. But when you get to where I am today, you celebrate it, and all the anomalies that go with it.'

'I'm trying to remember the last time I saw you,' said Clare, taking the offered teacup, giving Emily a shy smile.

Her snowy hair had been set in soft waves, a style from at least ten years before but which, Clare decided, suited her age and her status. No severe Victory roll for Great-Aunt Emily.

'Let me think. I certainly visited Harrow a few times after Anne got married and left for the Highlands. I used to go to the theatre in the West End. Your mother wouldn't come with me, unless it was a musical. I couldn't even tempt her with Laurence Olivier at the Old Vic. I wonder now whether perhaps I should have taken you to a matinee or two. That would have been a nice outing for us, wouldn't it? A ride on the Underground, up to the West End.'

Clare inwardly agreed. What a rare treat that would have been.

'Anyway, enough of me chattering. How are *you*, my dear?' Above her steaming cup, Aunt Emily's eyes focused on Clare's face and yet seemed also to sweep her entire body.

Clare wondered, did Emily know? Had her parents or Anne divulged her shame, never to be spoken of again?

In a moment of awkwardness, she glanced past her great-aunt through the French windows at the garden glowing gold and russet with the last dahlias, and sprinkled with fading-purple Michaelmas daisies. Something about the simplicity and the glory of the flowers comforted her. She felt, suddenly, as if she missed home. And yet did not know where that home might be.

'I am well, thank you,' said Clare, returning to the conversation. She spoke with care, keeping a ring of tact in her voice. 'I'm working for the Air Ministry. That's all I can tell you, I'm afraid.'

'Understood.' Emily tapped the side of her slender nose. 'But I didn't ask you that. I asked how *you* are, my dear.'

It seemed true what people said, Clare thought, as she watched Emily add another lemon slice to her own tea while she waited for Clare to answer: how looks jumped a generation. For something around her great-aunt's gestures, in the quality of her voice, and in the clarity of her smile, reminded her of herself.

From somewhere in her childhood, Emily's visits to Harrow emerged. Clare saw a slender, glamorous lady with shingled waves and floaty dresses and heels. Her hair, as today, had never been verging on the unruly, like Anne and Clare's. Now, Emily seemed to have shrunk into her body, her bones perhaps a little brittle, but her perfume smelt the same, and her eyes sparked with bottled mischief. And yet, Clare's father had been rather unkind about her, as if he had felt intimidated.

'My parents,' Clare said, conversationally, realisations settling inside her as she accepted another cup, 'they've gone on a long trip?'

'How well you have skirted my question.' Emily chuckled. 'But yes, at least a month, they said. Scouting out the West Country. Wanting to start afresh. Your father has decided to retire. Good luck to him – he'll be at a loose end in no time and begging his office to take him back. But it seems he has pinned his flag to a certain mast.'

Not quite grasping Aunt Emily's meaning, Clare mulled it over. She felt encouraged and able to confess.

'They do seem to always want to live their own lives, my parents,' she said. 'I don't mean that disparagingly. But I do feel I was a mistake, came along just as they had been planning some sort of escape. And now, at last, I am out of the picture, and they can do what they like.'

'Now, now,' said Emily. 'How sensitive you are. In a way, you are probably right. But there are always reasons behind people's behaviour. Try not to believe it is about you.'

Clare felt suddenly aware of her own shortcomings: her impatience with her mother, her avoidance of her father. 'It is hard not to think that sometimes,' she said.

Emily gazed past her for some moments, through her front window. From somewhere along the street, the sound of neighbours chatting on a doorstep drifted, and footsteps padded along the pavement. A normal Sunday morning.

'Celia does care,' Emily said. 'And I'm sure Michael does. Although he is one closed book. What it boils down to is that they are both too serious, stubborn, and buttoned up to show affection. But we've all been through it. Believe it or not, they – and we, my generation – have lived through, how shall I say this, not worse times, but just a different kind of *worse*.'

'It feels like the worse times now,' said Clare, feeling miserable for even voicing it.

'But I think young people, like you are and like I once was, feel aggrieved that their youth, their time, has been taken away by terrors beyond their control. Don't you agree?' Aunt Emily fixed her clear gaze on Clare, and Clare felt impelled to nod. 'My heyday was during the last years of Victoria's reign, believe it or not. I was all but twenty in 1896. I know you think I am ancient and should be crumbling away somehow. But I look back on that brief time as a bright jewel in my life. We had fun. We had light and laughter. And then it was all taken away. I lost my first husband in the Boer War of 1900. And my second in the Great War.'

'Goodness, Aunt Emily, I didn't even know you had been married. Let alone twice.'

Emily folded her hands on her lap, as if to concentrate her thoughts and give reverence to them.

'Poor Arthur was a bridegroom of two months when he was buried in the South African Veldt,' she said. 'Silly really, but I often used to worry that he'd feel so lost and lonely. You see, he wouldn't recognise that sky of stars, those constellations. It's a whole other universe there.'

Clare heard a break in Emily's voice. A softening of her spirited veneer.

'As for George. Well, they never found him. Parts of him are scattered wide in the mud of Passchendaele. He would be buried as "A soldier of the Great War". Or as the French sum it up so concisely on their own gravestones, "*Soldat Inconnu*". Unknown.'

'Oh, Aunt Emily.'

Clare's great-aunt quickly dismissed her astonished grief.

'I was older then, in 1917. Pushing forty-one. I dealt with it as best I could. I had no time to be a widow.'

Clare felt uncomfortable, detecting a tingle of shame for assuming her problems could be described as the most appalling. And yet, they, of course, seemed that way to her. But, sitting with Emily, seeing her cheerful poise and how she had survived, Clare sensed a way through it, too.

'I surprised everyone when I remarried dear George at the grand old age of thirty,' Emily continued. 'He was younger than me.' She laughed lightly. 'He called me a cradle snatcher. We married in '06. And then two years after your parents married, in 1908, we lost my sister. Ada. Your grandmother. The same year that Anne was born. It affected your mother profoundly.'

'Ah, yes,' said Clare. 'Poor Mum. Neither Anne nor I knew our grandmother Ada.'

'You may wonder why your mother is like she is. I think it all boils down to the fact that she will not relax. In case something worse happens. But it does anyway. That's what Celia should remember. But can I tell her. No. And Michael, well, I think he is always running after her on eggshells, trying to keep up.'

'I know what you mean,' said Clare, but tasted a bitter tang in her mouth. 'But they just seem so uninterested, and it feels like I am an inconvenience.'

'Surely not. Remember, whatever *that* is, it is not your fault.'

Below her voice, Clare added, 'But this was.'

'Sorry, dear?' Emily tilted her head, curious. 'What did you say?'

'I think the worst did happen for Mum, for them both, in my regard.'

'What's that?'

'Did Mum not tell you?' Pride in Mirren ballooned unexpectedly, thrillingly. She caught her breath. Swallowed hard. 'I have a daughter.'

'My dear Clare.' Emily sighed in wonder, her eyes widening. 'But where is she?'

The simple question struck Clare – the same question a quiet voice inside her had been asking since she left the last house on the lochan. She could ignore it no longer. Her sadness. The hollow ache for Mirren.

'She's with Anne.'

'My, my, you are all so good at keeping secrets. Not a peep from anyone.'

'Anne didn't—?'

'No, no. Which is commendable. She's a good girl.'

Emily stood up and went over to a cabinet in the corner. Clare heard a bottle clang, and glasses clink, and Emily pressed a tiny glass, cool and delicate, into her hand.

'Sherry, dear. Not the strongest alcohol I have, but it's Sunday morning. Drink it. Looks like you need to.'

She tapped her glass against Clare's.

'Bottoms up,' she said and swallowed in one go, while Clare gingerly sipped the soothing sweetness.

'I remember one time,' Emily said, gazing at Clare, her eyes fluttering with a reel of memories. 'It must have been one June. I was visiting. Possibly to go up to the Royal Academy summer exhibition. You came in from the back garden and your nose was scattered with pollen, like freckles of gold. You'd been smelling the flowers.'

'I don't remember,' said Clare, although an image nudged her mind, more of a feeling than a clear memory. A warmth, a cradling. An older stranger from another unfathomable generation. And Clare, the little person, receiving Great-Aunt Emily's unexpected, kind attention.

'That's better; you're smiling.'

Clare lifted her suddenly empty glass. 'May I have another one of these?'

Emily laughed. 'Yes indeed, you may, if you agree to stay for lunch. I have some good chicken pieces from the butcher's.'

Clare nodded, fighting unexpected tears of gratitude, and uttered that it would be lovely.

'How old is your daughter?'

Emily's inflection asked for the baby's name, her voice softening with honeyed compassion as she uncorked the sherry bottle, her bangles ringing.

'Mirren Anne. Six months.'

'Ah, that's lovely. And I want to say what a perfect age, but what do I know? Despite two husbands, having babies passed me by,' said Emily. 'I can see you are missing her.'

Clare gulped air. 'I am.'

'And the father...' Emily settled back in her chair, proceeded tentatively. 'May I ask? Where is he?'

Clare's hands, holding the little sherry glass, began to tremble.

'Clare, you look frightened.'

'I am... ashamed.'

'Oh, my dear.' Emily's slender hand patted her knee. 'It's a story as old as time – you get caught, the man runs off, disappears. Do you not think it has always gone on? A lot of girls are forced to give their babies up for adoption. Thank goodness for Anne.'

Clare breathed in slowly, nodding.

'And do not feel shame,' Emily said. 'Looking at you now, I certainly don't. You are doing sterling work in your important job, and will be a good mother. You need to get used to it. Give it time.'

'But, Aunt Emily,' Clare said, 'the man hasn't disappeared. I thought I'd got away from him.'

'*You* wanted to get away...?' Emily sounded aghast.

Clare nodded. 'But he has cropped up again. Where I work.' Her casual word to describe Leo Bailey's reappearance at Hillside and the shock that continued to grind her bones did it no justice. 'And he doesn't know. He has no idea what... what he did. Or if he does, he doesn't care.'

Clare's glass clanged on the side table as she set it down.

'Sit there,' Emily said. 'Rest a moment. You don't have to explain. Then come out into the kitchen with me and peel the potatoes. Tell me if you want to; I won't press you if you don't. I can see, Clare, that this has been appalling for you.'

With that, she left the room and Clare waited for some moments, gazing through the French windows at the little courtyard garden, her thoughts softening.

And, as she peeled and chopped while Emily prepared the meal, she found herself wanting to tell Cal McInnis about this visit to Great-Aunt Emily's. At last, she would have something to write to him about. And, as the smell of the chicken roasting intensified, and with the radio in the parlour tuned into the *Light Programme*, she was reminded of home. She felt settled, felt herself softening towards her parents. Perhaps even missing them.

* * *

'I wonder if I could come over again, when Mum and Dad are back from their trip?' she said later, as they cleared up after the most splendid meal Clare had eaten in a long while.

'Come over whenever you like. In fact, come for Christmas. If you can have some leave?' Emily, drying her hands on a tea towel, glanced at Clare. 'I do like those earrings, by the way. So pretty.'

Clare touched her earlobe. 'Ah, I bought them in a little shop at Loch Ness before Mirren was born. A small treat to myself.'

'I can't promise such dramatic landscapes as you got used to up there, but put on your coat and hat, Clare; we can take a walk.'

They went out of the back door, along the short, terracotta path, brushing past glowing chrysanthemums and dahlias reaching their faces to the low slanting sun. Pausing at the gate in the back wall while Emily fiddled with the latch, Clare glanced behind her at the house to see russet brickwork, with little casement windows upstairs tucked under the eaves.

'Goodness, Aunt Emily, it looks completely different from this side.'

'That's because the house was built in the 1680s, so Jacobean in style,' said Emily. 'In the upstairs rooms, you'll see all the original beams and plasterwork. But someone made their money a century later and did up the front. Added a new façade, that lovely white plasterwork, new sash windows, my lovely bow front window, and smartened it up. Put on a fresh face. Something we all do with ourselves, don't we, Clare, from time to time?'

Emily shut the gate and they laughed together as they took the footpath along the back of the houses, beside the little river that flowed through the Old Town. Fallen leaves bounced over the eddies and yet the water looked clear enough to see riverweed trailing underneath, healthy and green after a good, long summer.

'Ah, look at that current; the Misbourne is high,' said Emily. 'We have had a lot of rain. Come on, we'll go this way, out of the village.'

Once the houses had fallen away, the curves of the Chilterns filled the near horizon – a smaller vista compared to the landscape around Anne and Allistair's, but delightful in a different way. Beechwoods crested the hills, with wide meadows filling the valley bottom, fading now as the season drew on, poised to soak the spilling river water.

Away from her home, Emily seemed to be more her age, more fragile. She walked slowly in the chilled autumn air, a little out of breath on occasion, and she took Clare's arm as they stepped over the uneven ground.

'One day,' Emily said gently, her grip tightening on Clare's sleeve, 'you'll return to the Highlands and fetch your little girl.'

Clare found herself speechless with longing, the feeling almost pleasurable as it tore through her blood. And Emily offered her silence and the space for her to think, a reassurance that it was all right to feel the things she did.

On they walked, until Emily indicated that they ought to turn back, for the sun began to sink on the shortened afternoon and the little burnished beech leaves fluttered in a growing breeze. Clare understood that she would have to leave, catch her train, and return to Hillside where she'd have to face him, somehow.

Clare, suddenly agitated, turned to Emily. 'You see, the man—'

'What's that, Clare?' Emily said sharply and caught her arm to stop her on the path.

'Mirren's father...' Clare didn't want to say his name, for it would sound rotten, would contaminate the beautiful day she'd had.

She gazed at her great-aunt's kind and perceptive face and it tumbled out of her: the hot August evening in London, dinner at the restaurant, her new green dress, the offer of coffee – for wasn't having coffee with her boss, surely, Clare uttered, catching Emily's outraged eye, simply having coffee? And yet she could not bring herself to reveal the crucial detail. That she had told him *no*.

'And your mother does not know this? That your boss seduced you?' Emily interjected, aghast.

Clare shook her head with a violence that made her teeth rattle. She tried not to cry, thinking of what Emily had lived through, trying to match her resilience and her fortitude.

'I feel such a fool,' she uttered, and the rest of that night swirled like rancid liquid in her memory, right down to the way his eyes darkened and glazed over, and the sound of the button pinging to the floor. Tears flooded her eyes. 'How could I have been so stupid?'

'That's it, my dear, there's nothing wrong with a good old cry,' Emily said, pressing her arm gently to punctuate her meaning. 'You're not stupid, and not a fool.'

Clare took gulps of the fresh, Chiltern air and nodded, mopping her face with her cuff.

'Let's get you back home,' Emily said.

'Thank you, Aunt Emily.' Clare gathered herself and gave a smile.

Emily took her arm, as if, this time, Clare was the one who needed support.

'And while we walk, Clare, and tomorrow and the day after that, you will remember – *none* of this is your fault.'

19

MIRREN

The Highlands, Summer 1985

Gregor did the right thing for that Saturday. He had telephoned the week before and asked Mirren if it would be all right to take Kirstine out for lunch.

'Of course it is,' she'd said, lightening her voice, toning down the prickliness.

'It's just that she's finished her exams, finished school, I thought I'd treat her.'

'You don't have to explain why you want to take your daughter out to lunch, Gregor.'

Mirren heard his sharp, impatient sigh down the line.

'Sometimes I do, Mirren,' he uttered.

'Look, it's all right,' she said, steering the conversation back to being cordial. 'It's a lovely idea. But I won't tell her. She's at her friend's. Ring back later and ask her yourself.' She paused, bracing herself against her pulse of despair, a longing for the moments that had slipped into the past. 'She'll love it.'

'That's good. Thank you.'

Mirren held her tongue. She wanted to tell her husband that there was no need to thank her, but this would make her look like she was grasping the upper hand, make her sound snooty and cold. And that, she had come to realise, alone in the house in recent weeks, had been the problem here.

She said goodbye, put the phone down and wondered if Cal had *had a word*.

On Saturday morning, Kirstine came downstairs with a bounce in her step, wearing her customary pedal pushers and ponytail, and an enormous *Choose Life* t-shirt which she'd clinched with a wide belt and puckered at the shoulder with a handful of badges: The Cure, Siouxsie, and the *Rio* album cover. The anticipation and hope in her eyes reminded Mirren of her daughter's face on Christmas morning.

'Where is it you're going, hen?'

'There's that nice pub on the river.'

'Well, it's warm enough to sit outside. But you never know. Don't you want to take a cardie?'

Kirstine laughed, shaking her head. She stopped in front of the hallway mirror to tear out the elastic band in her hair and re-do it. Her eyelashes today looked spectacularly black and spiky.

'Will you come, Mum?'

Mirren uttered a negative sound. 'Not today, this is for you and Dad.'

'But what will you do?'

'Plenty.' She went to the window. 'Now, I think I heard a car just now. Goodness, is that *him*?'

Mirren watched as Gregor got out of a new silver Ford Sierra. He stood at the driver's side and waved up at the house.

'How can he afford *that*?' she said bitterly, her teeth gritted in outrage. 'Well, I suppose if he is living by himself in a rotten little flat, I suppose he can.'

'Mum, that's not a new car,' Kirstine, reading her immediately, chastised her with her light laugh. 'He's borrowed his friend's. The old one broke down.'

Kirstine opened the front door, waved to Gregor and hugged Mirren, laughing still, leaving the lingering scent of Body Shop musk in the air and, pleasingly, on Mirren's jumper.

Mirren turned and went back into the kitchen, cross with herself for being so affronted the whole time, for not wanting to witness their embrace and their laughter. They were always such good friends together, Gregor and Kirstine. Truth be told, over the years, she had often felt a little left out.

She sat at the table to finish her lukewarm coffee, gazed out at the summer garden, and wondered, indeed, what she should do today. She shrugged and whispered to herself, 'Plenty.'

As she was clearing up the kitchen, Mirren spotted the vacuum cleaner parked in the corner. Doing more housework could not have been further from her mind; the idea of it made her feel lazy and grumpy. And she did not want that sort of day. But there remained the question of the lost earring, trapped inside the bag of dirt.

Anne and Allistair, she conceded, thinking about the issue of her mother and her absence, had been way ahead of their time. In those days, the late forties, parents, teachers, anyone in authority, simply sat children down and dictated to them. But Mirren had a memory of Anne chatting breezily to her about Clare visiting, although, as always, not using her name.

'Your mother is coming to see us. To see you, Mirren. And, listen, hen, she wants to give you a fresh new life with her, in a new home, in a pretty cottage in England.'

Mirren, standing on a chair at the kitchen table and messily rolling out pastry dough with her child's baking set, hadn't understood, but Anne's words had gladdened her. So, she would *see* her mother? Anne had nodded, her smile bright and fixed. But it still didn't make sense. Didn't she already have a home, here at the last house on the lochan?

'Won't you be coming too?' she'd asked.

'Not this time,' Anne had said, and Mirren saw her glistening eyes, but could not tell whether her aunt had been crying or had been peeling onions. 'But we will come and visit very soon. We promise.'

'And Isla and the dogs too?'

'We'll see.'

They took a week to pack for her, choosing the largest suitcase they had, with Allistair joking that it looked nearly as big as Mirren. They took care and consideration over every treasure, and every item of what constituted a little girl's world: her clothes and shoes, her nightie and dressing gown. Slippers and books and colouring sets. A favourite teddy bear, her doll, and the doll's clothes. Not a lot to write home about, Mirren conceded now, sitting alone in her own kitchen, but then this had been in the aftermath of the war.

She rested her arms on the table, bent forward and pressed her forehead to the surface as the glaring reality scorched her mind: young Mirren had believed them all. That when her mother arrived at the last house on the lochan, when her mother hugged her and gave her the earrings, those enchanting, pearly-green stones, she had come to take her home with her.

Mirren shut her eyes, but try as she might, she could not see her mother's face, or hear her voice; she had no idea if they had the same sort of body, would be the same height. What about her hair? Her eyes? In an odd way, Mirren could *envisage* Clare, but always as if a mist obscured her. She even said to Gregor once that she remembered things *around* her and he had looked like he did not understand, and had peered at her, as if trying to read the small print.

And yet Clare had been there. She had been real. Mirren's suitcase had stood packed and ready in Anne and Allistair's hallway. And, later that day, had been unpacked, everything returning to how it had been, although Mirren now owned a pair of pretty earrings.

'An entirely inappropriate gift for a child, anyway,' Anne had said, taking them off in their purple pouch for safe keeping.

'Probably for the best, hen,' Allistair had said.

And to this day, Mirren did not know if he meant the guardianship of the jewellery, or the fact that Mirren had been *almost* gathered up, but at the last moment, rejected and abandoned.

But she couldn't sit around moping, Mirren thought, and went into the garden to yank up the weeds. She didn't want Gregor to think that she couldn't look after the house, the garden, or herself on her own. Her chuckling sounded dry as she knelt to ease up the dandelions around the rose bushes, realising how hard she tried to prove she did not need him, or any man.

She sat back on her heels, trowel in mid-air, and pictured the fellow who had been with Clare. The man standing by her as she wept; the man shaking Allistair's hand. Did they all think that Mirren did not remember; did they not realise how often she had wondered and assumed that he was her father? But a grown-up voice told Mirren that he can't have been. For this man had looked supportive and kind, standing beside Clare. Her real father, she knew deep down, had discarded her mother.

As she'd grown up, the dark, mythical days of the war, reminisced about by Anne and Allistair, had always seemed such a very long time ago. But now, Mirren decided, brushing the dirt from her hands and heading back inside, in the way that time ebbs and flows, they didn't.

She'd certainly heard stories of flings, during the war or otherwise. Isla's erstwhile husband for one. Accounts of how fear and hardship led to hysterical gaiety. People were ravenous for fun, determined to laugh and dance and hold each other while Glen Miller played and the bombs fell. Her father may well have been a married man. Or had he loved Clare and simply gone missing, like so many?

* * *

Mirren stood for a long while holding open the fridge door and peering inside. She gave in, pulled out the bottle of pinot grigio, and even though it was only half-past one in the afternoon, poured a large glass and switched the television on. The sudden sound of a massed crowd cheering and chanting filled the room.

'God,' she uttered to herself. 'How could I have forgotten *Live Aid* was on?'

She had been reading about it all week in the newspapers, the global music event, which seemed outrageously ambitious to match the enormity of what it aimed to address. And yet, with her recent self-absorption, it had fair slipped her mind.

Mirren watched while the rock and pop elite performed to the enormous crowd filling the pitch and the stands, right up to the gods, at Wembley Stadium. Shots from a helicopter overhead swooped over the iconic white towers, the surrounding suburban streets where it seemed every television set would be tuned in, indeed, hearing the music from their own back gardens.

Captivated, Mirren pledged money over the telephone for Ethiopia, and pushed her own troubles into a corner – apart from one thought. Would Clare be at home now, wherever that may be, watching along like the rest of the world? Would she see Bono there, all in black with his high boots and long mullet, going down into the crowd, or Geldof, pale and exhausted, swearing, demanding her money? Would she see, and have to look away, as the film showed people crouched in rags, limbs like broken sticks, dying of hunger on a Biblical scale, while she sat on her sofa?

Early evening, as Freddie Mercury took to the stage and sang 'aayy-oh' to the ecstatic crowd, Mirren heard the doorbell chime.

'Are you watching it?' Gregor asked as she opened the door.

She stared at him, on the edge of demanding what he thought he was doing, turning up like this. At the same time, devastated by how pleased she felt to see him, and wishing she didn't find him so attractive, standing expectantly in his smart trousers and new shirt. It felt so natural for him to be there, all smiles and excitement, brandishing a clinking off-licence carrier bag. She yielded and waved him in.

'Yes, yes, quick,' she said, 'I don't want to miss anything.'

'It was on in the pub,' he said, hurrying through. 'I didn't think it would be that good. But my God! I've brought a couple of bottles of white. But I see you've already started on the booze.'

He headed straight to the kitchen to rummage for a corkscrew.

'I dropped Kirstine at her friend's,' he said, sitting down in his usual chair, pouring wine. 'She is staying over there to watch. I thought...' Guardedly, he glanced at Mirren. 'I thought perhaps we could spend a quiet evening together. Maybe talk. If you want to.'

'Not through Queen, Gregor,' Mirren said, laughing, shaking off the suggestion. 'I'm not talking through Queen.'

As the evening unfolded, they watched the television together, singing along to the greatest songs of the past twenty-odd years: pretty much, Mirren thought, the soundtrack of their marriage. And outside, as it had done each summer they'd lived in the house, the pale, evening sky grew darker by degrees and the great loch below glowed in the twilight.

As George Michael sang with Elton John, Gregor reached his glass over to chink against Mirren's.

'This is better, isn't it?' he said.

'Better?'

'Me being here, like this.'

She wondered to what he alluded. 'Yes, but Gregor, we have been drinking and *Live Aid is* rather momentous.'

They hadn't switched on the lamps, to ensure they got the full glory of the show on the television screen. In the half-light, Mirren's husband looked half his age, relaxed, and at home. He'd put on a smart shirt for his lunch with Kirstine: pale-pink and loose fitting. It suited him, while Mirren felt a frump in her knee-length denim skirt and slippers.

'Gregor,' she said, with a prickle of fear behind her eyes.

He half turned in his armchair, gave her his full attention; something she'd felt he'd not done in a very long while. His eyes widened in expectation.

'Why did you leave us?'

He opened his mouth as if to protest, to wave away her question, but she stopped him.

'You said you wanted to talk, Gregor.' She sounded braver than she felt. 'You also said you needed space and time to think. Do you think you've had that?'

He ruminated for a moment, getting up to turn the volume down a little on the television.

'I have had that,' he said, and then, to the softer background of electric guitars, added, cautiously, 'and I have had the time to work out the reasons. To find out why.'

Mirren held his stare, felt another tremor of fear. She'd almost got used to him being gone, because in her mind, that had always been a temporary measure, while he 'worked things out'. But now, it seemed from the open look on his face, he was ready to move the situation on, widening the rift between them. To make the split permanent.

She topped up her glass, the bottle done. 'Your reasons?' She dredged up her strength. 'And they are?'

Gregor sighed long and deep. He waited while a Radio 1 DJ introduced the next supergroup on the telly.

'You see, Mirren, the problem all these years had been that you never wanted to talk.' His voice rose to a defensive pitch. 'And now, tonight, I feel I need to force you to listen to me, because from the look on your face, you don't want to hear this. It has got this bad, it has gone this wrong that we may never be able to fix it.'

Mirren shaped her mouth into an odd, grimacing smile, a cover for how tender and fragile she felt. 'But don't you remember, when we were young, you said we didn't ever need to say much.'

'Yes, when we were kids. That sounds like a whimsical pipe dream of mine. No, the reality is, Mirren, that you always shut yourself off from me. Not about Kirstine, or running the house, or where we were going on holiday, but I felt I was living with only what was on the surface. I knew what went on below, that so much of the time that you were down, you were hurting. And we both know why.'

Mirren felt a twisting inside, as if the truth needed to be wrung out of her. She peered dry-eyed at the television, sensing Gregor's discomfort and his pity.

'You mean my family situation?' In the strange way memory worked, time ebbing and flowing once more, the deer filled Mirren's mind's eye. The way it held her in its gaze, as if it knew her, would never forget her. 'You mean about my mother?'

'Yes, yes, I do.' Gregor softened his tone, his palm resting on her arm. 'And it has never got better, even after all this time, has it?'

The room seemed to grow hotter, even though the window stood open and the cool scent of cedar resin rose from the trees in the front garden.

Mirren pushed off her slippers, curled her legs under her, reached for her empty glass.

'Is there no wine left?'

Gregor looked relieved at her breaking the tension, relieved that she hadn't taken his delicate train of thought and run with it.

'Don't worry, hen; I got two bottles.' He leapt up and out to the kitchen, opened the fridge door.

Mirren watched him set the bottle down alongside two fresh glasses. As he poured, she smiled inwardly, delighted he had not forgotten her requirement for new wine, new glass. But then, why wouldn't he? They'd been married nearly twenty-five years.

It looked as if the concert was ending, the stage at Wembley filled with famous faces, arms around shoulders, sharing microphones.

'Do you realise,' she said, conversationally, 'that this is taking place not five miles from where my mother and Anne grew up?'

'Aye, right enough.'

The idea of Clare watching the concert with her companion, the man who'd been with her the day she left, flared through Mirren's mind. She wondered at the whole other life she had chosen.

'Gregor, my mother is only in her sixties. That's not old, not these days, is it?'

'No, I mean look at Anne,' he said. 'She's seventy-odd, and I wouldn't put her past fifty.' Gregor caught Mirren's eye. 'Must be something in the genes, hen, for you always look good.'

'That's enough of that,' she quipped, half joking.

'But that's just it!' Gregor cried, his chin jutting in anger. 'I can't even compliment my wife.'

'What do you mean?'

'You just won't take it from me, will you? You won't let me love you.'

Mirren turned her head against the clarity, the simplicity, of Gregor's accusation, tears stinging her eyes.

'I know I do that,' she began in a half whisper. 'I know I'm a nightmare. But I feel so cut off, Gregor, cut loose. I have always been, even though I am surrounded by family, people who care for me.' She dared not look Gregor in the face. 'I have realised, in these last few months, that love shown to me frightens me. Because if I am loved...' She swallowed the absurdity of her words. 'I will be rejected.'

She wanted to tell him that she felt frightened now, sitting here with him, in their own sitting room, surrounded by the trappings of their marriage, their family life. That if she demonstrated that she needed him, he'd only reject her, again. Like he did the day he left.

Gregor shook his head, appalled and confused.

'It's my fault.' He leaned across, gathered her hands loosely with his own. 'I should not have flounced off like that. But I tried hard, so many times.' He sounded utterly beaten, tired beyond words. 'I couldn't try any more, I'm sorry. I see how it must look. I should never had gone.'

His touch felt like static, like the air before thunder. And memories of his kisses, his warmth, and his way of loving her drowned her. Mirren's tears pooled around her mouth. She hadn't been aware she'd been crying. She eased her hands out of her husband's clasp and wiped her face.

'No, Gregor, it's not your fault. It's entirely mine.'

'Not true. I know it is incredibly difficult for you,' he said. 'Your mother leaving you when you were a child. I know how hard you find it. All of it.'

Mirren sank back in her chair, refreshed and encouraged suddenly by the spilling of tears, by revealing weakness, by the soul-deep trust she felt for Gregor. The man she thought she could tell everything. And yet, only now, had she been able.

He watched her, his eyes stretching wide in concern.

'Just think, Mirren, if Clare had taken you with her that day,' he said, 'we wouldn't be here. Kirstine wouldn't be here. We would have ploughed entirely different furrows.'

His words made sense. This was the Gregor she knew of old, who would take care of her, shield her from the playground bullies who had taunted her for having a different surname. The Gregor who'd stayed by her side on the school bus, who'd married her. And loved her.

A relieved giggle rose from Mirren's throat.

'Trust you, you always see the positive side.'

Gregor reached for her and tugged her towards him, his face close to hers. That smile, that deep gaze. Beside her. As he should be, as he had always been.

'Oh no, Gregor,' Mirren said, recoiling, the moment right, but also clumsy, awkward, and wrong. 'No, we have been drinking. And look, *Live Aid* has ended. You should call a cab.'

'But it is carrying on in Philadelphia.'

She stared at him aghast and they both burst out laughing.

'Listen to me,' he said, shaking his head. 'What a line.'

Yawning hard, Mirren switched off the television while Gregor went to the hall to call the local taxi firm.

'It's going to be at least an hour,' he said as he came back through. He gave her one of his quick yet thorough looks. 'You look *scunnered,* Mirren; go to your bed. I'll make myself a coffee and wait down here. If that's okay with you.'

'Well, you know where everything is.'

They laughed again, gently this time.

Mirren paused for a moment, capturing the peaceful look on his face, then headed for the stairs. She wanted to talk with Gregor, but the night felt old, both of them exhausted. But they had tomorrow, and if not tomorrow, they had the next day, and the next.

'Er, Mirren...' Gregor piped up from the kitchen. He'd switched on the kettle and was spooning his coffee. 'You are slipping.'

She paused, came back, leaned sleepily against the kitchen doorway. 'Am I, indeed?'

'The hoover. What's it doing out?' he teased. 'You always put it back under the stairs.'

In the old days, Mirren might have taken this as reproach, but tonight, his words vibrated with compassion, with knowing her entirely.

'I can see your mind is on other things.'

'It is, Gregor. So much so, I managed to hoover up one of my mother's earrings. But I haven't been able to face trying to retrieve it.'

'You mean, it's in the hoover bag, stuck inside all that dirt?'

''Fraid so, yes.'

'I'll do it,' he said, without question. 'Get yourself to bed. I'll take the cleaner and my coffee into the back garden. I'll get it sorted.'

Mirren gawped at him, could feel the tears rising. She thanked him quickly, turned on her heel, and went upstairs.

Sleep came for her almost straight away, pure and dreamless. But, at some moment during the night, she'd heard the comforting, low crackling of a cab radio down on the road, a car door shut. And the next morning, going down to the kitchen to make her first cup of tea of the day, Mirren checked the cupboard under the stairs. Gregor had put the vacuum cleaner back in its usual place. In the middle of the kitchen table sat one of her saucers, and on it lay a tissue, folded into a flat square. Like a gift.

While the kettle came to the boil, Mirren carefully unwrapped the layers of tissue, and Clare's earring, cleaned and shining as new, dropped into the palm of her hand.

20

CLARE

The Chilterns, December 1941

Winter had settled into the Hughenden Valley, the cold sinking into the earth, soaked up by damp, fallen leaves and held within the bare branches of slumbering trees. Daylight proved misty and short-lived and when Clare went for her afternoon tea break, the blackout was already down in the gloomy mess room, the 40-watt ceiling bulbs offering inadequate light compared to the stark illumination of the drawing offices with their white ceilings and Anglepoise lamps. Clare felt a chilly draught around her ankles as she sat in the canteen, leafing through last Sunday's newspaper from the pile on the table. Julia, sitting next to her, filled in a crossword from a month or so ago.

'Nearly done,' she said, with a flourish of her pen.

'Ah, but someone had already started it,' said Clare. 'Doesn't really count.'

'Gives me a boost, either way.' Julia frowned as she peered over Clare's shoulder to read the headline. 'Do you think this will make a difference, then?' she said, tapping the page. 'The attack on Pearl Harbour?'

'To us?' Clare asked.

'To our way of work here. To the maps we make, the intelligence coming in. I bet the briefing room telephone lines are buzzing. Strategy being realigned.'

'It has to make a difference, America entering the war, one way or another. But for us, I think it will be business as usual,' Clare said, not knowing, but trying to sound as rational and clear-minded as she could for Julia's sake. Already, according to the newspaper, the Japanese had started bombing British posts in Malaya and attacking Hong Kong, upping their game wherever their fighter planes could reach in their Far Eastern theatre of war. There was, Clare decided, and always had been, a price to pay. 'I know it's what people have been praying for. But perhaps we won't know or feel its true effect for months, maybe years.'

'Years?' Julia repeated beneath her breath. 'I won't be able to stand it if it goes on for years.'

Clare agreed with her but would never admit it. 'We have to,' she said.

'I know that,' Julia said, weakly, her delicate features drawn and pinched. 'For goodness' sake, I'm not being very patriotic, am I?'

'You show it in other ways,' she replied. 'You're here, aren't you, working all hours God sends.' She turned a few pages on from the news to a fashion story: a willowy model relaxed and elegant, seemingly not minding being photographed in her night clothes. 'Ha, this might cheer you up; look at this.'

Julia leaned in. 'Shelter wear?' She laughed. 'Posh pyjamas that you wouldn't mind being seen in the street in?'

'I think it is a smashing idea. I mean, who knows who you may encounter on your way to the shelter? They look cosy, don't they?

Just the ticket.' Clare thought back to the cold, uncomfortable nights during the Blitz in the back garden.

'Well, anything to get us through,' said Julia. 'How much are they? Gracious, nine coupons? I suppose it would be worth it. And they are quite snazzy.' She glanced towards the door and dipped her head close to Clare's. 'I wouldn't mind encountering *him* in the blackout.'

Clare followed her gaze and a ball of ice hit her in the stomach. Leo Bailey stood in the queue at the tea counter. He glanced her way with that expectant, quizzical look of his, and quickly away again, and the cold expanded, petrifying her flesh.

'I mean, although he is rather mature, he's quite the matinee idol, isn't he?' Julia continued, chatting on gaily. 'How old do you think he is?'

Clare knew he was thirty-three. From one scan of his file all that time ago, she could tell Julia his precise date of birth. She shifted to the edge of her seat, her nerves shredded, astonished each time by her extreme reaction, the physical blow at seeing him.

'But he doesn't really fit in here, does he? Keeps himself to himself,' Julia persisted. 'Quite the mystery. And he is not short of a bob or two, either. Look at that suit. That's certainly not utility. Don't you think he has a little bit of Clark Gable about him?'

Clare concentrated on realigning the newspaper pages, folding the paper neatly, sweat dampening her scalp and the inside of her collar. She liked Clark Gable, and Julia had ruined that.

'And he won't look over here, will he?' Julia giggled. 'He must be shy. Perhaps I can change all that.' She nudged Clare, expecting a response. 'You've gone all quiet. And you won't look at him! Do you *like* him, Clare Ashby?'

Speechless, Clare gave a violent shake of her head.

'Of course, I know,' Julia said, sounding satisfied. 'You like Bertie.'

Clare managed a shy smile. Yes, she liked Bertie. She thought his company pleasant, and she found him attractive in a way that she could not pin down, as if she were unsure and simply forcing herself.

'Anyway,' said Julia, still whispering, her eyes wide with gossipy pleasure. 'Susanna says she managed a quick chat with him the other day. A charmer, apparently. She says she could tell he loves women if you know what I mean.'

'A flirt?'

'Apparently, he is a widower. Which is sad, isn't it? Perhaps I can help cheer him up.'

Clare took a sharp, involuntary breath. 'A *widower*?'

'Yes, Clare. Widows, widowers – not such an uncommon thing these days.' Julia scrutinised her, puzzled. 'What with there being a war on. Hadn't you noticed?'

Clare stared down at her hands, at her damp fingertips covered in newspaper ink.

'Yes, yes, of course...' She offered a lame smile.

Perhaps the BBC personnel records had not been kept correctly after all, she thought, and that Mrs Jane Bailey as next of kin should have been crossed out by Clare's predecessor somewhere along the line. Or had his loss occurred more recently? After all, the Blitz in London had continued until May at least. Perhaps, then, this was the reason for his appearance at Hillside. A change in circumstances: a fresh start. Hadn't Mr Hedges said that he'd been a draughtsman before joining the BBC all those years ago? And here he was, turning up like a bad penny, putting those skills to good use.

'Clare, are you quite all right?' Julia asked, peering at her. 'You seem awfully pale. I know this isn't the most flattering of lights in here, but still...'

Leo Bailey sat down to drink his tea in the far corner behind Clare. It felt as if his shadow filled the room. The back of her neck burnt in discomfort, as if his stare might scald her skin. Still, she managed a nod for Julia and made a show of wiping her hands on her handkerchief.

'Is there something you want to talk about?' Julia asked, kindly. 'I mean, tell me to mind my own business, but you often seem to be on the edge of saying something, and stopping yourself.'

Clare nodded, smiled, conscious that her eyes shone with unshed tears.

'Listen, don't mind me. But if you ever want to talk...'

'Thank you, Julia. I ought to be getting back.'

As Clare drained her cup and gathered up the newspaper, she felt someone come up to the back of her chair and rest both hands on her shoulders as if to overpower her, hold her down.

'Not so fast, Miss Ashby.'

Clare froze, her jaw clamped. She yelped, shrinking down in her chair.

Julia laughed. 'Oh, Bertie, stop playing the fool. She's gone as white as a sheet. You scared the life out of her.'

'Sorry, my dear,' he said, sitting down in the chair next to Clare and shifting it closer. 'I shouldn't be such a buffoon. I merely wanted to secure your attendance at the pub tonight. Are you game too, Julia?'

'You and the Ice House Boys?' Julia asked.

'What do *you* think?' Bertie said. 'Clare?'

'I'm in,' said Julia, brightening at the prospect of a night out. 'And when Clare here gets her power of speech back, I'm sure she will be too.'

Everyone in the mess room had heard Clare cry out, the commotion of Bertie scraping his chair across the floor, Julia laughing. Over Bertie's shoulder, Clare dared steal a look behind her. Leo stared hard back at her and her heart turned rigid in her chest.

'Yes, yes,' she said faintly. 'Count me in.'

'That's my girl.' Bertie slipped his arm around her shoulder and pulled her towards him so that her head tucked under his chin. He planted a quick kiss on the top of her head. 'Ah, she's bowled over by me.' He chuckled.

Bertie's embrace felt secure and agreeable enough, and Clare simply gave in, allowing it. She thought of the jackdaws at the last house on the lochan. The pair of them, together, building a home, following their instincts. She lifted her face and kissed Bertie on the cheek. He looked pleased with himself, squeezing her tighter.

Clare hoped Leo Bailey had seen the kiss. She wanted to show him that she had her own life, her own friends. A man who cherished her. A man she could have an ordinary life with. Have something everyone else had.

* * *

That evening, it appeared, Lieutenant Fariner had other plans for Clare.

'I can't come,' she said when Bertie opened the door to the library, gave her a big smile and cocked his head as the mantel clock chimed for half-past five. 'The lieutenant needs me to stay here. The filing cards are in disarray. He's not blaming anyone. He just wants it sorted. Things are going to get sticky soon, he says. And we need this in order so we can be in some short of shape to handle it.'

Bertie pulled a face. 'Duty calls.'

'It does.' Clare hesitated, realising she didn't mind missing out on the pub that much. She would relish a peaceful moment on her own to deal with the methodical work in hand. 'Enjoy the ale and the dominoes.'

'Darts tonight. I'll come back in two hours and give you a lift home. It's perishing out there. Where is Fariner anyway?'

'Big meeting upstairs.'

'Sounds like things are hotting up.'

Bertie said cheerio and left Clare to sort through the small, wooden filing chest sitting on her desk, stuffed with index cards scored with intelligence and cross references. At first, the flicking and snapping of the cards as she pulled each one out, studied it and reordered it, felt restful but her fingers soon tingled with cold, her nose chilled, and the fire in the library grate had given up the ghost.

Clare took the filing chest, crossed the hallway and opened the door to Disraeli's dining room. She liked it in here. Smaller, square, and more intimate than the other rather cavernous rooms, wallpapered in swirls of deep-green foliage. Despite its grandeur, it felt like a cosy parlour. Above the marble fireplace hung a portrait of white-haired Queen Victoria in layers of black lace, with her inscrutable expression. And, mercy, a rather good fire burning in the hearth. Clare set herself up at the desk, close to the heat, turned up the lamp and set back to work.

The door opened and Clare, intent on a particular tricky alphabetised mess, did not look up. Perhaps Fariner had come to look for her.

The person did not speak, just stayed in the doorway, letting in cold air. She raised her gaze, reluctant, for she'd lost her place.

'Good evening,' Leo Bailey said. 'I thought I saw you come in here.'

Clare sat upright, bristling, and tight-lipped. She kept perfectly still as if she had solidified.

'Did you know,' he went on when she did not speak, glancing up at the portrait with a guarded smile, 'that Queen Victoria used to visit Disraeli a great deal? Has dined in this very room. Imagine that. Who can only guess at the conversations in the candlelight. If only walls could talk.'

Clare placed her pen down with care on the blotter, feeling her blood thinning, her head weightless. She gave a quick shake of her head.

'Sorry, didn't mean to disturb you. Thought you kids were all going out to the pub. Then I spotted you. Thought you might want company. This room is usually empty at this time of the day. I like to sit in here alone when I've finished work. Probably frowned on but, really, one can't waste a good fire—'

'I have a lot of work to do,' Clare said, thinly, 'and you are letting in the cold air, Mr Bailey.'

Immediately, she regretted it. She meant for him to go but he stepped into the room, shut the door, studied her for a second and his smile broadened.

'*Mr* Bailey. I see. Is that how it is?'

He gestured to the armchair on the other side of the hearth, hesitating, as if seeking permission to sit. Clare, perplexed by his imposition, did not acknowledge his request. And he sat anyway.

She refilled her pen, forcing her mind to clear.

'I have a lot of work to do.'

He crossed his legs impatiently, giving a sigh that transformed into a heavy groan, as if his reserves of energy had drained clean away.

'Always the way, Clare. Always the way.' His voice cracked with fatigue. 'And you were always so conscientious.'

Clare looked down at the index cards on the desk in front of her, as if to continue with her work. But the effort seemed futile. She replaced the lid on her pen, staring at him, remembering how she'd once admired him, around the Radio department offices and in the studios, and across the table in the little eatery on Charlotte Street, the way he dressed, the attractive shape of his head. His focus on her had felt like a dazzling sunbeam. But how young she had been, how naïve. There had always been apprehension around the edges, as if her regard for him had not been good enough anyway. Now, sitting in the chair by Disraeli's hearth, he seemed half the man, a fragment from another world, long past. His interruption an irritation. The energy he once exuded now felt like a nuisance.

Leo sat back in the armchair, rested his chin on his elbow, as if they were about to have an after-dinner chat, and irritation drew a sharp line up Clare's spine, gritting her jaw.

'Are we supposed to acknowledge each other, Clare, I wonder, from our former lives at the Beeb?' he asked. 'Because we all have previous lives, after all, before Hillside. *We* have previous lives.' He paused and caught her eye. 'I am wondering if the powers-that-be may frown on us having such *relations*, such a conversation as this. Careless talk and all that.'

His audacity, before, would have enriched her anxiety. The younger Clare may have felt affronted, trembled, wanting him to shut up and go away. But new courage settled in her bones. She no longer felt like the naïve girl in the BBC office. Leo Bailey did not scare her with mentions of *relations*. He did not have the power.

She casually sifted a set of index cards and looked him in the eye.

'How is Kay Pritchard?'

He batted his hand through the air. 'Oh, married with a baby and evacuated somewhere.'

Clare's scalp prickled. Kay's life had panned out *almost* like her own.

'And we know that Miss Stanford is doing well, working for the Ministry,' Leo went on. 'Hedges is retired. He couldn't hack it.'

Clare shook her head, dismissing the trivia.

'Why did you leave the BBC, Leo?'

His features flattened, his chin dipping.

'When my wife died—' His voice sounded high-pitched,

agony trailing in his eyes; he paused to cough. 'I wanted to do something better. Something more useful to shorten this blasted war.'

'I am sorry...' Clare's words weakened in her throat. She could hardly be outraged at the mention of his wife now, even though he had never spoken to Clare about her before.

Leo rallied. 'That's why working here is doing me some good. To stop the enemy in any small way that I can. My apprenticeship in graphic design certainly helped. Marking out those maps, those towns and cities, so we can get the bastards.'

Clare winced, hating how pleased he seemed with himself. And also, suddenly how simply *ordinary* he appeared. She'd been muzzled since that hot August evening while her life changed, and the bombs exploded all around her. She looked him in the eye and wanted to spoil his life, to remove that self-serving expression on his face. Drop her own metaphoric grenade. Tell him of the chaos he had caused.

Clare pictured Mirren, hundreds of miles away, and stopped herself laughing out loud at the ridiculous notion that Leo knew nothing about her. But even Clare, really, would have no idea how her daughter was keeping until Anne's next letter arrived. She didn't know what Mirren had for her tea, whether she slept through the night. Whether she had warm socks for winter, and whether she had a favourite jumper, knitted by Isla, no doubt.

Clare knew full well how it felt to hold a placid, sleepy baby through a long, light, Highland summer night; Mirren nearly slipping from her arms into the silky deep water. But would she ever know what it felt like to embrace Mirren as a wriggly, toddling child, with milk teeth coming through and a chatter all of her own? Or see her smart in her uniform, setting off for school?

Clare felt a prickling around her eyes. And what did Mirren look like now? *Who* did she look like?

'Leo...' she began, and his name sounded meaningless, when before it had been a spoonful of poison.

Misreading Clare's expression, he sighed. 'I know you think the worst of me, Clare. I appear to have gained a reputation with women. Nothing to be proud of. And I am sorry.' He peered at her, hoping, perhaps, for her understanding. 'You see, I liked you, liked your company. Such a good worker you were. A constant, throughout the pressure, the intensity of toiling all hours at Broadcasting House, which may as well have had a target for the Luftwaffe painted on its roof. The threat of metal raining down on my head.' He sounded bizarrely petulant, as if he'd been the only one. 'All that black humour, born of fear. Jane understood. But she didn't know. Clare, you *knew*.'

Clare glanced at the portrait and took in the old queen's resolute gaze. Her regal expression as if she had heard every word, and that truth and honesty must prevail. She began to methodically pack away her filing. Doing any more work tonight seeming utterly pointless.

'Clare?' Leo said, shifting in his chair, eager for her to say something.

Her confidence sparked, she grasped at the chance set before her, like finding her own shadow in the dark. She raised her voice.

'Leo, there is something you must know—'

His arrogance interrupted her. 'I think we misunderstood each other, Clare, from the start. And yes, I did not behave as a gentleman should have done. But it was for comfort, wasn't it, that night. For both of us. I thought you... I hope... I hope you were all right...?' His gaze latched on to hers, deepened with new, intimate meaning. 'You look well, you... you are not wearing the perfume... Was my gift inappropriate?'

'I never wore it. I— I gave it away. And yes, it was inappropriate,' she said through her teeth. 'Everything was inappropriate!'

'Ah yes, you see, I sometimes get carried away.'

'Carried away? Really, Leo,' Clare said, quietly, 'your poor wife.'

Leo sank back into his chair, his shoulders hunched, his paunch protruding. As she stared at him, a thought brightened Clare's mind: Leo Bailey was not Satan, but a sad, confused little man.

'I must say, it's a very odd thing,' he said. 'About the perfume. Jane, you see, actually, she—'

The door to the dining room opened and Bertie breezed in.

'Come on, Miss Clare Ashby, pub's over. We're all going home.'

Spotting Leo, he halted, took a moment. 'Ah, good evening. I don't think we've met.'

'Leo Bailey,' Leo said, standing and shaking Bertie's hand. 'I've seen you around, sir.'

'Flying officer Havill. Bertie. You too, sir.'

In her sudden confusion, the meeting of two very separate worlds, Clare dipped to the desk, collected her work together, her fingers flying inefficiently over index cards, desperate to pack up and go. Sweat settled on her upper lip, her cheeks burning with the secret she had not told either man.

Bertie continued with small talk. 'Yes, a draughtsman, aren't you? Tough work through the winter. The lack of light must send you all around the loop.'

'Be that as it may, I am not going to be at Hillside for long,' Leo said, and Clare caught his glance at her. 'I am being posted elsewhere after Christmas. Can't say where of course. Official Secrets and all that.'

Standing behind the desk clutching the filing chest, Clare gave an involuntary cry of relief.

Both men looked at her and her smile stretched uncomfortably.

'Well, good luck to you, Mr Bailey,' Bertie said. 'Come on, Clare. Let's get you home. Been a long day.'

She quickly followed Bertie out of the room, avoiding Leo's eye, her chance to tell him about Mirren shattered.

As they set off down the pitch-black drive in Bertie's car, her frustration jumbled up with relief made her want to sleep for a hundred years. Half listening to Bertie chatting about the evening at the pub and watching tree trunks loom out of the darkness, fleetingly brightened by the dipped headlights, Clare crossed her fingers and hoped that perhaps, one day, none of this would matter.

21

Outside the little dining room, with the blackout still down on this dark, Christmas Eve morning, a robin piped up in conversational fashion, chiming through the cold dawn. Mrs Bell came in with the toast rack for the breakfast table, Clare's ration of butter and a jar of jam. Clare thanked her and set to work scraping butter over toasted bread.

The landlady hovered with the teapot, a smile fixing her jowls. 'So, you're going to family then?'

Clare looked up in surprise. All these months, she had often wondered if Mrs Bell ever took off her flowery tabard or wanted to start a conversation.

'I'm going to my great-aunt's in Amersham,' she said. 'My parents will be there.'

Mrs Bell nodded, her eyes widened and wet.

'Well, you are lucky to have someone and somewhere to go to.'

Clare pensively spread jam. Realising Mrs Bell showed no signs of leaving her to it, she asked, 'And how will you spend Christmas?'

'Much the same as always.' Mrs Bell spoke quickly, as if she'd been waiting to do so. 'I'll go to the cemetery to put flowers on Margaret's grave.'

'Ah yes, of course,' Clare said.

Within a week of moving in, Clare had gathered the reason for her landlady's sharpness, her grief bottled and festering, materialising in fits and starts. Mr Bell had passed away before the war, their daughter Margaret more recently. Clare's gaze flicked to the framed photo on the shelf, taken possibly ten years before: Mrs Bell with her husband and teenage daughter.

'The florist in the village kept back some golden chrysthans for me. I know it's wartime and some folk may say it's an extravagance, but I want to do it for my Margaret. To brighten her up. And then, in February, the snowdrops will come through, all around her. And then, a year would have passed.'

'Snowdrops are so welcome, aren't they?' Clare said, hoping her sentiment didn't sound hollow.

There had never been the right moment to offer Mrs Bell her condolences. The landlady had never stood at the breakfast table and talked to her about it before. Only the family photograph greeted her each morning at breakfast. The smiling couple posing in a studio, with their radiant daughter between them.

Picking carefully over her words, Clare offered, gently, 'May I ask, Mrs Bell, what happened to Margaret?'

The landlady pulled out a chair, sat down, and poured herself a strong cup of tea, her proximity radiating misery across the table.

'Margaret joined the Wrens as soon as she turned eighteen,' said Mrs Bell, her mouth twitching as if she found it difficult to form the words. 'The posters said, "free a man for the fleet", so off she went into training. She loved it. She made so many friends. I have all her letters. She was stationed in Portsmouth, in Observation. On the Naval Dockyard, you understand, not on a ship. And then, one night, an air raid. A damn and blast, bloody air raid.'

Clare moved her hand across the table towards Mrs Bell's trembling fingers.

'You don't have to talk about it if you don't want to—'

Mrs Bell snapped her hand away into her lap. 'I do want to. But talking makes it more real. And I want it not to be. Real.' Her gaze fixed on Clare. 'You must need to get going, Miss Ashby. You have a train to catch.' She sounded generous, far from churlish. 'You have your family to go to.'

'Mrs Bell, I have a daughter,' Clare blurted. 'She's only young, seven months. A baby.'

Mrs Bell did not flinch. 'Ah, the most lovely age.'

'She's with my sister. Up in Scotland. And I... haven't seen her since the autumn. I don't know when I will ever again.' Clare stopped, to spare Mrs Bell's feelings, when really she wanted to talk passionately about Mirren, to whip out her photograph so Mrs Bell could admire her.

'But you will. You will. There you see. Your family, your daughter. She is safe where she is,' Mrs Bell said, and allowed a sharp little smile. 'Cherish it all, Miss Ashby. Cherish it while it is real.'

* * *

Walking along the pretty street in Old Amersham towards Emily's cottage, Clare thought about how apprehensive she'd felt before, arriving unannounced at her great-aunt's home. But this time, uneasiness gripped in a different way. Back in the autumn, she'd felt a dash of excitement and a little mischief, but now her pace slowed, her heels dragged. She hadn't seen her parents in well over a year and had barely corresponded with them. Now they'd be ensconced in Great-Aunt Emily's front parlour, waiting for her to arrive. And she could picture the disapproval on their faces.

Emily opened the front door with a suppressed whoop of joy

and held Clare in her slender embrace. When Clare caught the rose scent of her perfume, she smiled, and then smelt her father's pipe smoke, rustic and brown, and heard a rustling exchange of words emanating from the parlour.

'Come through, come through, and Happy Christmas,' trilled Emily, leading her along the hallway. 'We are about to open the sherry your father kindly bought.'

Clare set her bag down and followed her great-aunt into the room which seemed different to how it had been on her previous visit. Then, it had felt like an elegant sanctuary, filled with comfort and character. But now her parents sat either side of the fireplace with faces turned to the door, and charged the atmosphere by simply being there.

Clare stalled on the threshold, mustering her failing stamina, and chimed, 'Hello, Mum and Dad. How are you both?'

Her father got to his feet, taking care to rest his pipe down on the hearth before approaching her.

'Well, well, here she is,' he said, running his hand over his forehead to ensure his hair stayed in place over the bald area. He patted her shoulder, like he might a pet dog. 'Here's Clare. Our agent on the ground, doing very important, secret war work. Thought we might not recognise you, didn't we, Celia? Thought you might be in uniform, or at least wearing a wig and dark glasses.' He laughed ineffectively when no one else did, adding as an afterthought, as he caught her eye, 'You look well, anyway.'

Clare's mother made a big fuss of rewinding her knitting and stuffing it down the side of the cushion before hauling herself to her feet.

'Now, now, Michael, don't you be giving her big ideas. Secret agent indeed,' she said, throwing him a sharp look. Clare noticed her mother's temples speckled more with grey, and a widening of her hips. And far too much powder on her nose. She had taken to wearing her hair in the Victory roll, but it looked far too severe. 'Hello, Clare. It's nice to see you. How was your journey?'

Clare stepped forward for a restrained embrace, but instead felt a kiss somewhere near her ear, and her mother's hands pressing on her forearms as if to keep her at arm's length.

'That sounded like a test, Mum,' she said, laughing to cover the gaucheness of it all. 'I can't tell you about my journey here. You know full well that I can't reveal where I'm based.'

'There, I told you, Celia,' said her father.

'So you did, Michael.'

'But it seems to be going well,' Clare said. 'Long hours, difficult work, but—'

'Well, every bit helps, doesn't it?' said her father. 'You are doing your *bit*. It's admin work, I take it?'

Clare absorbed his offhand remarks with a nod and a smile. How could she ever explain the guilt she felt as she sat behind her desk, marking up the bombing maps? How precisely she mapped out murder. She did not want them to know. For how would they ever understand? Her parents, both contemplating her now with expectant yet vacant expressions, never seemed able to cross the void into understanding her.

'Well, you can't have come far, Clare, as it's only midday,' pressed her mother, glancing at the mantel clock. 'So, I'm thinking War Office in the city: Bentley Priory. Or perhaps Uxbridge?'

'Celia, really, stop fishing. She can't tell you. Official Secrets, and all that,' Clare's father said, settling back in his chair with his pipe. 'Although, you're right, Celia, like you always are. Clare, you must be stationed reasonably nearby.'

'And yet, in all this time, you have not been to see us here,' her mother grumbled, sitting down and rummaging for her knitting.

'That's enough of the third degree, you two,' said Emily, buzzing in with sherry glasses. 'Leave the girl alone. Let her get her coat and hat off at least. Now you are here, Clare, we can raise a toast. It's about time.' She lowered her voice. 'Your father doesn't allow alcohol before twelve.'

Clare took off her coat, perched her hat on the sofa arm and sat down. She felt suddenly, unduly tired.

'Can I please just have a cup of tea?'

'Anything you like, Clare. I have Christmas cake. A little meagre on the fruit but cake it is.'

Emily's tea and cake set to work to revive her, while the radiogram played the *Forces Programme* with choral carols, and Clare let their conversation drift over her, wondering at Emily's patience. Her parents, as unpaying guests, sipping their sherry, her father poking at the fire and ruining the stack of coals, seemed to be behaving like petulant children.

'Clare, we had a lovely Christmas card from Anne and Allistair,' her mother said. 'It's that one there with the huge robin on it.'

Emily had decorated the mantelpiece with sprigs of fir and holly foraged from the wood, and interspersed it with Christmas cards. Clare imagined the clean, green scent of the fir, which would take her straight back to the Highlands if only she could smell it through the heavy fug of her father's pipe.

'Oh yes,' said Clare. 'So did I...'

'And we must tell you...' Her mother leaned forward, animated. 'I assume you know Father is retiring. At last. We have given up the house in Harrow. We've decided to move to the West Country. We love it down there.'

'Oh, where will you be living?' Clare asked, swallowing the shock of having her childhood home so unceremoniously pulled out from under her feet.

'A little place called Dunsford. In the middle of nowhere. You won't know it,' said her father, and it sounded to Clare that she never would.

'It's on the edge of Dartmoor. It's glorious. I didn't want to be near the sea, you see,' said her mother, 'where the Germans might get us. And I don't want to be anywhere near London. Even here, there are planes going over all the time.'

Those planes, thought Clare, munching Emily's delicious cake, carrying the maps I've had a part in creating.

'And we asked Emily, didn't we?' said her father looking at Clare's great-aunt, 'Asked if you'd like to come with us. Set up home nearby.'

'But no,' Emily said and caught Clare's eye with a smile. 'No, I am staying put.'

* * *

Clare helped Emily lay out lunch on the dining table in front of the French windows. Her walled garden lay sleeping, plants cut back, or collapsed and grey, waiting for another year to begin, underlit by ranks of Christmas roses in a palette of purple and a particularly mysterious glowing green.

Clare placed the glossy but rather small piece of boiled ham in the centre, along with a dish of roasted potatoes and a bowl of steamed chard.

'I grow it at the back,' said Emily, bringing in a jug of parsley sauce. 'It keeps coming through and I keep eating it. It's good for you.' She placed a hand on Clare's forearm. 'You make sure you eat lots while you are here.'

'Well, well, what's this?' said Clare's father, as if he didn't know, settling himself at the head of the table. 'You'll be pleased to know, Clare, that your mother procured the ham. Got chatting to the butcher, didn't you, Celia?'

'The way you say it sounds like I got it from under the counter.' Clare's mother flushed, looking worried someone might come hammering on the door. 'I just dropped some hints at the end of November, that we'd like a ham for Christmas Eve. Perhaps he took a shine to me, as a new lady in the village.' She patted the back of her hair. 'And it's goose tomorrow.'

'Can be persuasive, can't you, Celia?' said her father, showering praise.

'Oh goose,' Clare breathed, 'my utter favourite. Haven't had it in... years.'

'Make the most of it,' her mother said. 'We pooled our rations. It cost an arm and a leg.'

'Ha, or a wing and a drumstick,' said her father, shaking out his napkin. 'Emily, shall I carve up Celia's delicious ham?'

Emily motioned that he should be her guest, and turned to Clare.

'Ah, you're wearing those lovely earrings again,' she said.

Self-consciously, Clare tapped her earlobe.

'Yes, remember, I treated myself, Aunt Emily,' she said, her voice quiet, not wanting to draw attention.

'A gift from a fellow?' asked her mother, not hearing.

'No, no,' Clare said, feeling she must explain. 'I saw them in a wee shop at Fort Augustus, the village at the head of Loch Ness, earlier this year and just thought how lovely they were.'

'A wee shop, Clare?' chuckled her father, Clare's slice of ham wobbling at the end of the knife as he manoeuvred it onto her plate. 'You're becoming Scotch.'

'I think the people prefer *Scottish*, Michael,' said Emily. 'Only the whisky is Scotch.'

'And the eggs,' said Clare's father, smothering his ham in sauce.

'Buying yourself jewellery?' Her mother tutted. 'I never did.'

'Well, Celia,' said Emily, 'perhaps you should have done.'

Clare's mother looked confused for a moment and then began

to blether to her aunt about how lovely everything on the table looked.

'We are lucky people to be sitting here in relative safety having our Christmas Eve lunch,' said Clare's father. 'The latest bulletin announced the Japanese are advancing through Malay. Hong Kong has surrendered.'

'Such appalling news,' said Emily, going pale. 'It is as if the whole world is being swallowed up.'

Clare shuddered as her view of the theatre of war switched from ports and cities in Germany, to an unknown continent and other, unimaginable terrors. She looked down at her plate but she'd lost her appetite.

'But rest assured, everyone,' said her father, tucking into his ham, 'our Navy is in Singapore.'

The conversation petered out to the sound of cutlery scraping china as they ate.

Emily, next to Clare, leaned in. 'You do look well, Clare.' And Clare caught her meaning. That perhaps, last time, she had not appeared so. 'Might there be a fellow,' she asked, gently playful, 'who might buy you more jewellery?'

Clare's father harrumphed. 'What's that. A fellow?'

Clearly, the dinner-table conversation did not meet with his approval, even though the horrors of war had done. Clare's mother looked startled, her eyes flickering, as if she were bracing herself.

'There are fellows I know, most of whom are my colleagues,' Clare said cautiously and then smiling as she thought of the Ice House Boys and their japes and jokes. She brightened. 'But there is one man who is very kind and attentive and we get on well. Bertie, Albert Havill. He is in the RAF.'

Her father squared his shoulders. 'Sounds like a capital chap.'

'We don't know that for sure, Michael,' snapped her mother.

'That's lovely, Clare. I am happy for you,' said Emily, ignoring them. 'I guessed as much. You're mixing with a great group of people, I am sure. A fresh start. Someone nice. And you can put everything behind you.'

Her father glared at Emily, her mother prickled and Clare felt that if Mirren had been sitting in a highchair at the table gurgling away, her parents would be doing their best to ignore her.

'When can we meet him, then?' her father asked, sharp with authority.

'It's not that serious yet,' said Clare, 'so I don't really—'

'Serious, Clare?' He looked at her. 'How would you rate *serious*?'

Clare pressed her lips together, not trusting herself to answer. Was he implying that *serious* meant going so far as marrying a man and *then* having a child with them? She looked at her father's scowling face, and then at her mother's. The thought of explaining what had really happened to her made her insides coil. And she knew that even the mention of Mirren by name would be intolerable to them.

But she wanted to tell her parents that, in her Christmas card from her sister, Anne had added a note to say that their granddaughter had cut her first tooth and had her first haircut, with Isla carefully snipping around her tender ears. Clare wanted them to know, to understand. She wanted them to love Mirren. But she didn't explain. She didn't answer her father, and he went back to his dinner, while her mother watched her across the table with watery eyes.

* * *

The chimes of Big Ben on the wireless marked the start of that evening's nine o'clock news, and the blue-blooded announcer's voice declared: 'This is the BBC Home and Forces programme. Here is the news...', sending a preconditioned shudder down Clare's spine.

Putting on a brave face all day had exhausted her. She'd forgotten what it had once been like to live with her parents and felt stupefied by their constant exchanges and comments, her mind drained and spinning. And she certainly did not wish to hear any more news. She said she would go to bed, leaving poor Emily downstairs admirably fielding their ripostes.

The heat from the fire downstairs radiated up to her great-aunt's snug attic room via the chimney flue. Clare slipped her hot water bottle under the sheet and quickly got ready for bed. After finding socks and slippers, for the attic stairway proved draughty, she went down to the first floor to use the bathroom. As she locked the door, she could still hear her parents' voices, carrying up the stairs. She felt dispirited, as if she'd reverted to being a child – silent and docile – and not the young woman who'd received praise for her secretarial skills at the BBC, had run through the London streets under fire, and now carried out precise, important work to help shorten the war in some way. Not forgetting, she thought, being the mother of a beautiful little girl.

Washing her hands and face in the bathroom, Clare thought of all the ways she wanted to make Mirren, and herself, feel safe. She allowed herself a small, encouraging smile.

As she crossed the darkened landing, her mother stepped out of her own bedroom, as if staging an ambush.

'I take it,' she whispered sharply, 'from something Aunt Emily said at lunch, that you have told her that you have a baby? She said... something about putting everything behind you?'

Clare clenched her jaw, anger rising. 'Yes, Mum, I told her, on my previous visit.'

'I thought as much. That's all very well but it's making your father feel very uncomfortable. We really didn't want people to know. You know your father is very old-fashioned, and a child out of wedlock—'

'Emily is not *people*, Mother,' Clare flashed back. 'She is family. And she has been very kind.'

Her mother's eyes glistened, two pin pricks of light in the gloom. 'Be that as it may.'

'But it was not just Father being old-fashioned and uncomfortable,' Clare said, their whispering hisses becoming louder. 'It was you as well, Mum.'

'He is my husband,' she said pulling her chin back in her defensive manner. 'And I have to stand by his decisions, his opinions. Whatever they may be. I mean, really, this sort of thing may happen in the East End of London, but not in the suburbs. And not to people like us.'

'Like *us*?' Clare's voice cracked as a jumbled mesh of emotion rolled over her.

She took a deep breath, realising in one piercing, lucid moment, that at the bottom of it all lay disappointment. Her parents simply did not know how to imagine what happened to Clare or express the words to explain it. They simply did not want to know.

Bracing against such bitter disenchantment, her eyes blurring with tiredness and wishing the day could end, Clare grasped the banister as if to make her escape up to the attic.

'It's not as if we don't care for you or the child.' Her mother's broadside stopped her. 'But it has been such a blow. The whole episode. So very unsavoury.' Her mother looked her up and down. 'I mean, the poor child. To be illegitimate.'

Clare inhaled, shook her head. 'But Anne and Allistair are taking good care of her.'

'It's all very awkward,' she said. 'I mean, what do we tell the child? It might have been better off all round if she had been adopted by strangers. A clean break.'

'I never wanted to give her up,' Clare uttered, floored by her mother's audacity.

Her mother's stare fastened on her, her face crumpling with sorrow. 'I see that now... Listen, Clare, you may wish to know... Anne sent me a photograph of her, with her Christmas card. I keep it in my handbag. Your father doesn't dare look in *there*.'

Clare wondered if it was a copy of the one Anne sent her a few weeks ago.

'I think...' Her mother's gaze turned wistful. 'I think she looks like you as you did at that age. I said as much to your father, but he didn't want to look at the photograph. Said it wasn't up for discussion. And anyway, he says he doesn't remember either you or Anne as babies.'

Clare jolted, had no way of responding.

'But I am concerned for your future, Clare,' her mother went on. 'The child's father disappeared into thin air. What do we know about him? Do you still... know him?' She peered at her, searching for a reaction, a clue.

'No, Mum.' As Clare's lie stuck to the roof of her mouth, she realised that she truly did not know Leo Bailey, or ever want to. Not like she wanted to know Bertie, or indeed, Cal McInnis.

'Well, not surprisingly. He was probably married...?' Her mother sighed. 'I do hope this Albert, Bertie, is a better sort. A fresh start, as Emily said. And the idea of Anne keeping the baby seems the right thing to do all around.'

'*Keep* the baby? For good?' Clare gasped. She had always considered the arrangement for Mirren to be temporary, at least until the end of the war. 'You're speaking as if that is the plan.'

'It is what your father and I assumed, now you're down here. You see, we felt it surely suited you to go to Scotland and be with Anne. Bring up the baby there. Not leave her there. I wonder why—

am surprised you left. I know you are doing war work, but that could also be done locally?'

Clare steeled herself to argue back. That she had been drawn to help with the war effort by Meryl Stanford. And, after all, it couldn't go on for ever. But what did she know, now with the Americans in and all this fresh horror in the Far East? Would there ever be an end? And what about Mirren? She pictured her daughter and wanted to cry, remembering how dangerous she'd been with her. How depressed and desperate, on the shore of the loch. Mirren would be safe with Anne and Allistair. And never safe with her. The crux of the matter.

'This Bertie chap,' said her mother, snapping her out of it, 'does he know?'

Clare shook her head.

'Perhaps if you give up Mirren for good, and let Anne keep her...' Her mother's voice mellowed with persuasion. 'Perhaps that will the best for everyone. After all, why would Bertie want to bring up someone else's child? He'd want his own children, surely.'

'Mum, you are getting ahead of things. Bertie and I are good friends... and really, I...' Clare gestured that she must get herself up the stairs and to bed.

'Think about it, dear.' Her mother placed her hand on her arm, stopping her. 'There may be another way. Let Anne keep her.' She bared her teeth in a twisted grin. 'Because, as soon as Bertie finds out, he will drop you.'

22

Clare wound her scarf around her neck, blew on her gloved fingers and began to climb the long hill to Amersham Station, her parents' puzzling, uncomfortable farewell buzzing in her mind. They'd seemed relieved that she was leaving, made the appropriate noises about her hurrying to catch her train, wondered aloud that, seeing as it was Boxing Day, whether the timetable had changed. They wished her luck, as if she were a stranger. Aunt Emily saved the moment by coming with her to the front door, hugging her on the doorstep, enveloping Clare in her perfume, gripping her shoulders, and whispering in her ear, 'Go find your happiness. Go fetch Mirren.'

Clare paused to catch her breath at the top of the hill, the station in sight in the rapidly falling dusk, and Emily's words still chiming in her mind. Had her great-aunt overheard the conversation she'd had with her mother on the landing and had felt compelled to pass on the refreshing, visionary message? Whatever the case, Clare thought as she continued on her way, Emily's empathy left her with a little more confidence, and hope.

Unexpectedly, through the cold air came the sound of the rails crackling and hissing, a train arriving from London. Clare stepped up her pace with a sense of urgency. It must be an earlier delayed service, which didn't surprise her. Journeys these days were often disrupted by unexploded bombs, damaged bridges, or some other mishap.

'Last train to Oxford!' called the station master.

The blacked-out carriages had already halted amid billows of steam, and she could hear the sound of train doors slamming shut as she dashed through the ticket office, dodging straggling, departing passengers, hearing the guard's insistent whistle.

'Last train to Oxford!' he bellowed through the growling of the engine. 'All aboard. Stand clear! Stand clear, I say! Madam!'

'Wait, please wait!' She ran, catching sight of his furious face.

She set her suitcase down on the platform and grasped the door handle, the whistle shrill and angry.

'Clare?' someone shouted. 'Clare!'

With no time to look around, she threw her case into the empty carriage, leapt up the step and landed sideways on a seat. The train jerked and the wheels began to turn as she leant forward and hauled the door shut. She sat back, puffed out, but laughing with relief, her heart hammering, and her neck slick with sweat under her scarf. Thank goodness her hat had stayed in place, and thank goodness she'd left Emily's cottage when she did, or she'd have to spend another night and endure another strained goodbye. But who had called out for her along the platform?

She wiped her face with her handkerchief, getting her breath back, thinking that it can't have been the guard or the station master shouting her name. Anyway, they both looked too outraged to speak. At least she'd soon cool down, she thought, for the gloomy single compartment felt icy cold.

The door slid open.

'Found you!' A man in an RAF blue great coat, forage cap and scarf wound high around his chin slipped in and shut the door. 'You made a brave run for it. Outraging the railmen. Well done.'

'Good grief, Bertie! It's you!' She laughed with pleasure. How happy she felt to see his friendly, familiar face.

Bertie sat on the seat opposite her, leaning forward. She reached without thinking and grasped his hands, enjoying the dizzy whirl of coincidence.

'Then I realised perhaps I shouldn't have called out for you at such a crucial moment,' he said, his smile beaming. He squeezed her hands back and held onto them. 'It might have distracted you, and you'd have missed the train. And you'd be stranded there on the platform in the cold. And I would have had to leap off the train like they do in the films. I couldn't leave you there, all alone, could I?'

'These blessed trains are always up the creek,' she uttered. 'I'm so glad I caught it.'

'I've never seen you move so fast. It was mayhem for me at Marylebone. Thought for a moment there I might not make it back to base. Would have to face the wrath of the wing commander. Not something I would enjoy. Have you had a good Christmas?'

'Yes and no,' she admitted, her surprise and joy at seeing Bertie dampened as reality returned. 'Great-Aunt Emily is wonderful,' she said, 'and her home so lovely. But my parents are... challenging, shall I say. Oh God, now I feel disloyal. What must you think of me?'

'It's all right,' he said, chuckling. 'You don't have to like *all* of your family. And what I may think of you... well.' He paused, grinning at her in the yellowish electric light. 'Look, it's perishing in here. Come back to where I was sitting. The heater was nearly burning my legs off.'

They made their way along the corridor and settled in a warmer carriage. Clare pondered what Bertie had said – about what he thought of her – wondering why he may tease her like that. But she let him chat away about his Christmas in London, and the various hilarious or tiresome relatives that he'd encountered. As she laughed with him, counting the cousins and aunts and uncles he mentioned, she found herself feeling a prickle of envy at his obviously large and merry family. But with Emily's nugget of wisdom bobbing around her thoughts, the future seemed brighter, as if she were recovering from a long and nasty illness. As Bertie chatted on, her own uncomfortable episode over the festivities shrank away; she felt light-headed with possibility and wanted to listen to Bertie for longer.

'So, how many cousins did you have staying in your big, old family house in Hammersmith?' she asked.

'Now let me see, there was...' Bertie looked distracted, glanced along the carriage. 'Hold on a moment,' he said. 'Where are we?'

'No idea,' she said. 'The blackout doesn't help. What was the last station?'

A passenger across the aisle spoke from behind his newspaper. 'High Wycombe, love.'

'God, we've missed our stop,' Bertie groaned. 'What a pair.'

Clare could sense the train slowing for the next station. 'Come on, we'd better get off, wherever we are. What a bother.'

'Let's hope the last London-bound train hasn't gone already,' uttered Bertie as they stepped down from the train.

The winter night had fallen, blanking out the sleeping countryside; the Chiltern hills appearing as dark masses against the black sky. They hurried along the empty platform, up the steps and across the footbridge to the other side, their footsteps echoing in cold air. The waiting room was locked, the ticket office looked closed. No light showed, and not another soul stirred. Sitting down on the cold bench, Clare felt as if time had halted, as if the deserted station had been captured in an eerie photograph.

'Who knows when the next train is?' she said, wrapping her scarf tighter and pushing each mittened hand up the opposite sleeve of her coat.

'Let's hope fortune is on our side this time,' Bertie said. 'It was rotten bad luck to miss our stop. But good luck that we both caught the same train. At least we are stranded together.'

'Yes, I suppose so.'

'We were obviously both enchanted by our conversation,' he said, and their breath puffed white clouds in the dark around them.

She shivered.

'Come here.' Bertie's gesture impelled her to get to her feet. He stepped close to her, tilted his head as if asking for permission before wrapping his arms around her. 'Does that feel better?'

Clare wanted to giggle. His embrace felt comforting and warm, and yes, it felt better to be held in his arms, but also a little silly. But she nodded, her chin brushing the coarse wool of his coat.

'Don't worry, we'll get back in one piece,' he said somewhere near her ear.

She uttered her affirmation.

'I told my family about you over Christmas.'

A strange, portentous creeping inched around her stomach. She did not know if she felt excited or afraid. 'You did? Who?'

'Anyone who felt inclined to listen. Mother, Dad. Uncle Albert, who I am named after, by the way.'

'Well, I must say,' she said, lightly, 'you came up in our conversation, too.'

'All positive reports, I trust.'

Clare's scalp prickled at the memory of her mother's warning, and she tried for a little humour. 'Well balanced, you'll be pleased to know.'

Bertie adjusted his embrace, as if getting used to holding her.

'I'll have a look down the platform for a timetable.' He rested his cheek against the side of her head in playful farewell. 'Don't go anywhere.'

She laughed lightly, dismissively. 'There's nowhere to go.'

* * *

While she waited, sitting alone in the moonless dark, she wondered if there would be a taxi for them at High Wycombe. It may mean another wait, but at least they could share the fare. No moon meant a quiet night for Bomber Command, and her mind turned with displeasure to the routine she'd soon get back into. But knowing that Leo Bailey would be leaving Hillside, or with any luck, had already left for good, gave her new strength. It meant she could close the door on that chapter.

She heard Bertie returning, and inhaled the refreshing, icy air.

'No timetable. Must be in case of invading German paratroopers and them wanting to catch the next train to London.'

'Oh, well, we will just have to keep our fingers crossed...'

'That's what I have been doing all along, Clare: keeping my fingers crossed. That, and praying to the god of good fortune. If there is one listening.'

'All along? Yes, of course...' Confused, she asked, 'Why? Because of the trains...?'

'Because I am going to ask you to marry me.'

'What in the world!' She laughed. 'Bertie, really...' She could not see his expression properly in the dark, but from the tone of his voice, she felt sure he was kidding her. 'But you are not on one knee,' she giggled.

She watched aghast as he knelt in front of her on the platform. He fumbled for her hand. Goodness, she thought, this is absurd.

'You are the kindest, sweetest, loveliest girl I have ever met,' he said, as if he'd been thinking this for a very long time. 'Will you do me the honour, Miss Clare Ashby, and be my wife? Will you marry me?'

She recoiled, and the creeping sensation in her belly switched to familiar, unmistakable nausea.

'Bertie,' she said, a whispered warning. 'Are you joking? Because if you are...'

'No, my darling Clare. Deadly serious.'

She stared at his face, saw a gleam of earnest light in his widening eyes. His mouth half open in expectation.

'Ever since I first met you,' Bertie's words discharged in a staccato rush, 'when I collected you from the police station, my darling, I have wanted to— Didn't you realise? The girls knew. Julia and Susanna. They encouraged me. I haven't dared tell the boys, of course. I'd never hear the end of it if you turned me down. And you might, of course. But think of all the lovely things between us. I keep my fingers crossed. God of fortune and all that. What were the chances, tonight, that you ran to catch the train I was already on? It's a sign. It has to be.'

'Please get up. Stand up. Please, Bertie. Get off the cold ground.' Her voice rasped in her throat.

She told herself she'd had no idea, had not seen any signals. Knew nothing of *the lovely things between us*. But something quieter spoke up, chastised her. She'd been too preoccupied with worrying about the comings and goings of Leo Bailey to take in the way Bertie Havill looked at her, cherished her, took care of her. And yet, his shock proposal lingered on, wave after grinding wave.

Bertie did as she commanded and sat beside her. He gripped her hand, and many moments passed while her mother's warning, delivered on Aunt Emily's landing, clanged like a bell. Clare suddenly wanted to fly in the face of it, to disobey her mother. She wanted, in a way, to test Bertie. Because, deep down, she realised it would not break her if he dropped her.

'Clare?' he said. 'What's the matter? You seem horrified. Is it the shock? I'm sorry, I have rather sprung it on you. Perhaps I should have waited. Found a better way. It's cold, dark and you want to get home. You don't need me asking you *that—*'

'I have something to tell you.'

He turned towards her and she forced herself to look at him, grateful for the night for shielding the expression on her face, and his.

'Bertie, I have a daughter.'

He gasped. 'You're already married!'

'No, not married.'

She heard his breath sucking in and out as if he were trying to clean out the inside of his head, plumes of mist vanishing into the dark.

'A daughter?' It sounded as if he had trouble forming the words. He ran his hands over and over along his thighs. 'How old?'

'Not yet a year,' Clare said, taking umbrage. She did not feel she needed to explain much more, for surely, this must be the end of the conversation.

'Where is she? What's her name?'

'Why do you want to know?' She felt certain her having a baby would be enough for him. And there would be no need to divulge any more information.

He said, tenderly, 'Because she is *your* daughter.'

Taken aback, Clare told him quickly, almost coolly, that Mirren lived in the Highlands with her sister and her husband. Bertie fell silent, his mouth moving and chomping with unspoken questions. She felt him staring at her and most likely judging, changing his mind about her, as many people would.

Clare waited, while, she felt sure, Bertie filled in his own narrative. She certainly did not wish to give him the full picture of how it all came about, for she felt unable to articulate it, the shame and self-blame always too difficult to form into words.

Confiding in Emily had helped but only Cal McInnis knew the whole, nasty truth.

And now, with Bertie, she felt impelled to spin the yarn.

'I was unfortunately *caught*,' she said into the quietness, wincing at the clumsy, prudish expression. 'One evening, in London, I met a soldier on leave and... it happened. And he disappeared into the war. He doesn't know.'

Bertie stood up, nervously stomping his boots, the soles scraping the ground.

'I'm not proud of myself,' she said. 'But I am proud of Mirren.'

'I don't doubt it,' Bertie said, pitched with bravado. 'But if I ever get to meet this chap, if I ever see him, I shall bop him on the nose.'

A weary, dragging disappointment pooled inside Clare, his comment feeble and inadequate in response to the enormity of what she had been through. His eyes looked flat, as if not properly focusing on her. The bulk of his body shifted as he subtly, unconsciously, retreated. And her disenchantment ballooned into frustration, edged with fear, as Bertie walked off along the platform, as if on patrol, watching, she assumed, for the train. But it felt like he'd left her to get on with her life alone.

Tears smarted in her eyes.

'Why am I crying?' she muttered to herself, pulling her scarf higher up her face to catch any tears that fell.

Clare looked around, beyond the station, her eyes adjusting to the dark. Beech trees on the wooded hill revealed themselves in a pleasing pattern of branches, the enormous night surrounding her felt like her whole world, expanding about her, empty and cold. With one tiny light, a distant star, out of reach. Mirren, 500 miles away.

Her mother had been right. Bertie had dropped her at the first mention of Mirren. He'd left her so that she would have to fend off Leo Bailey, whenever he decided to reappear in her life, alone. Clare shivered and a disjointed parade of memories taunted her. Dinner at the restaurant and the puzzling feeling, right there at the start, when she had seemed to know what was going on, and yet matters changed into something else entirely. Unwrapping the perfume bottle, discovering the truth of his marriage in his personal file. The churlish leaving of the perfume on the doorstep. Yes, Clare admitted, shivering on the bench in the dark, that she'd wanted his wife to find it, and to wonder. But, surely, Clare told herself, it must be the only thing she ought to be ashamed of.

She heard the ring of Bertie's boots on the platform, receding, pausing, waiting. Perhaps she had needed to hear a response like Bertie's. Without rage, resentment, or pity. But a lighter, kinder reaction, to help diminish her pain. And perhaps disappointment was a feeling that she must simply smile at and step over for the rest of her life. His footsteps sounded again. She must keep hold of the possibility that if this man, who she liked and trusted, accepted Mirren, her future may be good. Her future may be normal.

Bertie stood in front of her, his frame filling her view, with the deep dome of the night sky arcing over him.

'Is the train coming?' she asked, trying to sound conversational.

'No sign.'

'Perhaps we'd better start walking—'

He cut in. 'So, will you then?'

Clare inhaled, the cold stinging her throat. 'You still want to?'

Bertie reached down and hauled her up from the bench, his embrace enclosing her, shielding her from the cold, and it no longer felt silly. It felt necessary.

'What do you think?' he whispered. 'Did you not hear me? You are the kindest, loveliest girl.'

Clare held on tight to Bertie, her whole body exhaling in relief.

'And don't just nod this time,' he whispered.

She gave him his answer, and stayed inside his embrace, listening for the train in the prickling silence of the solstice darkness. An owl hooted from the beechwoods, the sound thin and fragile. Another responded, way over the other side, like a comforting conversation. And it didn't matter how long they would have to wait for the train.

PART III

23

MIRREN

The Highlands, Summer 1985

She did not remember Clare, but the sight of any deer disappearing into the heath set off the yearning, tugging at something fixed deep in her memory. Sometimes, the weather reminded Mirren in a more gentle way: the light shining across the lochan at Anne and Allistair's. But Clare knew nothing of the deer. Her mother knew nothing of Mirren's draining hunger. And did *she* ever think of the lochan?

That morning, wearing her earrings – now a reunited pair – to work seemed like a wonderful idea: a way of honouring her mother, despite everything, and a positive signal for Gregor, if he happened to drop by the library and see them dangling from her ears. But, heavier than her usual jewellery, she felt constantly aware of them against her skin while she stamped books and pushed her trolley. The reason she rarely wore them – they goaded her, spun her mind in circles to a black spot where Clare did not recall that she had ever given her earrings. Where she had forgotten all about her.

Mirren let out a weary groan as she walked up her steep path to the house. The library had been busy with school holiday clubs and gangs of lively children, and the weight of the day still clung to her shoulders. She paused in habit to look behind her at the great loch and the distant shore. Every time, a different view, a different sky. A quick lungful of Highland air usually did the trick. She had a lot to be thankful for, she thought, as she put her key in the door.

It had been a good month since Mirren and Gregor's unexpected, enjoyable, drink-hazed evening, capped by him rummaging through a bag of dust for her earring.

Hanging her jacket, she turned to the hall mirror and ran her fingers over her hair to tidy it. A sharp breeze had caught her as she got out of the car. Mirren gave her reflection a smirk. Gregor once said her hair had a life of its own.

Surely, his visit had to mean something. But as the weeks since passed in silence, everything that had happened, from the moment Gregor announced he wanted to leave to his latest friendly overture, felt puzzling. The reason behind the bickering that had stealthily crept up on them and ruined their marriage had once again been tidied away to be dealt with another day.

'Mum! Thank God, you're home!' Kirstine thundered down the stairs, her face pale and stretched with alarm. 'Anne called two hours ago. It's Isla.'

'My goodness, what?'

'They found her on the floor. Not sure how long she'd been there. Maybe a whole day.'

'Oh, dear God,' uttered Mirren, her stomach plummeting.

'They called an ambulance. She's had a stroke, they think. She's at the Infirmary.' Kirstine clung to Mirren, burying her face on her shoulder. 'Anne and Allistair are there with her,' she said, her voice muffled. 'But they are still waiting for the proper doctor to see her, Anne said.'

'Oh, hen, hen. She's in the best place.' Mirren held her daughter's shoulders tightly, shock escalating like pins and needles over her scalp. 'They'll do everything for her.'

Kirstine pulled back, her cheeks streaked with tears. 'Are you going to go to the hospital?'

'I will. Absolutely.' She grabbed her jacket, her mind whirling in panic, the awful fear she wanted to protect Kirstine from. 'But it may be best you stay here. They will be funny about lots of people visiting.'

Kirstine sniffed, wiped her eyes with the back of her hand. 'Do you have a tissue, Mum?'

'Not one you'd want to use.'

Kirstine's wry smile brightened her face and Mirren noticed again the subtle change in her. Ever since Gregor had taken their daughter to lunch, the afternoon of *Live Aid,* she'd seemed tender and hopeful, as if something he said had reassured her.

'I knew you'd want to go to the hospital,' Kirstine said. 'I made you some sandwiches. And a flask.'

She dashed into the kitchen for the packed supper and pressed the Tupperware eagerly into Mirren's hands.

Mirren thanked her daughter, and said she'd quickly pop to the lavatory.

As she climbed the stairs, her eyes swimming with tears, she knew that she for one, would never not think of Kirstine. Would not forget her own daughter.

* * *

Mirren hurried along corridors of varying tones of beige and grey, reading signs to wards and departments as she passed them, skirting busy doctors and people shuffling with walking frames, trying not to inhale the curious savoury hospital smell. Her panic had retreated while she negotiated the drive back to Inverness, the car park, and the ticket machine, but now surged in waves. She might – she will – lose Isla, vital, full-blooded Isla, the voice of reason, the wee grannie in everything but name.

Allistair emerged around a corner, looking as dazed as Mirren felt, his tall frame stooping of late, and appearing as any elderly gentleman might, blending into the background in grey trousers, cap, and sensible, brown, zip-up jacket. When he saw her, his face brightened with relief and she begged herself not to start crying.

'She's in there,' he said, oddly cheery. 'Has been giving the doctors what-for.'

'She's awake?'

'It's Isla, remember,' he said. 'Usually, a stroke at eighty-nine years old means it's time to close the curtains. But not Isla. I'm getting us a coffee. Would you like anything?'

Mirren lifted her flask with a quick grin and went on into the ward.

Isla lay in the last bed on the left, her body seeming to sink into it, as if consumed by stark-white hospital linen, with Anne perched on the chair beside her. Mirren slowed down, almost tip-toed in reverence, not wishing to disturb the poignant vignette.

'Ah, Mirren, thank goodness you're here,' Anne said, relief catching in her throat. 'The daughters will be descending also, no doubt, but they've a long way to travel.'

Mirren acknowledged her aunt with a quick nod, keeping her gaze on Isla, whose body, once stocky and strong, looked depleted, her limbs stick-like and wiry and at uncomfortable angles. She lay with her head to one side, eyes closed, her cheek sagging, her long, silky white hair a clumpy mess. Isla certainly would not be happy about that.

'Go and get another chair,' Anne said. 'Ask the nurse if you can borrow... go on.'

Mirren turned obediently to fetch a chair and, after much rearranging and scraping of furniture, sat down.

'That's better.' Anne patted Mirren's knee. 'Allistair's just gone to the coffee machine. I hope he has the right coins. He said he did, but he may have to ask someone to change a pound note.'

Isla made a grumbling sound and began to stir, although she opened only one eye; the other eyelid hovered between sleep and wakefulness. She moved her mouth side to side, as if chewing on something bitter.

'Ah, you're awake.' Anne leant forward over the bed. 'Would you like some water, Isla?'

'Aye but will you no' keep the noise down,' she croaked. 'I've a horrible headache.'

While Anne fussed with the jug of water and a plastic cup, Mirren reached for Isla's nearest hand and squeezed it. It felt papery and cool, verging on lifeless. Together, they helped Isla sip.

'I won't ask how you are, Isla,' Mirren said. 'I can see that for myself.'

'Gave us such a fright,' said Anne as she manoeuvred Isla's pillows unnecessarily behind her head. Isla flopped back to the same position. 'But the doctor says she is stable.'

Isla's face, carved with the lines of her life, looked blank and ghostly, not quite real, as if someone had taken her expressions away. Plastic tubes containing sharp needles fixed to the crook of her elbow and the side of her neck distended her skin. But Mirren peered past it all, determined to see Isla, the woman who'd endured throughout her life.

'They are talking about care homes, Mirren,' Isla murmured, a tad brighter after her drink of water but forming each syllable with caution.

'Already?' Mirren asked. 'But we have to get you well first.'

'There's a nice one in Fort Augustus,' she said, her mouth

drooping. 'But you know what happens. You go in and eighteen months later, you're done for. With me, we'll give it eight months.'

'Och, Isla,' Anne said. 'Stop that nonsense. You should not try to speak. The doctor said. You must rest.'

Isla grumbled in protest, fighting fatigue. She closed her eyes, tilted her head into the pillow and dozed.

'Where has Allistair got to? I'm parched and need caffeine,' Anne muttered. 'They used to come round with a trolley.'

'You can have my flask of tea,' said Mirren.

Anne shook her head, her customary energy surfacing through her tension, making it worse. 'No, I don't like the taste of tea in a flask.' She sighed, glanced at her watch. Now she was well into her seventies, though usually fresh-faced and her hair only marginally streaked with grey, anxiety made her look her age. 'We were talking about you,' she said, quietly, conscious of disturbing Isla. 'Allistair and I, just before you arrived. When you were a little girl, you once asked Isla why the birds sound different in the winter.'

Mirren giggled. 'Really?' And she relived the vague curiosity from way back in her childhood imagination. 'Of course, I know now. Because in winter, we have different birds.'

Anne said, 'It was quite sweet, really.'

Isla stirred, gestured with her good hand. 'Anne, if you are so worried about Allistair, and your blessed cup of coffee, will you no' go and find him?'

'You want me to hurry him up, Isla?'

Isla sighed. 'Aye.'

Anne rolled her eyes at Mirren, stood up, scraping her chair, hauled her knitted cardigan tighter around her hips and left, uttering grumpily about feeling dismissed.

'Has she gone? I cannae see.'

Mirren glanced behind her as Anne's mildly stooped yet statuesque frame disappeared through the doors.

'She's gone.'

Isla reached for Mirren's hand, her fingers crooked, and her grasp loose. A tenderness settled over her features like a mask over her face.

Mirren gazed at her with sudden fear.

'Are you all right, Isla? Shall I call the nurse?' She looked around. With the occasional beeping of machines and murmuring conversations, the ward seemed settled in quiet efficiency. 'Which one?'

Isla exhaled, gave a minute shake of her head.

'Let's not bother them,' Isla said, locking eyes with her. 'Mirren, I remember that sweet little thing you said, about the birds sounding different in winter. I told your mother.'

Mirren jolted, her scalp tightening, cold prickling shooting up her neck.

'What?'

'I used to write to her. All the time, over the years. But she rarely wrote back to me. She had a nervous breakdown.'

'*What?*'

'Clare. She was in a terrible state.'

'Isla, I...' Mirren shuddered, her breath hissing in and out. 'I didn't— I wasn't even sure— I never knew.'

'That's why she couldn't keep you.' Isla peered at her, or rather in her direction, her gaze glassy. 'My God. Poor lass. No one has ever been honest with you, have they?'

Mirren squeezed her eyes shut. The freeze-frame with Clare standing in the rain and staring up at the window at the last house on the lochan pinned itself to her mind. The chaos felt by her young, unformed self gaping at Clare, dazed and bewildered but unable to know or articulate her feelings, stupefied her. She gulped for air in the clinical-smelling hospital ward as she experienced the loss all over again. The little girl she must have once been, trembling behind the wet pane of glass. She must have felt nauseous, her mind tumbling with confusion, wanting to wave, to call out, as she watched her mother tear herself away.

'No one told me,' Mirren said, her tongue heavy, swallowing, it seemed to her, the same nausea. 'No one ever explained.'

Panic rose, her stomach like a queasy weight, the past pressing in as the subdued bustling carried on behind her.

'Oh, hen, she couldn't cope. She didn't want to hurt you any more.' Isla's voice sounded guttural and pained. 'To be in and out of your life. It was the war, remember. Such a traumatic time. I know you think we rattle on about it. But it changed so many things. It changed Clare.'

Mirren winced at the name as it rang with such light ordinary innocence. She had not grasped any of it. Isla had unburdened herself of the truth, but it drifted now, inadequate, treacherous, and lame.

'Isla.' Mirren squeezed the old woman's hand. 'Isla, I still don't understand.'

'Aye, aye,' whispered Isla, not catching on.

'All these years, Isla, I...' Mirren's sentence dried in her throat.

'I kept her letters in a shoebox.' Isla's slack face blanched, her eyes fluttering shut with exhaustion, wrinkle upon wrinkle folding in.

Mirren heard two pairs of footsteps approaching across the linoleum floor, her chance to ask more questions slipping fast. Isla looked *scunnered*. It seemed unfair to urge her any further.

'What are you two whispering about?' Allistair said, cradling two plastic cups of coffee, and then setting them on the bedside stand. 'Whatever gossip she's been telling you, it has fair old worn her out.'

Mirren, unable to answer, shook her head, her smile unnaturally straining her cheeks.

Allistair, who'd brought her up and knew her every tic and grimace, uttered, 'Good God, Mirren...?'

But Anne hadn't noticed. 'Took us ages to find a coffee machine that worked,' she said. 'The nurse just told us that visiting is nearly over, but you'll need some bits, Isla.' She placed a gentle hand on Isla's arm. 'A nightie, slippers, certainly a hairbrush.'

An insistent impulse to flee, to carve out space and time to think about what Isla told her, hammered inside Mirren's head.

'I'll drive back and fetch whatever Isla needs.'

Isla's eyes sprung open. 'The *dugs!*' she croaked. 'They'll be wanting their tea, and be let out for a walk.'

Anne soothed her. 'Isla, hen, you don't have the Scotties any more. They're with us now and they're fine.'

'Have been for a few months now,' Allistair said. He took a loud sip from his coffee.

'What about Hamish?' Isla asked. 'Won't they chase him?'

'Hamish is long gone,' Anne said. 'Chasing voles in cat-heaven.'

'Sounds wonderful,' Isla said.

Mirren stood, fumbled for her jacket and handbag. 'I best be off then.'

'I'll come with you, Mirren,' Anne said. 'Keep you company. And I know where Isla keeps her night-time things.'

Mirren felt a snap of disappointment. She longed to be driving back along the Great Glen alone, with a chance to unravel what Isla had told her, to start to make sense of her secret, and turn it inside out in her mind. But with Anne chattering in the passenger seat beside her, this would be impossible.

Perhaps, instead, this could be her moment to ask her, the woman who had nurtured her through the war and beyond, for the truth.

She glanced at her aunt as she tidied Isla's covers and smoothed her unruly hair, and saw how the care she took with her husband's elderly cousin had taken its toll. Worry now etched Anne's face, drawing tired lines down it, and as she sighed with barely disguised exhaustion, Mirren decided it did not seem such a good idea.

Mirren said a gentle goodbye to Isla, bending down to kiss her papery cheek. She appeared crumpled, a fragment of the person she once had been. It struck her that if Isla felt confused about whether she still had her Scottie dogs, and whether Hamish the cat was still alive, would she be confused about other things? Clare's letters, and the secrets they contained?

And yet, when Isla gazed up at Mirren with a slow, whispered farewell, her eyes flickered with the bright spark of her soul.

* * *

Outside in the hospital car park, Mirren heard someone call her name, and Gregor sprinted out of the dusk towards them.

'Well, hello, Gregor,' said Anne.

'How is she?' he said, panting mildly. 'Kirstine called to tell me, and I came over to see if I could do anything to help.'

Mirren blushed, conscious of Anne's curious gaze flicking from her face to Gregor's and back again as she explained to him that she and Anne were heading back to Isla's. For all Anne knew, they were still estranged, had not spent the *Live Aid* evening together in an amiable, wine-fuelled haze.

'Ach, Mirren, that's a long round trip all the way to the lochan to be doing after a day's work,' Gregor said. 'I'll drive you there and back, and you can collect your car afterwards.'

Although this meant Mirren's chance to talk with Anne had been snuffed out, his offer felt confusingly welcome.

Mirren consented and Anne said, 'In that case, I'll go back inside and wait with Allistair. I must say, I am nearly ready to go home.'

As Gregor drove, Mirren filled him in on what had happened with Isla like a polite and grateful acquaintance might. She did not want to draw breath, pause, in case he asked about other things, and awkwardness seeped in. And she felt sure it might, for they had not spoken since that evening. During the entire journey along the Great Glen, all twenty-five minutes or so, he listened, uttering compassionate responses, for through their marriage, Isla had become part of his family, too.

With the light fading, the hills around them growing inky purple, and the interior of the car dimmer by the minute, Clare thought about their evening together. She relished him touching on the troubled, tender spot about her mother, his genuine comfort and understanding, testament to him knowing her so very well. And yet, Mirren would not allow it. Mirren cut him off. And even when he said he should never have left her, she let the moment drift away.

At Isla's cottage, Gregor stayed downstairs to check the back door and put the milk away, while she went up to find the washbag and nightie.

'Don't forget her talcum powder,' he called after her. 'Old ladies do love it.'

She collected what Isla needed from the bathroom and slipped into the bedroom for her nightie and slippers, finding them in moments. But she waited, scanning the room. Opening wardrobe doors, flinching as they squeaked, she began to look for shoeboxes. She checked under the bed, in the fireplace cubby hole and gingerly opened each drawer in Isla's chest of drawers. How long could she do this, she wondered as she pushed aside Arran jumpers and thick, knitted socks, until she drew a blank, until sheer futility became reality.

'Are you all right up there?' Gregor called up the stairs. 'Got everything you need?'

'Almost,' she called back, and knelt on Isla's rug to thrust her hand to the back of the bedside cabinet.

The Clarks shoebox sat tucked behind a Tupperware tub of medication and Mirren grasped it, drew it out with an eager flash of elation. She lifted the lid. Letters, with faded postmarks dated from the early 1960s and up to the Eighties, not more than twenty or so, lay neatly inside. A precious, preserved collection. Mirren's scalp prickled and sweat spread through her hair. Dampness settled on her upper lip. Her jubilation faded swiftly to guilt, and mutated into dread, dragging hard through her stomach. She felt a terrifying, bright flash of realisation. Finding the letters may well mean finding the truth. A truth she did not want. That her mother never loved her, never wanted her.

'Hey, Mirren, do you need some help?' Gregor called.

She went out to the landing and stood at the top of the staircase holding the shoebox. Standing at the bottom, Gregor peered up, his expectant expression melting into worry.

'What have you found there? Mirren? Are you all right?'

'No.' She brandished the box. 'Clare's letters to Isla.'

'What? Clare's *letters*? Oh, hen...' He sighed, raised his arm, gesturing gently for her to come down the stairs to him.

She walked in a daze, taking each step with care and precision.

'I haven't looked at any. I don't want to know.'

He put his arm around her, lead her back into the parlour. 'Not surprised, Mirren. And they are Isla's private letters, after all.'

'But she told me about them. Just now in the hospital. Anne doesn't know. Isla kept it secret. No one knows.'

Her knees turned to straw, and she swayed. Gregor caught her arm, sat her down on Isla's fireside chair, still clutching the box.

'You're shaking Mirren. I'll get you a dram.'

She watched Gregor find a tumbler, unscrew the bottle, her estranged husband taking care of things, like his Uncle Cal might.

Lifting the lid, she extracted an envelope at random, with Isla's address on the front:

Lochan Cottage, near Foyers, Inverness.

Cal would have noted the address, and the English postmark. He would have sorted the letter and put it into his postman's sack, ready for delivery. Mirren recalled what he'd said, when they had their walk earlier that summer, that he still missed Clare. He might not have known her handwriting, but he might have guessed; he would, perhaps, have hoped. As Mirren had also been guessing and hoping all her life.

'Isla wants me to have them, Gregor, or at least to read them,' Mirren said, turning the envelope over in her hand. How light it felt, so flimsy and aged, with no weight at all in contrast to the information it may contain.

Gregor did not look convinced. 'Isla is very ill at the moment and rather confused. She may not have meant it.'

'She wants me to know. And I want to know. At least, I think I do,' Mirren said stubbornly, heard herself whimper. 'I want answers to the questions that have gone over and over in my mind since I was a child.' She fired at him. 'Why Clare did not take me with her. My suitcase was packed, Gregor. I was ready to go. And she left without me.'

He set the whisky tumbler down on the hearth by her feet. 'Mirren, the letters may not tell you that, precisely. This may not be a very good idea... perhaps when you are calmer, have had more time to think. That might be better. You are in shock, with Isla taken ill. This is a lot for you to take in.'

'But Isla meant to tell me. Perhaps she feels time is running out. And this is something I've never had.' Mirren tapped her fingertips on the box. 'This here is a wee snippet of hope. It is better than nothing at all, which is what I have had all my life.'

Gregor's eyes behind his glasses widened in shock and his troubled expression crumpled into disappointment. She knew that he took that as a snub: that he had been part of that 'nothing' in her life.

Her fingers trembling, Mirren plucked the single sheet of Basildon Bond paper from its envelope and unfolded it. She quickly took in the address top-right: *Town Cottage, Old Amersham*; and the date: *October, 1967*, the month Kirstine had been born.

'Are you sure you want to do this now?' Gregor asked sitting down opposite her, his voice low and soothing. 'What about getting back to Isla?'

Mirren nodded, defiant. A fiery thrill of sureness coursed through her veins.

As Isla's mantel clock ticked tenderly, her mother's neat, deep-indigo inked hand, on one side of the page only, began to speak to her. Immediately, after the first line, Mirren's blood thinned and she felt she must resist, to avert her gaze, but the letter, brief and lively, drew her in, softening the years and reaching through time.

Clare hoped Isla had been keeping well. She mentioned the autumnal weather in the Chilterns, and the dahlias in her garden. Touched on how fascinated she'd been by the younger generation's 'summer of love' and finished by thanking Isla for sharing the news that she had become a grandmother. Below her signed name, she had added a postscript.

The page vibrated in Mirren's hand.

She looked at her husband.

'What's the *angel's share*?'

'These are.' Gregor pointed out the neat row of empty bottles on the floor next to Isla's hearth.

Mirren stared at him, puzzled.

'The angel's share,' he said, 'is what's left behind, the vapour if you like, once you've finished your bottle of whisky, or drained a cask. We like to think of it as something ephemeral and fleeting. Something indistinct. But the angels cherish it.'

Mirren looked at Gregor, then at Isla's empty bottles in astonishment and felt a strange quickening of realisation, of understanding, inside her.

She swallowed on the aching dryness in her throat. 'Clare says here that all she had of me was the angel's share.' She glanced at the bottom of the letter again. 'But she dearly hopes that I will have a whole world of more time with my own baby so that I can treasure her.' Tears, sour and burning, flooded down her cheeks. 'We treasure Kirstine, don't we, Gregor?'

'Mirren, Mirren...' Gregor took the letter from her, lifted the box from her lap and put it on the floor. He reached over to comfort her, grasping her hand. 'Yes, we do. Of course we do.'

'But this... this angel's share... I don't understand. Clare did not treasure me?' Sobs wrenched painfully from Mirren's chest.

Gregor picked up the letter and read quickly. 'She says she was *unable* to treasure you, Mirren. She wanted the best for you. But she could not give it to you.'

Shaking her head, Mirren still could not believe him.

'Think of it this way,' Gregor said, coaxingly. 'You have two mothers. Clare and Anne.'

Mirren squeezed her eyes shut, shook her head. 'That doesn't help,' she said, blistering towards anger. 'Anne and Allistair never talked about Clare, and I was never allowed to ask any questions. I mean, they are good people. *Really* good people. But misguided. I was a bewildered and insular child, and became more bewildered and insular as time drifted on. I moulded myself to the world I was brought up in. And, Gregor, two mothers like that were not enough.

They did not make a whole.' Mirren thought she might choke on her tears. 'I felt as if I had no mother.'

'But I said before... if Clare had taken you with her, we would not be here now...'

Mirren gaped at him, wondered why he did not understand.

'Why are you here, Gregor? Why did you come to the hospital?'

'Because I heard about Isla, and I wanted to make sure everything—'

'But are you just being nice?' she snapped. 'Like Clare was being nice, by giving me some earrings? You were when you helped to find the lost one in the vacuum cleaner. Empty gestures which obviously don't mean anything.'

'Mirren, please. How do you know these things don't mean anything?'

She raised her hand to push away his logic, and uttered, 'It's the only way I can cope with any of it. Can't you see that?'

'I'm not just being *nice*, for goodness' sake,' he muttered beneath his breath, 'I'm your husband and you need to allow me to help you.' He picked up the shoebox and began to leaf through the letters. He took one out, and then another, scanning Clare's brief messages. 'There must be something more here, something to prove that you are wrong to say that about Clare. People have all sorts of reasons for the things they do. Things no one else can ever understand. Not being able to cope, wanting to disappear...'

Isla had touched on something: a nervous breakdown.

Even so, Mirren glared at Gregor, 'Yes. And leaving their family.'

He ignored her jibe, read another letter, put it aside. Picked up another.

Watching him, Mirren took a sip of whisky and realised how much she didn't like it. Why hadn't he remembered?

'We need to be getting back to Isla,' she muttered. 'They'll be wondering where we've got to.'

Gregor winced. He lifted his hand as if asking for silence. 'Oh God, Mirren, wait. Here we are,' he said, holding out the letter he'd been reading, although reluctant, a little frightened, to pass it over. 'This might be what you've been looking for.'

Mirren shrugged, held out her hand palm up so that he could place it there.

She skimmed down the page, dated sometime in 1961, discovering how Clare had filled her time one summer organising the local church fete, and how pleased she felt to hear that Mirren's wedding had gone off well.

'What do you mean, Gregor?' she asked, prickling and defensive. 'What clue? That we got married? I'm still reeling from the fact that my mother has all this time known the niceties about my life, and yet did not want to be part of it.'

'No, read on. Right to the end.'

Mirren sighed. How exhausted she felt, wrung out by the onslaught of emotion, a mixture of old and familiar, and entirely raw and new, fresh wounds menacing her and pecking around her head. She took a deep breath, willing herself to keep it all at bay. She read:

Isla, life is a struggle, and I cannot trust myself. I know what you are saying about Mirren, and that perhaps it is now time, now she is settled and married and will hopefully have her own family, for her to get to know me. But I suspect she won't want to. I will upset the happiness she has built for herself. I won't be the mother she needs or has needed. I am not that person. The war changed me. Isla, I helped to kill people. People like us. And it was my job. I find it hard to live with myself. Face the person I am each morning. I don't want to know me. And I suspect that Mirren won't want to either...

Clare's handwriting blotted on the page, the words melting into one another, obliterated by Mirren's tears. She dropped the letter, dashed the back of her hands over her eyes, wiping.

'Gregor, do you remember the deer?' she asked, her voice clogged and grainy.

'The *deer*? What deer? Why? No, I don't.'

'In the car with Cal. He was driving us back from school. The deer was by the side of the rode. We stopped. I stared at it. It, she, stared back. I'll never forget her.'

'I'm sorry, I...'

Mirren closed her eyes, drowning under the flood of memory, the look on her mother's face as she stared up at her behind her bedroom window seared on her mind. Clare's expression contained agony and defeat, the most natural, instinctive, animalistic realisation that leaving her behind could be her only option. Like a doe understanding it must leave behind her injured calf.

Mirren jumped at the shrill, shattering ring of Isla's telephone. Gregor marched out to the hallway. 'Must be Anne, hurrying us up. A washbag emergency.'

She heard him say hello. He waited for the pips to finish as Anne, somewhere in a hospital corridor, fed ten pence pieces into the slot.

'Yes? Anne, yes, we're still here, we're just... ah,' he said, and his voice dropped. 'When? Yes. I see. Oh God. Yes, of course. Thank you. Ah, I'm sorry...'

Gregor replaced the receiver and came back into the room, his face taut, his eyes clouding with dismay.

'What is it?' Mirren said, although her own instinct already knew.

She stood up and let herself be gathered into his embrace.

'She's gone,' he said.

Mirren felt no need to respond, or to ask any more questions.

Over Gregor's shoulder, she gazed around the little parlour with its lifetime of accoutrements, Isla's fingerprints on every object, from the Scottie dog figurines along the windowsill to the empty bottles of whisky by the hearth. She listened to its silence and sensed that the room knew already.

Gregor said, 'Anne is insisting that we don't need to go back to the hospital. They will be leaving themselves soon. I'll drive you home.'

Mirren leaned back while he held her, wanting to look at his face, read his expression to help her decide whether her instinct could be right, that by walking into his arms, she had returned somewhere familiar and loving. The place meant for her.

'Are you all right?' he asked. He kissed her lightly on her forehead.

'We need to get home, Gregor,' she said, with an urgent need to be there. 'Let's tell Kirstine together.'

Gregor went around switching off the lamps while Mirren gathered up the letters and fitted them inside their envelopes, before slotting them back into Isla's shoebox.

Closing the front door and walking with Gregor to the car, Mirren could smell rain in the night air, on its way in from the Western Isles. She heard a slow wind sighing in the pines nearby. The loss of Isla felt brutal and incompatible with the peaceful darkness, and she held onto the Isla's shoebox as if it may comfort her. An urgency gripped her, made her hurry to open the passenger door, to urge Gregor to drive quickly. She wanted to shake off the stagnation of the years that had drifted by without her knowing, without her ever asking. Why it took Isla to pass away for her to feel such resolve baffled her. But now, Mirren thought, as the car sped in darkness along the top road, someone needs to tell Clare about Isla.

24

CLARE

The Chilterns and London, Summer 1948

The attic bedroom looked ready, the floor swept, the bed under the eaves made up and pristine. Fresh, new curtains graced the little window. Clare spent time fiddling with the gathers; she wanted them perfect.

Clare's seamstress skills certainly did not match Anne's, and she'd asked the lady along the road to make them for her. When she'd returned the finished curtains, wrapped in brown paper, Clare discovered a little cushion made from a remnant and filled with lavender gathered from the lady's garden. Her neighbour's implicit kindness made Clare want to weep. But she fastened the feeling securely inside her; there would be time for that later. For now, she must keep a clear and practical head. She gave the bedroom one more check, and perched the cushion on top of Mirren's pillow.

'Kettle's on, Clare,' Bertie called up from the kitchen.

'Yes, all right,' she replied, with a tucked-in smile. Her husband always made the tea. He had tactfully informed her, a week into their marriage, that he made a better brew. And he liked to have a sit down and a cup of tea before setting out on a long journey.

The bedroom appeared in order, waiting to serve its purpose. The room may be prepared, Clare thought as she walked down the stairs, but she wondered in all honesty how ready she would be, to welcome her daughter here.

The size of Emily's cottage compared to the last house on the lochan troubled her, for a start. Would it be comfortable enough, large enough for a little girl who'd grown up in such a wild, free space? Would Mirren think her bedroom cramped? The view from the window in the slope of the roof limited, when she'd had such a glorious horizon to gaze upon? As she'd done for a few years now, Clare wanted to ask Emily about it, and hear what she had to say. But could only guess at what nuggets of wisdom that gracious lady may have tossed her way.

When her great-aunt passed away the day after VJ Day, as if she'd wanted to hold on to see the end of the war before succumbing to pneumonia, she left Town Cottage to Clare, along with her furniture, a small fortune, and a variety of pithy comments from her parents. Clare and Bertie kept most of the antiques but bought new, modern pieces including Clare's favourite, the Ercol nest of tables made from Chiltern beechwood. She hoped having such clean, streamlined style in the place where she felt so much at home would bring optimism into her new, peacetime world. And give her the confidence to do as Emily had suggested: *find her happiness, and go and fetch Mirren.*

As Clare went into the parlour, Bertie set the tray down on the largest of the Ercol tables and fussed with the tea strainer. He glanced at his watch, his nerves, Clare realised, poorly disguised.

'Right, we leave in an hour,' he said. 'I have booked the taxi. They better be on time, though. We don't want to be late before we start. The Underground might be slow, for one. The points are always tricky around Wembley. Are we ready to go, darling?' he asked, passing her an over-brewed cup of tea.

'Suitcases are packed, and you put them by the front door, remember,' said Clare. 'I nearly tripped over them when I came downstairs. I have the sleeper tickets in my handbag.'

The practicalities filled Clare's mind, helping her detach from the enormity of where they were going; what they were going there for.

'I think we are as ready as we will ever be.'

They drank their tea in silence, Bertie fidgeting, his eyes taking on the glazed expression that Clare had come to learn graced his face when he thought deeply. She wondered if he had got cold feet at this, the last minute, even though right from the start, when she'd told him about Mirren, he'd been loyal and compassionate, keen to demonstrate his love.

Soon after they got engaged, he'd rushed down to Hammersmith on his own to tell his parents about Mirren face to face. And Clare had been on tenterhooks waiting for his return, wary that their reaction may place another obstacle in her path to the ordinary life she craved. But Bertie had returned relaxed and enthusiastic, enveloping Clare in a joyful hug. They hadn't minded at all.

'They're both rather bohemian, you know. Mother's a bit of a blue stocking and began gushing about a ready-made grandchild,' he'd said. 'Dad seemed happy enough. I mean, he does vote for the Liberal Party. I should have known they would be all right about it.'

And Bertie's mother, not long after, had written to Clare to say how much she looked forward to meeting her, and perhaps one day, little Mirren.

When Clare wrote to her own parents, more recently, to let them know their plans to bring Mirren to Buckinghamshire, her mother's response read like disapproval scorched into the page. Her opinion, a mouthpiece for her father's no doubt, left Clare fully aware about how they felt. That her idea may prove disastrous; that Mirren was settled there with Anne and Allistair, so why disrupt everyone? And her parents retreated even further into their own lives, wanted nothing to do with Clare's. The West Country may as well be another country.

Clare sipped, grimaced, set down her cup and grabbed her handkerchief to wipe tea leaves from her lips.

'Sorry, darling. Forgot to use the strainer on yours,' said Bertie. 'I think this must be the worst cup of tea I have ever made.'

Clare laughed softly, assured him it didn't matter. For with Bertie, things never really mattered, were always normal and regular. He built for her the world she wanted. How relieved she had been when she first tentatively admitted to him, not long after their wedding six years ago, that she wanted to have Mirren with her. But the war years had stretched on, putting paid to a reunion in any practical sense. Only after Emily's death, and the end of the war when they'd settled in the cottage, did its real possibility begin to take shape. But her need for Mirren had always been there, the wondering and tugging inside her. So why, with this momentous day upon them, were doubts creeping up on her?

In the past, Clare would have sought Emily's counsel and taken on board her no-nonsense point of view: *it's nerves, Clare, pure and simple. Now, remember what you want, and go and find your happiness.* She might also, she realised, have confessed her fears to Cal, knowing he'd understand. Bertie tended to trivialise matters, his way of coping perhaps, and she often had to justify herself to him. Whereas Cal, for the brief time they'd known each other, had understood. She didn't have to explain.

She set down her cup. 'Come on, Bertie, let's give up on the tea,' she said, her disloyal thoughts making her words trip over themselves. 'I'll take it away to the kitchen and wash up.'

Here in Emily's cottage, they'd fallen into their husband-and-wife routines seamlessly. After the intensity of Hillside, Clare relished the calm. She'd worked part-time at something deliberately unchallenging – filing clerk at a local solicitor's firm – which gave her ample time for herself. Although, she often thought, there was only so much housework and gardening she could do, only so much dusting of Ercol furniture while she waited for Bertie to finish his shift.

She glanced at her husband, noticing the early receding of his sandy hair, inherited from his father. The usually level-headed Bertie, late of the RAF and now newly recruited to the police force, looked rankled. He really must be having kittens, she thought. But he had embraced the idea of fetching Mirren. He had looked into schools in earnest, satisfied that the local girls' grammar proved excellent. He had encouraged Clare write to Anne and drop the first hint.

As they finished up in the kitchen, she thought about how she'd started the first letter at least ten times. She had trod carefully, wanting to make it clear that she knew Anne and Allistair had done a marvellous job bringing up Mirren, raising and caring for her baby when she had been desperate and broken. She did not want them to think she resented them. But now life had improved, she wrote; she felt settled and content with Bertie. They would create a loving and caring home for Mirren. After all, she was Mirren's mother. But she'd felt a stab of doubt as she wrote it. She'd sounded like she had protested too much. And *mother* sounded like a foreign word.

Anne had replied, eventually, and there began a long exchange of correspondence. But even when they spoke on the telephone to finalise arrangements, Anne had not sounded like the sister Clare thought she knew. Anne had said, again and again, that she and Allistair agreed and understood. And yet there seemed to be resistance and caution, coming, Clare knew, from the place that had driven them to create the nursery for their own unknown, unborn child all those years ago. She needed to see Anne, to be standing in the same room as her, and look her in the eyes; then she would know for sure.

She heard the toot of a taxi and Bertie opened the front door. She went down the hallway, plucked him by the sleeve.

'Are we doing the right thing, Bertie?' she blurted. 'Is this for the best for Mirren?'

He stared at her, almost in horror.

'Darling, you *know* it is. And you *know* we are. We can't pull out now,' he half laughed. 'We've bought the train tickets.'

He looked and sounded so absolute and certain that Clare realised that she might not have been matching his enthusiasm.

* * *

Soon after lunchtime, their suitcases secured in Left Luggage at King's Cross, Bertie said cheerio.

'We shall rendezvous at seventeen hundred hours,' he said, tapping the face of his watch. 'Right here.' He pointed to the ground and then up to the platform sign. 'Which means you'll need to leave Miss Stanford's at sixteen hundred on the dot to give you plenty of time.'

'Bertie, it's only Hampstead. The taxi will get me here in twenty minutes.'

'Even so, it pays to build in contingency. Synchronise watches.' He turned her wrist to check. 'Good. They're telling the same time. Did you wind yours properly?'

Clare laughed. 'Goodbye, Bertie. Have fun with your RAF chums.'

'We may have a beer or two,' he said, blushing, and suddenly looked so young again, like he had when she'd first met him.

'And I may have some sort of tipple myself, if I know Meryl Stanford.' She kissed his cheek. 'I will see you later.'

The streets of Hampstead appeared as charming and gentile as they had seven years before, barely touched by the Blitz. They had that certain elusive, polished look, one which Miss Stanford also exuded when she opened the front door.

'Goodness, Clare, you do look well,' she said. 'Come in, come in.'

'As do you, Meryl,' she said, acquainting herself with the older woman's familiar style and energy, her full skirt, a nod to the New Look, swishing ahead of Clare as she led the way up the mansion stairs. Clare could smell fresh paint and the soles of her shoes all but bounced off the new thick carpet.

'We survived, didn't we?' Meryl said. 'And thank God this place did. As did my godmother.' She hooked her thumb over her shoulder. 'Still hanging on down there for grim death. I'm so glad you got in touch, Clare, suggested we have tea. We could have dashed down to Fortnum's, but this is nicer, more intimate. And you will meet Christine.'

Meryl opened the door to her apartment.

'Christine?' Clare asked.

'My friend. She won't make three a crowd, though. She is going to pop out so we can chat. Come on, sit yourself down and we can have tea.'

Meryl's living room had also been freshened up with a coat of paint, new wall-to-wall carpet and a gallery of paintings that seemed, to Clare's eye, simply to show a puzzling fusion of lines and discs in a variety of primary colours.

'Ah yes, they're Christine's pieces. And not so much my taste,' said Meryl, following Clare's gaze. 'But she has assured me I will get something out of them, eventually, the longer I view them.'

'Talking about me, Meryl?' A young woman, around Clare's age and wearing wide-legged trousers, a shapeless, silk shirt and a surprisingly short haircut, stalked elegantly into the room. 'Not that I mind. You know what they say... and I'm not entirely sure which I prefer. Being talked about, as opposed to not being talked about.'

'Christine, this is Clare,' said Meryl, 'My protégé. And, Clare, this is Christine. My friend.'

The younger woman shook Clare's hand. 'I have heard so much about you,' she said, eyes twinkling under her severe fringe. 'And it is wonderful to put a face to a name at last. Remember, Meryl, there's a bottle of Margaux in the sideboard but I will leave you both to it. I am sure you have eons to catch up on, and I want to catch the bus down to Charing Cross Road. Have a browse in Foyle's. I will see you later, my love.'

Christine bent over the arm of the sofa and planted a firm kiss on Meryl's lips.

'Bye, my love,' Meryl replied.

Clare watched a hazy blush bloom on Meryl's cheeks and saw her eyes shine as they followed Christine leaving the room, and distant and perplexing aspects of Meryl's life fell into place. The older woman sprang to her feet and, with a giggle, searched for the bottle.

'Forget tea. This is more the ticket,' she said, pouring large glasses of red wine. 'Good old Christine.'

'I should sleep well on the sleeper, then,' said Clare as they chinked glasses.

Meryl took a graceful mouthful of wine, taking a moment to appraise Clare thoroughly.

'So, you are on your way to Scotland? With your husband? How wonderful.' She curled her legs under her on the sofa. 'To stay with your family, I am guessing. Your sister. Anne, is it?'

'Anne yes, and...'

Clare hesitated. Ever since she'd arranged to drop in on Meryl today, she had been in two minds whether to mention Mirren. But, settled on her sublimely comfortable sofa and witnessing a small but fascinating portion of her friend's life, Clare decided Meryl seemed as liberal and bohemian, if not more so, than Mrs Havill. She took another sip of the rich, heady wine and, encouraged by Meryl's firm and compassionate gaze, she told her all about her daughter, and that she'd had her before she met Bertie.

'My good God.' Meryl exhaled and rummaged for the cigarette case on the coffee table. She sparked the lighter. 'These are Christine's. I have given up. But honestly, Clare, this minute, I need this more than oxygen.'

'I can see how shocked you are.'

'Of course I'm shocked!' Meryl blew a thin stream of smoke to the ceiling. 'Not in a scornful, hateful way. Shocked that you endured all of that at such a young age, and had the courage to go through with it, to make plans for you and Mirren. To settle her with your sister and come back down here to work with the Ministry. How I admire you. So...' Meryl peered at her with concern, 'you met someone in Scotland, then?'

Clare jolted at her assumption, but nodded. It felt safer to go along with it.

'Yes, I met someone in Scotland,' she said, her even tone ending that direction of the conversation. A sudden image of Cal jarred her mind, and she realised that, in a way, she'd spoken the truth.

'Ah,' said Meryl, seeing how unnerved she looked. 'I won't press you.'

Clare had felt comforted, from time to time, whenever she pictured Cal. But now, taking a mouthful of Meryl's fine wine, she felt crushed with regret. The morning he'd dropped her and Mirren back at the last house on the lochan, the last time she'd seen him, she hadn't had the courage to ask him how he felt, after what he'd witnessed by the lochside. She had never had the chance to ask him about his father, lost to the Great War, or his brother joining the Highlanders. Or anything more about *him*. And she would never know what had made him follow her down to the water.

Meryl, sucking on her cigarette, watched her closely. 'And, as hard as it may be for your sister now,' she said with caution, 'I can see why you want your daughter back.'

'You can?'

'You're missing her, I can tell. Christine is a tad older than you. And she wants children,' Meryl said. 'I am sure we can find a way. We have lots of male friends.'

Clare absorbed Meryl's startling revelation, realising bohemianism went further than unusual art and close female friendships, further than she could ever imagine. But something else Meryl said ticked over in her mind: that her desire for a new life with Mirren would prove difficult, even unbearable for Anne.

'Do you think that my sister has hoped that this day may never come?' she asked, already knowing.

'It is not for me to say. Only she can answer that. But she has brought the child up. She's seven now, is that right? All those formative years. There will be a strong bond, Clare. It won't be plain sailing.'

Clare set her glass down, slumping under the weight of the notion she'd tried to fend off for months. That by collecting Mirren, removing her, and gathering her into her own world, she'd devastate Anne.

Meryl stubbed out her cigarette and wafted her hand in a vain attempt to dispel the smoke. 'So, your husband... Bertie, is it...? Dare I ask, how has he handled it?'

'He has been wonderful.'

Meryl looked at her sharply, hearing agony in her voice.

'I'm glad he is such a support to you. Many men would have run a mile.'

Clare drank a little more wine. Bertie's noble striving to make their lives settled, to find normality within the unconventional, had indeed been wonderful. And yet in time, it had become his own project, and her private yearning for Mirren became somewhat smothered and displaced.

'So, I realise, when you came back to London, in 1941, and met me here, you'd already had your baby.'

Clare nodded.

'I must say, you disguised it very well. I had no idea. And you must have been distraught to have found yourself in that situation, and also to leave her behind.'

How could Clare explain that it had been paramount that she left when she did, and to leave Mirren safely with Anne before she did her harm.

'You could have confided in me, if you had wanted to,' Meryl said. 'In my line of work, discretion is my priority. The secrets I have kept. People come to me with all sorts of problems, and I have to be impartial, non-judgemental, which of course I would have been wholeheartedly with you. I only am sorry now that I could not have offered you any support because I simply didn't know.'

Clare, determined to buoy herself up, opened her handbag and pulled out the latest photograph Anne had sent her. Allistair must have taken it: Isla and Anne sitting on the steps of the last house on the lochan. Between them, Mirren, squashed up between the women who loved her, all of them laughing. Mirren, her curly hair in long, raggedy plaits, a limp bow at the side of her head, short socks, and sandals. And two Scottie dogs, one a complete blur, running out of shot.

'Ah, what a lovely picture. And such a pretty girl. She certainly has your looks, Clare. And something around her eyes? Well...' Meryl's sentence trailed off as if she had spoken out of turn. She knew she was probing. 'You must be very proud.'

'Proud? Yes...'

Clare trailed off. She certainly could not agree that she was proud of her own behaviour. She had left Mirren as a young baby – not even six months old. What sort of mother does that? Mirren would not know her; she had only known Anne and Isla. Fear rose inside her as she contemplated the reality of the reunion. And yet, still she wondered and hoped that Mirren would recognise her: her voice, her touch, perhaps even her smile.

Conscious suddenly of the plan to catch the sleeper, Clare checked her watch.

'I'm sorry, Meryl, it's just that Bertie is running us on a tight schedule, but I see I have an hour and a half to spare. If that's all right with you? I don't want to take up too much of your afternoon.'

'Absolutely. I will rustle up some sandwiches. I take it you're booked to have dinner on the train?'

'Yes,' Clare said, warming to the idea. The last time she took the sleeper, she'd been pregnant, nauseous, and yet hungry for most of the journey. 'It's Bertie's treat.'

With Meryl busy in the kitchen, Clare reminded herself of her objective, the whole point of this journey: to go back to Scotland and collect her daughter. She told herself to be stronger, to not let fear and waning confidence ruin everything. And yes, Bertie, her kind, loving husband, had been instrumental in all of it.

'Now, Clare,' Meryl said, ten minutes later, setting a selection of sandwiches before them. 'You know I am in the game of discretion, but I did wonder if you ever ran into Leo Bailey at Hillside?'

Clare stopped midway through a bite of her sandwich, the bread adhering to her gums. She gingerly removed it, set it down on her plate, and uttered an affirmative noise.

'I thought you might have done. There wasn't a huge number of staff there. You can guess that I recruited him, not long after you.' Meryl laughed to herself. 'The old rogue. Although when I met with him at that time, he had certainly lost his sparkle. He had lost his wife the year before, as you probably know...'

Clare bristled and continued with her sandwich. After her last encounter with Leo Bailey in Disraeli's dining room, when he had the nerve to ask her if she ever wore the perfume that he'd given her, she refused to feel entirely sorry for him.

'He was quite the expert draughtsman,' Meryl mused. 'I expect he had wanted to use his skills in a whole new environment. And I don't blame him. I knew Jane Bailey. I'd met her a few years before at BBC Club dinner-dances. One birthday, she gave me a scarf. Such a kind gesture. Such an adorable thing. I loved it. Wore it often.'

Clare gave an uneasy shudder, remembering the scarf, and the way Meryl wore it around the office with such easy panache. She took another sip of wine and found it did not taste as lavish as it had done a few minutes before.

'Here, let me top you up,' said Meryl. 'You look a little pensive. Perhaps talk of the old days at the Beeb is not such a good idea. They were harrowing times all round, truth be told.'

'That they were, Meryl,' she said, fluttering her fingers in the air, to try to convey nonchalance. 'In fact, it was my last day there, after my little farewell soiree in the office, when Broadcasting House was hit. I shall never forget that.'

'Nor I. I spent the night in the basement of the Langham Hotel with Mr Hedges. He'd been dining there too. Not an episode I wish to dwell on. At least it was a short walk to the office in the morning.'

Clare laughed lightly, delighting in the way Meryl could express humour while describing the direst of situations.

'I trust you were safely ensconced in BH basement?' Meryl asked.

'Ah, I left when the alarm went, and made it to the Underground...'

Meryl cradled her wine glass, peering into its cherry-red depths. 'That was the night it happened.'

'What? You mean when the bomb struck the BBC? I only found out a while afterwards when I was in the Highlands. They were reporting on the second hit in December. I only knew then that some staff had been killed that night in the October raid.'

'Yes, it was appalling. But also, Jane Bailey...'

'She was at Broadcasting House?' Clare leant forward. 'That evening?'

'No, no, the Baileys' flat was bombed. They lived just down the road in Marylebone.'

Clare made a supreme effort to clear her face, to pretend that she did not know this detail and to hide the unsettling horror that she'd been there, possibly minutes before it was hit.

'But actually...' Meryl's expression twisted briefly with distress, and she lit another cigarette. 'God, look at me. Christine won't be best pleased. She'll smell it as soon as she walks in. She says if I want to give up, then I should give up. And not shilly-shally around. Yes... Jane Bailey didn't die that evening. She was horribly injured, however. In a very bad way. They'd pulled her from the wreckage. Trapped on the landing outside their flat. The front of the building had come away. The roof caved in.'

Clare could picture the landing with its console and vase of chrysanthemums, the doormat with *Welcome* on it.

'Oh God...'

'Sorry, it is disturbing, isn't it? The futility and the horror return like a recurring dream. It must do for Leo, certainly. They put Jane in St Thomas's Hospital and tried to patch her up. Leo asked me if I'd visit her a day or so later. And, no question, it was all part of my duties as personnel officer, to offer support. But also, as a friend.'

'So, Jane lived,' Clare swallowed the dryness in her throat, 'for a few days?'

Meryl nodded. 'I tell you, I needed to brace myself, and strap my professional head on. She was lying in her hospital bed, dust matting her hair, even her eyelashes and in her ears. I expect the nurses tried to clean her up but must have had other more pressing things to do. Her skin was utterly grey, which I know is not a good sign. She looked elderly, and she was only thirty-five. But she was able to speak. She wanted to explain why she'd been caught in the raid. It seemed important to her. I had wondered, as most rational people would have headed straight for the shelter.'

Clare thought about how reckless she'd been that evening with her own and Mirren's unborn life, making her way along the streets while fire exploded around her.

'Jane had been delayed leaving the flat when the sirens first started as she'd been in the bath. And she loved her baths, she said, and was cross at the Luftwaffe for spoiling her evening. Leo was still at work, and she assumed he'd leave what he was doing in the studio and go down to the BH basement. You know, Clare, how hard it is trying not to look scared while going about our daily business. Anyway, Jane pointed at her handbag, there on the hospital bedside. It was dirty and battered, but seemingly rescued along with her. She wanted me to look inside.'

Clare leant forward in her seat, curiously fascinated with Leo Bailey's wife, and yet in honesty, not wanting to hear any more.

'Jane said there had been a lull in the air raid. She assumed the squadron had moved on, and so she quickly dried herself and got dressed, grabbed her handbag as any sensible woman might, and opened the front door. And there, she said, was the damnedest thing. A bottle of Chanel No 5. Just lying there on her doormat.'

Clare shifted in her seat, shivering as a chill notched its way up her spine.

'Jane was stunned, she said, and she had laughed,' Meryl went on, 'thinking for one bizarre moment that it had been dropped by a bomb. She went back inside, set it on her kitchen table and stared at it.'

'What?' Clare exhaled. 'Why didn't she get out of the building?'

'I know; in times of crisis, one can do such strange things. I think it was the shock. Such a peculiar thing to find on one's own doorstep. But she soon came to her senses, she said. She put the bottle in her handbag, again, not really thinking straight, and left the flat. And the bomb fell.'

'Is that when—' Clare began, her tongue sticking to the roof of her mouth, 'when she was injured...?'

Meryl nodded. 'Funny thing is, there in her handbag, the bottle looked unscathed. Good as new. Not even opened. And yes, I am wondering too, if she hadn't stopped to pick it up, she would have been out of the mansion block and down in the shelter. There is one just across the street. Oh, Clare.' Meryl bitterly ground out her half-smoked cigarette. 'Her confusion, her pain was hard to bear.'

A strange weightlessness took over Clare's body, as if she was skating over the top of everything Meryl had told her, not daring to look down and take it in. But she knew she must. She must face what she did. She left the perfume on the Baileys' doormat as a prank, yes, and as revenge. And it had made Jane Bailey hesitate, made her ponder, made her think her husband may be involved with another woman. For perfume is such a *particular* thing.

'Clare, you look terribly distressed. I know, it is an awful tale to tell,' said Meryl. 'But remember, you have come through it, the war, either scathed or unscathed. We both have. And you have your husband; you have your Mirren.'

'But Jane died...'

'I think my visit must have taken it out of her.'

'Were you with her?' Clare heard herself ask faintly, not wishing to be party to any more.

'No, but while I was there, she began not to be able to speak.

And I know now, the more noise someone makes, the more likely they are to live. Something seemed very wrong. The nurse came to give her morphine and asked me to leave. She died that evening.'

Clare sat up straight on Meryl's sofa, her face frozen in shock. 'I have to go.'

'Of course, I do rattle on.' Meryl sighed. 'It is certainly bringing it all back to me. We must concentrate on happier times. Your future with your little girl.'

Clare wondered if her expression, her suppressed horror would give her away. That Meryl would guess exactly what she had done. She grabbed her hat and Meryl handed over her coat, saying how lovely it had been, and she wished her a safe journey. But Clare barely heard what she said. The brutal recognition of the consequences of that terrible night felt like a whip lashing around her head, to catch her, sting her and snare her. She wanted to flinch and duck, while bleak shame, while guilt folded in on her.

Meryl kept up her polite conversation all the way down to the front door, and Clare seemed to float down the stairs, with no feeling in her legs. She must have smiled brightly, cheerily said her farewells, responding with a chuckle as her former boss asked her to say hello to Bonnie Scotland for her. But walking off along the gentile Hampstead cobbles, her spirit drained, her smile fallen clean away. And her body turned numb. She felt cut off from Meryl's jolly expectation, separated from normality.

For her world had never been ordinary, and she believed it never could be.

25

CLARE

The Highlands, Summer 1948

Allistair drove them away from the Royal Highland Hotel and out of Inverness through light rain that moved like a white veil, obscuring the hills and the Great Glen one moment, revealing fragments of dark-green and brown the next, feeding the burns and the Falls of Foyers, and the black water of the loch below.

'You'll no' leave too soon, will you, Clare? You'll stay a while, won't you?' Allistair said. 'That's what Anne would like. So, we can all have time to get used to the idea. And make it easier for Mirren, too.'

'Of course, Allistair,' Clare said, sitting in the back. 'That is the plan.'

But she wondered what the rules would be, and who would make them up. None of the grown-ups were truly prepared. And who would ever be equipped to make such decisions? She had no idea how much or how little Mirren knew. What Anne and Allistair had told her. Clare had, over the years, written sweet notes to her daughter, but never received a reply. She tried not to let this bother

her; after all, a young child would find it difficult, would have to be coached to respond to a letter to a stranger. Anne may have not had the time, and Clare simply felt gratified that she had made the effort, laying the foundations with Mirren for this day.

'Ah, good *auld* Scottish rain,' Bertie piped up from the front seat, as the wipers lashed across the windscreen.

'When the weather's bonnie, it truly is bonnie. I assure you, it's not always like this,' Allistair said, sounding prickly, and not his usual, affable self.

Clare understood her brother-in-law's discomfort. She watched through the car window as the hills peeled away from horizon to horizon and the long road along Loch Ness brought her nearer to her daughter, her apprehension mounting with every mile they passed.

Bertie turned his head to look at Clare and said conversationally, 'So, do you think Mirren will remember you, darling?'

Allistair glanced sideways at him in surprise.

Clare bristled. Had Bertie forgotten what she'd told him?

'No, Bertie. She won't remember me. She was not even six months old when I left.'

Her husband nodded vaguely and seemed to drift, his mind wandering even as she spoke about her daughter. Doing her best to disguise her anger, her disappointment, she turned her face to the rain-dotted window. The landscape emerged from the misted rain to greet her like an old friend.

Her mind cleared, and Cal walked through it. She had been expecting him. Blurting out her half-truth yesterday to Meryl about having met someone in Scotland had been on reflex, had come from a closed-off corner inside her. And now a light seemed to glow there, illuminating possibility. Being back in the Highlands, within miles of Cal and his life, his home, she enjoyed the satisfaction that he'd be sheltering from the same rain. For a moment, she pictured the way he had looked at her, his gaze like a hook. She wondered if she should ever witness such a moment again.

Clare shook herself. She did not want to walk down that path, for Bertie sat in the passenger seat, passing the conventional time of day with Allistair. Cal and Bertie came from different places, and she saw them in different lights, that's all, she assured herself. Cal, of course, a lot older. He must be in his late thirties now. But his maturity and his presence had awakened something, in those short months that she'd known him, of which she previously had not been aware. A grown-up, revelatory place, where she could be simply Clare.

She corrected herself: didn't Bertie help her do this too? After all, according to her father, before he'd even met him, he was a 'capital chap'.

Allistair turned onto the avenue of aspens and Clare's anxiety intensified to excruciating levels. Catching sight of the manse, solid and grey against the rain-washed sky, she said quickly and inconsequentially, her words juddering, 'Oh, Allistair, these trees have grown.'

Neither man responded. And she guessed they both felt as rotten with nerves as she did.

The sound of the car tyres on the gravel drew Anne and Isla to the front door. They sheltered under the porch, their beaming faces and instinctive waving of hands deflecting the tension. As soon as Allistair cranked the hand brake, Clare sprang from the car with sudden joy and found herself enveloped in hugs, with the Scottie dogs bouncing around for attention.

Everyone looked a little older, more ragged around the edges. Isla appeared wider, the plaid pattern on her trousers stretched somewhat, and Anne's usually elegant frame stockier. And Clare knew she must seem entirely different to the girl who had left seven years before. She hoped, these days, a touch smarter and better groomed. She introduced Bertie to Anne and Isla, and noticed they appeared relieved that he seemed a nice, ordinary man.

Isla grasped her hand. 'You'll be staying a wee while, won't you?'

'Yes, yes, Isla,' Clare assured her, wondering at everyone's concern that she'd abscond without warning. 'That's what we said.'

'Let's not stand on ceremony,' said Anne, cheerfully. 'Let's get ourselves inside, out of the rain.'

Despite her smile, Anne gestured formally, showing Clare into the house she once lived in as she might a stranger, while the men made a fuss getting the suitcases out of the boot. Clare could see the detachment she dreaded from her sister. The reluctance to lock eyes, looking everywhere but at her when she took her raincoat and hung it on the hallstand, reminding her of their mother. But Clare did not wish, or have the capacity, to ponder it.

Following Anne across the hall and into the parlour, she glanced around, expecting a child to be waiting for her, perched on a chair, or standing on the rug in readiness.

'Isla, will you serve tea to the gentlemen in the kitchen?' said Anne mechanically, as if trying to cling on to civility and control. 'Clare and I can have ours in the parlour presently.'

Isla bustled Allistair and Bertie through to the back of the house, and Anne indicated that Clare should sit. She closed the door.

'I had hoped for the rain to stop,' Anne said, reverting to the safety of the weather. 'Things always seem better when the sun is on the hills.'

'Anne, I wonder where—' Clare began.

'I hope your journey was smooth, and your room at the Royal Highland satisfactory. They've been doing it up recently.'

'Are we going to—?'

'I know. You want to see her. She's upstairs.' Her braced shoulders fell, as if she'd that moment given in. 'I thought you may want tea first.'

'No. No tea.'

She sighed, seeming thoroughly disappointed. 'Wait here, then. I will fetch her.'

Clare sat alone for some minutes in the room where she had spent long, pale, midsummer nights cradling Mirren, still filled with the same furniture, ticking clock, and painted screen by the door, the familiar view from the window. Clare's ears prickled when she heard a door close above and two pairs of footsteps treading lightly along the landing, coming down the stairs, and she thought her churning, smouldering stomach would burn its way through her flesh.

The door opened and they appeared, Mirren walking hesitantly in front of Anne who had each hand on the girl's shoulders, coaxing and pushing her forward into the room, as if presenting her to Clare. And Clare, acutely aware that, like the aspens, Mirren would have grown, didn't expect such a change from the last photograph sent to her, the one in her handbag taken at the beginning of the school holidays. Of course, she ought to know; children alter all the time. And found herself staring. Her daughter looked taller than she expected, a little fuller around her face, and yet her limbs appeared gangly, as if they had not caught up.

It took everything Clare had to stay seated, praying that she would appear friendly and loving and in no way formidable.

'Hello, Mirren, I'm Clare. I'm your mum.'

She had practised the phrase in her mind for months, for years, and yet it sounded stilted and rather too loud. She held out her arms, gesturing, offering herself to the little girl, as if this would soothe her primal wound.

Mirren kept still and said nothing. Her shoulders twitched as if to shake off her aunt's grip and her face stiffened with a wide-eyed, fearful look. And Clare, conscious that whatever she said or did may frighten Mirren and do her harm, mirrored her daughter, staying motionless but with her arms held wide.

Anne tapped the child, prompting her to move forward. And when Mirren at last took the two or three steps across the rug and reluctantly leaned with the top half of her body, Clare wrapped her arms around her, mindful of not squeezing too hard for she felt so fragile. She cradled her, breathed her in, relishing the moment she'd both dreamt of and feared, and exhaled hot tears down her face.

Ignoring Clare's silent weeping, Anne asked, with quiet, expectant authority, 'What do you say to your mum, Mirren?'

Mirren uttered that she didn't know, wriggled free, darted across the room and sat on the floor behind the painted screen. In comical fashion, as if playing and not hiding from Clare and the gravity of the encounter, she bobbed her head around and back again.

'Well, we can chat like this if you like,' said Clare brightly, coaxing her. 'Do you like the screen? All those lovely animals... It's a little like hide and seek, isn't it? Except I know where you are.'

Anne perched on the edge of the other armchair, as if on red alert, while Clare asked Mirren about what she liked to do best, what books she was reading, and did she enjoy her school. The little girl put her head around to give her answer, or not, as she saw fit, and then retreated. And in the silences, Anne chipped in with details.

'And who is your best friend, Mirren?' Clare asked.

Mirren's face popped around, and she even offered a smile. 'Gregor McInnis.'

And in saying the classic Scottish name, Clare detected her daughter's light accent. She felt mildly surprised, but in an instant, realised she shouldn't be, for even Anne now spoke with the odd burr here and there.

'Ah, so that's Cal McInnis's nephew,' said Clare. 'I remember seeing him as a little boy in a pushchair at Fort Augustus. When you were in my tummy.'

Mirren didn't seem to absorb the last bit of what Clare said. She shifted cross-legged around the edge of the screen, her face earnest with puzzled sadness. 'But if I go with you, will I no' see Gregor again?'

'Oh my goodness, yes, Mirren, of course you will.' Clare had expected a question like that, and hoped she would be able to soften her daughter's fears. For there would be many more questions like that to come. 'He can visit us in Amersham.'

But she hadn't expected the doubt in her daughter's eyes, the colour and quality of which were the image of Leo Bailey's.

'Yes, dear,' Anne leapt in. 'And you can come back to the lochan for school holidays. For Easter. For Christmas and Hogmanay.'

Hearing Anne commandeering all the family events, Clare stiffened, but she persevered.

'So, Mirren, you must be nearly at the end of your summer holidays now?'

'Will I have to go to a new school?' she asked, looking at her aunt for the answer.

'Now, Mirren,' said Anne. 'We did talk about this, didn't we?'

'Bertie, out there in the kitchen, he found a lovely school for you to go to,' said Clare. 'And I will take you there every day. And collect you afterwards.'

'Who's Bertie?'

'He's my husband, my dear.'

'My dad?'

'No, no...'

Mirren shrugged, as if holding her confusion within her frame. And Clare realised that they all had a very long way to go. And, yes, Bertie may well have found an excellent school, but Mirren would have to go there and endure it, reason with it, day in, day out, as she would have to suffer this awful muddle, day in, day out, in her own secret child's heart.

'Well, Mirren, I have a little surprise,' Clare persevered cheerfully. 'I have a gift for you.'

She dipped into her handbag for the silk pouch, walked over to where Mirren sat on the floor, squatted down and handed it to her. The child beamed as she stroked the softness of the fabric, poked her finger into the gathered top and tugged it open. The earrings fell into her palm. She looked up at Clare in astonishment.

'They are my earrings, but I want you to have them,' Clare said. 'Do you remember, I mentioned them in a little note I wrote to you a while ago?'

Mirren looked at Anne, puzzled. Anne gave a minute shake of her head.

Mirren held the earrings up to the light, the Scottish marble glimmering mysteriously, and she looked past them to gaze at Clare's face. And Clare sensed an exchange of trust between them, that Mirren may be on the way to understanding why Clare had visited.

'Show me, Mirren,' said Anne, holding out her hand, and the child dutifully gave them to her. 'They are beautiful, Clare. But a bit too grown-up for her. She hasn't got pierced ears.'

'Aw, but I like them,' said Mirren, her mouth twisting in disappointment.

'I'll keep them safe for now. Until she's old enough. You'll soon learn, Clare,' Anne said, flippantly.

Clare shrank back into her chair, recoiling from the first time in their adult lives that Anne had chastised her and put her down. It gave her the same feeling as sitting on the draughty stairs at home in Harrow and hearing something about herself that she did not want to know.

Controlling the tremor in her voice, her stomach flipping with mortification, Clare said, 'In a while, Mirren, you can show me your room, if you like. And your toys. You can bring whatever you like. But in the meantime,' she shot a hard look at her sister, 'I need some air.'

Anne, noticing Clare's distress, seemed relieved, welcoming the idea. 'Shall I fetch Bertie to go with you?'

Clare shook her head. She didn't want Bertie; she wanted someone else. The thought struck her like a blow on the face. She wanted Cal.

She went out to the hallway and fumbled her way into her mackintosh, aware of how disappointed she felt that Cal hadn't been standing on the front porch with the others to welcome her back – after all, the only other person who knew some of the truth of Mirren's conception was Emily, and Emily took it to the grave. This linked Clare to Cal, even as he carried on with his life, elsewhere. This felt such a comfort to her: that he existed; that he sometimes, perhaps, thought of her. And yet she felt too shy to ask after him.

Anne, beside her, finding her own coat, said, 'Clare, the rain has eased. I'll come with you. And, Mirren...' The little girl stopped on the threshold of the parlour, as if she had wanted to follow them. 'Isla's taken the dogs into the back garden now. Go find Jock and Jess. On you go.'

* * *

As the sisters walked to the lochan, the silence felt like static hissing between them. Clare sensed Anne ruminating, about to begin, stopping herself. They found the fallen log where they'd sat when Clare had first arrived, pregnant and reeling with shame.

Looking out across the water, the past rolled up to meet her like the miniature waves reaching the lochan shore.

'I can't believe how incredibly grim this is,' Clare admitted, breaking the spell, her sigh dragging out of her. She felt, then, that they were sisters again. 'I thought that I would feel happy, coming back here, at last...'

Anne breathed out, pleased that Clare had spoken first. 'Oh, Lumen, I wonder if we are both feeling as distressed as each other.'

Her pet-name sang to Clare, gave her courage. 'I love Mirren, you know that, and want her to be safe and happy.' Clare hesitated. 'But I stupidly imagined it being easier than this. I've waited so long...'

'I hate to say it, Clare: I think it feels odd because Mirren doesn't know you.' Anne spoke cautiously, but with reason. 'And you plan to take her away from her home.'

Clare flinched at the truth, and panic simmered. Was Anne going to stop her, keep Mirren for herself?

'But I wrote to her, didn't I? As soon as I guessed she would be able to read. Little cheerful notes, every so often, on her birthday, at Christmas, so she would get to know who I was. Not necessarily what I was to her. But that I was *Clare*.'

Anne shifted on the seat, clasped her hands on her lap, wrung them inside out.

'I didn't give them to her.'

Clare felt the log shift underneath her, as if everything she had tried to build for herself and Mirren, their futures, had fallen away. A sickening, tingling spread over her skin, tightening like a vice at the back of her neck.

'Oh, Anne, why did you do that?!' she wailed. 'I wanted her to *know* me, to be ready to meet me. I can't believe you kept them from her. Tell me you kept them safe?'

'Yes, I kept them. They are safe. But I didn't want Mirren to come to expect them, to have her hopes raised, and then you not come back into her life. For whatever reason. There never seemed to be a proper reason, one a child would understand, why you weren't here with her. I wanted to protect her. It all seemed so unstable.'

'Things have been beyond my control,' Clare uttered defensively, her fury weakening.

'And you can see how she asks questions I cannot answer. Only you can.' Anne turned to look at her. 'About her father.'

Clare lowered her head. 'I simply can't talk about him, Anne. I don't want to.'

Her sister's tone lowered in sympathy, switched to fear. She tried to catch Clare's eye.

'Why? Was it not— did he—?'

Staring out over the water, Clare said evenly, 'I don't wish to repeat myself.'

Anne's face flushed and she uttered her apologies.

Inhaling hard, Clare said, 'I know that I must have hurt our parents terribly. And you too, along the way. I don't think any one of us coped at all with the...' She wanted to say pain but knew it would sound too self-serving. 'The utter *disgrace*.'

'But we still loved you, Lumen,' Anne said, tears pooling in her eyes.

'*You* did,' Clare said churlishly.

'Our parents cared. That's why they reacted, and continue to react, like they did. But you must know that what we planned, what we all did, was the best for Mirren. And, I think for you, too. You were so young.'

Young, foolish, and easily persuaded, Clare admitted to herself, her bitterness spoiling whatever joy she may have clung on to, arriving back here at the last house on the lochan.

'I see that for Mirren to grow up here, with all of this, all around her...' Clare said, raising her hand as if to touch the hills on the horizon. 'Was so much better for Mirren than any alternative I could have offered. The war didn't help matters.'

'And times have moved on,' said Anne, ever sensible. 'The folks around here have accepted Mirren. You must understand, this is her world. And, Clare, you stayed away far too long.'

'I was doing important war work.'

Anne glanced at her.

'Which you know I can never talk about,' she added.

'That aside, the war has been over for three years.'

Clare faltered, not sure why she had to go so far to explain herself. After all, she was Mirren's mother.

'But I wrote to Mirren in the meantime, and you saw fit to keep the letters from her.'

'I told you, I had my reasons...'

'But I had to keep Mirren secret, and I lead a life of confusion. I had to shut her away in a little box and not tell anyone. I didn't know where I stood. Anywhere. It has been so immensely...' The last word caught in her throat. 'Gruelling.' Clare stood up, exasperated, angry, and silently imploring the past to stop its endless spooling through her mind. 'But that time is over, Anne. It is all over. Mirren needs her mother.' And something whispered in her ear, reminding her. Hadn't she made a vow with Mirren, and herself, to take care of her daughter?

Anne peered up at her, lines of tears streaking from her eyes. Clare looked away, unable to take in her sister's agony. She watched wisps of low rain cloud, delicate and white, folding over the crest of the far hills, moving towards them.

'I think, Clare, that what you mean,' Anne began, her sentence breaking as she struggled, '...is that you need Mirren. And I know what that means to you.'

Clare conceded, feeling age-old guilt again. 'Yes, Anne, but what about you—'

Anne raised her hand to stop her. 'Never mind that. I know, Lumen, because I feel it too.' She gave a little cry of pain. 'But I know... I *have* to know, and accept, because we agreed, that although this is killing me, that my tenure is over.'

'What are you saying? Do you mean...?'

'I mean that you should have Mirren. Of course you should; that is why you are here. That was always our intention.' Anne swallowed, her mouth contorting as if it hurt her to speak. 'Take Mirren home.'

* * *

Inside the manse, the atmosphere stretched and sparked with tension and even Isla looked wary as they came back through the front door. Clare went to sit with Bertie in the parlour and Anne announced that she would start preparing lunch and that everyone could sit around the table as a family.

'Clare, you and Bertie are in your old bedroom if you want to take your suitcase up. Just along from Mirren's bedroom. We've already packed her case, by the way, chosen her favourite things.'

'Yes, but do remember, Anne, that we do have to take everything back on the train,' said Bertie.

Anne turned her head quickly and headed out to the kitchen.

Bertie looked at Clare. 'That's right, isn't it, darling? We're staying here? We're not taking her back to the hotel today?'

Clare nodded, but said, 'Leave our suitcase down here for now.' Her contradiction matched the tangled confusion tightening inside her.

She could hear Isla's voice in the kitchen, Anne's muffled

response, and the gentle clatter of utensils, the running of the tap, Allistair suggesting they put the kettle on again.

Mirren popped her head around the parlour door and crept into the room tentatively.

'Here she is,' Bertie said playfully. 'What have you been doing, young lady?'

'Looking at the flowers,' she said. 'But I came in because it's started raining. Jock and Jess are all wet and have to stay in the back.'

Clare reached her hands out to her daughter, smiling broadly, and wanting to weep with joy. She had not yet heard Mirren be so expressive. She'd missed her first words, her first steps, her first smile, and the thought of it cracked her open.

'Come here, then, Mirren, and let me check. I want to see if you have any pollen on your nose,' she said. 'My Great-Aunt Emily told me once that when I came in from the garden when I was a little girl, I often had a little dusting of pollen. And she knew I'd been going round smelling the flowers.'

The child lingered by the door, glancing from Clare to Bertie and back again, collecting trust. Clare gestured again and she moved closer to Clare's armchair, taking pigeon steps, and tilted her chin for Clare to examine her. How her baby's face had bloomed but not altered much. How she had grown and yet endured as the exquisite human Clare had borne. The child leaned in further, her large eyes solemn and hopeful. There, so close that Clare could smell her sweet, little-girl scent, her gaze pierced Clare and turned her inside out.

Mirren waited patiently for her to tell her she had pollen on her nose.

'Ah, nothing today,' Clare faltered. 'Must be because Anne and Allistair have lavender out there. Those plants don't have much pollen, you see, that can land on your nose.'

Mirren wrinkled her face playfully, rubbing the back of her hand over her nose as if she had an itch.

'Well, never mind,' Clare said. Her hands began to shake, a vibration through her body. 'Ah, see the way you've plaited your hair...' she gabbled. 'Your Auntie Anne and I had to do that too, to stop our hair looking a fright. You, see, we all have the same hair.'

Mirren reached a fingertip to touch Clare's hair, behind her ear, locking her with her fascinated stare. With Leo's stare. Clare shut her eyes, telling herself that Mirren only looked that way at her because any child might stare like that. Mirren didn't know what Clare had done. That she nearly brought harm to her. Had harmed other people, many people, and one woman in particular.

'Are you my mum?' Mirren asked. She turned to look at Bertie. 'Are you my dad?'

'Ah well, young lady...' Bertie started.

Mirren looked at Clare and stated, 'But you are my mum.'

Clare's ears filled with a muffled scream, as if emitted by someone standing behind a door. The past crashed into her despite her will to deflect it. The London air raid filled her memory with fire. She twisted to the side and pressed her face into the arm of the chair, cradling her head against the cushion. The reality of her deed, leaving the perfume on Jane Bailey's doormat and luring her to her death, snapped through her mind. The scream had been her own.

'Clare? Clare?'

Bertie stood over her, his hand on her shoulder. She cringed away from his touch, wanting to scream again but this time heard only silence.

A little girl's voice uttered, 'Mum?' and Clare had no idea if Mirren had spoken, or indeed she had, pleading for her own mother's attention, her mother's kindness and understanding.

'I have to leave,' she said and struggled to her feet, twisting away from Bertie's embrace. 'I must leave this house.'

Clare darted across the hallway and out the front door.

The rain drifted in layers, the fine, cooling spray sprinkling her face. She raised her hands to capture the drops, wanting to feel something other than brutal, blinding shock. But the tidings Meryl Stanford had imparted to her about Jane Bailey surfaced and branded itself into her insides.

Astonishingly, it felt like old news, something for which she had been to blame for many years, even though she'd only known this awful fact about herself for twenty-four hours. Her actions on the night of the air raid sank to the dark place inside her where she kept all the maps of towns and cities she helped make for Bomber Command.

She heard shouting inside the house, Anne yelling, 'Mirren, did you not hear what I said? Go to your room!'

Isla and Bertie came towards her across the gravel, with Anne and Allistair following, hurrying down the steps.

'Hen, hen, whatever's the matter?' Isla asked. 'What's this to-do?'

'I can't do this,' Clare whispered. 'I can't do this to my child.' But her own voice inside her head scolded, *But you promised.*

Bertie, at her shoulder, looked her in the eye questioningly. 'What on earth, Clare?'

'Mirren's upset,' Anne said. 'Who screamed? What have you done?'

'Perhaps we should go to the hotel for now,' Bertie said, trying for appeasement. 'Come back another day.'

'No, Bertie,' Clare said through her teeth, 'I want to leave this place. Need to leave. Altogether.'

'Oh no, no, no, Clare!' Anne cried, in a flash of pure rage. 'Not acceptable. Not good enough. Think what you're doing to that child. Back and forth, back and forth. Your life is settled now, and you want to take her back, so now we all have to suffer? All *our* lives upended? What do you think you're playing at!' She gasped, her anger searing the damp air. 'What about Mirren? I've had enough of it.'

Catching his wife gently by the shoulders, Allistair said, 'Come now, hen, that's a bit harsh.'

'Annie, Annie,' Isla soothed. 'I know it's upsetting. We're all upset.'

'Why are you doing this, darling,' Bertie asked, 'after everything we've talked about?'

The fine rain dripped from the ends of Clare's hair, sending her curls into frizz. A dusting of minute drops clung to the knit of Isla's jumper. Clare stayed mute, focusing on the little, crystalline dots, trying to shake off the indignity of facing her family, surrounding her, talking at her, all at once, their eyes rolling in anger, bitterness, and confusion. How could she blame them? She had vowed to Mirren that she would take care of her, that she would come back for her. But by doing so, she would wreck her life.

Allistair sighed. 'I'll run you back to Inverness.'

'I knew this would happen,' Anne hissed. 'You're going home without her.'

Clare wiped the rain from her cheeks. 'I simply can't do it, Anne. I'm sorry.'

'Oh, stop crying, Clare,' Anne said, unrecognisable with anger. 'This is your own doing.'

'I'm not. It's not...'

Bertie took her arm and led her to the parked car, where Allistair busily hoisted their suitcases into the boot. Bertie opened the back door for her and leaned over to quickly shake Allistair's hand in an instinctive man-to-man ritual. Isla hurried back inside for her coat and passed it to her, her face rigid with alarm.

But Clare remained where she stood, letting the fine rain soak into her clothes.

'If you're going, go!' Anne cried, bracing herself against Isla, the smaller woman supporting her.

Clare glanced up at the manse, with its stone façade stained with rain, the drainpipes dripping. Movement at an upstairs window caught her eye and Mirren's pale face appeared, her eyes wide and fearful, as if watching the grown-ups play out some dreadful sketch. Clare stared back at Mirren, gathering the courage to endure the pain slicing through her middle and sever herself from her daughter.

Mirren moved closer to the glass, her breath misting the pane, and Clare heard a muffled cry: 'Mum!'

Anne jolted, turned on her heel and dashed back into the house.

'Coming Mirren,' she called. 'I'm coming.'

Mirren disappeared from the window and Clare, her legs giving way, gripped the car door and got into the back seat.

Bertie slammed the door behind her.

Settled in the passenger seat, he glanced over his shoulder.

'I'll ask again, Clare,' he said, evenly. 'Why are you doing this?'

Clare simply gave a shake of her head, unable to tell her husband that he had never known her, never understood her; that their life together had ended.

Allistair fired the engine and they sat in brittle silence while he completed a complicated three-point turn and finally drove away under the aspens. They headed off on the lane over the heath, the car bumping along through the wide, saturated landscape.

'Just let this car pass...' Allistair said as he slowed down to pull over, raising his hand in acknowledgement. 'Ach, if it isn't Cal McInnis. Over for a wee cup of tea.'

Clare uttered a cry of surprise, wanting to scream at Allistair to stop the car. She grabbed hold of the door handle, ready to spring out, run to Cal, sit beside him as his passenger and go with him wherever he was going. But her body froze, checking her, protecting her from making matters worse. After all, what would everyone think of her then? She held fast, stiffened in her seat, clutching the edge of it with both hands.

Through his own rain-soaked car window, Cal spotted her. He turned his head in disbelief, his eyes wide, his mouth opening in shock as his car continued past her along the lane. Allistair revved the engine, crunched the gears, and drove her away.

The battle over, and utterly vanquished, Clare sat back and stared around her to drink in the familiar views for which, she felt sure, would be the last time she'd be seeing them. But the Scottish rain, moving in its persistent way across the land, obscured everything she longed to see.

26

MIRREN

The Highlands, Summer 1985

Mirren picked up the service sheet from the little shelf in front of her.

In Memoriam: Isla Mirren Fraser MacKenzie

Tears shimmered in her eyes and she dabbed them with her handkerchief, unaware until that moment that she shared Isla's middle name. Kirstine, next to her on the pew, squeezed her arm, and Mirren gave her a watery smile.

She had never seen her daughter head to toe in black before. It should not have suited her, for she was far too young for widow's weeds. But Kirstine's creamy McInnis skin radiated in contrast, her lips tinted a discreet rose, and in that moment, the tailored jacket and skirt made her a stylish young woman, no longer Mirren's teenage girl. Kirstine smiled knowingly and pointed to her own earlobe. On reflex, Mirren tapped the Scottish marble earrings she'd put on that morning, checking they were safely in place.

Gregor leaned in on her other side. 'You all right, hen?'

'Silly question,' she said, but despite her grief, she felt bolstered by his quiet presence at her side, the weight of his thigh against hers, how splendid he looked in McInnis tartan, with his bare knees crammed up against the front of the pew. The look in his eye told her that she didn't have to explain herself, that there was no need for any words. That everything would be all right. After all, he had walked her in and out of the school gates, silently and safely for all those years.

He lowered his voice, mindful that Anne and Allistair sat at the end of the pew in front.

'Have you told your aunt yet that you found the box of letters at Isla's?'

Mirren shook her head.

He gave her a puzzled look. 'I thought you didn't want any more secrets. No more things brushed under the carpet.'

'It has all been a bit too much, Gregor,' she whispered. 'There has to be the right time. I want to wait until after the funeral. When all this is over. When things will be more settled.'

He nodded, agreeing. 'When you do so, and if you want me to, I will come with you. I just want to make sure you are okay.'

Mirren glanced past Gregor at his uncle, sitting on his other side, reading the service sheet. She remembered the journey in the car back from school, with Gregor in the back seat and Cal saying that she should memorise her address should she ever get lost. But learning 'the last house on the lochan' seemed so easy that she never thought she would. And yet, she obviously had, somewhere along the way.

'Thank you,' she whispered, resting her hand on Gregor's knee, touching the fine woollen weave of his kilt. He folded his hand over hers.

'And by the way,' she said. 'I am not lost any more.'

The church door creaked on its hinges and Mirren steeled herself not to look around, fearful of having her hopes dashed. But it was Isla's daughters, with matching heather corsages pinned to lapels, walking into the church. All into their sixties and grand-mothers themselves, the women settled their families at the front on the other side of the aisle, arranging and rearranging genera-tions of offspring.

'Who is that elderly man?' Mirren asked Gregor, noticing a frail, tearful gentleman with a geriatric tremor being helped to his seat by one of the daughters.

'Ah, Isla's husband,' he said. 'The infamous Mr MacKenzie.'

'Heavens,' uttered Mirren.

'His respect for her went the distance,' said Gregor. 'Despite the fact they hated each other.'

The church door opened, closed again, and villagers from Foyers, folk from Fort Augustus and pals from Inverness filed in, all for Isla, their collective murmuring rising as they filled the pews. And still, Mirren dared not look around. For she had not told Gregor that she kept another secret connected with the discovery of Isla's letters. Something else she had failed to mention to Anne.

The vicar, standing in his pulpit, gave a signal and the organ wheezed into a rendition of 'Amazing Grace'. Everyone straggled unevenly to their feet, and the coffin was carried in. Perched on the stand in front of the altar, the box looked plain, modest, and patient. And, Mirren decided, so unlike Isla.

She fumbled with the hymn book, finding the right page, her fingertips useless in her best gloves. Tiny words smudged and reeled. The musky old-book scent prickling her nostrils. Why did they always print it so small?

The vicar began his address. 'Dearly beloved, we are here to celebrate the life of our sister, Isla. In doing so, we remember the past. And it is important to do so. The past is a place we all return to, not only in our dreams, whether in joy or pain,' he said. 'It is the only place we will all in time belong.'

The creaking door announced itself again, louder this time, now that the congregation had settled, and quick footsteps of a late-comer hurried to the nearest pew.

Better that they arrive late than not at all, thought Mirren. And whoever it may be, she felt sure they would be more than welcome in this little Highland kirk.

Mirren kept her eyes fixed on Isla's coffin, imagining what she might have to say about it all.

27

CLARE

The Highlands, Summer 1985

Sitting at the back of the church, Clare slipped out as soon as the service finished. She walked down to the stone wall of the kirkyard on its rise above the marshy shore of Loch Mhor, the water shimmering in late-summer sunlight. Here, five miles or so from the lochan, and the same distance from Foyers, the gravestones seemed to only bear three different surnames: Fraser, McInnis, MacKenzie. Clare watched the people who owned those surnames file out of Isla's funeral service, mingling around the porch, exchanging consolation, all belonging here.

Memories of Isla spooled through her mind, like snapshots and old reels. Walking the Scottie dogs around the lochan in a summer squall, the roses at Lochan Cottage white against a stormy sky. Laughter in front of the fire and tots of whisky – ginger wine for Clare while she was expecting – in the silence of a winter's night. The row of empty bottles by the hearth, containing the angel's share.

'Dear Isla,' Clare whispered, breathing deeply on tender Highland air. 'I am sorry I was so late.'

The dogs, descendants of the originals and always called Jock and Jess whether boy or girl, sat obedient and alert, held on the leash by a young child, possibly one of the Isla's great-grandchildren. Both Scotties had a sad, seeking look in their eyes, even though everyone gathered around and made a fuss of them.

Clare waited in a curiously enjoyable, detached daze as Isla's close family filed down to the open grave, following the coffin. She caught sight of Anne and Allistair, ageing well, she noted, and holding back to let the daughters go first. And there, in splendid kilt and with his shock of silver hair, Cal McInnis.

Clare raised her hand instinctively as if to catch his attention but pulled it back instantly.

The other man, also kilted, she assumed must be Gregor, the image of Cal as a younger man, except with glasses and darker, greying hair. Beside Gregor stood a young girl, and there on his other side, Mirren, no longer in her dreams and in the depths of her wretched regret. Mirren, looking sad, yes, but animated, compelling, and beloved. Oh, thought Clare, and her beautiful hair.

Mirren's letter had arrived at the Amersham cottage not more than a week ago. And even though Clare had travelled overnight, all the way to be here today, she could not quite believe that she had made it, that she stood under the same sky and within shouting distance of the one person she had thought about, had longed for, every livelong day.

'God have mercy,' Clare breathed, reaching behind her to grip the stone wall.

She steadied herself, wanting no more to feel so separated and alone. The people here all belonged here; had a sense of belonging. Whereas she had always felt only *longing*.

The burial was over, Isla planted in the dirt-black grave. Mild air across from faraway hills ruffled the wreaths arranged around the hole and the groups began to disperse.

One person peeled away from the others.

Clare took a sharp breath, tried to compose her face, stop herself blinking so much, as Cal McInnis strode towards her, weaving his way through headstones, the pleats of his kilt buoyant in the breeze.

'Ach, you're still alive, then, Miss Clare Ashby,' he said.

She laughed her own greeting, grateful to him for lightening the mood, wondering whether to correct him and say that, even though she had been divorced for many years, she had kept Bertie's surname.

She found herself beaming at his lovely, peaceful face.

'Did Isla ever mention to you?' she confessed, matching his jovial tone. 'That we had written to each other over the years.'

'Of course I knew, hen,' he said. 'I am the postmaster, after all. I notice postmarks.' He gave her a brief, and yet considered, glance. 'Aye, I knew.' The breeze seemed to pluck the wistful words from his mouth. 'In any case,' he brightened, 'I'm retired now.'

My goodness, Clare thought, he looked good on it.

'I don't think Anne knew,' Clare said. 'About Isla and I writing to each other. Perhaps one too many secrets in this family, don't you think?'

Cal contemplated her, the light in his eyes changing. Gold flecks brightening against darker brown. She thought of it too. Their own secret: the bond that linked them. Cal had saved Mirren's life down on the Loch Ness shore, and indeed her own. And yet she knew, all these years later, they would probably never talk about it; something so momentous would be diminished if put into words.

'It has taken you a lot of courage to come here today,' he said, his voice deepening. 'And I am glad you did. But then I have always thought of you as the bravest woman I know.'

At the corner of her eye, Clare saw Anne, Allistair, Gregor, Mirren and Kirstine, oblivious to her presence, walking away toward their cars.

'But I'm frightened now,' she said, her pulse beating at the base of her throat. 'I want to tell her how sorry, how very sorry I am. I broke my promise.'

'I knew you were sorry,' he said, 'and I can see that you are.'

'Why did I allow this to happen to me?' she asked, the unbearable trembling reaching her fingertips.

Cal could not answer her. 'We've all missed you, Clare,' he said. 'Although many of us have kept it to themselves, one of us has said it out loud.'

Clare didn't grasp what he meant, the urgency and agony of her yearning running ahead of her.

'I need to see her,' she said. 'I want to talk to her.'

'Come on, hen,' Cal said and gathered her hand in his.

They walked across the kirkyard together, his firm grip firing her courage, his gentle voice offering her strength, as he had done when he guided her away from the water all those years ago in the thin, pale light of a midsummer night.

AUTHOR'S NOTE

When the Air Ministry left Hughenden Manor, Buckinghamshire, in 1946, they took everything with them except a collection of photographs left behind in the cellar. These pictures, of RAF men and women working at drawing boards, were found by the National Trust when it took over the manor in 1947, but no one had any idea what top-secret work Hughenden had been used for during the Second World War.

It wasn't until 2004 that the unravelling of the war secrets of Disraeli's former home began. A National Trust room steward overheard a visitor, Victor Gregory, telling his grandson about what he had done there during the war. After much detective work, the Ministry of Defence agreed to release the men and women who'd worked at Hughenden from their oath of secrecy, the Official Secrets Act, and it was only then that they were able to talk about their time there.

When I visited in November 2022, to discover for myself the secrets of Hughenden – code name Hillside – I had the pleasure of a personally guided tour by volunteer, Trevor Taylor. As with all of my writing, I depended upon my imagination, bolstered by fact, to try to convey what it would have been like to carry out such highly sensitive work and to create the story I wanted to tell. I would like to acknowledge the inclusion of the names of four real people who contributed to Hillside's wartime history – Mr Dawson, Mrs Askell, Sergeant Hadfield and Mrs Hadfield, who owned a black Scottie dog – while all the other characters are fictitious.

* * *

The quote read out at Isla MacKenzie's funeral is by Reverend Anthony Jones of the Great Glen Churches, Scotland.

ACKNOWLEDGEMENTS

I would like to thank my editor Emily Yau for her brilliant editing expertise, copy editor Emily Reader for the fine tuning and Camilla Lloyd for the finishing touches. I send my gratitude to the Boldwood team for their ongoing support, and to my agent Judith Murdoch for always believing in me.

ABOUT THE AUTHOR

Catherine Law writes dramatic romantic novels set in the first half of the 20th century, during the First and Second World Wars. Her books are inspired by the tales our mothers and grandmothers tell. Originally a journalist, Catherine lives in Kent.

Sign up to Catherine Law's mailing list here for news, competitions and updates on future books.

Visit Catherine's website: www.catherinelaw.co.uk

Follow Catherine on social media:

facebook.com/catherinelawbooks

x.com/authorcathlaw

instagram.com/catherinelawauthor

goodreads.com/catherinelaw

ALSO BY CATHERINE LAW

The Officer's Wife

The Runaway

The French Girl

The Code Breaker's Secret

The Land Girl's Letters

The Map Maker's Promise

Letters from
the past

Discover page-turning
historical novels from
your favourite authors
and be transported
back in time

Join our book club
Facebook group

https://bit.ly/SixpenceGroup

Sign up to our
newsletter

https://bit.ly/LettersFrom
PastNews

Boldwood

Boldwood Books is an award-winning fiction publishing company seeking out the best stories from around the world.

Find out more at www.boldwoodbooks.com

Join our reader community for brilliant books, competitions and offers!

Follow us
@BoldwoodBooks
@TheBoldBookClub

Sign up to our weekly
deals newsletter

https://bit.ly/BoldwoodBNewsletter

Printed in Great Britain
by Amazon